TRAITOR
TO THE THRONE

TRAITOR
TO THE THRONE

A REBEL OF THE SANDS NOVEL

ALWYN HAMILTON

VIKING

VIKING
An imprint of Penguin Random House LLC
375 Hudson Street
New York, New York 10014

First published in the United States of America by Viking,
an imprint of Penguin Random House LLC, 2017

LIBRARY OF CONGRESS CATALOGING-IN-PUBLICATION DATA IS AVAILABLE
ISBN: 9780451477859

Printed in U.S.A.

1   3   5   7   9   10   8   6   4   2

Set in Fiesole Text

For Rachel Rose Smith,

who's always got my back.

TO GALLANDIE / ALBIS / GAMANIX
Dev's Valley
Ghasab
Saramotai
Fahali
Dassama
REBEL CAMP
AMONPOUR
SAND
SEA
Deadshot
Dustwalk
Sazi
MIRAJI
W
E
S

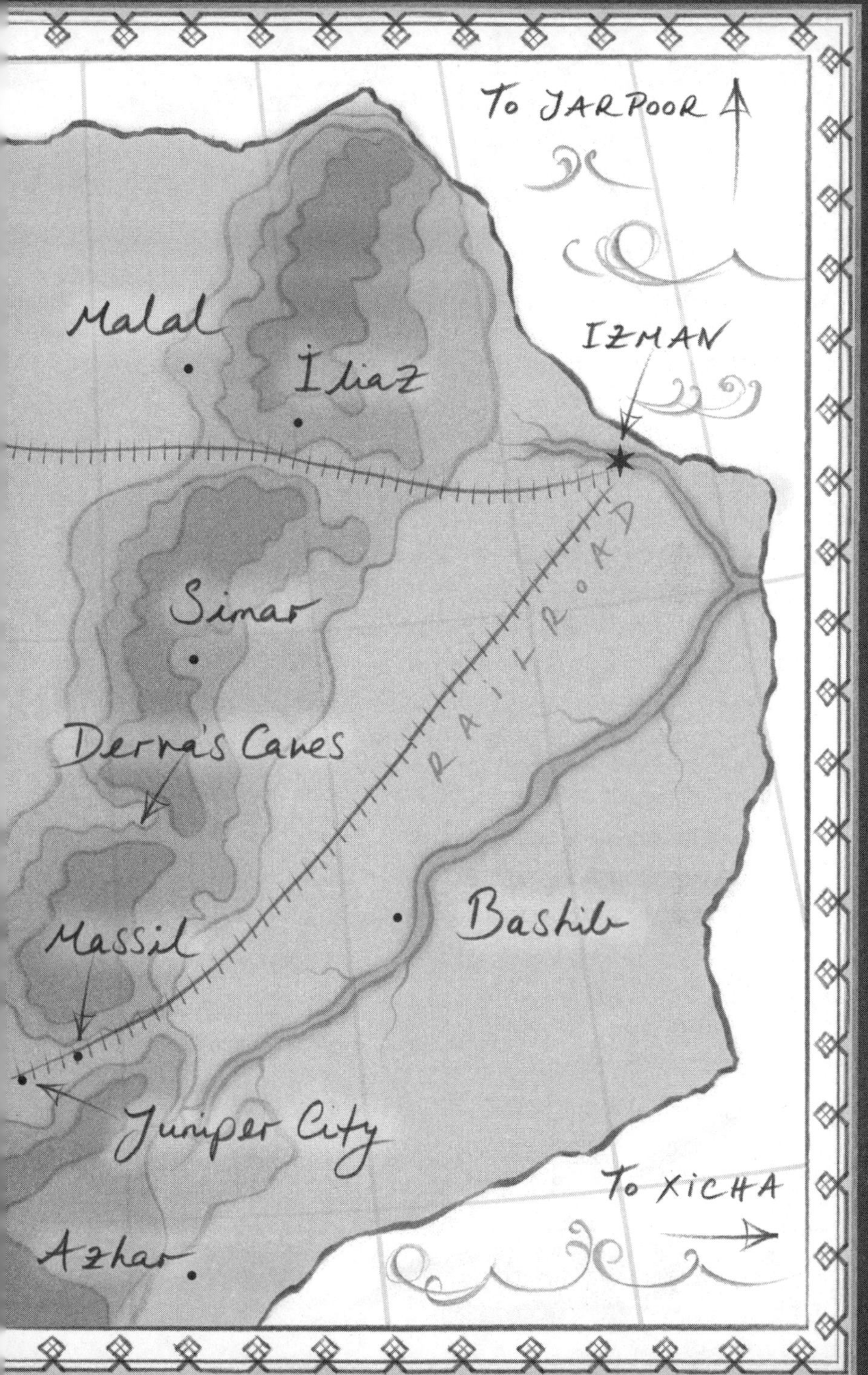

To JARPOOR
Malal
IZMAN
Iliaz
Simar
RAILROAD
Derna's Caves
Bashib
Massil
Juniper City
To XICHA
Azhar

CAST of CHARACTERS

THE REBELLION

Amani Sharpshooter, Demdji marked by blue eyes, able to control desert sand, goes by the moniker of the Blue-Eyed Bandit.

Prince Ahmed Al-Oman Bin Izman The Rebel Prince, leader of the Rebellion.

Jin Prince of Miraji, half-brother of the Rebel Prince Ahmed, full name Ajinahd Al-Oman Bin Izman.

Shazad Al-Hamad Daughter of a Mirajin general, among the original members of the Rebellion, well-trained fighter, strategist.

Delila Demdji marked by purple hair, able to cast illusions in the air, Ahmed's sister by blood, Jin's sister by adoption.

Hala Demdji marked by golden skin, able to twist people's minds into hallucinations.

Imin Demdji marked by golden eyes, able to shape-shift into any human form, Hala's sibling.

Izz and Maz Twin Demdji, marked by blue skin and blue hair respectively, able to shape-shift into any animal form.

Bahi Childhood friend of Shazad, disgraced Holy Man, killed by Noorsham.

IZMAN

Sultan Oman Ruler of Miraji, Ahmed and Jin's father.

Prince Kadir The Sultan's eldest son, Sultim, heir to the throne of Miraji.

Prince Naguib One of the Sultan's sons, army commander, killed by the rebels in the battle of Fahali.

Lien Xichian woman, wife of the Sultan, Jin's mother by blood, Ahmed and Delila's mother by adoption, died of an illness.

Nadira Ahmed and Delila's mother by blood, killed by the Sultan for bearing the child of a Djinni.

The Last County

Tamid Amani's best friend, Holy Father in training, walks with a limp due to a deformity at birth, presumed dead.

Farrah Amani's aunt, eldest sister to Amani's mother.

Asid Farrah's husband, a horse trader in Dustwalk.

Safiyah Amani's aunt, the middle sister, left Dustwalk before Amani was born to seek her fortune in Izman.

Zahia Amani's mother, hanged for the murder of her husband.

Hiza Amani's mother's husband, not Amani's father by blood, killed by his wife.

Shira Amani's cousin, Farrah's only daughter, whereabouts unknown.

Fazim Shira's lover.

Noorsham Demdji marked by blue eyes, able to produce Djinni fire that can annihilate a whole city, born in the mining town of Sazi, missing since the battle of Fahali.

Myths & Legends

First Beings Immortal beings made by God, including Djinn, Buraqi, and Rocs.

The Destroyer of Worlds A being from the center of the earth who came to the surface of the world to bring death and darkness, defeated by humanity.

Ghouls Various servants of the Destroyer of Worlds, including Nightmares, Skinwalkers, and others.

The First Mortal The first mortal created by the Djinn to face the Destroyer of Worlds, made out of earth and water and air and brought to life with Djinni fire.

Princess Hawa Legendary princess who sang the sun into the sky.

The Hero Attallah Lover of Princess Hawa.

ONE

THE FOREIGN PRINCE

O nce, in the desert kingdom of Miraji, there was a young prince who wanted his father's throne. He had no claim to it but the belief that his father was a weak ruler and that he would be stronger. And so he took the throne by force. In a single night of bloodshed the Sultan and the prince's brothers fell to the young prince's sword and the foreign army he led. When dawn came he was no longer a prince. He was the Sultan.

The young Sultan was known to take wives into his harem the same way he had his country: by force.

In the first year of his rule, two such wives gave birth

to sons under the same stars. One wife was a girl born in the sands. Her son belonged to the desert. The other wife was a girl born across the water, in a kingdom called Xicha, and raised on the deck of a ship. Her son did not belong.

But the sons grew as brothers nonetheless, their mothers shielding them from the things the palace walls could not. And for a time, in the Sultan's harem, things were well.

Until the first wife gave birth again, but this time to a child that was not her husband's—a Djinni's daughter, with unnatural hair and unnatural fire in her blood. For her crime in betraying him, the Sultan turned his anger on his wife. She died under the force of his blows.

Such was his rage, the Sultan never noticed the second wife, who fled with their two sons and the Djinni's daughter, escaping back across the sea to the kingdom of Xicha, where she had been stolen from. There, her son, the Foreign Prince, could pretend that he belonged. The Desert Prince could not pretend; he was as foreign in this land as his brother had been in their father's. But neither prince was destined to stay long. Soon, both left Xicha for the open seas instead.

And for a time, on ships going anywhere and coming from nowhere, things were well for the brothers. They drifted from one foreign shore to another, belonging in each place equally.

Until one day, across the bow of the ship, Miraji appeared again.

The Desert Prince saw his country and remembered where he really belonged. On that familiar shore he left the ship and his brother. Though the Desert Prince asked his brother to join him, the Foreign Prince would not. His father's lands looked empty and barren to him and he could not understand what hold they had over his brother. And so they parted ways. The Foreign Prince stayed on the sea for a time, raging silently that his brother had chosen the desert over the sea.

Finally the day came when the Foreign Prince could no longer be separated from his brother. When he returned to the desert of Miraji, he found that his brother had set it on fire with rebellion. The Desert Prince talked of great things, of great ideas, of equality and of prosperity. He was surrounded by new brothers and sisters who loved the desert as he did. He was now known as the Rebel Prince. But still he welcomed the man who had been his brother his whole life with open arms.

And for a time things were well in the Rebellion.

Until there was a girl. A girl called the Blue-Eyed Bandit, who had been made in the sands and sharpened by the desert and who burned with all of its fire. And for the first time the Foreign Prince understood what it was that his brother loved in this desert.

The Foreign Prince and the Blue-Eyed Bandit crossed the sands together, all the way to a great battle in the city of Fahali, where the Sultan's foreign allies had rooted themselves.

In that battle of Fahali the rebels won their first great

victory. They defended the desert against the Sultan who would have burned it alive. They freed the Demdji, another Djinni's child, whom the Sultan would have turned into a weapon against his will. They killed the young commander, their brother who would have shed blood until he could win praise from his father, the Sultan. They ruptured the Sultan's alliance with the foreigners who had been punishing the desert for decades. And the rebels claimed part of the desert for themselves.

The story of the battle of Fahali spread quickly. And with it spread news that the desert might be a prize for the taking again. For the desert of Miraji was the only place where the old magic and the new machines were able to exist together. The only country that could spit out guns quickly enough to arm men to fight in the great war raging between the nations of the north.

New eyes from foreign shores turned to Miraji, hungry ones. More foreign armies descended on the desert, coming from all sides, each trying to claim a new alliance, or the country itself. And while enemies from outside gnawed at the Sultan's borders and kept his army occupied, the rebels seized city after city from the inside, knocking them out of the Sultan's hands and rallying the people to their side.

And for a time things were well for the Rebellion, for the Blue-Eyed Bandit, and for the Foreign Prince.

Until the balance started to shift against the Rebel Prince. Two dozen rebels were lost in a trap set for them in the sands, where they were surrounded and outgunned.

A city rose up against the Sultan, crying out the Rebel Prince's name in the night. But those who did saw the next dawn with the blank eyes of the dead. And the Blue-Eyed Bandit fell to a bullet in a battle in the mountains, gravely wounded and only just clinging to life. There, for the first time since the threads of their stories had become tangled, the Blue-Eyed Bandit's and the Foreign Prince's paths split.

While the Blue-Eyed Bandit clung to her life, the Foreign Prince was sent to the eastern border of the desert. There, an army from Xicha was camped. The Foreign Prince stole a uniform and walked into the Xichian camp as if he belonged. It was easy there, where he did not look foreign anymore. He stood with them as they battled the Sultan's forces, spying in secret for the Rebel Prince.

And for a time things were well, hiding among the foreign army.

Until the missive came from the enemy camp, its bearer wearing the Sultan's gold and white and holding up a flag of peace.

The Foreign Prince would have killed for news of what came in that missive for his own side, but there was no need. It was known that he spoke the desert language. He was summoned into the Xichian general's tent to translate between the Sultan's envoy and the Xichian, neither of them knowing he was an enemy of them both. As he translated he learned that the Sultan was calling for a ceasefire. He was tired of bloodshed, the message said. He was ready to negotiate. The Foreign Prince learned that the ruler of Miraji was summoning all the foreign rulers to him to talk of a new alliance. The Sultan asked for any king or queen or emperor or prince who would lay claim to his desert to come to his palace to make their case.

The missive went to the Xichian emperor the next morning. And the guns stopped. The ceasefire had started. Next would come negotiations. Then peace between the Sultan and the invaders. And without the need to mind his shores, the desert ruler's eyes would turn inward again.

The Foreign Prince understood it was time to return to his brother. Their rebellion was about to turn into a war.

TWO

I'd always liked this shirt. It was a shame about all the blood.

Most of it wasn't mine, at least. The shirt wasn't mine, either, for that matter—I'd borrowed it from Shazad and never bothered to give it back. Well, she probably wouldn't want it now.

"Stop!"

I was jerked to a halt. My hands were tied, and the rope chafed painfully along the raw skin of my wrists. I hissed a curse under my breath as I tilted my head back, finally looking up from my dusty boots to lock eyes with the glare of the desert sun.

The walls of Saramotai cast a mighty long shadow in the last of the light.

These walls were legendary. They had stood indifferent to one of the greatest battles of the First War, between the hero Attallah and the Destroyer of Worlds. They were so ancient they looked like they'd been built out of the bones of the desert itself. But the words slapped in sloppy white paint above the gates . . . those were new.

WELCOME TO THE FREE CITY

I could see where the paint had dripped between the cracks in the ancient stones before drying in the heat.

I had a few things to say about being dragged to a so-called Free City tied up like a goat on a spit, but even I knew I was better off not running my mouth just now.

"Declare yourself or I'll shoot!" someone called from the city wall. The words were a whole lot more impressive than the voice that came with them. I could hear the crack of youth on that last word. I squinted up through my sheema at the kid pointing a rifle at me from the top of the walls. He couldn't have been any older than thirteen. He was all limbs and joints. He didn't look like he could've held that gun right if his life depended on it. Which it probably did. This being Miraji and all.

"It's us, Ikar, you little idiot," the man holding me bellowed in my ear. I winced. Shouting really didn't seem necessary. "Now, open the gates right now or, God help me, I'm going to have your father beat you harder than one of his horseshoes until some brains go in."

"Hossam?" Ikar didn't lower the gun right away. He was

twitchy as all get-out. Which wasn't the best thing when he had one finger on the trigger of a rifle. "Who's that with you?" He waved his gun in my direction. I turned my body on instinct as the barrel swung wildly. He didn't look like he could hit the broad side of a barn if he was trying, but I wasn't ruling out that he might hit me by accident. If he did, better to get shot in the shoulder than the chest.

"This"—a hint of pride crept into Hossam's voice as he jerked my face up to the sunlight like I was a hunted carcass—"is the Blue-Eyed Bandit."

That name landed with more weight than it used to, drawing silence down behind it. On top of the wall Ikar stared. Even this far away I saw his jaw open, going slack for a moment, then close.

"Open the gates!" Ikar squawked finally, scrambling down. "Open the gates!"

The huge iron doors swung open painfully slow, fighting against the sand that had built up over the day. Hossam and the other men with us jostled me forward in a hurry as the ancient hinges groaned.

The gates didn't open all the way, only enough for one man to get through at a time. Even after thousands of years those gates looked as strong as they had at the dawn of humanity. They were iron through and through, as thick as the span of a man's arms, and operated by some system of weights and gears that no other city had been able to duplicate. There'd be no breaking these gates down. And everyone knew there was no climbing the walls of Saramotai.

Seemed like the only way into the city these days was by being dragged through the gates as a prisoner with a hand around your neck. Lucky me.

Saramotai was west of the middle mountains. Which meant it was ours. Or at least, it was supposed to be. After the battle at Fahali, Ahmed had declared this territory his. Most cities had sworn their allegiance quickly enough, as the Gallan occupiers who'd held this half of the desert for so long emptied out of the streets. Or we'd claimed their allegiance away from the Sultan.

Saramotai was another story.

Welcome to the Free City.

Saramotai had declared its own laws, taking rebellion one step further.

Ahmed talked a whole lot about equality and wealth for the poor. The people of Saramotai had decided the only way to create equality was to strike down those who were above them. That the only way to become rich was to take their wealth. So they'd turned against the rich under the guise of accepting Ahmed's rule.

But Ahmed knew a grab for power when he saw one. We didn't know all that much about Malik Al-Kizzam, the man who'd taken over Saramotai, except that he'd been a servant to the emir and now the emir was dead and Malik lived in his grand estate.

So we sent a few folks to find out more. And do something about it if we didn't like it.

They didn't come back.

That was a problem. Another problem was getting in after them.

And so here I was, my hands tied so tight behind my back I was losing feeling in them and a fresh wound on my collarbone where a knife had just barely missed my neck. Funny how being successful felt exactly the same as getting captured.

Hossam shoved me ahead of him through the narrow gap in the gates. I stumbled and went sprawling in the sand face-first, my elbow bashing into the iron gate painfully as I went down.

Son of a bitch, that hurt more than I thought it would.

A hiss of pain escaped through my teeth as I rolled over. Sand stuck to my hands where sweat had pooled under the ropes, clinging to my skin. Then Hossam grabbed me, yanking me to my feet. He hustled me inside, the gate clanging quickly shut behind us. It was almost like they were afraid of something.

A small crowd had already gathered inside the gate to gawk. Half were clutching guns. More than a few of those were pointed at me.

So my reputation really did precede me.

"Hossam." Someone pushed to the front. He was older than my captors, with serious eyes that took in my sorry state. He looked at me more levelly than the others. He wouldn't be blinded by the same eagerness. "What happened?"

"We caught her in the mountains," Hossam crowed.

"She tried to ambush us when we were on our way back from trading for the guns." Two of the other men with us dropped bags that were heavy with weapons on the ground proudly, as if to show off that I hadn't gotten in their way. The guns weren't of Mirajin make. Amonpourian. Stupid-looking things. Ornate and carved, made by hand instead of machine, and charged at twice what they were worth because someone had gone to the trouble of making them pretty. It didn't matter how pretty something was, it'd kill you just as dead. That, I'd learned from Shazad.

"Just her?" the man with the serious eyes asked. "On her own?" His gaze flicked to me. Like he might be able to suss out the truth just from looking at me. Whether a girl of seventeen would really think she could take on a half dozen grown men with nothing but a handful of bullets and win. Whether the famous Blue-Eyed Bandit could really be *that* stupid.

I preferred "reckless."

But I kept my mouth shut. The more I talked, the more likely I was to say something that'd backfire on me. *Stay silent, look sullen, try not to get yourself killed.*

If all else fails, just stick with that last one.

"Are you really the Blue-Eyed Bandit?" Ikar blurted out, making everyone's head turn. He'd scrambled down from his watchpost on the wall to come gawk at me with the rest. He leaned forward eagerly across the barrel of his gun. If it went off now it'd take both his hands and part of his face with it. "Is it true what they say about you?"

Stay silent. Look sullen. Try not to get yourself killed. "Depends what they're saying, I suppose." Damn it. That didn't last so long. "And you shouldn't hold your gun like that."

Ikar shifted his grip absently, never taking his eyes off me. "They say that you can shoot a man's eye out fifty feet away in the pitch dark. That you walked through a hail of bullets in Iliaz, and walked out with the Sultan's secret war plans." I remembered Iliaz going a little differently. It ended with a bullet in me, for one. "That you seduced one of the Emir of Jalaz's wives while they were visiting Izman." Now, that was a new one. I'd heard the one about seducing the emir himself. But maybe the emir's wife liked women, too. Or maybe the story had twisted in the telling, since half the tales of the Blue-Eyed Bandit seemed to make out I was a man these days. I'd stopped wearing wraps to pretend I was a boy, but apparently I'd need to fill out a little more to convince some people that the bandit was a girl.

"You killed a hundred Gallan soldiers at Fahali," he pushed on, his words tripping over each other, undeterred by my silence. "And I heard you escaped from Malal on the back of a giant blue Roc, and flooded the prayer house behind you."

"You shouldn't believe everything you hear," I interjected as Ikar finally paused for breath, his eyes the size of two louzi pieces with excitement.

He sagged, disappointed. He was just a kid, as eager to believe all the stories as I had been when I was his age. Though he looked younger than I ever remembered being. He shouldn't be here holding a gun like this. But then, this was what the desert did to us. It made us dreamers with weapons. I ran my tongue along my teeth. "And the prayer house in Malal was an accident . . . mostly."

A whisper went through the crowd. I'd be lying if I said it didn't send a little thrill down my spine. And lying was a sin.

It'd been close to half a year since I'd stood in Fahali with Ahmed, Jin, Shazad, Hala, and the twins, Izz and Maz. Us against two armies and Noorsham, a Demdji turned into a weapon by the Sultan; a Demdji who also happened to be my brother.

Us against impossible odds and a devastatingly powerful Demdji. But we'd survived. And from there the story of the battle of Fahali had traveled across the desert faster even than the story of the Sultim trials had. I'd heard it told a dozen times by folks who didn't know the Rebellion was listening. Our exploits got greater and less plausible with every telling but the tale always ended the same way, with a sense that, while the storyteller might be done, the story wasn't. One way or another, the desert wasn't going to be the same after the battle of Fahali.

The legend of the Blue-Eyed Bandit had grown along with the tale of Fahali, until I was a story that I didn't wholly recognize. It claimed that the Blue-Eyed Bandit was a thief instead of a rebel. That I tricked my way into people's beds to get information for my Prince. That I'd killed my own brother on the battlefield. I hated that one the most. Maybe because there'd been a moment, finger on the trigger, where it was almost true. And I had let him escape. Which was almost as bad. He was out there somewhere with all of that power. And, unlike me, he didn't have any other Demdji to help him.

Sometimes, late at night, after the rest of the camp had gone to sleep, I'd say out loud that he was alive. Just to know whether it was true or not. So far I could say it without hesitation. But I was scared that there would come a day when I wouldn't be able to anymore. That would mean it was a lie, and my brother had died, alone and scared, somewhere in this merciless, war-torn desert.

"If she's as dangerous as they say, we ought to kill her," someone called from the crowd. It was a man with a bright yellow military sash across his chest that looked like it'd been stitched back together from scraps. I noticed a few were wearing those. These must be the newly appointed guard of Saramotai, since they'd gone and killed the real guard. He was holding a gun. It was pointed at my stomach. Stomach wounds were no good. They killed you slowly.

"But if she's the Blue-Eyed Bandit, she's with the Rebel Prince." Someone else spoke up. "Doesn't that mean she's on our side?" Now, that was the million-fouza question.

"Funny way to treat someone on your side." I shifted my bound hands pointedly. A murmur went through the crowd. That was good; it meant they weren't as united as they looked from the outside of their impenetrable wall. "So if we're all friends here, how about you untie me and we can talk?"

"Nice try, Bandit." Hossam gripped me tighter. "We're not giving you a chance to get your hands on a gun. I've heard the stories of how you killed a dozen men with a single bullet." I was pretty sure that wasn't possible. Besides, I didn't need a gun to take down a dozen men.

It was almost funny. They'd used rope to tie me. Not iron. If ever there was iron touching my skin, I was as human as they were. So long as there wasn't, I could raise the desert against them. Which meant I could do more damage with my hands tied than I ever could with a gun in them. But damage wasn't the plan.

"Malik should decide what we do with the Bandit anyway." The serious-eyed man rubbed his hand over his chin nervously as he mentioned their self-appointed leader.

"I do have a name, you know," I offered.

"Malik isn't back yet," the same one who'd been pointing the gun at me snapped. He seemed like the tense sort. "She could do anything before he gets back."

"It's Amani. My name, that is." No one was listening. "In case you were wondering." This arguing might go on for a while. Ruling by committee never went quick. It barely ever worked at all.

"Then lock her away until Malik gets here," a voice from somewhere in the back of the crowd called.

"He's right," another voice called from the other side, another face I couldn't see. "Throw her in jail where she can't make any trouble."

A ripple of agreement spread through the crowd. Finally the man with sad eyes jerked his head in a sharp nod.

The crowd parted hastily as Hossam started to pull me through. Only they didn't move very far. Everyone wanted to get a look at the Blue-Eyed Bandit. They stared and jostled for space as I was pulled past them. I knew exactly what they were seeing. A girl younger than some of their daughters, with a split lip and dark hair stuck to her face by blood and sweat. Legends were never what you expected when you saw them up close. I was no exception. The only thing that made me any different from every other skinny, dark-skinned desert girl was eyes that burned a brighter blue than the midday sky. Like the hottest part of a fire.

"Are you one of *them*?" It was a new voice, rising shrill above the din of the crowd. A woman with a yellow sheema shoved to the front. The cloth was stitched with flowers that almost matched my eyes. There was a desperate urgency in her face that made me nervous. There was something about the way she said *them*. Like she might mean *Demdji*.

Even folks who knew about Demdji couldn't usually pick me out as one. We children of Djinn and mortal women looked more human than most folks reckoned. Hell, I'd even fooled myself for near seventeen years. Mostly I didn't look unnatural, just half-foreign.

My eyes were what gave me away, but only if you knew what you were looking for. And it seemed like this woman did.

"Hossam." The woman staggered to keep up as he dragged me through the streets. "If she's one of them, she's worth just as much as my Ranaa. We could trade her instead. We could—"

But Hossam shoved her aside, letting her be swallowed back into the crowd as he dragged me deeper into the city.

The streets of Saramotai were as narrow as they were ancient, forcing the crowd to thin and then dissipate as we moved. Walls pressed close around us in the lengthening shadows, tight enough in some places that my shoulders touched on both sides. We passed between two brightly painted houses with their doors blown in. Gunpowder marks on walls. Boarded-up entryways and windows. There were more and more marks of war the farther we walked. A city where the fighting had come from inside, instead of beyond the walls. I supposed that was called a rebellion.

The smell of rotting flesh came before I saw the bodies.

We passed under a narrow arch half covered by a carpet drying in the sun. The tassels brushed my neck as I ducked under. When I looked back up, I saw two dozen bodies swinging by their necks. They were strung together across the great exterior wall like lanterns.

Lanterns who'd had their eyes picked out by vultures.

It was hard to tell if they'd been old or young or pretty or scarred. But they'd all been wealthy. The birds hadn't gotten to the kurtas stitched with richly dyed thread or the delicate muslin sleeves of their khalats. I almost gagged at the smell. Death and desert heat made quick work of bodies.

The sun was setting behind me. Which meant that when sunrise came the bodies would blaze with light.

A new dawn. A new desert.

THREE

The prison almost smelled worse than the corpses. Hossam shoved me down the steps that led underground into the jail cells. I had time to glimpse a long line of iron-barred cells facing each other across a narrow hallway before Hossam pushed me inside one. My shoulder hit the ground hard. Damn, that was going to bruise.

I didn't try to get back up. I lay with my head against the cool stone floor as Hossam locked the jail cell behind me. The clang of iron on iron set my teeth on edge. I still didn't move as the footsteps faded up the stairs. I waited three full breaths before struggling to my feet using my bound hands and elbows.

There was one small window at the top of my cell that gave just enough light that I wasn't fumbling around in the dark. Through the iron bars I could see into the cell across from mine. A girl no older than ten was curled up in the corner, shivering in a pale green khalat that had gone grubby, watching me with huge eyes.

I leaned my face into the bars of the cell. The cold iron bit deep into the Demdji part of me.

"Imin?" I called down the prison. "Mahdi?" I waited with bated breath as only silence answered. Then all the way at the other end of the prison I saw the edge of a face appear, pressed against the bars, fingers curling around the iron desperately.

"Amani?" a voice called back. It sounded cracked with thirst, but an annoyingly nasal, imperious note remained. The one I'd gotten to know over the last few months since Mahdi and a few others from the intellectual set in Izman had made the trek out of the city and to our camp. "Is that you? What are you doing here?"

"It's me." My shoulders sagged in relief. They were still alive. I wasn't too late. "I'm here to rescue you."

"Shame about you getting captured, too, then, isn't it?"

I bit my tongue. It figured I could count on Mahdi to still be rude to me even from the inside of a jail cell. I didn't think a whole lot of Mahdi or any of the rest of the weedy city boys who'd come to the heart of the Rebellion so late. After we'd already spilled so much blood to claim half the desert. But still, these were the men who'd supported Ahmed when he first came to Izman. The ones he'd traded philosophies with, and first started to fan the spark of rebellion with. Besides, if I let everyone I found annoying die, we'd be mighty thin on allies.

"Well"—I put on my sweetest voice—"how else was I meant to get through the gates after you bungled your mission so badly that they put the entire city on lockdown?"

I was met with a satisfyingly sullen silence from the other end of the prison. It would be hard for even Mahdi to argue that he hadn't failed from the wrong side of a prison door. Still, I could gloat later. Now the last of the daylight was starting to retreat, I was going to have to move quickly. I stepped away from the iron bars. Rubbing my fingers together, I tried to work some blood back into my hands.

The sand that had stuck between them when I'd pretended to trip at the gates shifted in anticipation. It was in the folds of my clothes, too—in my hair, against the sweat of my skin. That was the beauty of the desert. It got into everything, right down to your soul.

Jin said that to me once.

I brushed aside that memory as I closed my eyes. I took a deep breath and pulled the sand away from my skin—every grain, every particle answering my call and tugging away from me until it hung in careful suspension in the air.

When I opened my eyes I was surrounded by a haze of sand that glowed golden in the last of the late afternoon sun streaming into the cell.

In the cell across from mine, the little girl in the green

khalat straightened a little, leaning out of the gloom to get a closer look.

I sucked in a breath and the sand gathered together into a shape like a whip. I moved my tied hands away from my body as far as I could, shifting the sand with the motion. None of the other Demdji seemed to understand why I needed to move when I used my power. Hala said it made me look like some Izmani market charlatan of the lowest order. But she'd been born with her power at her fingertips. Where I came from, a weapon needed a hand to use it.

The sand slashed between my wrists like a blade, severing the rope. My arms snapped free.

Now I could do some real damage.

I grabbed hold of the sand and slashed my arm downward in one clean arc, like the blow of a sword. The sand went with it, smashing into the lock of the cell with all the power of a whole desert storm gathered into one blow.

The lock shattered with a satisfying crack. And just like that, I was free.

The little girl in green stared as I kicked the door open, careful not to touch the iron as I gathered the sand back into my fist.

"So." I sauntered down the length of the hallway, tugging away at what was left of the severed rope on my wrists. The rope came away from my right hand easily, leaving a red welt behind. I worked at the knot on my left hand as I came to a stop outside the cell that held Mahdi. "How're those diplomatic negotiations going for you?" The last of the rope on my hands slithered away to the floor.

Mahdi looked sour. "Are you here to mock us or to rescue us?"

"I don't see any reason I can't do both." I leaned my elbows into the cell door and propped my chin on my fist. "Remind me again how you told Shazad you didn't need us to come with you, because women just couldn't be taken seriously in political negotiations?"

"Actually"—a voice piped up from the back of the cell—"I think what he said was that you and Shazad would be 'unnecessary distractions.'"

Imin moved to the door so I could see him clearly. I didn't recognize his face but I'd know those sardonic yellow eyes anywhere. Our Demdji shape-shifter. Last time I'd seen Imin, leaving camp, she'd been wearing a petite female shape in oversized men's clothes—to lighten the load for the horse. It was a familiar body I'd seen her wear more than once now. Though it was just one in an infinite deck of human shapes Imin could wear: boy, girl, man, or woman. I was used to Imin's ever-changing face by now. It meant that some days she was a small girl with big eyes being dwarfed by the horse she was riding, or a fighter with the strength to lift someone off the ground with one hand. Other days he was a skinny scholar, looking annoyed but harmless in the back of a cell in Saramotai. But boy or girl, man or woman, those startling gold eyes never changed.

"That's right." I turned back to Mahdi. "Maybe I'd forgotten, on account of how amazed I was that she didn't knock all your teeth in then and there."

"Are you done?" Mahdi looked like he'd bit into a pickled lemon. "Or are you going to waste more time that we could be using to escape?"

"Yeah, yeah, all right." I stepped back, reaching out a hand. The sand answered, gathering itself into my fist. I pulled back my hand, feeling the power build in my chest, holding it for a moment before I smashed the sand down. The lock exploded.

"Finally." Mahdi sounded exasperated, like I was a servant who'd just taken an unreasonably long time to bring him his food. He tried to shove past me, but I stuck my arm out, stopping him.

"What—" he started, outrage already rising. I clapped my hand over his mouth, shutting him up, as I listened. I saw the change in his face the moment he heard it, too. Footsteps on the staircase. The guards had heard us.

"You had to be so loud?" he whispered as I removed my hand.

"You know, next time I may not bother saving you." I shoved him back into his cell, my mind already rushing ahead to how I was going to get us out of there alive. Imin pushed past Mahdi, stepping out of the cell. I didn't stop him. I couldn't have if I'd wanted to. He was already shifting as he went, shedding the harmless scholar's body until he was two heads taller than me and twice as wide. I wouldn't want to meet this shape of Imin's in a dark alley. He rolled his shoulders uncomfortably inside his shirt, now tight across his body. A seam split at the shoulder.

Full dark had almost fallen by now. The cells were lit only by a dim gloom. I could see the swing of lamplight on the staircase. Good, that'd be an advantage. I flattened myself to the blind spot at the bottom of the stairs. Imin followed my lead, doing the same on the other side.

We waited, listening to the steps on the stairs getting louder. I counted four sets of boots, at least. Maybe five. We were outnumbered and they were armed, but they'd have to come single file, which meant numbers counted for nothing. Lamplight played across the walls as they descended. I had the element of surprise on my side. And, like Shazad always said, when you were fighting someone twice your size you had to make the first blow count. The blow they were never expecting in the first place. All the better if you could make it your last one, too.

Across from me the little girl in green had shifted so she was right up against the bars, watching us, fascinated. I pressed my finger to my lips, trying to make her understand. The girl nodded. Good. She was young but she was a desert girl all the same. She knew how to survive.

I moved the moment the first guard's head came into view.

One violent burst of sand knocked straight into his temple, sending him careening into the bars on the little girl's cell. She staggered back as his skull cracked against the iron. Imin grabbed the soldier behind, hoisting him off the ground and slamming him to the wall. His startled face was the last thing I saw as his lamp hit the ground, shattering. Extinguishing. And I was as good as blind.

A gunshot sounded, setting off a chorus of screams, inside the cells and out. Underneath I heard one voice shouting a prayer. I whispered a curse instead as I flattened myself to the wall. I was least likely to get hit by a stray bullet if I wasn't out in the open. I had to think. They were as blind as we were. But they were armed and I had to figure they wouldn't mind killing a prisoner with a stray bullet as much as I would. Another gunshot went off, and this time there was a cry that sounded more like pain than fear. My mind struggled to think through the sudden rising panic, as I strained to follow the sounds. It'd been a long time since I was alone in a fight. If Shazad were here she'd know a way out of this. I could fight back in the dark, but I was as likely to hit Imin or the little girl in green as an enemy. I needed light. Badly.

And then, as if in answer to a prayer, the sun rose in the prison.

Starbursts filled my eyes. I was still blinded, but this time by the sudden glare of light. I blinked wildly, trying to see through the sunspots.

My vision cleared dangerously slowly, my panicked heartbeat reminding me that I was useless and blind and surrounded by armed enemies. My surroundings came into focus one little piece at a time. Two guards on the ground. Not moving. Three more rubbing their eyes, guns loose in their fingers. Imin pressed against the wall, bleeding from his shoulder. And inside the cell, the little girl in green, with a tiny sun, no bigger than a fist, cupped in her hands. Her face glowed in the pale light, casting strange shadows over her face from below that made her look a whole lot older. And I could see now that those huge eyes she'd been watching me with were as unnatural as mine or Imin's. The color of a dying ember.

She was a Demdji.

FOUR

There'd be time to worry about my new Demdji ally later. For now I had to use the gift she was giving us. The guards' guns were already rising toward me—a burst of sand knocked them out of their hands. One guard staggered back into Imin. Imin grabbed him, and with one sharp twist I heard a neck crack.

A guard sprung at me, knife drawn. I split the sand in two, using half to knock his hand aside before he could get near, even as I turned the rest solid in my hand, forming it into a curved blade of sand. It cut clean across his throat, drawing blood. Imin grabbed a fallen gun. He might not be as good a shot as I was, but in a space this closely confined it'd be hard to miss. I ducked as Imin fired. More screams came from inside the cells, the sound of gunshots bouncing off the stone walls drowning them out.

And then silence. I straightened. It was over. Imin and I were still alive. The guards weren't.

Mahdi stepped out of the cell, his lip curling up in faint judgment at the bodies as he took in the carnage. That was the thing about the intellectual types. They wanted to remake the world, but they seemed to think they could do it without any blood. I ignored him as I turned toward the cell holding the little Demdji girl in a green khalat. She was still cradling the tiny sun, staring at me with somber red eyes. They were unsettlingly bright.

I splintered her lock with a burst of sand. "You're—" I started as I dragged the door open, but the little girl was already on her feet, shoving past me out of her cell toward the other end of the prison.

"Samira!" she called. She got close to the bars, but didn't touch them. She knew enough to stay away from iron. More than I had when I was her age. I leaned against the stone wall. I was starting to feel the exhaustion creeping in on me now that the fighting was done.

"Ranaa!" Another girl pushed her way to the front of the cell, kneeling on the floor so she was eye level with the young Demdji. She looked like she'd been beautiful before prison got to her. Now she just looked tired. Dark eyes sunk into a drawn face. I checked her over quickly for any sign of a Demdji mark but she looked as human as they came. She was probably of an age with me. Not old enough to be the girl's mother. A sister maybe? She reached through the bars, resting a hand against the little girl's face. "Are you all right?"

The young Demdji, Ranaa, turned to me, her mouth already twisting into an angry pout. "Let her out." It was an order, not a request. And from someone who was used to giving them, too.

"No one ever taught you to say please, kid?" It slipped out, even though this wasn't the place to start teaching manners. And I probably wasn't the person to, either.

Ranaa stared me down. That probably worked on most folks. I was used to Demdji and even I found those red eyes unsettling. I remembered some stories saying that Adil the conqueror was so evil his eyes burned red. She was used to getting what she wanted with those eyes. But I wasn't all that used to doing what I was told. I twirled the sand around my fingers, waiting.

"Let her out, *please*," she tried, before stomping one bare foot. "Now."

I pushed away from the wall with a sigh. At least I'd tried. "Move back." I could give orders, too.

The second the lock shattered, Ranaa fell forward, flinging her small arms around the older girl's neck, still carefully holding the ball of light in one hand as the other one clutched the dirty fabric of her khalat. I could see into the rest of the cell from the glow of the tiny sun in her hand. The cramped space was stuffed with prisoners, so close together they didn't have room to lie down, a dozen women piled on top of each other. They were already scrambling to their feet, collapsing out of the cell with relief, gasping for freedom, leaving Imin and Mahdi to try to get them in some sort of order.

They were all girls or women. The remaining cells were no different, I realized, glancing around at the cautious, anxious faces pressing out of the gloom against the bars, wary of us but tentatively hoping for rescue. Mahdi and Imin had found a set of keys on one of the dead men and were busying themselves freeing the rest of the captives. I supposed that was easier than shattering the locks. Prisoners spilled from one cell after another, sometimes rushing to embrace someone else, sometimes just staggering out, looking like skittish animals.

"The men?" I asked Samira as she disentangled herself from Ranaa, figuring I already knew the answer.

"They were more dangerous." Samira said, "At least that's what Malik said when he—" She cut herself off, shutting her eyes like she could stop herself from seeing them die at the hand of the man who'd usurped power in her city. "And they were less valuable."

It took me a moment to understand the significant gaze she gave me over Ranaa's head. Then it sunk in. The women who were staggering out of the cells were young. There were a lot of rumors lately about slavers taking advantage of the war. Kidnapping girls from our half of the desert and selling them to soldiers stationed far from their wives, or to rich men in Izman. And then there was the matter of a Demdji's value . . .

"Ranaa." I riffled through my mind. I'd heard that name once already today. The woman wearing the sheema stitched with blue flowers, I realized. The one who'd wanted to know if I was a Demdji. Now I understood why she recognized me. "Your mother is worried about you."

The little girl gave me a disdainful once-over, her face still pressed into Samira's chest. "Then why didn't she come get me out?"

"Ranaa," Samira hissed reproachfully. I guessed I wasn't the only one who'd tried to teach the little Demdji manners. Samira had steadied herself against the door of the cell. I reached down a hand for her, helping her to her feet from where she was kneeling. Ranaa still clung to the edge of her dirty khalat, making it that much harder for Samira to move, weak as she was. "Forgive her," Samira said to me. She had a finely cut accent that reminded me of Shazad's, though it was a whole lot gentler. "She doesn't often have cause to speak to strangers." The last was followed with a pointed look at the little girl.

"Your sister?" I asked.

"After a sort." Samira rested one hand on the younger girl's head. "My father is"—she hesitated—"*was* the Emir of Saramotai. He's dead now." Her voice was flat and matter-of-fact, hiding the hurt underneath. I knew what it was like to watch a parent die. "Her mother was a servant in my father's household. When Ranaa was born looking . . . different, her mother begged my father to hide her from the Gallan." Samira searched my face. Usually I could pass for human, even with my blue eyes. But there were a few people who were more than a little familiar with Demdji who could spot me, like Jin had. "You would understand why, I expect."

I'd been lucky. I'd survived the Gallan for sixteen years without being recognized for what I was because I could pass for human. Ranaa would never be able to. And to the Gallan anything that wasn't human was a monster. A Demdji was no different from a Skinwalker or a Nightmare to them. Ranaa with her red eyes would be dead as soon as they caught sight of her.

Samira ran her fingers gently through the little girl's hair, a soothing motion that spoke of too many nights coaxing a scared little girl to sleep. "We took her in and hid her. After she started doing . . . this"—Samira's fingers danced over the light in Ranaa's hands—"my father said she must be Princess Hawa resurrected."

The story of Princess Hawa was one of my favorites growing up. It was from the very early days of humanity, back when the Destroyer of Worlds was still walking the earth. Hawa was the daughter of the first Sultan of Izman. Princess Hawa's voice was so beautiful that it brought anyone who heard it to their knees. It was her singing that brought a Skinwalker to her, disguised in the shape of one of her servants. He stole her eyes straight from her head. Princess Hawa screamed and the hero Attallah came to save her before the Skinwalker could take her tongue, too. He tricked the ghoul and won her eyes back for her. And when Hawa's sight was restored to her and she saw Attallah for the first time her heart stopped in her breast. What Hawa felt was so new and strange that she thought she was dying. Hawa sent Attallah away because of how much it pained her to look upon him. But after he was gone, her heart only hurt more. They were the first mortals to ever fall in love, the stories said.

One day, news reached Hawa in Izman that a great city across the desert was besieged by ghouls and that Attallah was fighting there. The city tried to build new defenses each day, but every night the ghouls came along and tore them down, forcing the city to start again at dawn, when the ghouls retreated. On hearing that Attallah was almost certainly doomed, Hawa walked out into the desert beyond Izman and cried such agonized tears that a Buraqi, the immortal horses made of sand and wind, took pity on her and came to her aid. She rode the Buraqi across the sand, singing so brightly that the sun came into the sky as she rushed to Attallah's side. When she reached Saramotai she held the sun in the sky, and the ghouls at bay, for a hundred days, long enough for the people of Saramotai to build their great, impenetrable walls, working day and night until they were safe. When the work was finally done, she released the sun and, safe behind the walls of the great city, she married her love, Attallah.

Hawa stood watch on those walls as Attallah rode back out into battle each night and returned to her at dawn. For a hundred more nights Attallah went beyond the gates to defend the city. He was untouchable in battle. No ghoul's claw could so much as scratch him. She stood vigil every night until, on the hundred and first night of her watch, a stray arrow from the battle reached the walls and struck Princess Hawa down.

When Attallah saw her fall from the walls, his heart

stopped from grief. The defenses that had guarded him so well for a hundred nights fell away and the ghouls overwhelmed him, tearing his heart from his chest. But in the moment that they both died, the sun bloomed in the dead of night one last time. The ghouls could not fight in the sun. Instead they burned, and the city was saved with Hawa's and Attallah's last breath. The people of the city named it in her honor: Saramotai. It meant "the princess's death" in the first language.

I wondered if it was a Djinni's idea of a joke to give his daughter, born in Hawa's city, the same gift that she had.

But Hawa was human. Or at least that was what the story said. I'd never wondered about it before. Folks in old stories sometimes just had powers that came from nowhere. Or maybe Hawa was one of us, and centuries of retellings had buried the fact that Hawa was a Demdji and not a true princess. After all, retellings of the Sultim trials made gentle, pretty Delila out to be a hideous beast with horns growing out of her head. And some stories of the Blue-Eyed Bandit left out the small matter that I was a girl.

"After Fahali we thought it would be safe for her." Samira pulled Ranaa closer to her. "Turns out even if they don't want to destroy her, some folks want her for other things." It was stupid superstition that a piece of a Demdji could cure all ills. Hala, our golden-skinned Demdji, Imin's sister, carried a reminder of that every day: two of her fingers had been cut off and sold. Probably to cure some rich man's troubled stomach. "The rumor is even the Sultan is after a Demdji."

"We know about that," I cut her off, sharper than I meant to. I'd been more worried about the Sultan tracking Noorsham down than anything else after we'd heard that rumor. I'd figured the chances there was another Demdji out there who could match my brother's pure destructive power seemed mighty slim. Even I couldn't raze a city the way Noorsham had. Still, we'd been careful the last few months not to let word spread that the Blue-Eyed Bandit and the Demdji who summoned desert storms were one and the same. Not that it mattered. I wasn't ever going to let the Sultan take me alive. But now I considered the tiny sun in Ranaa's hands. It was harmless enough, cupped in her palms like that. It might not be so harmless multiplied a hundredfold. The Sultan's chances were looking better now.

"Your rebellion has kept him out of this side of the desert so far." Samira said. "How long do you think you can keep him out?"

As long as it took. I'd be damned before I'd let the Sultan do to any other Demdji what he'd done to Noorsham. Ranaa might be a cloistered brat who'd developed a big head from being told her whole life she was the reincarnation of a legendary princess. But she was a Demdji. And we took care of our own.

"I can get her to safety." I couldn't leave her here. Not when there was a chance they might find her and I might find myself staring over the barrel of a gun at her next. "Out of the city."

"I don't want to go anywhere with you," Ranaa argued. We both ignored her.

"Prince Ahmed wants to make this country safe for Demdji, but until then, I know where she can be protected."

Samira hesitated a moment. "Can I come with her?"

My shoulders eased in relief. "That depends. Can you walk?"

Imin helped Samira, keeping her standing upright as she limped toward the stairs, Ranaa still clinging to her. I was about to turn away when Ranaa's light grazed the far wall. The cell wasn't quite empty. A woman in a pale yellow khalat was still curled in the corner, not moving.

For a second I thought she was dead, weakened by days in the dark cramped prison. Then her back rose and fell, just slightly. She was still breathing. I crouched down and laid a hand on the bare skin of her arm. It was hotter than it ought to be down here away from the sun. She was sick with fever. My touch started her awake, and wide wild eyes flew open. She gaped at me through a dirty curtain of hair, in panic. Blood and muck caked it against her cheek, and her lips were cracked with thirst. "Can you stand?" I asked. She didn't answer, just stared at me with huge dark eyes. She looked worse than anyone else I'd seen stumble out of these cells. She could barely stay awake, let alone make a run for it.

"Imin!" I called. "I need some help here. Can you—"

"Zahia?" The name was whispered almost as a prayer, rasping out of a throat that sounded bone-dry, a second before her head lolled backward and she lapsed back into feverish sleep.

I stilled. Every part of me. I wondered if this was what Hawa felt when her heart stopped in her chest.

Suddenly I wasn't the Blue-Eyed Bandit. I wasn't a rebel giving orders. I wasn't even a Demdji. I was a girl from Dustwalk again. Because that was the last place I had heard anyone say my mother's name.

FIVE

W hat is it?" Imin appeared at my elbow.

"I—" I stumbled over my words, trying to pull my mind out of the past. There were other women in the desert named Zahia. It was a common enough name. But she'd looked at me like she *knew* me and said my mother's name. And that wasn't all that common.

No. I wasn't a restless, reckless girl at the end of the desert anymore. I was the Blue-Eyed Bandit, and this was a rescue. I nodded toward the unconscious figure on the ground. "Can you carry her?" My voice was steadier than I felt.

Imin, still wearing the shape he'd fought in, lifted the unconscious woman off the ground as easy as a rag doll.

"This is ridiculous, Amani," Mahdi hissed, pushing through the crowd of freed women as I followed Imin out of the cell. They didn't look so good, but they were alive and standing on two feet. "Freeing people is one thing, but you want us to escape while *carrying* someone out?"

"We are not leaving her behind." I'd made the mistake of leaving someone in need behind to save myself before—my friend Tamid, the night I'd fled Dustwalk with Jin. I'd been scared and desperate and frantic. I'd taken Jin's hand without thinking, and I'd left Tamid to bleed out in the sand. I'd left him to die. I couldn't undo what had happened that night. But I wasn't the girl from Dustwalk anymore. I could make sure nobody got left behind again.

"Who knows how to use a gun?" I asked the group of women. No one moved. "Oh, come on, it's not that hard. You point and shoot." Samira's hand went up first. A few more followed her lead nervously. "Take them off the bodies," I ordered, swiping one for myself. I flicked the chamber of the gun open; the slightest touch of iron instantly made my power slip away. But there was a full round. I flicked it shut again and tucked it against my hip, careful not to let any part of it touch my skin. I didn't strictly need a gun. I had the entire desert. But it was always nice to have options. "Let's move."

• ● •

IT WAS AFTER dark and the streets of Saramotai were empty. A whole lot emptier than they ought to be this soon after nightfall.

"Curfew," Mahdi explained in a low whisper as we moved. "The peasant usurper's way of keeping the population under control." He didn't need to say *peasant* with quite that much disdain, but I wasn't about to come to the defense of Malik after he'd taken Saramotai by force and corrupted Ahmed's name.

Curfew was going to make things a whole lot easier or a whole lot harder. Right in front of the prison the road split. I hesitated. I couldn't remember where I'd come from.

"Which way to the gates?" I asked in a low voice. The women following us stared at me with huge, terrified eyes. Finally, Samira loosed her arm from Ranaa's grip and pointed silently to the right. She almost managed to hide the fact that she was shaking. I kept my finger on the trigger as we pressed forward.

I hated to admit that Mahdi was right, but we weren't exactly inconspicuous sneaking out of the prison trailing dozens of wealthy-looking women in torn khalats. And I wasn't counting on the women I'd given guns to—they held them like baskets to market instead of weapons. I had my suspicions that Mahdi could talk someone to death, but otherwise he was useless. And carrying the unconscious woman who'd called me by my mother's name made it more than a little difficult for Imin to fight if we ran into trouble.

I supposed I'd just have to keep us out of trouble, then. That wasn't exactly my strong suit.

Still, we didn't meet with any resistance as we passed

quietly through the deserted streets of Saramotai, retracing my steps from earlier in the day. I was just starting to think we were going to make it, when we rounded the last corner and two dozen men with rifles looked up at us.

Damn.

They were clustered around the city gates in gleaming white-and-gold uniforms. Mirajin uniforms. And not the makeshift ones of the guards who'd blundered into the prison and to their deaths. Real ones. Which meant they were the Sultan's men. On our side of the desert for the first time since Fahali.

I let out the most colorful Xichian curse Jin had taught me as my gun leapt into my hand on instinct. I knew it was too late, though—we were caught. One of the women behind me panicked, and before I could stop her she was gone, darting toward the maze of city streets like a frightened rabbit looking for cover.

I'd watched birds of prey hunt. The rabbit never made it.

A shot went off. Another chorus of screams behind me. And a cry of pain, cut off by a second bullet.

The woman was sprawled on the street, blood mixing with dirt. The bullet had torn straight through her heart. No one else moved.

I kept my finger steady on the trigger. Two dozen guns were up and pointing at us. I just had the one. No matter what anybody had heard about the Blue-Eyed Bandit, it wasn't actually possible to take out two dozen men with one bullet. Or even with my Demdji gift. Not without someone else getting shot.

"So this is the legendary Blue-Eyed Bandit." The man who spoke wasn't wearing a uniform. Instead he was dressed in a gaudy blue kurta that he'd paired with a badly matched purple sheema. He was the only one who didn't have a rifle pointed at my head.

So Malik, the usurper of Saramotai, had returned.

I was dimly aware of Ikar, perched at his watchpost above the gate, legs dangling as he craned over the scene. "I'd just been informed you were gracing our city with your illustrious presence."

He used awfully big words that didn't seem all that comfortable in his mouth. His hollow face was skeletal in the buttery glow of the lamp. I'd grown up in a desperate place; I knew the look of someone who'd been ravaged by life. Only instead of lying down and taking his fate, he'd decided to take someone else's fate from them instead. I could guess that the kurta on his back was the emir's. He had the shape of someone who'd worked and scraped and wanted and suffered, dressed in the clothes of someone who'd never known true want. My finger twitched on the trigger. I was itching to shoot something, but that wouldn't get us out alive.

The small contingent of Sultan's men shifted nervously, looking at me, like they were trying to decide whether I really was the Blue-Eyed Bandit. It looked like stories about me had made it all the way to Izman.

"And you're Malik," I said. "You know, I'd heard when you hanged that lot of people, you did it in the name of my prince. But it looks to me like your loyalty lies elsewhere." I gave the soldiers a mock salute with my free hand. "Not so much a revolutionary as an opportunist, by the look of things."

"Oh, I believe wholeheartedly in the cause of your Rebel Prince." When Malik smiled in the light of the lamps held by the nearby soldiers, he looked like he was baring his teeth. "Your prince calls for freedom and equality in our desert. I've spent my whole life bowing to men who thought they were greater than me. Equality means I should never have to bow again. Not to the Sultan, not to the prince, and not"—he turned and spat toward Samira, making her flinch under his sudden attention—"to your father, either." The movement dashed light and shadow across the walls of Saramotai. Two huge figures hewn into the stone flanked the gates on this side: Hawa and Attallah, joining hands across the curve of the arch.

I hadn't seen them on my way in, not with my back to them. I wondered what they would think if they knew that the city they'd fought so long to save from the outside had rotted from the inside.

Paint had long since faded off the stone, though I thought I could make out the red of Attallah's sheema. And I'd swear Hawa's eyes were still flaked with blue.

"I'm making my own equality," Malik said, pulling my attention back to him. "What does it matter if I'm raising up the low or bringing the folks up on high to their knees, so long as everyone winds up with their feet in the same dust? And she"—he pointed at Ranaa—"is going to buy our freedom."

"Your feet aren't in the dust." Samira pushed Ranaa behind herself protectively. She was doing a mighty fine job of hiding her fear. There was nothing but hate in her as she stood between the man who'd already killed most of her family and the one tiny piece of it left. "You're standing on the backs of the dead."

"The Rebel Prince will lose this war." One of the Sultan's soldiers stepped forward. "Malik is a wise man to see it." The words sounded forced and false, like it pained him to pander to Malik. "The Sultan has agreed to give Saramotai to Lord Malik when he reclaims this half of the desert. In exchange for the Demdji girl." The Sultan might want another Demdji to replace Noorsham, but I wouldn't stake a single louzi that he was willing to give up part of the desert for her. Malik was just stupid enough to think that the Sultan would keep his promise.

"You're outnumbered." That had never mattered much to me before. "Drop the gun, Bandit." Malik sneered.

"There's only one man who gets to call me that," I said. "And you're not near as good-looking as him."

Malik's temper snapped faster than I expected. The gun that had stayed so arrogantly by his side was out and in his hand in the space of a breath, pressing to my forehead in the next. Behind me I felt Imin shift forward, like he might try to do something. I held up a hand, palm flat, hoping he would take the hint and not get us both killed. From the corner of my eye I saw him go still. The women from the prison were watching the scene unfold with huge terrified eyes. One of them had started crying silently.

It would've been nice if the bite of an iron barrel next to my skin was unfamiliar. But this was far from the first time I'd been threatened like this. "You've got a smart mouth on you, anyone ever tell you that?" That wasn't a first, either. But telling him that didn't seem all that smart.

"Malik." The soldier who'd spoken stepped forward, looking like his patience was wearing thin. "The Sultan will want her alive."

"The Sultan is *not* my master." Malik's face had turned savage. He pushed the gun harder against my skull. I could feel the barrel of the pistol pressing between my eyes. My heart quickened instinctively, but I fought down that fear. I wasn't going to die today.

"You just cost me twenty fouza," I sighed. "I made a bet I could make it out of this city without anybody threatening to kill me, and thanks to you, I've just lost."

Malik wasn't smart enough to be worried that someone with a pistol between her eyes was talking back instead of crying and cowering. "Well"—he pulled back the hammer on the pistol—"lucky for you, you're not going to be alive long enough to pay up."

"Malik!" The soldier stepped forward again, his irritation falling away now. Seemed they had only just figured out they were dealing with an unstable man. By some unseen signal from their captain the weapons were shifting, away from the women behind me, toward Malik.

"Any last words, Bandit? Maybe you'd like to beg for your life?"

"Or . . ." A voice seemed to float out of midair by Malik's ear. "Maybe *you* would?"

Malik tensed visibly, in that way men did when they were in danger. It was a stance I'd become intimately familiar with in the past half a year. A thin bead of blood ran down his throat, even though it seemed like there was nothing around him but air.

The tension in my shoulders finally eased. The trouble with having invisible backup was that you never knew exactly where she was.

The air shimmered as the illusion cast by Delila dropped, leaving Shazad standing where there'd been nothing a moment before. Her dark hair was tightly braided to her head like a crown, a white sheema hung loose around her neck, and her simple desert clothes looked expensive. She was everything that Malik hated and she had him helpless. She looked dangerous, and not just because one of her blades was pressed to Malik's throat, but because she looked like her deepest wish was to get to use it.

Finally, and far too late, fear dawned slowly across his face.

"If I were you," I said, "now'd be the time I'd drop that gun and start reaching for the sky."

SIX

I was so close to Malik, I could see his face vacillating between despair and desperate action. He chose the second one. But I was faster than his stupid brain could work. I dropped to my knees a second before the gun went off, the bullet burying itself harmlessly in the wall behind me. Malik hit the ground next to me a second later, a new red necklace from Shazad's sword gracing his throat.

But we weren't done yet.

"That took you long enough," I said to Shazad, rising to my feet as I whipped my hands up. On the other side of the walls of Saramotai, the desert surged in answer. After using nothing but a handful of sand down in the prison, the power of having the whole desert at my fingertips was almost intoxicating.

"I see you managed not to get yourself shot this time." Shazad whirled to face the remaining soldiers as I did the same. "You still owe me those twenty fouza, though."

"Double or nothing?" I offered over my shoulder as we met back to back.

The captain was already giving orders to the confused soldiers, recovering awfully quick considering a new enemy had just appeared out of thin air.

"Delila!" Shazad called an order of her own. "Drop our cover."

The illusion lifted like a curtain before a show. Suddenly half the Sultan's men who'd been standing a moment earlier were crumpled on the ground, and our rebels were in their place, weapons drawn. Behind them was Delila, face still round with innocence, her purple hair that came from not being wholly human falling into wide, frightened-looking eyes. She dropped her hands, shaking with effort and nerves. She was scared but that wasn't stopping her.

"Navid!" From behind me, Imin spotted him instantly among the crowd of rebels.

A tall, desert-built man, Navid was one of our recruits from Fahali. We hadn't been trying to recruit people there, but after the battle it was hard to stop them joining up. Navid was one of the best. He was tough as anybody would need to be to survive this war we were fighting. And as earnest as you needed to be to think we stood a chance. He was hard not to like. But it still surprised me that Imin loved him.

Navid's eyes went wide with relief as he spotted Imin, recognizing his beloved no matter the shape. It was a moment of distraction, his defense lowering in his relief that Imin was alive. I saw it, and so did the soldier on his right.

The desert poured over the edge of the walls of Saramotai, cascading around the carving of Princess Hawa, knocking soldiers off their feet. I wrenched my arm up, flinging a burst of sand toward the soldier who would've killed Navid, knocking him down, and startling Navid's attention back away from Imin.

"Watch your back, Navid!"

I was already turning away. The sand turned into a hurricane around me. I swung one arm down, crashing sand across a soldier's face as he lunged for Delila, pushing him away from her. A shout came from behind me. I spun in time to see a soldier lunging for me, sword up. I started to gather the sand into a blade in my hand but I was too slow. And I didn't need to. Steel screamed against steel. Shazad's blade landed a breath away from my throat, kissing the soldier's weapon. The blood that would've been all over his sword pulsed noisily through my ears. In one move that was too quick for me to see, he was on the ground.

"You ought to take your own advice." Shazad tossed me a spare gun.

"Why would I need to watch my back when you've got it?" I caught the pistol a moment too late to shoot. Instead I slammed the handle straight into the face of the nearest soldier, the blow cracking up my arm, blood from his nose spurting across my hand.

The fight would be short and bloody. There were already more soldiers on the ground than standing. I fired. And now there was one more. I turned, looking for my next target.

I didn't see exactly what happened next. Only splintered moments.

Another gun at the edge of my vision as I raised my own weapon. Exhaustion making me sluggish. Making my mind slow to understand what I was seeing.

That the gun wasn't pointed at me.

It was pointed at Samira. And the soldier already had a finger on the trigger.

Everything happened then in the same second.

Ranaa moved, swinging herself in front of Samira.

His gun went off. So did mine.

His bullet tore through green khalat and skin mercilessly.

One split second and it was over. The fighting was done as quick as it had started. In the silence all I heard was Samira screaming Ranaa's name as the little Demdji's heart pumped out her blood onto the street, the tiny sun in her hand dying with her.

SEVEN

Ahmed was waiting for us at the entrance to camp. That wasn't a good sign.

Our Rebel Prince might not have the pretenses of most royalty, but he didn't usually wait for us like a wife whose husband had stayed at the bar one drink too long, either.

"Delila." He took a step out toward his sister, leaving the cover of the archway. Shazad checked the canyon walls for danger on instinct. The location of the camp was still safe as far as we knew, but if our enemies ever found out where we were, the top of the canyons surrounding us gave any attackers a clean shot with a rifle. At least one person had to care for Ahmed's safety, even if he wasn't going to do it himself. He didn't even seem to notice Shazad's concern; all his attention was on his sister. "Are you all right?"

A part of me wanted to tell Ahmed that he ought to have enough faith in us to bring his sister back in one piece. But then again, my shirt was now more red than white, which didn't exactly scream *Everything's fine!* Probably better to not draw attention to myself just now.

It was my blood. My attacker's blood. Ranaa's blood.

We'd tried to save her. But everyone could tell it was too late. She died quickly in Samira's arms.

People die. I tried to remember that. It was what happened on missions. She wasn't the first, and unless we managed to kill the Sultan tomorrow and put Ahmed on the throne, she wasn't going to be the last. *This is the cost of starting a war,* said a nasty voice in my head that sounded too much like Malik.

Only she was a Demdji. We'd never lost a Demdji in the fighting before. Or a child.

This was the Sultan's fault. Not ours. He'd let the Gallan across our borders and let them kill Demdji in the first place. And he was the one hunting our kind down to use as weapons now. It was his fault she was dead. But we were still alive—me, Imin, Delila—and we weren't going to become another Noorsham. We were going to topple him before he could find another Demdji. I'd make sure of that.

"I'm fine." Delila squirmed as her brother checked her over for injury. "Really, Ahmed, I'm fine."

Shazad gave me a significant look that she hid behind the guise of scratching her nose. After half a year I could read Shazad like an open book. This one meant we were about to be in trouble.

So we hadn't exactly had permission to take Delila with us. But we'd known we'd need help if we were going to get past Saramotai's impenetrable walls. We'd also known that if we asked Ahmed if we could take Delila on a mission he'd say no. So we just hadn't asked him. It wasn't technically disobedience if we'd never been forbidden from doing it. Even though we both knew that excuse would fly just about as well as either of us could.

Personally I'd been hoping Ahmed might not notice that Delila was gone at all. He was busy running a whole rebellion, and we were gone only a handful of days. But then, unlike me, most people seemed to be able to keep track of their siblings.

"She did good, Ahmed," I offered. "A lot of folks would be dead if it weren't for her." *A lot more folks.* But I didn't say that aloud. I knew Shazad heard it in my silence all the same. Delila just beamed at her feet as Ahmed finally tore his eyes off his sister to survey the state we were in and the rabble behind us. Some were riding, others were on foot if they were strong enough. Mahdi was among those who had declared he needed a horse after his ordeal. Imin had shifted to a girl's shape, riding double with Navid, whose arms were wrapped around her protectively.

"I see you managed to bring back Imin and Mahdi, and then some." There was a wry hint under his indulgent smile.

Some of the ex-prisoners had stayed in Saramotai, but plenty of others had decided to leave with us. Women who had nothing to stay for. Whose husbands and sons had been among the bodies hanging from the walls. The woman who'd called me Zahia was one of them. The Holy Father in Saramotai had seen to her as best he could. Enough to tell me that she wouldn't die on the journey to camp. Mahdi argued about bringing her, but Shazad didn't question me when I said it seemed wrong to leave her helpless in the city that had tried to kill her. I could tell Shazad knew there was something I wasn't telling her. The woman had been weaving in and out of consciousness since we'd left the city, riding mostly tied with a sheema to another woman in front of her so she didn't slip off.

It wasn't exactly uncommon for strays to come back from missions. I ought to know—half a year ago, I was one. Jin had been meant to come back with news of the Sultan's so-called weapon. Instead he came back with me. And in the six months that'd passed since then, I'd long stopped being the rebel camp's newest arrival.

We'd been joined by rebel sympathizers like Navid, ignited to action after the battle at Fahali. Orphans picked up in Malal, clinging to the hem of Jin's shirt the whole way back to camp. A defecting soldier who'd been guided our way by Shazad's father, General Hamad. Sometimes Shazad would slip and refer to them as troops. Ahmed called them refugees. After a few weeks everyone was just a rebel.

"We need to debrief." The words came with a significant look directed specifically at me and Shazad. Ahmed wasn't about to dig into us in front of everyone. But that didn't mean we were off the hook.

Shazad was already talking as we pushed through the gateway that led to camp, telling Ahmed what had happened in Saramotai. She danced around arranging to get me captured and skipped to how she and Delila, invisible under Delila's illusion, had slipped in behind me the moment I'd pretended to trip in the doorway, waiting for nightfall to let the others in behind us. The less she could remind Ahmed we'd put his sister in danger, the better. The way she told it, you'd barely know there'd been a fight. We'd left Samira in charge of the city, Shazad told him.

"We need to send her reinforcements," she said as we felt our way through the inside of the cliff toward camp. "We left everyone we could to help." "Everyone we could" meant the half a dozen other men who had come with us to Saramotai. Navid would've made seven whole people but he wouldn't be separated from Imin again. It wasn't exactly an army that could hold a stronghold but it was what we had. "It's not enough to hold the peace. We should send fifty well-trained soldiers, before somebody else develops any ambition and steps into Malik's shoes. And we need to reinforce the city against the Sultan. Ahmed"— Shazad lowered her voice, casting her eyes behind us to where the newly recruited rabble was feeling their way nervously through the dark tunnel—"your father's troops were in our half of the desert."

Ahmed didn't answer her right away, but as we neared the end of the tunnel I could see he understood the significance even better than I did. A whole lot of the power we held relied on appearances. Truth be told, we wouldn't be able to match the Sultan's army on a battlefield if they tried to take the desert back from us by force. Keeping our half of the desert relied on the Sultan's believing our numbers were greater than they were. And that deception relied on his men never straying into our half of the desert to find out the truth.

As we stepped through the other side of the cliff face, I blinked against the sudden brightness. The summer light made the rebel camp look like one of Delila's illusions— too beautiful and alive in this desert full of dust and death. A world apart.

The camp was twice the size it had been when I'd first seen it. I couldn't keep myself from glancing over my shoulder at the women of Saramotai following us. I'd gotten into the habit of watching the new refugees' faces when they first set eyes on the camp. I wasn't disappointed this time. One by one, they stepped out of the tunnel and got their first look at my home. For just a moment, grief and fear and exhaustion parted, giving way to wonder as they took in the oasis rolled out below them. Watching them, it felt for a second like I was seeing it with fresh eyes, too.

Except in the past six months I'd gotten used to coming home. I knew everything about the camp. I knew the faces that waited here and the scars they wore. Both the ones that brought them to our war, and the ones they'd gotten fighting for us. I knew which tents were slightly lopsided, and what the birds sounded like in late afternoon from the bathing pools, and that the smell of fresh-baked bread meant Lubna was on cooking duty for the day.

I half expected to see Jin sauntering toward me, like he had the last time I'd gotten back from a mission I'd been sent on without him. A smile on his face, his collar loose so I could see the edge of his tattoo, sleeves rolled up to his elbows so when he pulled me to him, making my own shirt ride up, the bare cool skin of his arms pressed against the desert-flushed heat of mine.

But it looked like he still hadn't come home.

Shazad was arguing with Ahmed over the details of whom to send to Saramotai and how many, leaving me to take charge of our new refugees. I gave Imin and Navid instructions to get them settled. Take the sick and wounded to the Holy Father. Get everyone else working. Navid didn't need instruction; he'd been on the other side of it himself. But he still smiled genially as I gave it. When I was done, Imin started to help him guide the women to the other side of camp.

I caught Ahmed's gaze over Shazad's shoulder as she kept talking, with Mahdi interjecting every so often. Ahmed's eyes flicked pointedly to Delila. I understood. He didn't want her any more involved than she already was in this. "Delila," I said, catching her attention, "would you go with Navid and Imin and make sure they can keep their hands off each other long enough to settle everyone?"

Delila might be naive, but she wasn't stupid. She knew what I was doing. I thought she might make one last stab at standing up for me and Shazad. But she ducked her head, pushing her purple hair behind her ears with false brightness, before following Imin and Navid and their gaggle of women from Saramotai.

Ahmed waited until she was out of earshot before he started. "What were you two thinking?" He hadn't taken his eyes from his sister's back. "Delila's a child and she is not trained to fight."

"Not to mention that your plan almost wound up getting you shot in the head," Mahdi butted in.

"Your total *lack* of a plan got you locked up in a jail cell, so I wouldn't point fingers if I were you. You know what they say: those who point fingers wind up with them broken so badly they point straight back at them." Shazad had even less patience for Mahdi than I did. She'd known him longer. From the days before the Sultim trials in Izman.

"I'm pretty sure that's not a saying," I said.

"You almost *died*," Mahdi said again, like we might be too stupid to understand.

"You say that like it's the first time I've ever had a gun pointed at me," I retorted as Shazad rolled her eyes. "It's not even the first time this *month*."

"My sister is not as accustomed to near death as you two." Ahmed started walking, an unspoken signal that we should fall into step.

"We wouldn't have let anything happen to her, Ahmed," Shazad said as she and I dropped into pace easily on either side of him, leaving Mahdi trying to elbow his way in.

"Besides, Delila's as Demdji as I am." We passed out of

the glaring sun at the edge of camp and into the shade of the oasis trees. We were headed towards Ahmed's pavilion. I was trying to remember just when I'd gotten quite so comfortable talking back to royalty. "She wants to help, same as everyone else here."

"That's not why you took her, though, is it?" Ahmed didn't look at me as we walked. "You took her to prove a point."

He was talking about Jin.

It'd been two months back that I'd gotten shot and nearly died while Jin and I were on a mission in Iliaz. I'd been lucky to survive. When I woke up, back at camp, stitched and bandaged, Jin was gone. Ahmed had sent him to the border while I was unconscious. To infiltrate the Xichian army, which had been gnawing at Miraji from the eastern border, trying to get a foothold in our desert ever since the Sultan's alliance with the Gallan had shattered.

I wasn't so petty as to drag his sister into danger just because he'd sent his brother into it when I might've been dying.

But then, I wasn't sure I could say that out loud, either.

"We can need her and prove a point at the same time." Shazad stepped in, taking the bullet for me. We'd nearly reached Ahmed's pavilion as he halted, turning to face us. I staggered to a stop and for a moment, all I could see was the Rebel Prince facing me, outlined by the gold sun on his pavilion, standing half a pace above us like he could bring justice down on our heads at any second. Like he was our ruler instead of our friend.

It was then that I noticed the entrance to the pavilion was closed. That was why I could see the sun stitched into the tent flaps radiating from Ahmed like he was stepping straight out of the sun. I'd only ever see those closed when Ahmed was holding a war council. Something was wrong. Shazad realized it the same second I did.

"Hala's back," Ahmed said. Something was wrong to get him to drop the subject of his sister so quickly. "She got back from Izman just before you. Maz spied you on the horizon from the air, so we thought we'd wait, to . . . talk." His eyes danced to Mahdi, and then away so quickly I wouldn't have noticed if I hadn't been watching him so closely.

"What happened?" Shazad asked. "Why didn't you tell Imin that Hala was back?" Imin and Hala were siblings. They shared a Djinni father. If Hala hadn't already been in Izman when Imin was captured, then there was no question we would have taken her instead of Delila. She would've torn through the mind of every inhabitant of Saramotai to get Imin out.

"Is Sayyida with her?" Mahdi butted in.

Sayyida. The reason Hala had been sent to Izman in the first place.

I'd never met Sayyida, but I'd heard plenty about her. She was the same age as me. She'd been married at fifteen to one of Shazad's father's soldiers. Shazad was the one who'd noticed she had more broken bones than her soldier husband. She was the one who had contrived to move Sayyida out of her husband's home to the Hidden House, a Rebellion safe house in Izman. From there she had gotten tangled up with the Rebellion. And with Mahdi, from the sound of things.

In the early days, right after the Sultim trials, Sayyida had managed to maneuver herself into a position in the Sultan's palace as a spy for the Rebellion. A month back, she'd missed sending her regular report. Ahmed waited a week. It was possible something else had gone wrong. And the last thing anyone wanted was to blow her cover if it was just a delay. A week of Mahdi nagging Ahmed every day to send someone for her before Hala finally went to find out what was happening.

"Is Sayyida all right?" Mahdi pressed. He sounded hopeful, though I could see the apprehension in his eyes as he looked over his prince's shoulder at the shut pavilion.

Ahmed's silence was answer enough.

●●●

INSIDE THE PAVILION Hala was kneeling on the ground, slumped over a pretty Mirajin girl, her golden hands resting on the girl's head. Hala didn't look up as we came in, and her eyes stayed screwed shut. She looked tired. Tired enough that she wasn't using an illusion to hide her missing fingers like she usually did. Her Demdji skin moved like molten gold, as every shuddering breath she took shifted the lamplight across it. A thin sheen of sweat clung to her. Not from heat, I realized, but from effort. She was using her Demdji powers, just not on her own vanity. She was using them on the girl on the ground. Sayyida, I guessed.

Sayyida's eyes were wide and unseeing, fixed on something far away that none of the rest of us could make out. Hala was inside her mind.

Mahdi dropped to his knees on her other side, across from Hala. "Sayyida!" He gathered her up in his arms. "Sayyida, can you hear me?"

"I'd appreciate it if you didn't do that." Hala's familiar clipped voice sounded strained. She still didn't open her eyes. "It's a little insulting to try to shake me out of her head like I'm a bad dream, seeing as I've been holding an illusion for the better part of a week to try to *help*." A week? That would explain why Hala looked like she was cracking. It was hard for any of us but the shape-shifters to use our powers for more than a few hours at a time. Let alone a week.

"She was easy enough to find, waiting for me in a cell." Hala slumped on the ground. She was shaking visibly. Barely hanging on. "Getting in her head was the only way I could carry her all the way here quietly." She looked desperately at Ahmed. "Did you bring something to knock her out?"

Ahmed nodded, pulling a small bottle of something clear from his pocket.

"What happened to her?" Mahdi shifted so he was cradling Sayyida. I'd always figured Mahdi for a coward, but I realized now I'd never actually seen him look scared before. Not even on the wrong side of a prison door. And this fear wasn't for himself. It was possible he did belong in this rebellion after all.

Hala glanced to Ahmed for permission. He hesitated for a second before nodding. The only sign Hala gave that she was letting go of her power was the small sigh that slid out between her lips before she sat back on her heels. But the change in Sayyida was like watching night fall at high noon. Her blank peace turned to screaming, her head arching back as she writhed out of Mahdi's grip. She was thrashing blindly, like a trapped animal, clawing at Mahdi's clothes, at the ground, at anything.

Shazad took the bottle from Ahmed's hand and the sheema from her neck and poured the contents of the bottle into the cloth. Just the smell of it made my head spin a little. She latched one arm around Sayyida's body, trapping the screaming girl's arms against her sides, and pressed the soaked cloth against Sayyida's nose and mouth. Shazad pushed slightly on the girl's middle, forcing her to take a gasping, panicked breath, inhaling the full force of the fumes.

Mahdi hadn't moved. He just stared with hollow eyes as Sayyida's struggling got weaker until unconsciousness claimed her, making her go limp in Shazad's grip.

"Mahdi." Ahmed broke the silence finally. "Take Sayyida to the Holy Father's tent. She can rest there."

Mahdi nodded, grateful for the escape. He wasn't a strong man; a scholar, not a fighter. His arms shook with the effort as he gathered her up. But none of us was about to insult him by offering him help.

"Rest isn't going to help her," I said as the tent flap closed behind him. "She's dying." The truth came easily. Us Demdji couldn't tell a lie. Whatever they had done to her, it was killing her.

"I know," Ahmed said. "But trust me, it does very little good to tell someone that the one they love is dying." He looked straight at me when he said that. I wondered what had passed between him and Jin when I was at death's door.

"What did they do to her?" Shazad's voice was tight. "Did she tell them anything about us?" Of everyone in this camp, Shazad had more at stake than any of us. She belonged to a family at the heart of Izman, and if it ever got out that Shazad was on the Rebel Prince's side, there were a lot of people close to her the Sultan could easily reach for.

"Oh, forgive me, I didn't ask after the particulars of her torture while I was rescuing her all by myself, while also trying not to hand my Demdji self straight over to the Sultan," Hala sniped. "Maybe you'd like me to go back and trade myself in for some useless information?" Hala was normally short-tempered, just not with Shazad. Folks didn't exactly do well when they got smart with Shazad. Hala must be worse off than I'd realized.

"If the Sultan knew about you, we'd already have heard," Ahmed said.

"We need a new spy in the palace." Shazad drummed her fingers across the hilt of the sword at her side. "Maybe it's time for me to return from my holy pilgrimage." As far as anyone in Izman knew, Shazad Al-Hamad, General Hamad's devastatingly beautiful daughter, had come down with a bad bout of holiness. She'd retreated to the sacred site of Azhar, where the First Mortal was said to have been made, to pray in silence and meditate. "It's nearly Auranzeb. It would be a good reason to go back."

"You get invited to Auranzeb?" My ears perked up. Auranzeb was held every year on the anniversary of the Sultan's coup for the Mirajin throne. A commemoration of the bloody night when he struck a bargain with the Gallan army and slaughtered his own father and half his brothers.

Even down in Dustwalk, we'd heard stories about the celebrations. Of fountains full of water flecked with gold, dancers who leapt through fire as entertainment, and food made of sugar that was sculpted so fine the folks who made it went blind.

"General's daughter privileges." Shazad sounded bored already.

"No." Ahmed cut across us quickly. "I can't spare you. I might not be as good a strategist as you, but even I know you don't send your best general into the fray as a spy if you can help it."

"And I'm so very dispensable?" Hala asked from where she was still slumped on the ground, a tinge of sarcasm in her voice. Ahmed ignored her. It was impossible to respond to every sarcastic thing Hala said and still have time to do anything else with your day.

I reached out a hand, offering to help her up. She ignored me, stretching to steal a half-peeled orange from the table instead.

"We have to do something." Shazad smoothed her hands compulsively over the map that was rolled out on the table. It used to be a single clean, crisp sheet of paper showing Miraji. Now it was a dozen different pieces showing far corners of the country. Cities with the names of rebels stationed there scrawled and crossed out; other pieces of paper overlapping one another as the desert shifted in our hands. There was a fresh note next to Saramotai. "We can't just hide out in this desert forever, Ahmed." I recognized the beginning of the same argument that Shazad and Ahmed had been having for months now. Shazad kept saying we needed to take the Rebellion to the capital if we wanted a shot at winning. Ahmed would say it was too risky, and Shazad would say nobody ever won a war on the defensive.

Ahmed rubbed two fingers across a spot at his hairline as he started his reply. There was a small scar there, almost invisible now. I'd noticed he rubbed it like it still hurt, though, every time he sent one of us off to do something that might be our death. Like that scar was where he kept his conscience. I didn't know how he'd gotten it. It was from the life Jin and Ahmed had before they came to Miraji.

Jin had told me the stories behind some of his scars once. On one of those dark nights in the desert between camp and a mission. Right after he'd earned a wound that would make a new scar right below the tattoo of the sun on his chest. We were a long way from any Holy Father to patch us up. Which left me. In the dark of his tent my hand had traveled across his bare skin, finding new bumps and marks while he told me where they'd come from. A drunk sailor's knife in a bar brawl in an Albish port. A broken bone on deck in a storm. Until my fingers found the one on his left shoulder, near the tattoo of the compass that was on the other side of his heart from the sun.

"That one," he'd said, so close to me that his breath stirred the hair that had escaped from the hasty knot on my head, "was from this bullet I caught in the shoulder when a pain-in-the-ass girl who was pretending to be a boy ditched me in the middle of a riot."

"Well, it's a good thing that pain-in-the-ass girl stitched you up, too," I'd joked, tracing his tattoo with my thumb.

Out of the corner of my eye I saw Jin's mouth pull up in the smallest edge of a smile. "God, I knew I was in trouble even then. I was running for my life, bleeding on your floor, and all I could think about was kissing you and damn if we got caught."

I'd told him that would've been idiotic. And then he'd kissed me until we were both stupid from it.

"What about Jin?" It slipped out without my meaning it to, interrupting the argument that had been going through its usual steps while my head was in a tent in the middle of the sands.

Ahmed shook his head, knuckles still resting against his forehead. "No word."

"And you don't think it's worth sending someone after him like we did for Sayyida?" It was out before I could check the anger in my words.

"So, you *are* angry about Jin." Ahmed sounded tired.

"We're in the middle of a war." It would be petty of me to be mad about Ahmed sending Jin away while my life hung in the balance. I supposed I was petty, then.

"We are." Somehow his calm made it that much worse. From the corner of my eye I caught one of Shazad's looks. Only this one was traded with Hala instead of me, too quick for me to read. Hala shoved the last piece of the orange into her mouth, finally getting to her feet, stepping away so she was clear of me.

"That wasn't an answer," Ahmed said to me. "You think I was wrong for sending Jin to spy on the Xichian? When foreigners warring with my father are the only thing keeping him at bay?"

"Well, it doesn't seem like it matters anymore," I snapped. "The Sultan is back on our territory anyway, judging by all those dead soldiers we left in Saramotai." Damn, I hadn't meant to say that. I tried a different tack. "I just think there might've been another way." That didn't come out right, either. Even if I had been thinking it for months.

Ahmed linked his hands on top of his head. The gesture was so much like Jin it made me even angrier. "You don't think I should've sent my brother out for the good of the country for *your* sake?"

"I think you could've waited to send him away." My temper broke, and suddenly I was shouting. Shazad drew forward like she was going to stop me from saying something I might regret. "At least until I woke up from being shot for *your* rebellion."

I'd never seen Ahmed's temper flare before. But I knew I'd pushed too far even before his voice rose. "He *asked* to go, Amani."

The words were simple enough, but it took me a heartbeat to understand them all the same. Shazad and Hala had both gone still, watching the exchange.

"I didn't send him away." Ahmed's voice wasn't raised anymore but it hadn't lost any of its strength. "He *asked* me for something that would take him away from here and from you. I tried to talk him out of it, but I love my brother enough that I didn't want him to have to watch you die, either. And I have spent the last two months lying to protect you, but I don't have *time* to keep you from acting out some misguided defiance against me because you think it's my fault he's gone."

Hurt and anger warred inside me and I didn't know which one I wanted to pay attention to first. I wanted to call him a liar but I knew I wouldn't be able to. Everything he was saying sounded true. Truer than Ahmed sending Jin away with no care for either of us. Truer than Jin going against his will. I had almost died and Jin was going to let me do it alone.

"Amani—" Ahmed knew me as well as anyone. He knew my instinct was to run. And I knew it, too. I could feel the itch building in my legs. He went from ruler to friend again, reaching for me. Trying to stop me. But I was already out of his reach, pushing out of the stifling dark of the pavilion and into the mockingly bright sun of the oasis.

EIGHT

Last time I'd seen Jin had been a few heartbeats before I was shot in the stomach.

We were in Iliaz, the key to the middle mountains. So long as Iliaz was in the Sultan's hands, there was no easy way into eastern Miraji. Meaning there was no way to take Izman, and with it the throne.

It was supposed to be a simple reconnaissance mission.

But it turned out we weren't the only enemies of the Sultan to figure out that winning Iliaz could mean winning Miraji. Iliaz was under siege from both the Albish and the Gamanix armies. I didn't know where either of those countries were, but Jin pointed out the flags on their tents as we lay flat on the mountaintop looking over their camps. And it turned out the young prince who was leading the army in Iliaz was a damn sight better as a commander than his brother Naguib had been.

He was holding his own in the mountain fortress against two armies at once, with minimal losses. Even Shazad was impressed. But she thought she could find a way through the siege all the same.

That was, give or take, how we wound up in the middle of a skirmish between the Emir of Iliaz's first command and two foreign armies. And the Iliaz first command was a whole lot bigger than any of us had expected.

I didn't remember much from that fight. Blasts of gunpowder sparking the night air from both sides, cries in tongues I didn't know, and blood dashing across the dusty rocks. Shazad a whirlwind of steel cutting our way out of the fight, me with the desert at my fingertips, Jin leveling his gun at Mirajin and foreigner alike. A scrape of bullet grazing my arm, untethering my power with just one iron kiss. Seeing the knife that was about to go through Jin's back a heartbeat before he saw it. A heartbeat that mattered in keeping him alive. Grabbing the pistol off my belt.

I stepped out of my cover and straight into the line of fire. The man with the knife went down with one pull of my trigger. Only there was another gun behind him, aimed at me by a dark-haired Mirajin soldier with a steady hand. His bullet tore straight through me. Like I wasn't Djinni fire and desert sand at all. Just flesh and blood.

Everything I knew about what happened next were things I was told after I woke up. Jin had grabbed me as I'd fallen, cutting three men down between us as he went.

I was bleeding so badly it looked like half my life was already on my clothes by the time he got to me. Shazad carved a path out of the last of the fray with a few swings of her swords and they got me onto Izz's back; he was shaped as a giant Roc, come to rescue us. Only there was no time to get me all the way back to our camp. I would have died first. They stopped at the first town they saw with a prayer house. It was on the Sultan's side of the country. Enemy ground. Izz, back in his human shape, made the Holy Father swear he would heal me, not harm me, then repeated it to make sure it was true before they handed me over. Shazad dragged Jin away when he tried to make the Holy Father work with a gun to his head.

The Holy Father didn't try to kill me, though I heard I came pretty close to dying once or twice all on my own. The bullet had just missed about three different ways of killing me. I'd only barely stopped bleeding by the time they had to move me again. The Holy Father warned them against it but Izz had been spotted. They got me back to camp as quickly as they could and handed me over to our Holy Father.

It turned out it was being a Demdji that'd saved me. I'd burned away any chance of infection, quick and hot, all on my own. So the only thing the Holy Father had to worry about was the bleeding.

Near a week had passed the next time I opened my eyes, fighting my way out of a haze of drugs that'd been forced down me along with water. Shazad was asleep next to me. That was how I knew I must've been close to death. The sick tent had been Bahi's territory. She hadn't set foot in it since he'd died. Not even when she'd gotten hurt herself, the one time I'd ever seen a sword get past her guard. I'd stitched the thin slice across her arm instead.

She woke instantly as soon as I shifted, her eyes flying open, going for a weapon that wasn't there before focusing on me. "Well, look who's back from the dead."

● ● ●

SHAZAD FOUND ME in one of the pools of water that had been designated for washing. Dark cloths hung between the trees on all sides to shield it from view of the camp. It was shallow enough that I could sit in it and be covered up to my shoulders, and clear enough that I could see my toes at the bottom. The bottom of the pool was scattered with white and black pebbles smoothed by the water. I pushed them around the bottom with my toes. I'd been in here long enough that I'd scrubbed the dust out of my hair, and it had already dried in strange wild waves, curling around the edges of my scalp, like it had a habit of doing.

I was carefully using sand to scrub away the flecks of blood that were still clinging to the wound at my collarbone from Saramotai. I'd thought about going to the Holy Father for stitches but I figured he had enough on his hands with the refugee women. Including the one who had called me by my mother's name. I didn't know if she'd have woken up yet, but if she had, that was another reason to steer clear of the sick tent.

Shazad had stripped the desert off herself, too. She was wearing a white-and-yellow khalat that reminded me of the uniform of Miraji. It made her desert skin look all that much darker against the paleness of the linen. She had a bundle tucked under one arm.

"Jin has as much flight in him as he has fight, you know," Shazad said. "That's how Ahmed wound up alone in Izman in the first place." I knew the story. When Ahmed had chosen to stay in the country where he was born, Jin had decided to move on, staying on the ship they'd been working on. He'd come back a few months later with Delila, after his mother died. "He did it at the Sultim trials, too." She shucked off her shoes. "Vanished the night before and came back with a black eye and cracked rib he never explained to any of us."

"He got in a brawl in a bar with a soldier about a girl."

"Huh." Shazad considered that, rolling up her shalvar. She sat at the edge of the pool, dipping her feet in to cool off. The sounds of the camp drifted around us on the slight breeze. Birdsong mingling with indistinct voices. "All right, we're low on time. So I'm going to hurry this up. You're going to ask me if I knew he'd asked to leave. And I'm going to tell you that I didn't. And you're going to believe me because I've never lied to you before. Which is half the reason you like me so much."

Well, she wasn't wrong about that. "What's the other half, if you're so clever?"

"That you'd be *constantly* undressed if it wasn't for me."
The bundle under her arm unfurled into a khalat I'd seen
at the bottom of her trunk of clothes before. It was the color
of the sky in the last moments before it turned to full desert
night and dotted with what looked like tiny stars. I realized
as it clinked in Shazad's hands that it wasn't stitching. They
were gold beads. I hadn't exactly arrived at the Rebellion
with enough clothing to fight a war, but Shazad had enough
for the two of us. Even if nothing of hers ever fit me exactly
right. But this was by far the most beautiful thing I'd ever
seen her pull out of that chest of clothes.

"What's the occasion?" I asked, dragging myself through
the water to lean on the edge of the pool next to her.

"Navid has somehow convinced Imin to marry him."

I sucked in a breath so fast I inhaled some of the water and started coughing. Shazad slapped me on the back
a few times.

Navid had been totally taken with Imin from the moment he arrived at the camp. It didn't seem to matter what
shape Imin wore; Navid could spy the object of his af-
fections across the camp without hesitating. He had very
drunkenly declared his love on equinox a few months
back, in front of the entire camp. I remembered grabbing
Shazad's arm, bracing myself for the inevitable mockery
and rejection from Imin. For some baffling reason it never
came. Baffling, because Imin treated everyone but Hala
with the sort of disdain that came only from true hurt.
The kind the Rebellion had saved the Demdji from in the
first place.

Imin had glanced around at all the staring faces with sardonic yellow eyes before asking us why we didn't have anything more interesting to stare at. Then Imin slipped a hand into Navid's, pulling him away from the firelight and our stunned silence.

"You have to attend," Shazad said as I recovered from my attempt to breathe in water, "and you have to be dressed to do it. Imin has already stolen three khalats from me for the occasion, because, and I quote, 'none of my own clothes fit at the moment.'"

I raised my eyebrows at her. "Did you point out that Imin's a shape-shifter and can make anything fit?"

"You know I did." Shazad pulled an annoyed face. "It went down about as well as you would expect and now I'm down three more khalats."

"You're going to run out of clothes at this rate."

"And when that day comes I will lead a mission to Imin's tent to reclaim the spoils. But for now I managed to save this." She gestured at the white linen clinging to her perfectly. "And this. And I know where to reclaim this one from because you sleep four feet away from me."

I ran my finger and thumb along the hem of the khalat she held out to me, my hand already dry in the unforgiving sun. I remembered something she'd told me once, on one of those dark nights when neither of us could sleep, and we stayed awake talking until we ran out of words or out of night. When she'd told her parents she was throwing her lot in with Ahmed, her father gave her those swords to fight the Rebellion with. Her mother gave her that khalat.

"That's the khalat you're supposed to wear into Izman. When we win this war." *If we win.*

"We're still a long way from Izman," Shazad said as if she'd heard the *if I* didn't voice. "Might as well not let it rot at the bottom of my trunk. You can wear it if you swear to me you won't get blood on it."

"It's dangerous to ask a Demdji to make a promise," I said. Promises were like truth-telling. They would come true. Just not in the way you might expect.

"It's a wedding, Amani." Shazad reached a hand down to help me out of the water. "Even you aren't that good at getting into trouble."

• ● ●

IN DUSTWALK, MARRIAGES happened fast. Most girls just dug out their best khalats, worn thin from years of sisters and mothers handing them down, and draped their sheemas over their heads to hide their faces in that uncertain time between engagement and marriage, lest a ghoul or Djinni notice a woman who belonged to no one, no longer a daughter but not yet a wife, either, and try to claim her for his own.

We didn't have a prayer house in camp, but we'd always made do. The Holy Father had prepared the ceremony in a clear space at the edge of the sand where the ground sloped up just enough to give a good view of the whole camp below in the last of the light. The wedding began at dusk, the sun setting over the canyon. Like they always did. A time of change in the day for a moment of change in two lives.

Imin wasn't wearing a repurposed sheema. It was a true wedding covering, made of fine cloth stitched with bright thread, and when the sun hit it, I could just see the outline of the face she had chosen through the thin yellow muslin. It wasn't one I'd seen on her before. Imin was our best spy, staying alive by looking unremarkable. But the face she'd chosen today was stunning, and she was beaming like I'd never seen Imin smile.

Hala caught my gaze as the two of them knelt in the sand side by side. It'd been an unspoken pact between us Demdji to keep one eye on Imin after that night Navid declared his love for her. None of us had ever seen Imin's walls drop for anyone in camp before Navid.

Imin and Hala might share a Djinni father, but by the sound of things they couldn't have had more different mothers. Rumor had it Hala had torn her mother's mind apart, driving her crazy on purpose because she hated the woman so much. The Rebellion had found Imin in a prison waiting for execution at the hands of the Gallan. Imin had spent sixteen years hidden in the house of grandparents who shielded their daughter's Demdji child. Alone and lonely, but safe. Until the day Imin's grandmother collapsed from the heat on their doorstep. Imin was otherwise alone in the house. The sixteen-year-old waited, hoping a neighbor would notice. But finally, desperate, Imin ran out to help wearing the same slender girl's form she'd donned to fight the heat that morning.

The body was too weak to drag a grown woman, though. Imin shifted into a man's shape out in the open.

Word reached the Gallan. They killed Imin's whole family on the same doorstep, as they tried to block the soldiers' path.

Until Navid, Imin had treated anyone who wasn't a Demdji with distrust. Even me, on account of how I'd thought I was human for sixteen years.

It would take the slightest misstep from Navid to send Imin back behind walls. But even Hala hadn't been able to find anything wrong with him, and she'd been trying real hard. Anyone could see the way Navid looked at Imin. And it didn't change no matter what body our shape-shifter wore, woman or man, Mirajin or foreign.

The Holy Father stood between Navid and Imin as they faced us, sitting in the sand, legs crossed. He recited the usual blessings for a wedding as he filled two large clay bowls with fire. He handed one to Imin and one to Navid. He spoke of how humanity was made by the First Beings out of water and earth, carved by wind, and lit with a spark of Djinni fire. He reminded us that when Princess Hawa and Attallah became the first mortals ever to wed their fires were twinned and burned so much brighter for it. All these centuries later we still uttered the same words they had.

As he spoke we came up, one by one, the women of the camp to Imin, the men to Navid. Each of us dropped something of ours into their fire to bless the union. In Dustwalk I'd always given an empty bullet casing or a lock of hair. I didn't have anything else to give.

For the first time in my life I had more, and I'd had to think about what I ought to give, as Shazad and I got ready. For just a second my fingers had drifted over the red sheema. The one Jin had given me in the burned-out mountain mining town of Sazi. As I closed my eyes for Shazad to press dark kohl into my lids, I could picture myself tossing it into the fire, watching the red cloth catch. It would go up in seconds. I was angry but I didn't hate him. I'd fastened it around my waist like a sash instead, the way I always did with Shazad's clothes.

I stood behind Hala, who held her hand above the fire, pricking each of the remaining three fingers on her left hand with a needle in quick succession. Blood was the traditional offering from family members, even if the father Imin and Hala shared didn't bleed. Bright red dots welled at the tips of her golden fingers, then sizzled noisily as the blood hit the fire. As Hala moved out of the way I held up my gift above the fire and a handful of desert sand slipped out between my fingers, scattering into the flames. I caught the slightest hint of a smile from Imin as I stepped aside, leaving room for Shazad to drop a small comb of hers into the fire. Next to her, Ahmed dropped a Xichian coin into Navid's bowl. He wore a clean black kurta edged with red that made him look like he belonged more in a palace than in a rebellion. He and Shazad made a well matched pair, standing side by side in front of the twinned wedding fires.

Behind Ahmed, the twins, Izz and Maz, were holding a blue feather, alternately snatching it out of each other's hands and shoving each other in a silent war over which one would get to drop it into the fire. The warning look Shazad gave them as she turned around was loud enough to get them both to behave. When they spotted me standing on Imin's side of the fire they waved frantically. I hadn't seen the twins since I'd been injured. They must've gotten back while we were in Saramotai.

When the whole camp was done, finally Imin and Navid turned to face each other to speak their vows.

"I give myself to you." Imin carefully tipped her fire into the third bowl that the Holy Father held between them, the ashes of our gifts mingling with bright coal embers and sending up sparks as they spilled from one bowl to another. "All that I am I give to you, and all that I have is yours. My life is yours to share. Until the day we die."

Navid repeated the same as he tilted the contents of his bowl in after hers until a single fire, larger and brighter than the ones they had held alone, burned between them. The Holy Father waved his tattooed hands over it in blessing.

There was a moment of silence as the sun disappeared entirely behind the canyon wall, casting the camp into a gloom broken only by the fire. And then Navid sprang to his feet, unabashedly picking Imin up, arms around her waist, before pulling her into a kiss. The whole of the camp cheered. The ceremony was over. It was time for the celebrations to begin.

"Amani!" I didn't have a chance to turn around to see who'd called my name. A pair of bright blue arms grabbed me around the waist, spinning me around gleefully.

I laughed, shoving Izz off as my feet found the ground again, staggering. Maz was wearing clothes, but Izz had already stripped down to nothing but his trousers. The twins had a real aversion to clothes. Their animal shapes didn't need them and it seemed to confuse them that their human shapes did.

Izz gestured at the bare blue skin of his chest and my khalat. "We match." He beamed stupidly at me.

"And luckily only one of us had to take off our shirt. I see you both survived Amonpour." The Albish had made an alliance with our western neighbors of Amonpour after losing Miraji to the Gallan twenty years ago. According to Shazad it had been nothing more than some men's signatures on paper. Until the Albish suddenly got the news of the Gallan being turned out of the desert. And then suddenly they were using that piece of paper to convince Amonpour to let them camp on their borders, waiting for an opportune moment to try to claim Miraji as a prize again. They were getting a little too close to us for comfort so the twins had been sent to spy on the Albish troops camped along our western border. In case they got itchy feet and decided to march through our half of the desert. The last thing we needed was a fight on two fronts.

"Elephants!" Izz flung up his arms so excitedly I staggered back, nearly stumbling into the fire at the strange, foreign word. "Amonpour has elephants. Did you know about elephants?"

"Were you holding out on us?" Maz slung an arm around his brother's bare shoulders, pointing at me accusingly. It was easy to forget one of them was blue and the other one just had blue hair when they were like this, moving and talking like one person. Maz's dark-skinned arm almost seemed like an extension of his brother's body.

Izz winked. "Fess up, Demdji."

I rolled my eyes at them. "If I did I probably would have kept it from you anyway, judging by the slightly crazy look in your eyes."

"Do you want to see one?" Maz was already kicking off his shoes.

"We might need more space." Izz started to gesture around himself, as if trying to get people out of the way.

There was no way this could end well. "Is this going to be like the time you learned what a rhinoceros was all over again?"

The twins froze, swapping a sheepish expression. "I mean—"

"Elephants are—"

"Slightly bigger, so—"

"Then how about you show me sometime when there aren't quite so many people, who aren't quite so full of liquor, around?" I suggested.

The twins traded a look as they seemed to silently debate the wisdom of that versus how badly they wanted to show me their new trick. Finally they nodded and contented themselves with giving me a very detailed explanation of what elephants looked like, and telling me nothing else about how Amonpour had gone. Well, I supposed we weren't invaded yet.

Torches were lit. Music had started and with it, dancing and eating and drinking. I was grateful to know that for a few hours we wouldn't be fighting a war. It was on nights like this in the rebel camp that I believed more than anything in what we could do. Nights when everyone stopped fighting long enough to live like we were promising the rest of Miraji it could.

• ● •

IT WAS A few hours after dark when I spotted him through the crowd.

I'd had enough to drink that I didn't trust my eyes at first. He was a flash of an impression as I spun. Head tilted back, laughing, at ease, like I'd seen him a thousand times. I lost my step, staggering too close to the fire. Someone grabbed me, pulling me back before I could set Shazad's clothes aflame. I tore myself out of the dancing and looked back, searching for him through the hazy mess of faces in the dark. But he was gone, as quick as if I'd imagined him. No, there, the crowd split.

Jin.

He was back.

He was standing on the other side of the fire, still wearing his traveling clothes, dust clinging to his dark hair. He looked like he hadn't shaved lately, either. I had a sudden flash of the last time he'd kissed me when he'd been a few days without a razor. My heart stumbled toward him, but I caught it, fighting to right it.

I turned away quickly, before he could spot me. I wasn't

in any kind of state to face him now. My head was fuzzy with alcohol and exhaustion. I looked for Shazad. She was a few paces away, deep in conversation with Ahmed, hands moving as quick as the dance of insects around a fire as she argued something passionately. And a little tipsily. Shazad wasn't much for unnecessary motions when she was sober. But when she caught my eye she read me like an open book all the same. I gave a small nod behind myself. Her gaze steadied. Like it did when she was trying to track down an enemy in a fight. I saw the shock register on her face the moment she spied him. Good. That meant it was really him, not some conjuring by Hala designed to torture me.

I had hoped that by the time I saw him again I'd be ready to face him head on. But now I felt split open. Like if I faced him it was all going to come spilling out in words. I wiped away the sweat on my neck. My hand came away red.

For one stupid moment, I thought seeing Jin really had split me open. No—the wound across my collarbone had reopened. The rushed patch-up job in Saramotai hadn't fared all that well against the dancing and drinking. Shazad had called it a scratch, but right now it looked a lot like an escape to me.

Jin had run away. Fine. I could do the same.

• ● •

THE WARMTH AND noise of the camp faded behind me as I picked my way toward the Holy Father's tent, set far to one side of the camp. It had changed some since it'd been Bahi's domain, the place I'd first woken up in camp, under a canopy of cloth stars. But that didn't make it any easier when I had to step inside. Half a year since Bahi had died at my brother's hands and I still thought I could smell burning flesh sometimes when I got too close to where he'd worked. It was no wonder Shazad steered clear. I'd known him a handful of weeks. She'd known him half her life. The new Holy Father had kept his patchwork of stars. It was the first thing I saw as I pushed my way into the tent.

A woman's head darted up from one of the beds. I hadn't been expecting anyone to be here. Leastways not anyone awake. In the bed nearest to the entrance Sayyida was sleeping still as the dead. Across from her was a young rebel whose name escaped me, bandaged from elbow to wrist, where there used to be a hand. He'd been dosed with something that would keep him dreaming he still had ten fingers, by the look of things. And in the third bed . . . I'd almost forgotten about the woman we'd brought unconscious from Saramotai. The one who'd called me by my mother's name.

Seemed she wasn't unconscious anymore.

"I—sorry." I hovered, holding one tent flap back, looking for an excuse. Only I didn't need one. I belonged here. More than she did. So why was I shuffling my feet like I was a kid back in Dustwalk again? "I didn't mean to wake you. I'm just bleeding." I held up my hand. Like I needed to prove it to this stranger.

"The Holy Father isn't here." The woman pushed herself to her elbows. Her eyes darted around frantically in the dim lamplight, like she was looking for some escape of her own.

"He's still at the celebrations." I finally stepped over the threshold and let the tent flap fall shut. I tried not to look at Sayyida as I pressed forward. "I just came for supplies."

I'd been stuck in this tent for a good long while after I woke up from nearly dying. I could've drawn every corner of it from memory. Down to the iron-and-wood chest emblazoned with holy words, where the Holy Father kept his supplies.

"It's locked," the woman said as I dropped down next to the chest.

"I know." I reached up for the small blue glass oil lamp that the Holy Father always kept burning when there was someone in the sick tent overnight. Nobody ought to be left to suffer and die in the dark. I felt around the base until my fingers closed around the tiny iron key that he kept lodged there. The trunk lock gave way with a satisfying click.

Inside were rows and rows of bottles and needles and powders and tiny knives all neatly lined up. It was so unlike Bahi's mess of tools and supplies scattered out across the ground that it almost hurt a little. Like there was less of him left in camp every day since he died.

"Believe it or not, this isn't my first visit," I said over my shoulder, as I picked out a bottle of something clear I'd seen the Holy Father clean wounds with before and put it to one side. I held the set of needles up to the light, squinting. I'd never noticed how big they looked until now, but I had to figure one of them was smaller than the others.

"You're going to sew yourself up?" she asked from behind me, like she didn't know whether she ought to be appalled or impressed.

"Not the first time for that, either." I picked a needle at random before turning around to face her head on. She looked a whole lot better than she had when we'd found her in that cell in Saramotai and she'd barely been able to focus on me. Her fever seemed to have broken and she was alert now, her face almost a normal color.

"I—" she started and then hesitated, running her tongue along cracked lips. "I've got some talent with healing. If you'd rather not."

I didn't need her help. I could take the supplies and leave. I could forget I'd ever been the girl from Dustwalk who had a mother named Zahia. But if I left now I'd have to face Jin. And I was having trouble thinking of a single time running away from my problems had actually worked. Besides, it wasn't like I was all that excited about shoving a sharp object into my own skin.

I sat across from her, handing over the bottle, thread, and needle. She seemed skittish as she pulled away the collar of the khalat. Her fingers drifted over the wound, dabbing the liquid over where the blood had caked, making a hundred tiny pinpricks of pain sing behind it. But I wasn't paying it much mind. I was watching her face in the dim glow of the lamplight. Trying to recognize something there I might know.

"You've been drinking," she said finally. "I can smell it on you. That'll be why it started again. Thins the blood. You don't need stitches, just a bandage and to learn how to hold your drink."

It was the way she said *drink* that made me sure. Her accent had been worn smooth by years in other places, places that didn't swallow that word like they were always thirsty, but there was no mistaking it. Not with the way the rest of the words dropped and rose. I could've picked out that accent in the cacophony of a bazaar. It was my accent.

"You called me Zahia," I said, biting the bullet so fast I didn't have time to lose my nerve. "That was my mother's name. Zahia Al-Hiza." I watched her close for a reaction. "But she was born Zahia Al-Fadi."

The woman's face folded like a bad hand of cards. She pulled away from me, dropping the collar of my khalat, and pressed the back of her hands to her lips, stifling what sounded like a sob.

I stared at her, unsure of what to do. I ought to give her some privacy or some comfort. But I couldn't tear my gaze away from her.

"That would make you Amani, then." Her voice sounded choked when she finally spoke again. She shook her head angrily, as if to dispel the tears. Desert girls didn't cry. "You look exactly like Zahia at your age." I'd heard that before. She reached out a hand like she was going to touch me. There were tears in her eyes. "It's like seeing my sister the day I left Dustwalk all over again."

"Your sister?" I pulled away before her fingers could so much as graze my cheek. "You're Safiyah Al-Fadi?" I saw it as soon as she said it. I might be the spitting image of my mother but I saw her in this woman, too. She was the middle sister of the three Al-Fadi girls. My mother and Aunt Farrah's mythical third sister. The one who had famously vanished out of Dustwalk to make her own life. Who my mother always talked about running away to find. Who I'd been headed for when I first left Dustwalk. Before I'd chosen Jin and the Rebellion. "You're supposed to be in Izman."

"I *was* in Izman." She suddenly busied herself, pulling bottles out of the Holy Father's trunk, checking them over with a quick, practiced eye. "I went there to find my fortune. I was there for nearly seventeen years." She uncorked one without a label to sniff the contents, carefully avoiding meeting my eye.

I didn't like that she was here. It didn't seem right that in this whole huge sprawling desert we would find each other somewhere neither of us was ever meant to be. It seemed like the world had bent itself over backward trying to push us together. Had I done this? I raked my mind for the things I'd said in the days Jin and I had walked across the desert, when I'd still thought I was going to wind up in Izman. Had I told some truth by accident? Before I'd known I was Demdji and that I couldn't lie— before I'd understood how dangerous it was to speak truths about the future, that it would twist the universe to make them true? All I'd have to have done was tell Jin I was going to find my aunt and the universe would rearrange the stars to make it so. And give me some kind of poisoned version of the truth.

Or was this just dumb luck?

Her nervous fingers finally settled on a bottle. She tipped out something thick and foul-smelling onto her fingertips and dabbed it across my wound.

"So how come you left Izman?"

"Because fortune is a funny thing." I waited, but it seemed that was all the explanation I was going to get for how she'd wound up in Saramotai. "Though I must admit I didn't think it was going to lead me to being imprisoned by a revolutionary who wanted to overturn the world order."

"Malik wasn't ours," I argued, wincing against the pressure of her fingers on my collarbone.

"Do you handpick all your followers?" She pressed a little harder on my wound than she needed to. "He did things in your prince's name; that's enough for me. He nearly killed me doing it, too. You know, some of this desert didn't ask for a rebellion that might get us killed." She pulled away from me, wiping her fingers on a cloth. "But I suppose, as the Holy Father in Dustwalk would have said, Fortune and Fate."

Three words and I was standing back in the prayer house in Dustwalk all over again, being preached to. That was an old expression the Holy Father used when times were hard. *Fortune and Fate*. It meant that fortune and fate weren't always the same.

I understood that better than anyone.

"Here." My aunt Safiyah dusted her hands off quickly, pulling out another of the bottles from the Holy Father's chest. "Take this for the pain. It'll help you sleep."

It was her accent, mingled with those words, talk of sleep and medicines, that drew the memory out of the corner of my mind.

Tamid.

It hit me like a blow to the chest.

I'd pushed down all thoughts of him for months now. But it was as if she'd summoned him here, with her Dustwalk accent, the tiny bottle of medicine in the dim light, the sick longing for people I used to know. He was the only friend I had before this place and the Rebellion. Who used to stitch me up and sneak me things until the pain went away.

Who I left to die in the sand.

Was this how truth-telling myself to my aunt would twist around on me? Reminding me of who I was before Ahmed's rebellion? Of the people who'd suffered and died because of things I did?

All of a sudden, taking something that would send me to sleep and away from that memory seemed awful tempting.

But before I could take the bottle, the entrance to the tent flapped open violently. My head snapped around. My first thought was that Jin had followed me here. But through the lingering haze of drink I saw two figures sil-houetted in the light of the lamp, against the backdrop of the dark outside. Jin would have come after me alone. And they were tangled together like two drunk wedding rev-elers looking for some privacy, stumbling into the wrong tent.

Then they shifted, and the light caught the knife.

I was on my feet in a heartbeat even as I heard a voice I knew well choke out my name.

It was Delila.

NINE

The figures staggered backward out from the tent. But it was too late to run. I was already on my feet. "Stay here," I ordered Safiyah, swiping up a knife as I went.

"Stop!" The order came at me as I burst out of the sick tent after them. Before I could see clearly. Before I even recognized the second figure holding Delila hostage. Dark hair flopping over his proud brow, his eyes panicked in a way I'd never seen before. Surprise staggered the strength in my voice. "Mahdi?"

He was holding Delila around her waist. A knife was pressed across her throat so hard he'd already drawn blood. I could see it running in a fresh trickle down her skin and under her khalat, staining it.

"Don't come any farther!" He was shaking hard.

"Mahdi." I kept my voice level, even though my mind was making a mad dash for an explanation. "What the hell are you doing?"

"I'm saving her." Mahdi's voice rose frantically. I checked how far we were from the wedding. Too far for anyone to hear him, no matter how loud he got. "I'm saving Sayyida. Raise your hands where I can see them!"

I kept eye contact with Delila as I did what he said, desperately trying to tell her it was going to be all right. I was not going to let her die here.

"What's in your hand?" he called out, urgently.

The knife.

"I'm letting it go," I said, keeping my voice level. I unclenched my fist and let it drop. It planted blade-down in the sand. "I'm unarmed now."

"No, you're not." Mahdi pulled at Delila, and she whimpered. He was frantic, manic—and that knife was awfully close to her throat. "You've got an entire desert around you."

He wasn't wrong. I could have him down in a handful of seconds if I wanted. But I couldn't make sure that knife didn't go through Delila as he fell.

"Mahdi." I spoke carefully, the same voice I'd use to soothe a skittish horse. "How exactly do you think sticking a knife to Delila's throat is going to help Sayyida?"

"She's a Demdji!" He spat out the words like it was obvious. "Some people think that it's having *part* of a Demdji that cures ills. But they're wrong. That's just peasant superstition. A few pieces of purple hair aren't going to bring my Sayyida back." He was unbalanced. He was desperate. He had a knife to Delila's throat. I'd never wished more that I could move the desert without needing to move my body. I tried anyway, tugging at the edge of the sand with just my mind. It crept along reluctantly before sagging back down. I needed help. "I've read books. *Whosoever takes the life of a Demdji shall have their life in equal measure.*" He recited like it was holy text even though I knew it wasn't anything I'd ever heard preached.

"What's that supposed to mean?" I had to buy some time. Enough to think of a distraction.

"It means Sayyida can survive if she kills Delila. I'd trade any Demdji's life for Sayyida's. In a heartbeat."

There. Something behind him. A flash of movement in the moonlight. It darted silently from one shadow to the next. In a moment, as he passed from one tree to another, I got a clear view of him.

Jin.

I caught myself just quickly enough to flick my eyes back to Mahdi before he could notice where I was looking. He'd followed me after all. And he had a shot at getting us all out of here without bloodshed if I could just hold Mahdi's attention long enough. I didn't need a distraction. I was the distraction.

"And then what?" I had to give Jin a chance to get close to him. "What's your plan? Ahmed would never forgive you for killing his sister—you must know that."

"I don't *care* about Ahmed." Mahdi's accent was becoming more grating the more frantic he got. "This whole rebellion is going to hell on a fast horse, anyway."

"I'm pretty sure we're not the ones going to hell in this situation," I said. Jin was only ten paces behind him now. Close enough so I saw the corner of his mouth pull up at my barb, even though his eyes never left his sister.

"Even you can see it, surely." Mahdi didn't seem to hear me. He was leaning forward, desperately, like he could convince me, too. Like I might step aside and let him past. "Ahmed has bitten off more than he can chew. Saramotai is just the beginning—there will be other uprisings, and the war with the foreigners will end and the Sultan will destroy us. Ahmed is too weak to hold this whole country. We can't save everyone. So I'm saving someone I can."

Jin was close now. Too close. The moonlight hit him as he left the cover of the trees, sending a spike of shadow across Mahdi's path. Mahdi's eyes went wide as he spun to face this new threat. His blade bit into the soft skin of Delila's throat with the sudden motion, drawing blood.

Delila screamed.

The time for distraction was done. I flung my arm in an arc, exploding a burst of sand right into Mahdi's face, blinding him as Jin darted forward. His hand latched over Mahdi's, twisting the knife away from Delila's neck. It changed course, plunging toward Jin's chest instead. I whipped my palm flat, and the sand shifted below Mahdi's feet, throwing him off balance, the knife sailing harmlessly by Jin's shoulder.

Mahdi went down, his fingers snapping like dry kindling in Jin's grip, the knife falling from his hand. He hit the sand with an agonized cry, even as Jin caught Delila.

And then it was over. Delila collapsed into Jin, sobbing, a smear of blood from her neck darkening his desert-white shirt. His eyes met mine over his sister's head.

So much for avoiding him.

TEN

The stitched sun in the crown of the pavilion glowed dimly in the lamplight. It wasn't enough to fill the whole of the pavilion, and the dark seemed to press in around the five of us.

Me, Shazad, Hala, Jin, and Ahmed.

There should have been more of us. If Bahi was alive. If Delila wasn't being patched up by my aunt. If Mahdi wasn't a traitor now locked up and under guard. If we hadn't all agreed Imin should be given *one* night away from the Rebellion for the wedding.

"You should have killed him outright, if you ask me." Hala's eyes were far away, but I knew she was talking to me.

"No one did ask you," I retorted. All I could think of

was the fear in Mahdi's eyes as he held Delila, shaking. Reasoning with me for Sayyida's life because he was too proud to beg. "You trying to tell me you wouldn't have done the same if Imin was the one dying in that tent?"

"No." Hala's voice was low, in that threatening way she got sometimes when it came to her sibling. "I'm trying to tell you that it just as easily *could* have been Imin. Or you, or me, or the twins. Every single one of us risks our life every day for selfish people like him and *this* is how they repay us." Selfish was what this desert did best. I knew that better than anyone.

"Love makes people selfish," Jin said, so softly I almost believed I wasn't meant to have heard it. A sudden hot, angry rush rose up in me. But before I could snap anything back, Hala spoke up again.

"I don't believe half of what's been done to me was for love. Unless you want to count love of money." Hala raised her left hand into the light pointedly, with its missing two fingers. "Why should the rest of us suffer just because Amani seems to get to pick and choose who gets to live based on how she feels that day?"

"Hala, that's enough," Shazad warned.

But Hala ignored her. "You seem exceptionally good at putting the rest of us in danger. Today it's Mahdi. Last time you seemed to think your brother's life was worth more than everyone else's in this desert. How long before another burned-out crater appears where a city used to be? Or he finds us and turns another one of us to dust like Bahi? Or maybe someone will manage to hunt him down like they did Imin and they'll take his eyes and he can die slowly when you could have given him mercy."

I went at her like a bullet from a gun.

Shazad was between us in a second. Before I could get to Hala, before Hala could conjure some horror in my mind in retaliation.

"I said, *that's enough*." She held me back, arms on my shoulders, bracing me as Hala sneered at me over her shoulder. I strained against her, but familiar hands grabbed me, dragging me back away from the fight. Jin. I didn't bother to fight as he pulled me against him easily. The familiar heat of his body as my back met his chest.

"Stop. You know you don't really want to fight her, Amani." He spoke in my ear, low enough so that I was the only one who heard him. So that his breath stirred the hair at the nape of my neck. Everything in me wanted to lean back into him, feel his heartbeat against my spine, and relax back into his presence. But I stilled before I could, forcing myself to pull away from him. To put air between us.

"Let me go." His grip loosened as he felt my body lock up below his touch. I shook him off and his hands dropped away. I could still feel the heat of his palms lingering on my upper arms. Like burn marks. Except Demdji weren't supposed to burn so easily.

"Everyone in this tent has people we'd turn the world inside out to protect." Shazad turned to Hala. "This is not about blood or love. This is about treason. Mahdi has committed a crime against us, and there is judgment to be passed."

Ahmed hadn't said a word yet. But now we were all looking at him.

Finally, he spoke. "My father would choose execution."

"It's what your brother would choose, too," Jin said from behind me. He'd retreated a safe distance from me. Even without looking at him I was keenly aware of him.

"You're advocating revenge?" Ahmed said. "An eye for an eye?"

"It's not an eye for an eye," Jin said. "Delila is still alive. Thanks to Amani. So I'm only advocating for one eye."

Ahmed's fingers drummed along the map. "It doesn't seem to me that a Sultan should hand out rulings out of spite."

Mahdi's words whispered into my mind. *Too weak to hold this whole country.*

Jin took a step toward Ahmed. "Our sister—"

"She's *not* your sister." His hand slammed against the table, bringing silence instantly. None of us had ever heard Ahmed lash out at Jin like that. Even Shazad drew back, her eyes flicking between the two brothers. Like she might have to hold one of them back, too. Jin and Delila might not share any blood—not like she did with Ahmed through their mother, or like Jin and Ahmed did through their father—but they'd been raised together. Jin had never called Delila anything but his sister and Delila considered both princes her brothers. But Ahmed was the one who tied them together. "And it's not your decision. It's mine."

Jin tightened his jaw. "Fine. While you make *your* decision, I'll go watch over *your* sister. Like I watched over her after my mother died. My mother who saved your life, lest we forget. And who died while you were here playing savior to the country that enslaved her and tried to kill your sister."

"Everyone get out." Ahmed never took his eyes from his brother as he gave the command. "This conversation is between me and my brother."

"Don't bother." Jin pushed open the tent flap in one violent movement. "We're done here." The night air spilled into the pavilion behind him, pouring the light from Ahmed's tent across the sand like a beacon.

That was when the gunshot came.

The whole world seemed to slow around us as we stood frozen, our minds struggling to catch up. A bullet was buried in the middle of the table, embedded a hairbreadth to the left of Ahmed's hand. Straight above it was a hole in the canopy, right through the yellow of the fabric sun.

Shazad reacted first. Grabbing Ahmed by the front of his shirt, she wrenched him to the ground and under the table a second before the next gunshot sounded. Then another one.

Jin grabbed me at the same moment, sending me sprawling, knocking the air from my lungs. I hit the ground hard, and a stab of violent pain tore through my right shoulder. I cried out. Not a bullet, though. I knew what that felt like. Jin shielded me with his body as bullets tore through the flimsy canvas of the tent.

Sayyida.

The idea hit as hard and sudden as a bullet to the brain.

The timing was too perfect. She hadn't "escaped" with Hala. She'd been bait. A trap. They'd followed her straight back to us.

Screaming started outside, followed by more gunfire. Another bullet struck near us, sending up a spray of sand dangerously close to where Jin and I were. The soldiers were shooting blind, but that didn't mean they weren't going to hit us.

I reached for my power, but it danced tauntingly out of my grasp. I felt something cold against my hip. I twisted to get a better look. My shirt had ridden up, and the iron of Jin's belt buckle was pressing into my bare skin, stripping me of my Djinni half. We both winced as another bullet slammed into the table above Ahmed's and Shazad's heads.

"Jin." The fall had knocked the air out of my lungs, and there was a shooting pain in my right arm, like it might be broken. It was hard to talk with Jin's solid weight on top of me. "Belt buckle," I finally gasped, my chest burning.

Jin understood. He shifted quickly away from me. I felt the iron leave my skin. And suddenly the panic wasn't a roaring sensation trapped in my chest anymore. It was pouring out of me. Into the desert. Into the sand.

I called the desert into a storm.

I felt it rise in the sands outside, picking up strength as it went. I pushed it as far from us as I could, to the edges of camp, but sand whipped at the torn walls of the tent all the same. I closed my eyes and let the desert work itself into a frenzy. The gunfire stopped, faltering under the force of the whirlwind even as it crashed into the side of the pavilion, lifting it from the ground, carrying it away like it was nothing.

Outside, the sandstorm had whipped the camp's fear into chaos. Rebels were rushing to tie sheemas around their faces as others gathered supplies or tried to calm horses. Everybody knew what our evacuation plan was. But it was one thing knowing it, another trying to execute it in the dead of night with bullets tearing through the air.

I fought for better control. I tried to breathe as I rose onto my knees. The gunfire had come from above. That meant they were on the walls of the canyon. I shifted, pushing my hands outward, pushing my power toward them, creating a shield from the gunfire as best I could.

As the sand moved, I saw the first rebel's body. Fresh red blood was spilling out of the bullet wound in his chest. I felt my control slip and grabbed at it again.

Shazad was on her feet, already giving orders as I kept the air raging around us, pulling the chaos into order.

"Amani! We have to go!" Shazad screamed over the roaring of sand, reaching for me.

"I can cover your escape!" I called back. "Get everyone else out!"

"Not without you." Shazad shook her head. Her dark hair was already coming free from its braid, whipping into her face frantically. Behind her I could see people desperately saddling horses, some clambering onto the backs of the twins in the forms of giant Rocs.

"Yes, without me!" I screamed back. I wanted to tell her that I'd be fine. But Demdji promises weren't safe to make. "Get everyone else to safety. Get Ahmed to safety. They need you with them, and you need me here."

Shazad hesitated a moment. My friend was fighting it. But our general knew I was right. Half the camp would die without some kind of cover. And right now I was the only cover we had.

Shazad half turned. She glanced over her shoulder to where Ahmed was trying to calm the panic enough to get people away, then back to me. "If you don't follow behind"—she dropped down in front of me, clasping my shoulder for just a moment—"you'd better believe I'll come after you."

And then she was gone. I turned everything I had in me outward. I emptied myself into the desert, a perfect cyclone shielding the edges of the camp, cutting our people's escape off from the soldiers' sight.

I didn't know how long I held it. As long as I could, before my arms started to shake. I was distantly aware of the chaos around me. Of supplies being loaded, of horses being led to the entrance of the camp, of Izz and Maz shooting into the air under a hail of gunfire. Of shouting, far away.

But all I really knew was the desert. I was wholly part of the sandstorm until I thought I might scatter to dust and whip away with it. I was losing control. It wasn't just my arms. My whole body was trembling with the effort. The sand was whipping through my hair instead of toward the enemy. I needed to let go. And if I had any shot of getting out, I needed to do it now.

I pushed myself to my feet. My legs buckled hard below me. Arms around my waist caught me before I could hit the ground.

"I've got you," Jin said in my ear. "Let go; I've got you."

A horse was rearing and kicking, panicking as the storm started to close in around us as my control wavered. "Why . . . are you . . . still here?" I gasped out. "Shazad—"

My head was swimming with the effort of keeping a grip on the sand. If I let go, the sand would race in and bury this place, drowning anyone who hadn't made it out yet. "She's got most everyone else out." The solidness of Jin's body was the only thing propping me up now.

"Not you."

"Like hell I'd leave you behind to get yourself killed." His voice was low and sure in my ear as his body curled around mine. Protecting me as he urged the horse forward. He pushed me into the saddle, swinging himself up behind me. A gun went off nearby, too close for comfort. "Amani. Let go. I've got you, I promise. Trust me."

So I let go.

ELEVEN

We rode like we were trying to beat the sunset to the horizon. The army was behind us. We had to get far enough into the mountains to outstrip them.

I slipped out of consciousness somewhere around leaving camp and slept away the few hours of darkness we had left. When I woke up, leaning against Jin, a new dawn was on us and we had an army in pursuit. The last of my power went into raising the desert behind us, creating as much of a shield as I could between the soldiers and our little party.

Jin and I weren't alone. About a dozen stragglers from camp who hadn't managed to get out with the twins or Shazad's first wave of riders were with us. Some of them were riding double on the last of our horses. I couldn't make out their faces as we raced across the burning sands. And I didn't know who had gotten away with Ahmed and Shazad or if whoever was with us could ride well enough to keep up. They didn't really have a choice right now.

My arm was a constant shooting pain up my side that got worse every time I checked behind. It took everything in me to keep it up and keep the pain from shattering my focus.

Finally I couldn't hold on any longer, and neither could the horses. If we hadn't outrun them by now, we would have to stand and fight. I dropped the shield behind us. Jin seemed to feel the tension flee my body. He wheeled the panting beast around, gun drawn, checking behind us for pursuers. My vision blurred from the sheer relief of not using my power anymore. I shielded my eyes against the last of the desert sun. We were all perfectly still as we scanned the horizon for any sign of movement. But there was nothing behind us but open sand. We'd lost them.

"We can pitch camp here," Jin commanded, his voice reverberating through his chest, into my back. He was hoarse with thirst.

"We're not safe," I started to argue.

"We're never safe," Jin said, so only I heard.

"We've got no cover, and the horses—"

"The horses aren't going to make it any farther without a rest and we can't outrun them on foot," Jin said in my ear. "And we can't outrun them without you, either. We'll post a watch, move again if there's even a cloud of dust on the horizon."

He slipped off our horse and started giving orders to pitch tents and go through the supplies people had grabbed as we evacuated. He uncapped something at his side and took a swig before passing it to me.

I brought the waterskin to my mouth and with shaking hands sipped slowly, cradling my injured shoulder close to my body. There were a dozen of us, give or take. That meant a whole lot of missing faces who were now just bodies in the sand if they hadn't gotten away with Ahmed and Shazad. I was the only Demdji among us. Hopefully that meant Hala and Delila were together, and between them, they could hide even a big group of moving rebels. And Shazad would get them all to safety. I had to trust they'd be waiting for us.

My aunt, Safiyah, was among those who'd escaped with us, as were two of the other women from Saramotai. I supposed it was hard to follow an escape plan when you didn't know it. Safiyah was helping dole out food. A few other familiar faces were dotted around. Relief eased my heart a little.

There'd be no fire tonight. It left us vulnerable to Nightmares or Skinwalkers but we were a lot more vulnerable if we lit a beacon to the Sultan's army. We'd just have to ring the camp in whatever iron we had and hope for the best.

Everyone was ravaged from the escape. Some were already stuffing bread into their mouths and simply collapsing as the sun sank low. We'd need to set a watch, and divvy up the supplies among the horses and pitch the tents. And there were a thousand and one other things to think of. But my head was spinning and I couldn't think of them.

I downed the water until my head steadied. We wouldn't have to make it last that long anyhow. By now I knew our part of the desert. We were a three-day ride from the port city of Ghasab, but at the pace we'd set, riding all night and through the day, we'd be there by sunset tomorrow. From there we could resupply and rejoin with everyone at the meeting point in the mountains. Well, everyone who'd gotten away.

I stowed the water away and gingerly tried to slide off the horse, testing my weight on my tender right arm as I braced myself against the saddle. It surrendered instantly, buckling me toward the sand in a messy heap.

"You're hurt." Jin reached down toward where I was sprawled. I ignored his hand and pulled myself up with my good arm, using the stirrup. The horse was so tired it barely protested.

"I'll survive." I tried to hold my arm as normal as I could as I turned away from him. "I always have."

"Amani!" He raised his voice as I walked away, loud enough so a few of the rebels glanced our way, before quickly getting back to work. Everyone knew enough to stay out of it. "I watched you walk across an entire desert. I've memorized the way you move. And right now you're moving like you've dislocated your shoulder. You need to let me take a look at it."

"I can give you something for the pain," Safiyah interrupted, brushing sand off her fingers. *Almost* everyone knew enough to stay out of it.

"She doesn't need something for the pain," Jin said evenly. He was talking to Safiyah, but his eyes never left me. "She needs someone to pop her arm back in its socket before we have to saw it off."

That made me stop.

I turned back to face him. He had unwrapped his sheema and wound it around his neck and I could see his face clearly. Jin had always been good at bluffing. A faint smile reappeared, like he could read what I was thinking more easily than I could. That smile always meant trouble. "Willing to chance it, Bandit?"

I was almost sure he was lying. But I wasn't more sure than I was fond of having two working arms.

"Fine." I extended my arm to him as far as I could, like a kid holding out a wounded animal she'd found in the desert. Jin didn't take it. Instead he put a hand on my back. The familiar thrill rushed up my spine. My body didn't seem to know I was angry at him. He led me into the small blue tent I claimed when we were on the move. Someone had pitched it for me. He let the tent flap fall shut behind us, sealing us in privacy.

The tent was too low to stand in. I stooped stubbornly until Jin pulled me to the ground to sit across from him. Night was descending fast around us, but there was still just enough light to see by. Outside I could hear the shuffle of the camp as it got ready for a night in the desert.

"I need to see it." His voice was gentle now that we were

alone. It took me a second to understand what he meant.

"Fine," I said again, avoiding his gaze.

Very carefully, he put one hand on my upper arm and slid the other one under my khalat at the collar. His fingers were warm and familiar. Once he would've made a joke about getting his hands under my clothes. But now a silent tension hung between us—until I couldn't stand it anymore. "You sure you know what you're doing?"

"Trust me." Jin wasn't looking me in the face, though he was so close to me it was almost the only place he could look. "I had to learn on the *Black Seagull*, before this all started." *This.* I knew he meant the Rebellion. I almost laughed. It was such a small word to mean all of us and everything we'd done and everything we still had left to do. "A lot of sailors got hurt getting tangled up in ropes."

He did something that sent a stab of pain through my side. I hissed through my teeth.

"Sorry."

"You goddamn should be." Pain sharpened my tongue. "This happened when you shoved me, you know."

"You're right," Jin deadpanned, fingers still prodding gently at me. "I should've let you get shot; that's so much easier to recover from."

"And what would you know about that?" We were running for our lives. This wasn't the right time to be picking a fight, not in the middle of a war. But I hadn't been the one to bring it up. "You weren't around when I did."

"You'd rather I'd stayed to watch you die?" Jin's jaw was tight.

"I didn't die."

"But you might have."

"And you might've died off spying on the Xichian!" Silence dropped between us. But we didn't move. Neither of us pulled away or forward. Jin's fingers still explored my tender shoulder.

He finally spoke again. "It's dislocated. But not broken." He was just above me now, so all I could see was his mouth and the shadow of stubble along his jaw. My shoulder braced between his two hands. "This part is going to hurt like hell. You ready?"

"Well, when you put it that way, how could I say no?" That slight curve to his mouth that always made me feel like we were in this together appeared. "I'm ready."

"All right." He shifted so we were face-to-face. "I'm going to pop your shoulder back in on three." I gritted my teeth and prepared myself. "One . . ."

I took a deep breath.

"Two . . ."

Before I could tense in anticipation of "three," Jin wrenched my arm out and up.

Pain stabbed from my elbow to my shoulder and tumbled out of my mouth violently. "Son of a bitch!" Another curse ripped out after it in Xichian, then one in Jarpoorian that Jin had taught me while we crossed the desert, the pain drawing out every insult in every language that I knew. I was halfway through a colorful curse in Gallan when Jin kissed me.

Any more words I might have had died cataclysmically

the second his mouth found mine. My thoughts fell to ruins right behind.

I'd almost forgotten what being kissed by Jin was like.

God, did he ever know how to kiss me.

He kissed me like it was the first time and the last time. Like we were both going to burn alive from it. And I folded into him like I didn't care. The Rebellion might be falling apart around us, the whole desert even, but for now we were both still alive and we were together, and the anger between us had turned into a different fire that drew us both into the middle of it until I wasn't sure which one of us was consuming the other one.

He pulled away with sudden, gut-wrenching speed, breaking us apart as quickly as we'd come together. My own ragged breathing filled the silence that followed. It was full dark now. All I could make out was the rise and fall of his shoulders and the paleness of his white shirt.

"Why did you do that?" It came out in a low breath. I was close enough that I saw the rise and fall of his throat when he swallowed. I had the sudden urge to rest my mouth there and taste whether his breath was as unsteady and as uncertain as mine.

But when Jin spoke, his voice was as steady as a rock. "To distract you. How's the pain?"

I realized that the screaming pain in my arm had gone silent as the rest of my body came alive in answer to Jin's kiss. He was right; it didn't hurt half as bad as it had when he'd twisted it back into place.

He picked something up off the ground—my red sheema, I realized. It must've slipped off. Jin touched my arm again, but this time his hand was just flesh and blood on my elbow, not fire invading my skin. He tied the sheema around my arm and looped it over my neck like a sling, tying it behind my neck in one firm knot before pushing himself to his feet. "Besides . . ." His voice was light, like it was all a joke and we were just two strangers flirting with each other before parting ways again. Not two people who were as tangled as we were. Who had crossed the desert together. Who had faced death together over and over. "Who could resist a mouth like that?"

He stole another kiss from me so whip quick that he was gone before I even fully felt it.

I sat in the dark long after he went, not rising even when I heard the sounds of a hastily thrown together meal being eaten outside. I wasn't that hungry anyway. I felt raw. Burned out. Scorched earth. I distantly remembered that phrase—Shazad had taught it to me. It was something to do with war strategy. I wasn't sure if Jin and I were at war or not.

I listened to the camp settle around me as everything ran through my head. Everything we had gone through. Everything left ahead of us. Everything that he wouldn't say. The more silence fell over the camp, the more noise my anger made.

We were both as stubborn as hell, but one of us was going to have to crack eventually.

I was on my feet before I could think about it, tearing away the tent flap. The camp had gone completely silent now, everyone settled into their tents except whoever had been set to keep watch. I strode across the camp. I knew Jin's tent on sight, red and patched on one side and set up straight across from mine. I wasn't sure what I was going to do—shout at him or kiss him or something else entirely.

I'd decide when I saw him.

I was almost there—two paces from his tent—when something clamped over my mouth, hard. Panic spiked in my chest as a cloth covered my face like a gag, smelling sickly sweet, like spilled liquor.

Instinct took over. I drove my elbow backward. A scream of pain tore through my injured shoulder. A mistake. My mouth opened in a gasp. I inhaled and the smell invaded my mouth, clinging to my tongue, my throat, all the way down to my lungs.

I was being poisoned.

The effects were instant. My legs buckled and the world tilted sideways.

The Sultan's army had found us.

Why hadn't we had warning? I could've done something. I could've raised the desert. I could've stopped them. Now I could barely fight. I thrashed helplessly, my fingers clawing at the hand on my mouth. I twisted to the side, struggling to throw my weight downward. Mostly knowing it was already too late. As I fell I saw two bodies slumped in the sand, not moving.

The watch, already dead.

I needed to warn the others. The world was fading. I was slipping away. I was going to die. Jin. I needed to give him a chance to escape. To save the others.

I opened my mouth to scream a warning. The darkness swallowed it with me.

TWELVE

I woke up being violently sick. Vomit splattered next to me across the wooden floor, by a bucket. I grabbed it before the second heave came.

Everything left in my stomach came up.

I squeezed my eyes shut and tightened my arms around the metal bucket. I ignored the cloying smell of vomit climbing up from the bottom. My head was still spinning, my stomach still churning. I didn't move straightaway, even after I was sure there was nothing left to choke up but my own liver.

I seemed to still be alive. Which was unexpected. I'd feel good about it when I stopped retching my insides up. And which meant I'd been drugged, not poisoned. The army ought to have killed me. They ought to have killed all of us.

Maybe they'd kept me alive because I was a Demdji, and I was valuable. Or because I was a girl and I looked helpless. But they didn't have any reason to take the rest of the camp alive. They'd have no reason not to take one look at Jin, who always looked like he could be trouble, asleep, and put a bullet through him to keep him out of the way.

There was one way I could know for sure. I couldn't speak anything that wasn't the truth. If I couldn't say it out loud, then he was gone.

I swallowed the bile in my throat.

"Jin is alive."

The truth slipped out like a prayer into the dark, so huge and so certain I felt like I finally understood how Princess Hawa had been able to call the dawn. The words felt as important as the rising sun, easing the panic in my chest.

Jin was alive. Probably a captive in this place like I was.

I started listing names quickly. Shazad, Ahmed, Delila, Hala, Imin—they were alive, one after the other. Not once did my tongue stumble. They were all fine. Well, trying to say they were fine out loud might be pushing my luck, seeing as we'd all just lost our home. But alive. And so was I. And I wasn't about to let that change.

I was going to live long enough to get back to them.

The room was moving, I realized then. Was I on a train? The floor shifted below me and my stomach heaved again. No, this was different. There was no steady, juddering feeling. This was more like being rocked in a cradle by a drunken giant.

As my head cleared I took stock of things. I gingerly set the bucket down again and eased myself up. I could sit up. That wasn't nothing to start with. And thanks to the light coming through a small window above me, I could see.

I was on a bed in a cramped room with damp wooden walls and a damp floor. The light had the feel of late afternoon. Burned sky after a long day in the desert. It'd been night when I was taken, so that meant I'd been asleep nearly a whole day. At least a whole day.

I shifted, trying to stand up, but my right hand pulled me up short. I was tied to the frame of the bed.

No. Not tied. Chained.

Iron was biting into my skin. I could feel it the moment I reached for my power. I shoved up the sleeve on my arm to get a look at it. The iron was clamped like an angry hand on a child's wrist. Only not completely. A sliver of light leaked between my skin and the iron.

I could work with that.

Without thinking, I reached for my sheema. My fingers scraped across bare neck instead. It felt like being punched in the stomach.

It was gone. I remembered now. Jin had tied it like a sling. I'd been struggling as the drug filled my nose and mouth, and the sheema slipped off me. Gone in the sand.

It was stupid. It was just a thing. Just a stupid strip of red cloth against the desert sun. Except it was a stupid thing Jin had given me. Snatched off a clothesline in Sazi, the day we'd escaped Dustwalk. I'd never stopped wearing it since then. Even when I was angry at him. It was mine. And now it was gone.

But there were other ways out of this.

I worried at the stitching on my shirt until the side of it gave way. Tearing off a strip of cloth, I started to stuff it between my skin and the iron manacle. It wasn't exactly easy work—the manacle was tight and the cloth was awkward and thick. But I kept going all the same, working the piece of cloth in one bit at a time.

There. I felt it the moment the iron stopped touching my skin. My power rushed back in.

I was tired and thirsty, and my mouth tasted of vomit and some unknown drug that was still lingering in my lungs, but I could do this. I reached for the desert outside with everything I had. I felt it surge in answer, only to have it slip away. I pulled again, but nothing came. It felt like reaching for something just a little too far away.

I fought down the panic. There were still other ways. Like there'd been in Saramotai. I took a deep breath and closed my eyes. I could feel it now as I calmed myself. Even against the strange lurching of the room and my dizzy head. The sand that clung to my skin.

I raised my free hand in one quick violent motion, tearing the sand from every part of me that I could find, scraping skin off with it. I slashed the sand down toward my arm in one sharp motion.

The chain on the manacle splintered like wood under an axe. And I was free.

I bolted for the door, fighting the haze that was clinging

to my mind like a lingering desert exhaustion. The floor tilted below me, pitching me out into a long dark hallway. At one end light leaked through from whatever was above. The floor heaved again below me.

Something connected in my mind, pieces from stories. Some I'd heard around campfires, and some Jin had told me.

This wasn't a train.

I was on a ship.

Wooden steps rose to meet me in the spot of sunshine, and I bashed my shin into a step as I scrambled upward, the ground tilting yet again. And then I was up in the sunlight and fresh air.

I was momentarily blinded by the sudden glare after the dark. But I'd never been the sort to stop running just because I couldn't see where I was going. As my vision cleared I bolted forward, focusing on the place where the ship seemed to end.

Shouts followed me, but I didn't stop. I pushed my legs forward into one last violent whip of speed. I crashed full force into the rail at the edge of the ship. My escape.

Only there was no escape.

I'd once asked Jin if the sand sea was like the real sea. He'd given me that knowing smile he used to use when he knew something I didn't. Before I stripped all his secrets away and that smile became mine.

But now I knew.

There was water as far as the eye could see. More water than I'd seen in my whole life, more water than I'd known even existed in the world. I'd seen rivers and I'd seen pools, and I'd even seen some desert cities that had the luxury of fountains. I'd never seen anything like this.

It was as vast as the desert. And it kept me as trapped as I ever had been in Dustwalk by the miles and miles of burning sand.

Hands grabbed me from behind, yanking me away from the railing like someone thought I might throw myself off and into the mouth of the sea.

The haze of the world was starting to fade, and I was becoming aware of other things around me now. The strange smell that I could only guess was the drowned, endless stretch of sea around me. Shouts and cries, someone asking how the hell I'd gotten out.

It was a rabble of men who surrounded me. Mirajin, and no mistaking it—their skin was desert dark, and darker still for some of them. Bright sheemas covered their faces, and their hands were hard from work and raw with welts. I held on to my handful of sand, even though I knew I couldn't take down half their number before someone would shoot me. Not when there were already three pistols aimed at me.

And then there, standing among the crowd of men in a white khalat so brilliant it hurt my eyes, was the reason Jin was still alive. It wasn't the Sultan's army who'd taken me after all.

It was my aunt Safiyah.

"You drugged me." My voice sounded scratchy. My aunt whose hands danced with practiced ease through the medicines in the Holy Father's supply chest. She'd made the food. She could have slipped anything into it to knock out the rebels so she could escape. How easy would it have been for her to grab me as I stormed to Jin's tent, and knock me out with something stolen when I'd left her alone with his supplies unlocked. Twice she'd tried to push bottles that would put me to sleep. *For the pain.*

Shazad always said I was bad at watching my back. That was why she did it for me. Shazad would've also said this was one of those times to keep my mouth shut. But Shazad wasn't here. Because this woman had kidnapped me. "You know, last time *I* drugged someone who trusted me," I said, "I had the decency to leave him where he was."

"God, I wish you didn't sound so much like her, too." She spoke low enough so I was sure I was the only one who heard. Safiyah circled around me, to where the sailor was still holding my arms. I felt her touch the strip of torn shirt still stuffed between my skin and the manacle. "Clever." She almost sounded proud of me. "So you can use your Demdji tricks."

I tried to pull away but the sailor held me fast. "You know what I am." It wasn't a question, but that didn't mean I didn't want answers.

"I've been trading medicines in Izman since before you were even born." She pulled the cloth free from my wrist almost gently. "Do you really think you're the first Demdji I've ever come across? Your kind are a rare breed. And worth a small fortune each. People in my trade learn to recognize the signs. I guessed because of your eyes, but

I knew when that sandstorm saved us out in the desert. And your mother was always so secretive about you in her letters."

She was in Saramotai for no good reason. No good reason except that the Emir of Saramotai had just started bragging to the world he had a child with eyes like dying embers who wielded the sun in her hands. Ranaa has been worth something. But my aunt had missed her chance to take the little Demdji girl. So she'd taken me instead.

"It's not true, you know." I remembered what Mahdi had told me, his knife held to Delila's throat. "What they say about carving us up like meat to cure your ills."

"The thing is," she said, not quite looking at me as she twisted the piece of cloth back around her own hand, "what really matters is that they're saying it at all." She was right. Stories and belief meant more than truth. I knew that as the Blue-Eyed Bandit. But I wouldn't be the Blue-Eyed Bandit anymore after she took my eyes.

Then to the man holding me, she said, "Put her with the other girls for safekeeping."

• ● •

WE WENT DEEPER into the ship than I'd come from. Far deeper. Back down into the deepest dark of its heaving wooden stomach and then down farther still. I didn't know where we were going, but I knew we were getting close. I could hear the crying long before I could see them.

The room where the other girls were being kept made the tiny cell I'd woken up in look like the lap of luxury. They were chained to the wooden walls by both arms, and a shallow swamp of water sloshed around where they were sitting, lapping in the dark at their shivering bodies.

There were about a dozen of them. I caught glimpses of their faces in the swinging lamplight as I was led through. A pale girl with ivory blonde curls, in the rags of a foreign blue dress that looked like it had once been shaped like a bell; a dark-skinned girl whose eyes were closed, her head tipped back—the only sign she was still alive was her lips moving in prayer; a Xichian girl with a curtain of jet hair and pure murder in her eyes as she tracked the man holding me; a single other Mirajin girl in a plain khalat shivering against the cold. They looked as different from each other as day and night and sky and sand, but they were all beautiful. And that was what frightened me the most.

I'd heard the stories from Delila of how Jin's mother had been brought to the harem. A Xichian merchant's daughter who lived her life on the deck of a ship—a deck that turned slick with the blood of her family on the day they were boarded by pirates. Lien, sixteen and beautiful, was the only survivor, taken in chains and silk rags to the new Sultan of Miraji, who'd just killed his father and brothers to take the throne for himself. Who was building a harem to assure his succession.

She was sold for a hundred louzi into those walls, where she would bear a son to a man she loathed. Where only the death of a friend she loved like a sister would give her the chance to escape back to the sea, clutching a newborn, with two young princes clinging to her hem.

Sometimes I doubted if Jin even knew those stories of his mother. They weren't the sorts of things women told their sons. They were the sorts of things women told other women. *Beware,* they told their daughters. *People will hurt you because you're beautiful.*

I wasn't beautiful. I wasn't here because of that. I was here because I was powerful.

This time the iron manacles bit hard into my skin. Safiyah and the man turned to go, taking the light with them. I couldn't just let them leave me here in chains. It was too much like surrendering.

"You know what they say—that betraying your own blood means you'll be forever cursed in the eyes of God," I called after Safiyah. The water was already lapping at my clothes. I was still wearing Shazad's khalat, I realized. The water was soaking through it to my skin. "The Holy Father preached that a whole lot in Dustwalk, too."

I didn't expect Safiyah to stop. But she did. She stood in the doorway a long moment, her back to me, as the man vanished ahead of her.

"That he did." She turned back to face me. And for the first time, she scared me. It was the calm in her face. It told me she hadn't hesitated in doing this to me. Not even for a minute. "Your mother and I always used to go to prayers. Every single day. Not just holy days, not just prayer days. Every day. We'd take up prayer mats next to each other and squeeze our eyes shut and pray like we were told to. We prayed for our lives. To get out of Dustwalk." I hadn't noticed it before, this coldness in Safiyah. But it was clear as daybreak now as she crouched across from me. "I loved my sister like the sun loves the sky. I would have done anything for her. And then she died, and left you. And you look so like her. It's like seeing a Skinwalker wearing my sister's face. Do you have any notion of what that's like? Looking at the thing that killed someone you loved, a thing that isn't even wholly human but seems to think she is?"

I watched the lamplight swing threateningly across her face, casting her into startling light and then darkness as it went. "Dustwalk killed my mother."

"Because she was protecting *you*. She was protecting you from the man who called himself your father. Would you like to know what her last letter to me said?"

I wanted to say no. But that would be a lie.

"She told me you weren't really her husband's. That he knew. He'd always known. That she feared for you now that you were older. That it was time to run. That she would die to protect you if she had to, but if she did, she would take him with her."

I was back in the desert, that day. The day the gunshots had come. They said my mother had gone crazy. She hadn't. She had killed her husband knowing full well that she might die. And she'd done it for me.

"She was going to come and join me, you know. Before you. I hated you from the moment she told me that she would have to delay leaving because she couldn't cross the desert while she was with child. Or when you were too small. And yet still, I built my life thinking one day I would be able to share it with my little sister. I did terrible things to make a life for both of us. Dustwalk killed my sister. But she died because she was your mother. And now I'm going to take the life I should have always had. And you are going to buy it for me."

"If you hate me so much, why not take my eyes out here and now?" I spat out at her. Let her show if she really hated me as much as she thought she did. "Just get it over with."

"Believe me, if I could have saved myself from carrying you across the desert I would have." My aunt tossed a smile back at me lazily. "But you're worth your weight in gold, you know."

I'd heard that before. In Saramotai, about Ranaa. And again from Hala, after rescuing Sayyida from Izman.

She wasn't just going to take my eyes to sell on to some rich Izmani whose heart was going to give out on him. She was taking me to the Sultan.

THIRTEEN

I was blind. Everything I saw was inside my mind, and outside that was just a darkness that went on forever and ever, sometimes punctured by noises.

In my better moments I knew it was the drugs. I was trapped in nightmares of fire and sand. Of sand on fire. A desert full of people burning. People I knew but whose names didn't exist in this dream. And a pair of blue eyes like mine watching it all. Because I still had eyes. I just couldn't figure out how to open them.

At some point I became aware that something had changed. I was being moved. And I could hear voices. Like I was listening from the bottom of a well.

"You know the Sultim likes Mirajin girls."

The Sultim. I knew that name. Far away, I knew what it meant.

"This one isn't for the harem." Another voice. A woman's. One I knew. It made me want to reach for my power. I stretched out my mind for it. The darkness started to creep in again. I lost my grip on the sand and the voices. The last thing I heard before it swallowed me again was "—dangerous."

A spark of consciousness woke at the very back of my mind.

Dangerous.

They'd better believe I was.

• ● •

I CAME TO all at once, a dozen bits of awareness competing for my attention. The cold of the table under me, the sharp pain riddling my body. The crystal-white glare of sunlight on my eyelids, a cacophony of birds, and something else, something that tasted unnatural. More drugs, I realized.

But I finally managed to open my eyes. The room was bright and airy and flooded with light reflecting brightly off a marble ceiling above me. The stone was the color of every sky I'd ever seen all at once. It was the pink and red of the wounded dawn, the dark violet of a calm dusk, and as brilliantly unsettling as the clear blue glare of high noon.

I'd never been anywhere this rich before. Not even the emir's house in Saramotai.

The palace. I was in the Sultan's palace.

We'd spent long hours trying to figure out ways to get more spies into the Sultan's palace. Months easing people from our side in through the kitchens. And I'd just been carried unconscious over the threshold like it was nothing.

And now I needed to get out.

I might've laughed at the irony of it if I didn't think it'd hurt so much.

The world was starting to put itself back together as I took stock of the situation. I was weaker than I ought to be. And I could already feel my eyelids getting heavy again, wanting to return to sleep. I had to sit up. I pressed my elbows into the cold marble slab and tried to push myself up. Pain stabbed across my entire body at the movement. I hissed air through my teeth and the sheet that'd been covering me slithered away.

I grabbed at it, and pinpricks of pain screamed back at me across my arms. Then I caught sight of myself for the first time. Under the soft white sheet I was wrapped in bandages. They covered almost every part of my body. Wrists to shoulders. Around my chest and all the way down my back. Tentatively I reached down and grazed my fingers over my legs. My hand met cloth instead of skin. I looked like a doll sewn out of linen. Only dolls didn't usually spot fresh blood like I was.

And here I'd been figuring nothing would be worse than waking up shackled on a ship.

I didn't exactly like being proven wrong.

And as the pain of whatever was under the bandages

subsided, I realized I was alone. That was a nice surprise. I spied a familiar blue khalat flung over a nearby chair. The one Shazad had given me before Imin's wedding. I didn't even know how many days it'd been since then.

Moving awkwardly with my sore muscles and bandaged limbs, I retrieved the stained fabric and pulled it on, fumbling with the tiny buttons that ran up the front. At least my hands seemed undamaged. Now I just wished I had a fistful of sand or a pistol to fill them. Hell, at this point I'd even take a knife. But I couldn't see any weapons among the clutter of the room.

Gauzy pink curtains fluttered from a huge archway. I moved gingerly toward them. Wind that tasted of familiar desert heat rippled them as I passed out onto the balcony.

Izman sprawled out below me.

It was like nothing I'd ever seen. A flat, blue-tiled roof with a gushing fountain on it leaned close enough to its neighbor to whisper city secrets. Beyond that, yellow flowers tumbled down sun-baked walls that were competing for space in the shade of their neighbors. Purple canopies crowned another house, and a golden dome pressed against minarets that jutted up like spears challenging the sky.

Jin said once that I couldn't understand how big Izman really was. If I ever saw him alive again, I might even be glad enough to admit that he'd been right.

It looked like a jumble of rooftops that went all the way to the end of the world. Only I knew that wasn't right. Somewhere out there was the desert I'd come from. I reached for it with my mind. For the sand and grit. But I couldn't feel anything. The desert had been ruthlessly polished out of here. I'd have to reach beyond the palace walls for that.

I gauged the distance between the top of the wall and the balcony.

I could probably make that jump on a good day. The throbbing pain in my body reminded me today was not a good day. But all it would take was one leap of faith, and I could be in the city. If I made it. If not, I would be a broken body in the garden below. Which still might be better than getting stuck here.

No. I was going to live to see Shazad again, like she'd asked me to promise. I was going to live to see Ahmed on the throne. And I was going to live to make Jin explain just why he thought he could kiss me after leaving me.

I'd have to go through the door. Only I wasn't about to try to walk through it like I was a guest instead of a prisoner. There would be a guard outside, no doubt about it.

There were no weapons in the room, but there was a glass jar filled with dried flowers. I picked it up off its shelf and positioned myself with my back flat against the door. And then let it go. It shattered on the colorful tiles.

That ought to get someone's attention.

I dropped to my knees, ignoring the screaming pain in my body, as I searched through the glass for the biggest shard. It had worked; I could hear footsteps through the door, someone coming to investigate. My hand closed around a piece of glass the size of my thumb, shattered to a sharp point. I curled my hand around it just tight enough not to draw blood, staying in my crouch, back flat to the wall by the door—ready for whoever came through. It had worked in Saramotai and I didn't believe the Sultan's guards were any brighter than Malik's.

The door swung open. I stayed low, heart pounding. All I saw was a flash of pale gray fabric before I moved. I slashed toward the back of the knees. It sliced through thin linen, gouging straight for the soft flesh underneath.

Instead, the glass scraped noisily off something hard.

A wound gaped in the fabric of the trousers where my makeshift weapon had struck, revealing gleaming bronze joints underneath.

For a second all I could think of was Noorsham in the bronze armor designed to control him. Heavy words in his Last County accent echoing around inside a hollow shell. But the voice that came now was a different one.

"Careful!" It sounded familiar, although it wasn't talking to me. I tipped my head back slowly, looking up at the man staring down at me dispassionately. "She's armed."

I thought I was ready for whatever I was facing here. I was dead wrong. Because in the doorway, with a new slice in his clothes, carefully parted hair stuck to his forehead, was Tamid.

The world tilted out from under me even as a guard in uniform stepped around him, weapon drawn. He grabbed me, ripping my meager glass weapon out of my hand. It was already stained red from where I had opened my palm with it, gripping it in shock.

I didn't even feel it. I didn't even fight as the guard wrenched me back to the middle of the room, forcing me against the cold marble slab where I'd woken up.

I twisted in his grasp. Not to escape. But because I couldn't stand to lose sight of Tamid.

Tamid who I'd grown up with. Tamid who, after my mother died, had been the only person in all of Dustwalk I'd cared about. Tamid who'd been my only friend for years. Who I'd last seen bleeding out in the sand while I rode away on the back of a Buraqi with Jin.

You're dead. The words shot from my brain to my mouth and stopped short. The untruth couldn't get any farther. Because he wasn't dead. He was alive and stubbornly collecting the broken glass from the floor. Like he didn't even know me. Only the slight furrow between his brows betrayed that he was focusing far too hard for such a simple task. Avoiding looking at me at all costs.

He wasn't using a crutch, I realized. Last time I'd seen Tamid, Prince Naguib had put a bullet straight through his twisted knee when I wouldn't give him the answers he wanted. I'd seen Tamid fall to his side, screaming. My fault. I'd seen men take lesser injuries than that and lose a leg, but here he was standing on two. I heard a small click as he moved, metal on metal, like the repeating system in a revolver. Through his torn pant leg I saw what looked like a joint made out of brass. My heart lurched. One flesh-and-blood leg and one metallic leg.

"What should I do with her?" the soldier asked.

"Tie it down to the table." Tamid picked up the last

piece of glass. He'd called me *it*. Like I was less than a friend he'd chosen to turn into an enemy. Like I was less than human.

The soldier's hands pressed painfully into my bandaged skin as he tried to hold me. I cried out without meaning to. The noise startled Tamid into looking at me.

"Don't—" he started, drawing the guard's attention. I saw my opening.

Make the first hit count.

I slammed my head forward. My skull connected with his, sending a crack of pain through my head. "Son of a bitch!" I cursed, as the soldier stumbled back, clutching his forehead. I rolled off the table and made for the door. But I was too slow—the soldier was already grabbing the front of my khalat, raising his fist, angling for my face. I turned away like Shazad had taught me, aiming to catch the fist with my shoulder.

The blow never came.

Weighty silence fell over the room.

I looked up. A man was holding back the soldier's fist. For a sliver of a second I thought it was Ahmed. Sunlight still danced blearily across my vision after days in darkness, edging his profile with gold. Dark hair with the hint of a curl in it fell over a proud desert-dark brow. Sharp, determined dark eyes smudged with a sleepless night. Only his mouth was different. Set in a steady, sure line, it didn't wear the soft uncertain question that sometimes hovered on Ahmed's.

But he was cast from the same mold. Or rather, Ahmed

was cast from the mold of this man. I shouldn't have been surprised. Sons tended to take after their fathers.

"You should know when you have been bested, soldier," the Sultan said, keeping hold of his fist.

The soldier's hand unwound itself from the front of my shirt quickly. I pulled back, out of reach. And just like that, all of the Sultan's attention turned on me.

I'd never figured the Sultan would look so much like my prince. I'd imagined him like every faded color drawing in the storybooks about cruel rulers who were overturned by clever heroes. Fat and old and greedy, and dressed in clothes that cost enough coin to feed a family for a year. I ought to have known better. If I'd learned anything from being the Blue-Eyed Bandit, it was that stories and the truth were rarely the same thing.

The Sultan had been the same age Ahmed was now when he took the throne. Ahmed and Jin were both born barely a year into his rule. I was decent enough at arithmetic to know that meant the man in front of me now hadn't seen four decades yet.

"You've brought me a fighter." He wasn't speaking to me. I noticed a fourth figure, hovering in the door. My aunt. Anger flooded out all my common sense. I moved again, lunging at her on instinct. I knew I wouldn't make it far, but the Sultan caught me before I'd gotten a step, hands on my shoulders. "Stop," he ordered. "You'll do yourself more harm than you will to her." He was right. The sudden motion had made my head light. My strength was draining out of me, even if the will to fight wasn't. I sagged in his grip.

"Good," the Sultan praised me gently, like I was an animal who'd done a trick. "Now let's take a look at you." He reached for my face. I recoiled on instinct, but I had nowhere to go. I'd been here before—on a dark night in Dustwalk and with Commander Naguib, another son of the Sultan's. I'd had the bruises he gave me across my cheek for weeks.

But the Sultan cupped my chin gently. He'd been a fighter when he'd taken the throne. They said he'd killed half his brothers that day himself. Two decades didn't seem to have made him any weaker. His fingers were calloused from use. For hunting. For war. For killing Ahmed and Delila's mother. But they were terribly gentle peeling my matted hair away from my face so he could see me clearer.

"Blue eyes," he said, without taking his hands away. "Unusual for a Mirajin girl."

My heart caught in my chest. What had my aunt and Tamid told him? That I'd come from the Rebellion? Would he believe them? Had the stories of the Blue-Eyed Bandit reached as high as the Sultan? "Your aunt has told me all about you, Amani."

"She's a liar." It spilled out, fast and angry. "Whatever she's told you, she can't be trusted."

"So you're saying you're not a Demdji, as she claims? Or are you just accusing her of being faithless to her own flesh and blood?"

"Don't bother, Amani," my aunt interjected. "You might have everyone else in Dustwalk fooled, but your mother confided in me." I understood the heavy look she was giving me over the Sultan's shoulder. She'd told him we'd come straight from Dustwalk. She *was* a liar. Not on my account, but she'd lied all the same. She hadn't told him about the Rebellion. And she was warning me with those veiled words. It would be bad for both of us if the Sultan found out where I'd really come from. He'd have questions for her, no doubt. Besides, I was valuable as a Demdji, not as a rebel.

"She wouldn't be the first, you know," the Sultan said to me. "To bring me a false Demdji. I've already had plenty of fathers and mothers travel from little towns at the end of my country just like yours, bringing me daughters with their hair dipped in saffron to make it look yellow, or their skin painted blue, thinking I would not know the difference."

He ran his hand across my cheekbone. There was a wound there; I could feel the dull throb of it under his thumb. I couldn't remember how I'd gotten it. His eyes traveled between me and my aunt. "You despise this woman. And I don't blame you. Do you go to prayers?" I kept my eyes on him, although I could feel Tamid watching me, tucked against the wall, like he could become part of it. Last time I'd truly attended prayers had been in Dustwalk and he'd been beside me, trying to make me be quiet as I shifted restlessly. "The Holy Books tell us worse than traitors are those who betray their own flesh and blood. Aunts who sell their nieces. Sons who rebel against their fathers." I tensed. "So, I will strike a deal with you. The same one I have struck with all the false

Demdji who've come before you. If you can tell me that you are not the daughter of a Djinni, I will release you, with as much gold as you can carry, and your aunt will be punished in a way of your choosing. If you need any inspiration, the girl whose father dyed her skin chose to have him strung up by his toes until all his blood rushed into his brain and killed him." He tapped my cheek, like we were sharing a joke. "All you have to do is say six little words: *I am not a Djinni's daughter*, and you can have your freedom. Or stay silent and your aunt will walk away with all that gold."

It was a damn good offer. Freedom and revenge. Only I'd have to lie for it.

"Go ahead," he said. I focused on his mouth as the words formed, that one part of him that didn't look like Ahmed.

I couldn't lie, but I could be deceitful. I'd done it before. I'd dodged my way out of plenty of things without speaking a single word that wasn't true.

"I didn't know my father." *Tamid will vouch for me.* But I didn't want to bring him into this just now if I didn't have to. The Sultan gave no sign that he knew that anything connected me and Tamid. Tamid could've told the Sultan that he knew me as more than a Demdji. He knew me as the girl who'd gotten a bullet put through his knee and ridden off with the Rebellion. But if he hadn't already, I wasn't about to be the one to sell us out. "My mother never said a word about him to me, and the whole of Dustwalk figured he was a Gallan soldier—"

The Sultan pressed his fingers to my lips, cutting me off sharply. He was leaning in so close now he filled my whole world. There was something unsettlingly familiar about him—more than just the face he shared with Ahmed. I just couldn't quite put my finger on what it was.

"I don't want to hear tricks or half-truths." He spoke so low only I could hear. "My father was a fool and he died at my hands, with a surprised look on his face. I am clearly not a fool, or else my rebel son would have done the same to me already. Now"—he carefully peeled one last strand of hair away from my face—"all I want is six simple words from you."

The Blue-Eyed Bandit might be the stuff of campfire stories, but Demdji, we were the stuff of legends. Half of Miraji wasn't even sure we were real. But the Sultan seemed well informed.

I had to lie. I couldn't lie, but I had to. Everything depended on it. Not just me getting out of here, and not just my life. Everyone's. If I couldn't lie now, he might pull truth after truth from my lips—maybe even about the Rebellion. He'd pull knowledge out of my silences. And he'd turn me into a weapon like he had with Noorsham. Into a slave.

I reached desperately for the lie that would get me out of there. Get me away from this enemy wearing the face of my prince.

I fought with everything in me. But everything in me was Demdji.

And Demdji couldn't tell lies.

The Sultan laughed. It was an unexpectedly honest sound. "No need to strain yourself. I knew what you were from the moment I saw you, little Demdji." He'd been toying with me.

"Reward this good woman." He gestured to my aunt lazily. The soldier snapped to attention and gestured for my aunt to follow him. His shoulders seemed to sag in relief as he left the room. She looked so damn pleased with herself as she turned, disappearing from the room. And I hated her. God, I hated her.

From the corner of my eye I noticed Tamid shifting in the corner, like he was expecting a dismissal, too. Like he'd rather leave than watch whatever the Sultan was about to do to me.

"Sit down, Amani," the Sultan ordered.

I didn't want to sit. I wanted to stand and face our enemy. But suddenly, and against my will, my body moved on its own, folding my legs under myself until I was sitting back on the marble slab where I'd woken up.

Panic rose up, almost choking me. I'd never been betrayed by my own body like that before. "What did you do to me?"

The Sultan didn't answer right away. "Your eyes betrayed you from the start." *Traitor eyes.* "There was another Demdji before you. He had blue eyes, too." Noorsham. He was talking about Noorsham. "It's one of the great justices of our world that your kind, for all your power, are yet so vulnerable to words." They'd had Noorsham's true name. That was how they'd controlled him. Noorsham had worn a mask, made of bronze, engraved with his name. The Sultan knew Noorsham's true name. "What do you think the chances are there are two Demdji in the desert with blue eyes who *don't* share the same father? I would say they were small." Which meant the Sultan knew our father's name. And my true name. My eyes shot around the room, looking for a bronze suit like the one they'd encased Noorsham in. But the room looked like nothing more than a Holy Father's chambers. Tamid had always wanted to be a Holy Man.

"We lost our last Demdji, unfortunately," the Sultan was saying. "It was our young Tamid's idea to make things a little more secure this time." He nodded to my one-time friend. Tamid was still looking anywhere but at me.

And finally I understood what was below the bandages.

"You put metal beneath my skin." It would be bronze. Bronze with my name on it. My true name. Including the name of my real father. I looked for a bronze ring on his hand like the one Naguib had used to control Noorsham. Something I could wrench off his fingers, breaking his control over me and letting me make a run for it. Instead I spied a small bandage across the Sultan's forearm. Like mine. He was taking precautions.

"Bronze." The Sultan touched one of the scars. "And iron."

Iron.

My stomach lurched at that. They had cut my skin open, put iron underneath it, and stitched me back up.

I was powerless.

Only . . . the Sultan had wanted Noorsham so he could use his power as a weapon. If that wasn't why he wanted me, then what had he just paid my aunt so highly for?

"You're wondering why," the Sultan said. I wished I wasn't so easy to read. "I made the mistake last time of thinking I could control a Demdji. But there are so many loopholes. So many small gaps in my orders you could squeeze through. As a girl you are largely harmless if you do wriggle through those loopholes. As a Demdji . . . well, the chance of harnessing your power is not worth the price if you disobeyed and turned it against me. It would be like letting you loose in my palace with a gun." He mentioned guns in a cast-off comment, but it still made me nervous. He couldn't know I was the Blue-Eyed Bandit. If he did, he'd know I was part of the Rebellion and I doubted we'd be having such a pleasant conversation. "The iron was Tamid's idea again. He has been *very* useful since coming to the palace. He is from the Last County, too, you know—where was it, my boy?"

"Sazi," Tamid said. It was a bare-faced lie. Sazi was near enough Dustwalk, but far enough away that I'd never been there until I went with Jin. It was where Noorsham was from. Where Naguib had been encamped before coming to Dustwalk. Tamid was hiding from the Sultan that we were from the same place. He hated me enough to stick iron under my skin but not to put a noose around my neck, it seemed.

I willed Tamid to look at me. But he kept his eyes firmly on the ground. I was so stupid. I'd seen him and for just a second I'd felt like nothing had changed. But I was wrong. I should've known that. Last time I was with Tamid I was a girl who left people behind. And he was a boy who'd never have betrayed me.

"Your part of the desert remembers things that most of the rest of us have forgotten," the Sultan was saying.

"So what good am I to you as a Demdji with no power?" I carefully turned my attention back to the Sultan.

The Sultan smiled enigmatically. "Follow me and find out."

And against my will, I felt my feet move. I just had time to glance over my shoulder to see Tamid finally look up at me, his face marked with something that looked a lot like worry, before the door closed between us.

FOURTEEN

I had to follow him, but I didn't have to shut up about it. "Where are we going?" Smooth marble echoed my own words mockingly back at me as we wove our way through the palace. "Where are you taking me?"

The Sultan didn't answer any of the questions I shouted at his back as I trailed him. Finally he stopped in the middle of a hallway. I halted a few paces from him. Behind us an archway twice my height opened into a small garden filled with roaming peacocks. Across from it, so as to be framed in the line of sight from the door, was a mosaic of Princess Hawa. She stood on what I guessed were the walls of Saramotai, hands spread wide as the sun rose behind her. Her eyes stared straight ahead. They were blue in this picture, too. Just like they'd been in Saramotai.

The Sultan pressed a hand to Hawa's. I heard a click, and then the section of the wall that extended from one of Hawa's hands to the other shifted, swinging out like a door. Behind it a long staircase plunged downward into darkness.

We'd passed the last guard a ways back now. And there were none here. Whatever was at the bottom of those stairs was truly meant to stay secret. "What's down there?" My voice bounced eerily down the stone steps.

"There are some things that are better to do in places where God is blind." The Destroyer of Worlds came from the place where God was blind, they said. Deep inside the earth. "After you."

Pressing a hand to the wall for balance, I counted the steps as we descended. Thirty-three was a holy number. It was the number of Djinn who gathered together to forge the First Mortal in their war against the Destroyer of Worlds.

I stumbled in the dark at the bottom. The Sultan was close behind me. He steadied me with a hand on my waist. For a moment I was back in the camp, Jin's hand on me. *I've got you.* I pulled away quickly.

This wasn't like the rest of the palace. Instead of smooth marble, the walls were rough-hewn stone. A low ceiling was supported by squat pillars that went on line after line into the shadows, like ancient soldiers standing to attention. The only light came from a hole in the ceiling, casting a bright circle in the dark vaults. As we got closer to the light, I could see the pillars were carved with patterns that had been worn down, like centuries had run them smooth. Maybe longer than centuries. I wasn't sure how old the world was. But this seemed like a place that was here at the beginning of it. The years had buried this place, but it had survived.

Standing under the light was like being at the bottom of a well. The circle of light was about as wide as my arms stretched out. But the sky above was only the size of a half-louzi piece. My bare toes brushed something cold. Looking down in the lamplight, I realized that there was iron set into the ground in a perfect circle, patterns woven through it. An identical circle glinted off to my left. And another, just beyond that, covered in dust and dirt.

"What are these?" I pulled away from the iron instinctively.

"You're from the edge of the desert," the Sultan said. "You are a descendant of the nomads who carried stories across the sands. You must know all the ones of the old days, in the times that the Djinn walked among us openly. When they still loved mortals. Well." He gave me a sly glance. "You are walking proof that they do still, occasionally. But there was also a time when *my* ancestors ruled with the help of the Djinn. That was what the Sultim trials were, thousands of years ago. Tasks set by the Djinn to choose the worthiest among the Sultan's sons. Not a series of foolish tests designed to turn men on each other." A series of foolish tests which Ahmed had won outright. "In those days, princes would climb mountains and ride Rocs to bring back a single one of their feathers. They drank water under the sleepless eye of the Wanderer. True feats. But though we cling to those traditions, the days of worthy princes are long gone. As are the days when the Djinn used to come here and surrender their power inside these circles in good faith, while the Sultan surrendered his weapons, and they traded counsel."

I ran my toe along the edge of the circle. I'd heard of these in stories. Places where the Sultan summoned a Djinni by his true name and then released him again. It was a sign of trust. If I counted the circles, would there be thirty-three of those, too?

"You are going to summon a Djinni here, Amani," the Sultan said.

My head shot up. I'd seen plenty of things that were created before mortals. Buraqi. Nightmares. Skinwalkers. But the Djinn were different. They weren't just the stuff legends were made of. They were our creators. Nobody saw Djinn anymore, though a few folks in Dustwalk claimed to have found one at the bottom of a strong bottle. And, I supposed, my mother had. "So desperate for greater counsel in these troubled times, Your Exalted Highness?" He didn't take the bait.

"The stories make it sound easy—you can simply call a First Being so long as you have their true name." Like princesses and paupers alike in the stories, calling for help at their hour of need with a true name earned through some virtuous deed at the start of the tale. "But you need so much more than that. You also need to be able to call them in the first language." The Sultan pulled a folded piece of paper from his pocket. "And you need one more thing. Care to venture a guess?"

I didn't take the paper. "If I were taking a stab in the dark"—I heard the bile on my own tongue—"I'd say it was a Demdji."

So this was why he was willing to pay a Demdji's weight in gold. This was why he'd shoved iron under my skin. He didn't need my powers. He was going to order me to summon a Djinni.

I knew the stories of the wars that the Djinn had fought alongside humanity. Adil the Conqueror who leashed a Djinni in iron and brought cities to their knees before he came face-to-face with the Gray Prince. The Djinni who built the walls of Izman in a single night as a gift to his beloved. A Demdji's power was nothing compared to what I knew a Djinni could do.

I thought he'd order me to take the paper. But the Sultan just smiled indulgently. "A true language." A language without lies. "A true tongue." A Demdji who couldn't lie. Who could say *You will come to me* in the first language and make it so. "And a true name. In this case, the same one buried under your skin. Part of your true name." My eyes shot to the paper without meaning to. "Your father's name."

My father's. My real father. The Sultan hadn't ordered me to take the paper. But still my hand twitched toward it against my judgment. My father was in my reach.

"Take it," the Sultan ordered finally. "If you want to."

My fingers closing around the paper at the order betrayed me. I wanted to let go of the paper. I wanted to fight it. But I wanted to know, too. I raised the paper so I could see it in the light from the well.

And there it was.

Black ink scrawled onto white paper. My father's name. Bahadur.

For the first time in my seventeen years I knew my real name. The same one that was etched into bronze and slipped beneath my skin.

I was Amani Al-Bahadur.

"Read it aloud." It was an order. And I couldn't disobey.

My mouth moved against my will, reciting the ancient language written on the paper. The words almost fell out, so easily for a language I didn't speak, like they belonged there. Like the Djinni half of me recognized this language better than any other.

I got to the end too quickly, and my father's name slid across my tongue as easily as fat over a fire. And then I was done. I fell silent.

Nothing happened for a moment.

Then the iron circle burst into flames.

FIFTEEN

I staggered back as a huge column of blue fire rose up from the circle in front of me. It was higher than the low-vaulted ceiling, filling the well all the way up to the sky. It burned hot and quick and brighter than any flame I'd ever seen. It fought for a few moments at the edges of the iron circle, at some invisible barrier, before, just as suddenly as it had appeared, pulling itself into the center of the circle, taking a shape.

I blinked against the light floating in my eyes, like I'd just stared straight at the sun and gone blind for a moment.

Then my vision cleared and I saw my father for the first time.

Bahadur looked like a man who had been made out of fire.

No. That wasn't right. I might not be so devout as some, but I knew my holy stories. Djinn weren't humans made out of fire. We were Djinn made out of dirt and water with just a hint of their flame to give us life. A spark from a bonfire. We were a far duller version of them.

Bahadur's skin shifted and moved with dark blue flames. Flames the same color as my eyes.

I didn't feel heat pouring off him. But I could feel something else, something that I couldn't name but that went past my skin and struck me in the soul. He stood as tall as one of the huge pillars down here in this ancient palace vault. Only he wasn't just holding up a palace. He was holding up the world. One of God's First Beings who had made the First Mortal. Who had made all of mankind.

Who'd made me.

I realized that what I was feeling was power. True, raw power, the kind that didn't come from a title or a crown but from the soul of the world itself.

He kept shifting as I stared at him. And I realized he was shrinking and shifting at the same time, changing his appearance. It reminded me of the way Imin shifted when changing shape. Until he wasn't blue fire and light anymore. He was dark skin and dark hair, as much flesh and blood as any desert dweller. Still, even blunted to look like us, there was no mistaking that he was different. He was too handsome, too carefully carved, too perfect to look like a mortal man. And he hadn't made his eyes look human. They were made of the same changing fire as the rest of him, except they burned more steadily. They burned white-hot around the edges, and bright blue around a perfect black pupil. And they seemed to scrape me inside out.

"You called me." Three such mundane words that carried so much weight. His attention shifted slowly to the Sultan. "Though not, I see, for yourself."

The Sultan was a powerful man. But he was a man just the same, and standing next to a Djinni he looked like nothing more than a spark hovering around a bonfire.

"Now." Bahadur sounded almost bored as he spoke to the Sultan. "What would you ask of me? Is it gold? Power? Love? Eternal life? All four, perhaps?"

"I'm not foolish enough to ask anything from you."

Bahadur considered him without blinking. I realized I was watching him closely, searching his features for something familiar, something I might share with him other than our eyes. "I have seen more days and met more mortals than there are grains of sand in your desert. I have met paupers and kings and everything in between. I have never met a man who didn't want something. It does not matter if you are a dirty-kneed child on the street or a man who already has more power and gold than you know what to do with. You always want something."

"And you always use our wants against us," the Sultan said. "You take our needs and our desires and you twist them until our only wish is that we hadn't asked for your help at all." He wasn't wrong. I'd read those stories, too. The ones of Massil, and of the Djinni who destroyed an entire sea in revenge on one merchant. The tinker who died in the desert looking for gold he was promised by a captured Djinni. "And in the end"—the Sultan swept his foot over the edge of the circle tauntingly—"we never get what we want."

"So you do want something."

"Of course," the Sultan said. "Everyone wants *something*. But I am not foolish enough to ask you for it. You are going to give it to me, with no strings attached."

When Bahadur laughed it echoed all the way down the vaults. "And why would I do that?"

"She is one of yours, you know." He meant me, though his eyes never strayed from his Djinni prize.

"Of course I know." Bahadur didn't take his eyes off the Sultan. *Look at me*, a part of me wanted to shout at him. Another wanted to shout at myself for wanting him to. I'd done just fine my whole life without a father. I didn't need one now. "Why do you think we mark them?"

The Sultan pulled a knife out of his belt. "Little Demdji. Take this and drive it through your stomach." My body went cold. It was an order.

"No." I said it out loud, like refusing could make it real. But it was no good—my hands had already started to move.

"Do it slowly," the Sultan ordered, "so that it hurts."

There was nothing I could do. My hand was moving, reaching out for the knife, curling around the handle, turning the blade so it pointed at my center. I fought it. My arms trembled with effort. But there was no helping it. The knife was slowly driving itself toward my stomach.

"Your daughter will die here." The Sultan addressed

Bahadur. "Unless I stop that knife." Stomach wounds killed you slowly. "Give me the names of your fellow Djinn, and I will order her to drop the knife."

Bahadur still didn't even glance my way. He watched the Sultan with flat blue eyes as the blade inched toward my body. He was an immortal First Being. Second only to God himself. To him even the Sultan, the ruler of the whole desert, was nothing. I was nothing, and I was his daughter. He sank down in the circle, crossing his legs gracefully as he went.

"All of you die eventually." He smiled in that indulgent way parents do at children. Except it wasn't at me. "It's what mortals do best."

The knife was still inching toward my stomach and he didn't care. He was going to let me die. The knife pressed against the cloth of Shazad's khalat. I was always getting blood on the clothes she lent me. This time she probably wouldn't forgive me. She'd never forgive me for dying on her in the middle of the war.

"Yes," the Sultan agreed. "Everything dies eventually." He turned away from the Djinni, like *he* was the one who was nothing. If he was disappointed in Bahadur's refusal, it barely showed. "Drop the knife." The order was thrown at me.

I wrenched the knife away from my stomach, letting it clatter to the ground. My body was my own again. It had been a bluff. A stupid failed bluff against an immortal being. I was shaking. Hard. But anger chased out fear fast. Anger at my own body. At the Sultan. But most of all, that

Bahadur would look on, so indifferent to me, as I died.

He had made me drop the knife. But he hadn't told me not to pick it back up.

My fingers curled back around the hilt, and I moved, plunging the knife toward the Sultan's throat. One final gesture to end everything.

"Stop." The order came a second too soon. Seizing my muscles with the knife a hairbreadth from his skin. I'd been a second from killing him.

For the first time Bahadur was watching me with interest.

The Sultan's gaze flicked from the knife to me. I expected rage. I expected retribution. But none came. His lip just twitched up. "You're a dangerous little Demdji, aren't you?" And then I knew why his mouth looked familiar.

His face was Ahmed's, but that smile—that smile was all Jin.

SIXTEEN

I was valuable.

That was why I was still alive.

That was why he'd stopped the knife.

I was going to be kept in the harem. That was what the Sultan said. Kept. Not like a prisoner. More like an especially nicely crafted gun. Stored until I was needed again.

Other orders came with it as I was handed over to a servant woman in a khalat the color of pale sand, her dark hair bound up in a sheema. Like she might have to worry about the desert sun in the shaded halls of the palace.

"You will stay in the palace," he instructed calmly. I wanted to fight. But while my mind might be able to rebel against it, my body wouldn't be able to. "You won't set foot beyond the walls of the harem without permission from a member of the palace." He understood Demdji too well. He chose his words carefully. *Don't leave the harem.* Not, *Don't try to escape.* Trying and succeeding were two different things to a Demdji.

I spared a glance down the steps as the Sultan ordered me back up. Toward Bahadur. My father—though the word felt unnatural. He watched us go from where he sat inside the small circle. Darkness folded around him as our lamp retreated but I could still see him long after I ought to have been able to. Like he still burned with his own fire, even in human form. He was a thousandfold more powerful than I was. He had lived countless lives before I was even born. But he was as trapped as I was here. What hope did I have of getting out if he couldn't?

"And you will not harm any person here. Or yourself." He worried that I'd kill myself. That I'd try to slip through his grip into nothingness. I didn't want to know what he had planned for me that was so bad that killing myself might be better. "But if any harm comes to me—if I die— you will walk up to the highest tower in this palace and throw yourself off it." If he died, I died.

A dozen other orders took root inside my bones as I was led through more polished marble hallways by the woman dressed in the color of false sand. My legs obeyed the Sultan's last orders. "Go with her. Do what she says."

We passed under a low stone archway. I could just make out figures of dancing women twined together carved into the stone. I felt steam in the air before we'd gone much farther, the cloying scent of flowers and spices already winding their way to my body. As easy to get drunk on as liquor when you'd been in the dried-out desert for too long.

We emerged into the most immense baths I'd ever seen. The room was tiled in iridescent blues and pinks and yellows in wild, hypnotic mosaic patterns from floor to ceiling. The steam climbing from the heated pools gave everything a slick sheen, from the walls to the girls.

And there were a lot of girls.

I'd heard stories about the Sultan's harem, where women were kept for the pleasure of the Sultan and the Sultim. And to breed future princes to fight for the throne, and princesses to be sold for political alliances. Here they were, running soap in long languid circles across their bare shoulders or floating at the edge of the water, eyes closed as attendants ran oils through their hair. A few lay on the nearby beds, long limbs being kneaded by clever hands as they dozed.

The attendant started to undress me without speaking, undoing the tiny clasps at the front of Shazad's khalat as I stared. I let her.

And then I spied the man. He looked like a fox in the henhouse. And a hungry one, too. He lounged on a bed, propped up by a stack of pillows, stripped to the waist. Probably a year or two my senior, he looked like something hewn out of stone, with heavy square features without a single graceful subtlety to offset them. He ought to have been handsome, but there was a nastiness to the tilt of his mouth that meant he'd never be.

Three impossibly pretty Mirajin girls were draped around him, wrapped in nothing but long linen sheets, long dark hair hanging in thick wet waves around their bare shoulders. One of them sat at his feet, trailing her legs lazily in the steaming water, leaning into the knee of a slighter girl who was folded into his side. The last one lay with her head in his lap, eyes shut as he trailed his fingers through her hair absently, pouty lips pressed into a contented smile.

His attention wasn't on any of them, though—it was fixed on two girls standing across from him, both bare as the day they were born, being inspected inch by inch by an attendant. Like the servants were looking for any flaw that might keep these girls from being admitted into this world of perfect, beautiful women. I recognized them, I realized as the attendant peeled away my khalat and wrapped me in a plain linen sheet, though it took my tired mind a moment to place them. They'd been on the ship with me, brought by the slavers to be offered to the harem.

What had happened to the girls not chosen for the harem? Had they been sold to other men in less prestigious houses? Or were the rumors true—that slavers drowned any girl rejected by the Sultan's harem?

As if she sensed me staring, the small girl pressed into his side looked my way. Something passed over her face as she leaned in to whisper to the girl lounging across the man's lap. The girl with the pretty pout. Her eyes snapped open, focusing on me so quickly it was plain as day she'd only been pretending to sleep. She pursed her full mouth pensively as she twisted so that she could whisper something to the other two. The laugh that followed bounced off the tiles around me.

It drew the man's attention my way.

"You're new," he addressed me as the girls pretended to try to hide their smiles. I hated his voice instantly. It stuck to his words like it was tasting them, and in turn they seemed to cling to my skin.

"You should bow to the Sultim." The pout-lipped girl yawned, stretching conspicuously across his body like a cat in the sun. So this was the Sultim—the firstborn of the Sultan's sons. Prince Kadir. Heir to the throne we were fighting for. The son who had faced Ahmed in the last challenge of the Sultim trials.

I'd long since passed the time when I might've been impressed by a prince. In the last handful of days alone I'd kissed one and yelled at another. But this one was my enemy.

So I didn't bow as the attendants carefully unwound my bandages, conscious of this man's eyes on me, as more of my skin was bared to the air.

There were ugly red welts where the iron had been shoved under my skin. The girls let out a bark of laughter as they appeared. "Maybe the tailor Abdul made her, my love," the pout-lipped one said, considering me. The other two girls tittered.

That stung.

"The Tailor Abdul" was a story about a man who was too picky with his wives. He married his first wife because her face was so lovely. He married his second because her body was desirable; and the third because she had such a good heart. But he bemoaned that his first wife was cruel, that his second wife had an unsightly face, and that his third wife had an ugly body.

And so he hired the tailor Abdul to make him the perfect wife. The skilled tailor did as he was told without objection. He sewed the first wife's head onto the body of the second wife, and then he sewed the good heart of the third wife into the body so neatly that he didn't even scar her perfect chest. What was left of the women was tossed out into the desert. In the end the wives got their revenge, as the husband was eaten alive by a Skinwalker who wore all the discarded pieces of his wives.

I stopped my hand from drifting to the marks on my arms. I was a Demdji, a soldier of the Rebellion, the Blue-Eyed Bandit. I'd faced a whole lot worse than bratty harem girls.

But Kadir only smiled. "In that case, she was tailored for me."

"It looks more like he made her for the menagerie," another girl started, failing to read her Sultim's mood. "Or he mixed her arms up with a monkey's." The girls' titters burst into laughter. But they had lost the Sultim's attention. He pushed himself to his feet, almost spilling the girl in his lap off him.

"You look Mirajin." The spark of interest in his voice was dangerous as he closed the short distance between us. "It's so rare they're able to bring me Mirajin girls. Your kind are my favorites, though. You're western Mirajin, I suppose." I didn't answer. He didn't seem to need me to. He grabbed my chin, tilting my face to catch the light and looking me over like a merchant might look at a horse. I would've hit him but the Sultan's orders kept my hands at my sides. "At least my brother's rebellion is good for something. Wars mean more prisoners."

It had long been known that the harem was a dangerous place to be. I'd heard in the days of Sultan Oman's father some women did come to him by choice. But more were prisoners of war. Slaves bought from foreign shores. Women captured off ships like Jin's mother. Now we had a war in Miraji. That would mean more slavers taking advantage of the chaos to take Mirajin women.

"Has the blessed Sultima even seen you yet?" the girl who'd been displaced from her Sultim's lap called out, trying to regain his attention.

"All the new girls for the Sultim are meant to be seen by the Sultima," the petite cohort agreed, like she was parroting something someone else had said.

"Yes, she needs to deem you worthy." The girl who'd been at his feet butted in, too, eager to please.

"Or not worthy." The pout-lipped girl smirked.

"Be quiet, Ayet, there's no need to disturb the Sultima." The Sultim's hand left my face, traveling down my neck, across my collarbone, making my skin crawl.

"She is off-limits." The servant with me spoke up just as Kadir's hand reached the border of the white linen sheet that covered me. She had the clipped, matronly tone of a mother without much patience. The Sultim opened his mouth with a dismissal that never came as she cut across him. "Your father's orders."

Mention of the Sultan drew Kadir's hand up short. For a second he seemed to blaze with defiance. And then it was gone, covered as he dropped his arm and shrugged, brushing past me instead, like that was what he'd intended to do all along. His wives gathered themselves up, following him. Ayet's eyes dropped to Shazad's discarded khalat as she passed. So fine a few days ago at the wedding. Before we were attacked. Before I was kissed and kidnapped and cut into. But still beautiful. Her left foot caught the fabric, flicking it and sending it flying into one of the pools, soaking the fabric through.

"Oops." Ayet flashed me her teeth. "Sorry." She flicked one last droplet off her hair at me as she left, followed by a burst of giggles and whispers that bounced off the walls of the baths.

I felt the back of my neck go hot.

When Ahmed took this palace, I was going to burn the harem to the ground.

SEVENTEEN

The harem stripped me of the desert.

The attendants dumped water over my head and scrubbed at my skin until it was screaming and raw. Until they'd robbed me of the skin that'd been caked with sand and blood and sweat and gunpowder and fire and Jin's hands.

They pulled me out of the steaming water. I let one of the girls wrap me in a big, dry linen sheet and lay me down gently next to the bath. Something warm dripped across my skin, like oil. It smelled of flowers I didn't know. The other girl ran a comb through my hair, scraping gently at my scalp.

I'd spent my whole life fighting. Fighting to stay alive in Dustwalk as the girl with the gun. Fighting to escape death in that dead-end desert town. Fighting to get across the desert. The Blue-Eyed Bandit. Fighting for Ahmed. For the Rebellion. *A new dawn. A new desert.*

But as the comb scraped through my hair over and over again, I wasn't sure I had any fight left in me.

I let sleep claim me.

Tomorrow. I'd fight tomorrow.

• ● •

IT DIDN'T TAKE a whole lot of time for me to figure out that the harem was full of invisible chains and walls meant to look like they weren't there.

It felt like a maze, designed to turn me around, over and over, until I wasn't sure how I'd come in or if there was a way out anymore. There were dozens of gardens, which fit together like honeycombs. Some of them were plain stretches of grass, with a single fountain gushing endless water and pillows scattered throughout. Others were so thick with flowers and vines and sculptures I couldn't even see the walls anymore. But the walls were always there.

I couldn't count how many folks lived in the harem. Dozens of wives belonging to the Sultan and Sultim alike. And children, too—the princes and princesses born to the Sultan's wives. All of them younger than sixteen. The age they were finally released from the harem. To pass from their father's hands to their husbands'. Or to die for him on the battlefield like Naguib had. All of them Ahmed and Jin's brothers and sisters.

Finally I found one of the borders: a gate crafted out

of iron and gold that stood ajar. My legs stumbled to a stop as I tried to pass through. I fought against the feeling holding me back, but it was no good—my body seized like I'd been grabbed by some invisible hand. My blood turned to stone and a fist twisted in my gut, pulling me back.

I'd been ordered not to leave.

I couldn't go any farther.

I needed to get word back to the Rebellion. Even if I didn't know exactly where the Rebellion was. Shazad's family was in Izman, though. And Izman was on the other side of these walls. A few feet away. It might as well have been a whole desert between us.

There had to be a crack, some way out of the harem. Even if I couldn't get out, there had to be some way to get out a warning, at least, that the Sultan had a Djinni.

That he had my father.

I pushed that thought away. He wasn't my father any more than my mother's husband had been.

If he were my father he would've cared if I'd died or not.

My mother had raised me on a thousand stories of girls who were saved by the Djinn, princesses rescued from towers, peasant girls rescued from poverty.

Turned out, stories were just stories.

I was on my own.

It ought to be a familiar feeling. I used to think I was on my own in Dustwalk, too. But that had never been true. I'd had Tamid back then. Now there were dozens of tiny incisions healing all over my body reminding me why I couldn't trust my oldest friend. My fingers found one of the tiny pieces of metal under the skin of my arm. It hurt when I pressed my thumb against it. I pushed harder.

For the first time in my life I really was alone.

● ● ●

IT WAS ON my third day in the harem that I stumbled into the menagerie.

The noise was the first thing I noticed—a riot of different screams coming from iron cages crowned in intricate latticework domes. There were hundreds of birds perched among the iron bars, dressed in colors to make a Djinni jealous. The yellow of fresh lemons. Green like the grass in the Dev's Valley before we fled. Red like the sheema I'd lost. Blue like my eyes. Only not quite. Nothing was really the same blue as my eyes. Except for Noorsham's. And Bahadur's. The ones that had watched, burning low with indifference, as the knife inched toward my skin. The ones that hadn't even blinked or deigned to turn away. Like watching me wouldn't cause him any pain.

I turned away from the birds.

Huge peacocks fanned their tails as I passed another cage. In another, a pair of tigers lounged in a patch of sunlight, sprawled across each other, yawning wide enough so I could see teeth the length of my fingers. There had been some painted on the walls of the secret door leading into the rebel camp, too. But those were pictures, a thousand years old, the size of my hand. These were far from that.

I stumbled to a stop at the farthest cage.

The thing inside was nearly as big as a Roc. A solid behemoth of gray skin and thick limbs and unnaturally large ears. I caught my body pressing up against the bars. Like I might be able to squeeze through and touch it.

On the opposite side of the cage was a girl, sitting with her knees drawn up to her chin. She couldn't be more than fifteen. Too young to be one of the Sultim's wives. She had to be the Sultan's daughter, then. One of his brood of princesses, who were never spoken about half so much as the princes. Something about her reminded me of Delila, even though, I realized, she'd share blood with Jin, which Delila didn't. But still, there was a softness in the curve of her cheeks, like she hadn't fully finished unsticking herself from childhood yet, either. And she was handling something that looked like a toy she was modeling out of red clay around a metal skeleton, making a tiny model of the beast. She nudged one of the legs as I watched; it bent naturally, guided by small metallic joints inside.

"What is it?" I asked. She looked up, startled out of her work, staring at me through the bars of the cage. The words had slipped out without meaning to.

"An elephant," she said quietly.

My heart twisted painfully as I thought of Izz and Maz excitedly explaining elephants to me.

This was what they had seen across our borders. A real live elephant.

"Come to visit your family?" The sneering voice behind me was far from welcome. I turned to meet it all the same.

It was Ayet, the wife who'd kicked my khalat into the pool my first day in the harem. With her were two other girls who always seemed to flank her like some sort of personal guard. I'd learned from overheard conversations they were called Mouhna and Uzma.

"And your families are in the Sultan's kennels, I suppose." I watched the insult dawn across all three of their faces at once. Ayet recovered fast.

"You seem to think that we are your enemies," Ayet said. "But we can help you. Do you know where we are?" She didn't wait for me to answer. "This is the very menagerie where the Sultan's wife Nadira met the Djinni who gave her a demon child." Nadira was Ahmed and Delila's mother. Everyone knew that story. One day the Sultan's wife was wandering the gardens of the palace, when she stumbled upon a frog that had accidentally leapt into one of the Sultan's birdcages and could not find his way out again.

I glanced at the birds in the cage.

The birds kept pecking at him. Nadira took pity on the creature and, opening the cage, reached in with no care for the way the birds pecked at her own hands, turning them bloody and scratched. As soon as she set the frog back down, he transformed into his true form, that of a Djinni.

"See, here's the thing." Ayet and her girls circled me like a pack of roving animals. "Girls who don't find their right place in the harem don't tend to last long. The Sultim likes Mirajin girls." Ayet's hand slammed into my chest, surprisingly hard, knocking me back toward the nearest cage. One of the tigers glanced up, curious. "But he's only ever got room for three of us on display. So when someone new comes in, another one has to go. And none of us wants to disappear. Which means *you* don't have a purpose here."

"I've got no interest in your idiot husband." I wanted to shove her hand away. But I couldn't. The Sultan had given me orders. I couldn't fight back.

Ayet wasn't convinced. "Do you know what else happened here? This is where the Sultan killed Nadira after she gave birth to an abomination." She took a step toward me. "Because here, nobody can hear screams over the birds." Sure enough, the birds in the cages were in chaos now, their voices drowning out the rest of the harem just spitting distance away. "Go ahead. Call out for help."

"You should leave her alone." The voice wasn't strong. It was barely a squeak among the chorus of wild-feathered birds. But it was loud enough to be heard. It was the girl with the toy elephant. She was watching this all play out from the opposite side of the cage. Her eyes were wide with fear. But she'd spoken up all the same.

Ayet sneered, but a sharp-tongued insult never came. "This is our business, Leyla. The Sultan hasn't taken a new wife in a decade, which means she's clearly here for our blessed husband the Sultim, not your father."

"If you're so sure of that"—Leyla got to her feet uncertainly, clutching the clay elephant like a child a dozen years younger—"I can just go ask *my father.*"

Invoking the Sultan was like uttering a magic word. The kind that summoned powerful spirits and opened doors in cliff faces. All Leyla had to do was mention him and it was as if he were here.

Ayet caved first. She rolled her eyes, like she wanted me to think I wasn't worth her time, and turned away.

"Consider this a warning." She tossed the words over her shoulder as she swanned out. I watched her go, hating her. Hating that I couldn't break her nose like I wanted to.

Across the menagerie Leyla was winding the mechanism in her hands absently. "You'll get used to them." I didn't plan on having to get used to them. I was getting out of there before I had time to.

• • •

SINCE ARRIVING IN the harem, I'd stayed in my rooms when I wasn't looking for a way out. The attendants brought me fresh clothes and a basin to wash in and meals, seeming to anticipate what I needed without me ever needing to speak a word. But that night, no food came.

I couldn't help but think Ayet might have something to do with that. Just because she couldn't tear me apart like a wild animal didn't mean she was done trying to make me suffer for some imagined designs I had on her Sultim. The last thing I needed was another prince in my life. I had a hard enough time with the two I'd already acquired.

I waited until it was dark outside before finally giving in to my growling stomach. Even I wasn't stubborn enough to starve to death.

Women were dotted all over the garden where the meal was served, sitting in tightly knotted clusters around dishes of food that they shared between them. So tightly knotted that it'd be impossible to untie one long enough to get to the food. I was suddenly back in my first night in the rebel camp, before I'd known everyone's name. When I'd been an intruder. Except I'd been an intruder with Shazad and Bahi to guide me then.

I spied Leyla then, the only person I could see sitting by herself. She was almost done making the toy elephant, by the looks of things, and the modeled clay was taking shape around the articulated metal joints. As I watched her, she wound up a small key in the back of the toy. It marched with jolting, violent steps toward one of the small children sitting with the huddle of women nearest her. The little boy reached for it excitedly, but his mother snatched him away, pulling him onto her lap, knocking the thing over in the process.

The moment of joy that had bloomed on Leyla's face at operating the tiny thing disappeared, as she ducked her head. A girl like that would be eaten alive in the desert. Then again, a girl from the desert could get eaten alive in the palace.

I picked up the toy from where it was now lying use-lessly on the ground, legs still jerking forward. I held it out to her. She looked up at me with eyes that seemed to take up her whole face.

"You helped me today, in the menagerie." She just stared at me. I wanted to say that I could've handled myself. And that would've been true if I weren't trapped by a hundred tiny pieces of metal under my skin. "Thank you."

She nodded and took the toy. I sat down next to her without invitation. I didn't really have anywhere else to go. I was being nice to her because I was going to need allies in the harem. That was what I told myself. Not because she had big lost eyes that made me think of Delila's.

Ayet and her two parasites were in a tight knot a little ways off. Waves of disdain were rolling off them even from this far away. When they caught me looking back Ayet whispered something to Mouhna. They descended into fits of giggles like crowing birds.

"They're afraid of you," Leyla volunteered. "They think you'll take their place with Kadir."

I snorted. "Believe me, I have no interest in your brother."

An attendant appeared, handing me a plate heavy with savory-smelling meats. My stomach growled in grateful answer.

"He's not my brother." Leyla's jaw set firmly. "I mean, yes, I suppose. We're both children of my most exalted father the Sultan. But in the harem the only people we call brother or sister are those who share the same mother. I only have one brother, Rahim. He's gone from the harem now." She sounded far away.

"And your mother?" I asked.

"She was a Gamanix engineer's daughter." She turned the small toy over in her hands. Jin had told me about that country. It was where the twinned compasses he and Ahmed each always kept had been made. A country that had learned to meld magic and machines. This explained how she'd learned to make little mechanized toys. "She vanished when I was eight years old." Leyla said it so calm and straightforward it caught me off guard.

"What do you mean, vanished?" I asked.

"Oh, it happens in the harem," Leyla said. "Women disappear when they lose their use. That's why Ayet is so afraid of you. She hasn't been able to conceive a child for the Sultim. If you replace her, she could vanish just like the others. It happens every day."

I took a bite of my food absently, listening to Leyla talk. It hit my tongue like an ember, igniting my mouth. Tears sprang to my eyes as I spat the food in the grass, coughing violently.

"Can't handle our fine food?" Mouhna called from across the garden. Next to her Ayet and Uzma were doubled over in fits of giggles as Mouhna popped a piece of bread in her mouth, puckering her lips at me deliberately as she savored it. "A present from the blessed Sultima."

Leyla picked up something red from my plate. Her nose wrinkled. "Suicide pepper," she said, tossing it into the nearest fire grate.

"What in hell is a suicide pepper?" I was still coughing. Leyla pressed a glass into my hands. I downed it, cooling the burning on my tongue.

"It's a foreign spice. My father tries to keep it out of the harem, but it's—" She ran her tongue over her lips nervously. "Sometimes girls here use it . . . to escape." It took me a heartbeat to realize what she meant by "escape."

Suicide pepper.

So some folks had found a way out. It wasn't the sort of escape I had planned. But if those peppers were coming in from the outside, there had to be a way to get things out, too. Some way for the whispers to make it through these walls.

"Who is the blessed Sultima?" I'd heard her mentioned already. When I first arrived. In the baths.

"The Sultim's first wife." Leyla looked up, surprised. "Well, not the first that he took. He took Ayet as a wife the day after he won the Sultim trials. But the blessed Sultima is the only one of Kadir's wives who has been able to conceive a child."

They must hate her. My aunt Farrah had hated Nida, my uncle's youngest wife. But Farrah's place as first wife had been secured by three sons. It was Nida who had to kiss her feet to get anything. They might be talking about the Sultim instead of a desert horse trader, but they were still just jealous wives. And I understood how these things worked. The first wife was the most powerful woman in the household—in this case, in the harem.

"Where would one find the Sultima?"

EIGHTEEN

The Sultima was a legend in the harem.

Chosen by God to be the mother of the next heir of Miraji. The only woman worthy of conceiving a child by the Sultim. She kept herself locked in her rooms most of the time. Women in the harem whispered that it was because she was praying. But I remembered something Shazad had told me once: if you could stay out of your enemy's line of sight, they'd always count your forces stronger than they were.

And from the whispers I'd heard, the harem was full of the Sultima's enemies.

But if there was one thing I knew about legends, it was that we were still flesh and blood. And flesh and blood had to come out of her rooms eventually.

Two days after Mouhna fed me the suicide pepper, Leyla woke me up with news. The blessed Sultima had finally emerged to bathe.

I spotted the Sultima before I'd even fully emerged from the hallway into the baths. She was sitting with her back to the entrance, dangling one leg in the water, with the other braced under her, twisted just enough toward me so that I could see the swell of her stomach. Her age singled her out. I'd seen other pregnant women in the harem, but they belonged to the Sultan. He'd stopped taking wives nearly ten years back; his wives were nearer in age to him now—most had seen at least three decades or close to it. Even from afar I could tell the Sultima hadn't seen eighteen years yet. She was running her hands over her middle over and over in soothing motions, head tilted forward in thought.

From here, the blessed Sultima looked just like any other heavily pregnant desert girl. It wasn't so much that I'd expected her to go to the baths draped in pearls and rubies, but after all the rumors and whispers, I figured I'd get something more than a girl in a thin white khalat.

She wasn't alone. At the other side of the water, Kadir was sprawled, wearing a loose shalvar and nothing else. He was bare from the waist up. I hadn't thought Jin shared anything with this brother, but the aversion to shirts seemed to be a family trait.

There were about a half dozen other girls I recognized from the harem in the water, too. A collection of Kadir's wives, splashing around in the water, giggling, long white khalats sticking to them.

I'd been here long enough to realize that most of the women in the harem weren't Mirajin. They were pale northern women stolen off ships, foreign-featured eastern girls sold as slaves, dark-skinned Amonpourian girls taken in border skirmishes. But there was no mistaking this girl for anything but desert born, even from behind. The linen stuck against her body from the steam that curled up from the baths; damp dark hair clung to her face. She didn't exactly look like the all-powerful Sultima, the chosen vessel of the future Sultan of Miraji.

And then she looked up, startled by the sound of my footsteps, eyes darting over her shoulder toward me, and my heart leapt into my mouth.

Oh, damn every power in heaven and hell, what did I do to deserve this?

I was face-to-face with the Sultima I'd heard so much about. The only woman pure enough to conceive a child by the Sultim Kadir. The girl sent by God to assure the future of Miraji.

Only I knew her as my cousin Shira. And the only thing God had ever sent her to do was make my life a living hell.

Jin told me once fate had a cruel sense of humor. I was starting to believe him. First Tamid and now Shira. I'd crossed an entire desert but it was like I'd been dragged back home to face everything I'd left in my dust when I ran.

Shira looked as surprised as I was. Her mouth formed a small O before pressing tightly into a hard line. We stared at each other across the narrow stretch of tiles left between us. Our wills locked, the same way they'd done a hundred times across the tiny bedroom in my aunt's house.

"Well," Shira said. She'd lost her accent. I could hear it even in that one word. Or maybe not lost—smothered under something that passed for a northern accent. "Paint me purple and call me a Djinni if it isn't my least favorite cousin."

There was a retort on the tip of my tongue. I caught it from slipping out by the skin of my teeth. *The Sultan has a Djinni,* I reminded myself. *He has a First Being trapped at his will and nothing is stopping him from using it against the rebels at any second. And then it could be over. For me. For Ahmed, Jin, Shazad, and the whole Rebellion.*

I didn't know much about other families, but I reckoned most of the time when you had to pretend to be nice to them, there weren't this many lives at stake.

"I thought you were dead," I said. *You and Tamid both.* Last time I'd seen Shira she'd been on a train racing toward Izman with Prince Naguib, taken captive because they figured there was a chance she'd know where I was going. And if they found me, they found Jin, and if they found Jin, they found the Rebellion.

After Jin and I had gotten off the train, she'd lost her use. Noorsham had told me she'd been left in the palace to die. Only she wasn't just still alive. She was thriving. I wondered if she knew Tamid had survived being abandoned to fend for himself in this palace, too. If she knew what he was doing for the Sultan. If she even cared. She never had.

I shoved away thoughts of Tamid angrily. Shira was easier to face. It'd never been that complicated between us. We hated each other. Old hate was easier to face than Tamid's new disdain.

"You ought to know better than that." My cousin smiled that seductive smile at me. "Us desert girls are survivors. Although I'm curious about how you plan on surviving long here." I stepped under the iridescent stones of the archway and into the harem baths proper. I ignored the tendrils of steam curling around my body like clinging fingers. "Last time I saw you, weren't you riding off with some rebel traitor? Traitors don't survive long here." Her eyes darted across the baths pointedly toward where Kadir was lounging. The bathing hall was as wide across as the whole of Dustwalk, far enough that Kadir hadn't noticed me yet. He picked something up from a pile at his elbow and tossed it in a high arc into the middle of the pool. As it caught the light I realized it was a ruby as big as my thumb.

It hit the water with a careless splash. A chaos of screeches and giggles followed as the six girls in the water dove toward where the ruby had disappeared under the surface, splashing and piling over each other as Kadir watched them hungrily. The shrieking and the splashing covered our voices.

"Now, what do you think my prince would make of your allegiance to his traitor brother if I told him?"

My sudden fear must've been scrawled all over my face because Shira smiled like a cat who'd eaten a canary.

God damn her. I'd come here for help, not to get sold out by her. "Shira." I closed the last few steps between us from the entrance to the edge of the water, dropping down in a crouch next to her, lowering my voice. "If you tell Kadir I'm part of—" I caught the words back before I said them out loud. "—what you know," I said carefully, eyes darting toward a girl who'd just surfaced near us in the water. "I swear to God, Shira, if you breathe a word, I'll—" I scrambled for something to threaten her with, just like the bargaining games we used to play in Dustwalk. She wouldn't tell her mother I'd been out all night with Tamid and I wouldn't tell her father she'd been in the stables letting Fazim get his hands under her clothes. Only this wasn't Dustwalk anymore, and if she told on me, I'd get more than a switch to the back—I'd get myself, and probably a few hundred other people, killed. And then it slipped out: "I'll just have to go ahead and tell him that kid of yours isn't his."

Shira's whole face went still.

"Oh, God." The truth of my own words hit me. "The baby isn't the Sultim's."

"Keep your voice down," Shira hissed. Across the baths, one of the girls surged out of the water with a scream of triumph, her fist fastened around the ruby, tight as a noose. She kicked her way to the edge of the pool, showing the red stone proudly to Kadir, who leaned down to steal a kiss from her. She dropped the ruby into a small pile of colorful jewels on the side of the baths, keeping it separate from the piles of the other girls. When they were done, the Sultim would set their prizes into a necklace and gift it to them. It was like watching children play a game. Only the games in this harem could end with losing your head. The Sultim pulled another small yellow diamond from his dwindling pile.

"What the hell were you thinking?" Infidelity meant death in the harem—even I knew that. It had happened to Ahmed's mother when she gave birth to Delila. And it had happened to other women, too; there were countless stories, too many to ignore. Men who slipped into the harem without permission. Servants, princes who were not heirs . . . in every single tale it cost everyone involved their lives. Shira was a lot of things, but stupid wasn't one of them.

"I wanted to survive." Shira's fingernails clicked dully against the tiles at the edge of the bath. I realized they'd been filed down low. She always used to keep them longer in Dustwalk. "You left me and Tamid to die in Dustwalk so you could stay alive."

She said Tamid's name different from how she used to back in Dustwalk. It didn't stick to the roof of her mouth with disdain. I supposed whatever they'd gone through together was the sort of thing that was bound to turn you into allies.

"Is Tamid the one who—" I started, already dreading the answer.

"Don't be ridiculous," Shira snapped. "I wouldn't risk giving the Sultan a cripple for a son."

"And you really wonder why I think you're awful?" I

clenched my fists, fighting the old urge to defend Tamid. He wouldn't fight for me. I wondered if she was why he loathed me now. Had she infected him with her hatred of me on the journey? Or had I made him hate me all on my own?

"Is what I did to survive any worse than what you did?" She moved her foot in slow circles through the water, sending out ripples. "Naguib abandoned me here after I was no good to him anymore. I would have died if I hadn't proved myself more interesting than the other girls in the harem." A new chorus of shrieking emerged from the gaggle of girls, as another jewel sailed into the water. "But even being the Sultim's favorite will only keep you alive here so long. So I've done the only thing I could that really ensured my survival." She ran her hands along her swollen stomach, her jaw working. "And you can tell whoever you want. No one will believe *you*."

Good God, she was not making this easy. It'd been a long time since we'd last bickered in Dustwalk. I'd faced a whole lot of folks worse than her. But she was making me feel like we were right back under her mother's roof and there was nothing I wanted more than to best her just once.

"Yes, they will, Shira." If she wasn't going to flinch, neither was I. Because if I knew one thing for sure, it was that if anyone found out Shira was carrying some other man's child and pretending it was the Sultim's, she'd lose her head. I held her life in my hands just the same as she did mine. "And I reckon you know that."

Shira stared me down. Being Sultima suited her; even I had to admit it. There was weight in those eyes that'd make most folks want to drop their gaze first. But I'd grown up shooting; I could outlast her.

"Fine, it's a deal." Sure enough, Shira blinked first. "I won't tell on you if you won't tell on me."

"You're going to have to do me one better than that, cousin."

"You want something else?" She scoffed, still running her hands across her stomach over and over. She had a whole lot of power here. But she didn't have any over me. Finally she pursed her lips, as if the words she was about to spit out tasted bitter. "Of course you do. Fine." Then Shira tossed her head back and laughed like I'd just said the funniest thing in the world. For a second I thought she'd lost her mind. Her voice echoed around the tiled walls, carrying over the commotion in the water and making Kadir look up. And he saw me. Damn it. Shira gave me a satisfied smirk. "Better talk fast, cousin. I'm guessing you're the new toy Kadir keeps talking about. The one he's not allowed to have. So you have until he gets here to play with you to spit out what you want."

I really wanted to push her into the water. "Rumor has it you've got a way to pass contraband in and out of the harem."

"Who says that?"

"People," I evaded. "Do you or don't you?" I kept one eye on Kadir as he got to his feet, sauntering lazily around the iridescent blue tiles of the pool toward us. It was like being tracked by a hungry Skinwalker. I wanted to get out before he got to me.

"I might," she said, hedging. Wasting time. "What is it you're so desperate to get in that you'd threaten my life for it? A bottle of liquor? New clothes? That certainly seems worth the price of my head." It wasn't a half-bad attempt to make me feel sorry about blackmailing her. Anyone else and I might've actually *been* sorry.

"I don't want anything brought in." I kept an eye on Kadir, getting closer now. "I need to get a message out. Can you do that?"

"I suppose so." Shira ran her tongue over her teeth, deliberately slowly. She was trying to keep me here. "I'd need some time."

"I don't have a whole lot of that. Can you help me or do I tell your husband that you climbed into another man's bed and get you hanged?" He was halfway across to us now.

"I can help." Shira set her jaw angrily, resting her hand on her middle. "If you—"

"Come to join the game?" Kadir called, interrupting whatever Shira had been about to say next. He was close enough to be heard. His eyes traveled up and down my body. "You're a little overdressed."

I pushed myself to my feet. Shazad had taught me enough to know that you didn't stand against an enemy from lower ground. "I'm dressed just fine for leaving, Your Exalted Highness."

Kadir made a noise at the back of his throat, like a hum of agreement. Except it sounded an awful lot like a laugh. "You are free to leave, of course." He was rolling a perfect white pearl between his thumb and forefinger. He circled around in front of me, standing between me and the way out. Then he tossed the pearl carelessly aside, letting it land in the water. The girls, who'd been watching the exchange, didn't scramble for it. "As soon as you bring me back that pearl."

"I can't swim," I said. Anywhere else I'd be able to stand up for myself. I'd be able to fight him. But I was helpless. I tried to hold myself like I wasn't.

"Then you can't leave." He smirked. "That pearl is very precious to me."

I couldn't fight him. Just the thought of raising my fist and putting it in his too-pleased-with-himself-looking face made the tug of the Sultan's orders twinge in my stomach. And I wasn't sure what he'd try to do if I walked out. What he could do. Or whether the Sultan had warned him against hurting me.

If the Sultan cared whether his Demdji prize got hurt. I didn't even know why I was still alive. He had his Djinni.

The silence was broken by a splash as one of the other girls dove under the water and sprang back up a moment later, the pearl between her fingers. "I got bored waiting," she said, pouting prettily, her pale hair sticking to her forehead as she brandished the pearl. But there was a tightness to her smile. And I understood what she'd done. For me. The risk.

The tension broke as Kadir lounged over to her. Shira was on her feet, grabbing me by the elbow, pushing me out of the baths. "Tonight." She shoved me back toward the safety of the gardens. "Meet me by the Weeping Wall after dark."

NINETEEN

The Weeping Wall was the easternmost wall of the harem, a small, closed-off part of the garden dominated by the biggest tree I'd ever seen in my life. It would've taken three of me to get my arms all the way around it, and the branches stretched so far they touched the top of the walls on either side.

According to the women of the harem, it was the place where Sultima Sabriya had waited for Sultim Aziz a thousand years ago. He had gone to war on the distant eastern border and left his love in the harem. The Weeping Wall was the closest she had been able to get to him while he was away in battle. She stood there every day, waiting for him, her tears watering the tree so that it grew higher and higher every day. Until one day it was finally high enough for her to climb to see over the walls of the harem to where her husband's army was. That day, the other women found her on the ground, screaming and wailing and clawing at the wall. She couldn't be consoled and she cried until her voice left her; and the tree grew greater still.

Three days later the news came that Aziz had been killed in battle. That was what Sabriya had seen from the top of the tree, across the walls, across deserts and cities and seas.

The wall looked just like every other in the harem in the dim light of my oil lamp. Ivy blooming with flowers all the color of the setting sun climbed from the earth up the stone wall, trying to hide the fact that we were in a prison. I pushed the ivy aside, setting my hands against the solid stone. My fingers met an uneven surface. When I held the lamp up I realized it looked like a gouge—several of them. The kind fingernails might leave.

"And her wailing carried on for seven nights and seven days." I jumped at Shira's voice behind me. She was draped in a dark blue khalat that made her melt in with the shadows. "Until the Sultan could listen to her grief no more and he strung her up where only the stars could hear her wail."

I dropped my hand. "Who knew such love could exist in the harem."

Shira didn't miss the sarcasm in my voice. "Anyone less self-centered than you." I was about to retort that she didn't love Kadir, no more than she'd loved Naguib. But then I realized that her hands had drifted to her pregnant stomach as she spoke. Folks did terrifying things for the ones they loved. That, I'd learned from stories. I even had a bullet wound scar across my hip from Iliaz to prove it.

"So what now?" I raised an eyebrow at her expectantly, a trick I'd learned from Jin.

"Oh, now we wait, cousin." Shira leaned against the huge tree, tilting her head back.

I was going to have to play along with Shira's game. I flopped against the tree next to her. "How long?"

Shira tipped her head back further. "It could be a while. I can't tell. It's hard to see the sky properly from the city."

I leaned my head back against the trunk, my hair snagging in the rough bark. She wasn't wrong. Through the crisscrossing branches of the huge tree I could see the dark sky, but with the lights from the palace and the city, I couldn't make out the stars.

"So." Shira broke the silence after a moment. "Are you really with the Rebel Prince?" She was fiddling with something, and I realized it was a rope that ran the length of the tree, like a pulley. She was tugging it absently, up and down. At the top, above the line of the harem walls, a piece of cloth stirred in the wind.

"I really am." She was signaling someone. It could be a trap for all I knew. I couldn't do much about it if it was except face it when it came.

"Who would've thought it?" Shira smiled. "Two girls from Dustwalk, with royalty. What was it the Holy Father used to say?" Her accent was slipping. I wondered if she noticed. "Men who worship at the feet of power either rise with it—"

"—or get trampled," I said, filling in the saying. "Good thing we aren't men, then." I didn't know why I was buying into her game. But I was real low on people I could talk to in this place. Leyla was sweet enough, but she was still the Sultan's daughter. And Tamid wasn't worth thinking about. He might be alive, but my friend had still died in the sand in Dustwalk. Shira's dark eyes met my pale ones. A moment of recognition passed between us. We'd both hitched our wagons to powerful folks, just on different sides. If that was the choice, to rise or be flattened, chances were one of us was going to wind up rising and the other one dead.

"Shira—" I started. I wasn't sure how I was going to finish.

I never did. Because a man stepped out of the Weeping Wall.

I'd seen a whole lot of Demdji do impossible things, but I'd be lying if I said I'd been expecting that.

The man was flesh and blood, and though at first glance he was dressed in desert clothes, he was distinctly un-Mirajin. He had hair the color of sand, held back by a sheema that looked like it had been tied by someone with no hands, and pale skin that glowed in the lamplight. And his eyes were nearly as blue as mine. For a second I thought he was a Demdji.

"Blessed Sultima," he said, his voice low and tinged with an accent. Not a Demdji, then, just a foreigner.

He pulled himself to his full height, giving me a better view of him. Dark polished boots different from anything I'd ever seen in the desert rose to his knees, his loose desert trouser legs stuffed inside, and he wore a white shirt open at the collar. I got the strangest impression he was pausing for effect. After a beat, he stepped forward dramatically.

That was when his arm got stuck in one of the vines that hung from the wall.

It sort of ruined the effect.

He recovered as well as he could, untangling his arm. Then he plucked one of the flowers from the vine and offered it to Shira with an extravagant bow. "Your beauty grows with every passing day."

His badly tied sheema flopped open, falling off his face so I could see him clearly. He wasn't a whole lot older than we were, and a light constellation of freckles over his pale nose made him look even younger. He was northern but not Gallan; his words sounded wrong, and I'd seen enough of the Gallan to know he wasn't one of them. He straightened and flung the sheema over his shoulder like the sweep of a cloak. Shira took the flower and pressed it to her nose.

So this was how Shira smuggled things into the harem. And, judging by the look he was giving her, this was how she'd managed to get herself pregnant, too.

Finally the foreign man seemed to notice me.

"This is—" Shira started, but he didn't let her finish.

"Allow me to introduce myself." He snatched up my

right hand without asking. I resisted the urge to yank it out of his grip. Shazad would call that undiplomatic. "Especially to such a beautiful young woman." He raised my hand to his lips, in some strange foreign gesture, and kissed it. "I," he declared, straightening dramatically, "am the Blue-Eyed Bandit."

I choked on a snort that got stuck in my throat and turned into an uncontrollable cough. Shira patted me awkwardly on the back as I doubled over, bracing my free hand against my knees.

"Yes, I know, my reputation precedes me." My *reputation precedes you*. But I still couldn't talk through my coughing. "Don't let it intimidate you. I didn't really defeat a thousand soldiers in Fahali." He leaned forward conspiratorially, still clutching my hand, now twining his fingers through mine. "It was merely hundreds."

"Is that right?" I'd finally managed to catch my breath. I remembered Fahali like a blur. Gunpowder and blood and sand, and myself in the middle of it. "So tell me, how did you flood the prayer house at Malal?"

"Well." There was a glint in his eyes. He talked from the top of his mouth, unlike the Gallan, who talked from the back. "I could tell you, but I'd rather not give you any dangerous ideas."

I probably ought to stop enjoying this. But I couldn't remember the last time I'd had something to laugh about in this damn rebellion. Definitely not since we'd fled the Dev's Valley. "And how about the fight at Iliaz? Is it true what they say? That the Blue-Eyed Bandit was outgunned and outnumbered and surrounded by enemies on all sides?"

He didn't miss a beat, his chest swelling as he drew me toward him. "Oh, well, you know, what others call outnumbered, I call a challenge."

"I heard the Blue-Eyed Bandit got shot in the hip." I'd let him pull me close enough that we were almost chest to chest now. "Can I see the scar?"

"My lady is very forward." He grinned widely at me. "Where I come from, you have to know a girl more than a few minutes before she'll try to get your clothes off." He tilted his head forward, winking at me.

"Well, how about I take my clothes off, then." Before I could think better of it, I stepped back and tugged up the side of my shirt. The huge ugly scar was hard to miss, even in the dark. "Because I heard the scar looked something like this." I was pretty sure nothing he'd ever brought into the harem for Shira was as priceless as the look on his face just then. It was almost worth the risk of giving him my identity. It might not have been a smart thing to do, now I thought about it, but it sure was satisfying. He dropped my hand as I let my shirt fall back, pulling away from him. "And, see, I was in Fahali, and I don't remember you being there."

He scratched the back of his head sheepishly as I went on. "I remember fighting the Gallan soldiers in the sand and I remember men burning alive on both sides, but I don't remember you." The act was gone now—he was watching me with real interest. "But I gather you're the reason everyone thinks I can be in two different places at once. And why I keep hearing rumors about the Blue-Eyed Bandit seducing so many women." That part made sense now. He was as handsome as anything, even when he looked ridiculous at the same time. And he knew it, too.

"What can I say, I walk into their homes to take their jewels and they give me their hearts." He winked at Shira, who smiled enigmatically into the flower he'd given her. No, Shira was too clever to give anything away to a man she couldn't truly have. She'd taken from him. She'd used him for her child and she was still using him.

"So this is your way to the outside world?" I asked my cousin.

Shira was twirling the flower he'd given her between her fingers, looking pleased with herself. "Sam was sneaking in and . . . wooing one of the Sultan's more gullible daughters, Miassa. I noticed she kept disappearing and coming back with her hair and clothes all mussed. It didn't take long to catch her—very silly of her to start running around with other men when she was already engaged to be married to the Emir of Bashib. I promised not to turn them both in to her father if Sam helped me."

"It all worked out for the best." The foreigner, Sam, shrugged again, as if to say it wasn't her brains he was interested in anyway. "The Emir of Bashib leaves his wife alone a great deal; it's not hard for the Blue-Eyed Bandit to visit her still now and again."

There he went, using my name again. My temper flared.

"Believe me when I tell you, I know the Blue-Eyed Bandit, and you're not me. So who are you really?"

"Well." He leaned his shoulder back against the wall. "You can't blame a fellow for cashing in on a very good story. Nobody told me the real Blue-Eyed Bandit was so much more . . ." He looked me up and down, eyes seeming to linger on the places I'd fleshed out recently. Half a year of decent meals with the Rebellion meant I wouldn't be able to pass for a boy anymore. I raised an eyebrow at him in a challenge. He coughed. "So much more. And I *am* a bandit. Well, more of a thief, I suppose. When all these stories started spreading, it was only sensible that I take advantage of my God-given looks." He winked one of those mocking blue eyes at me. "You wouldn't believe how much easier it is to strike a good deal when you're practically a living legend. They say you're very good. Though you're obviously not that good if you wound up locked in here."

I wished I could punch him.

"How did you get in here?" I asked instead.

"I'm Albish." He said it like it explained everything. When he was met with my blank expression, he continued. "Our country is crawling with magic. My mother is a quarter Faye and my father half." Faye. That was the northern word for their Djinn. Only they were creatures of water and soft earth. "If it's stone, I can walk through it. See?" He'd allowed himself to sink back while he was talking to me and was now elbow deep in the stone wall of the palace.

It was as impressive as anything I could do; I'd give

him that. "What's an Albish thief doing in Izman?"

"My talents were wasted in Albis." He righted himself and the stone shifted just a little bit back into place. "Thought I'd bring them to your desert, where people wouldn't expect a man of my talents to come after their jewels. The habit of locking valuables in an iron box doesn't seem to have made it here yet." He wasn't lying. I could tell that much. But he was hiding something I couldn't quite put my finger on. There were easier places to go than Izman if it was just money he was after. Countries that weren't in the middle of a war, for one. But he was what I'd been waiting for, someone who could get in and out of the palace at will. And I'd been raised in Dustwalk, where we didn't look gift horses in the mouth.

I grabbed my cousin's arm and pulled her away from the wall, out of earshot of Sam, the Blue-Eyed Bandit imposter. She shook me off with a roll of her eyes that needled at me, but this wasn't the time to get annoyed at her. "Can I trust him? Truthfully, Shira—can I trust him with something important? A whole lot of lives?"

"I've had him send letters for me to Dustwalk," she said after a moment. "To my family." I wondered if I was imagining the hardness in the way she said *my*. Even now she couldn't help but remind me that, though we shared blood and had lived under the same roof, I'd never truly be part of her family. "Well, letters and some money." I'd barely given any thought to Dustwalk in months, except to thank God that I was out of there. But I cast my mind back now. Dustwalk without a factory, with nothing, destroyed. It would be a miracle if the whole town hadn't decamped or starved to death by now.

Shira trusted this man with her family. I could trust him with mine. I turned back to Sam, who was incompetently trying to tie his sheema back up. "Could you carry a message out for me?"

"Of course." I winced as he tucked the edge of his sheema in all wrong. It was painful to watch. A toddler could do better than that. "How much?"

"How much what?"

"How much will you pay me to carry this message?" He repeated it carefully, like it might be his Mirajin that was at fault.

I glanced at Shira, who splayed empty hands at me pointedly. "The Sultim thinks I'm too modest to wear any of the jewelry he gives me." Now that I thought about it, I realized she was surprisingly unadorned for the harem. Ayet wore gold bangles from wrist to elbow some days. She clacked with metal with every gesture. "Truth is, I just put them to very good use. Everything that happens within the walls of the harem is a trade. The sooner you figure that out, the more likely you are to survive."

"I don't have any jewels," I said to Sam. "You've already taken my reputation. Isn't that enough?"

"Well, you weren't making very good use of it. I think I've done you a favor. Besides, stories belong to the people," he said. "And considering you are very much trapped, it's going to take more than that."

I ran my tongue across my teeth, thinking. I could probably get something to trade with if I had a few days.

Some of the girls in the harem weren't all that careful. It wouldn't be that hard to take a bangle off them when they slept. But I wasn't sure I had that much time to waste. And there might be another way. "The message I need you to carry, it's for Shazad Al-Hamad, General Hamad's daughter, he's—"

"I know who General Hamad is," Sam said, and for a moment the cocky, smiling man was gone.

"Then you ought to know he's got money. A lot of it. And so does his daughter." I paused, then added, "His breathtakingly gorgeous daughter." Shazad would have my head if she could hear me describe her like this to some foreign thief. I wasn't even sure she was in Izman, but she was still my best shot.

"I like her already," Sam said. But there was a note of sarcasm under there. He rubbed a spot on the base of one of the fingers of his left hand. It was a distracted gesture, far away. I got the feeling he didn't even wholly know what he was doing. "Why should she believe me? The general's rich, spoiled daughter." Shazad would definitely have Sam's head for calling her spoiled. Here was hoping he had the good sense not to do it to her face.

"Just tell her the Blue-Eyed Bandit is in the palace." I didn't dare give him anything else to pass on to her. Not about the Sultan having a Djinni or anything else. Not yet, anyway. I'd risked enough by giving him my identity. "The real one. And that she needs someone to watch her back."

TWENTY

THE NAMELESS BOY

In a kingdom across the sea, a farmer and his wife lived in a hovel with their six children. They were so poor, they had nothing to give their children but love. And quickly they learned that love was not enough to keep their children fed or warm. Three of their children died in their first winter, too weak to survive the cold. So when their seventh child was born, a son, on the darkest, coldest day of the bleak winter, they did not give him a name, so prepared were they for him to die.

But their nameless son survived that darkest day. And the one that followed. He lived through his first winter and into the spring. And he lived through his second winter. And, in his second spring, he finally earned a name.

The once-nameless boy was quick and clever and had a talent for going places he was not meant to be, so long as the walls were made of stone. And he saw that his family was poor while others were rich and he did not think this was fair. So when his mother became sick, in the boy's seventh winter, he took food from kitchens with more shelves than his to feed her and he took silver from other houses to buy her medicine. That was how he walked into the castle on the hill that belonged to the lord of that county, and into the life of the lord's young daughter.

The lord's young daughter was lonely in the great castle, but she was rich, too, and she had learned she could have anything by asking for it. So when she asked for the boy's friendship, he gave it to her gladly. He taught her games and she taught him to read. She learned she was gifted at skipping stones across a pond on a bright summer day and he learned he was gifted at languages spoken in distant corners of the world.

As they grew older, he became healthy and strong and handsome. So handsome that the lord's daughter noticed. She was still rich and there had never been anything in the world that she could not get simply by asking. So when she asked for the boy's heart, he gave that to her gladly, too.

The two met secretly in all the hidden places they had found together as children.

The once-nameless boy's brothers warned him against the lord's daughter. They had all married poor girls who lived in the shadow of the great castle and though they were poor, they were all happy enough. But the once-nameless boy had read too many stories of worthy farmers' sons who married princesses, and highwaymen who stole rich ladies' hearts, to heed his brothers' warnings. He believed that he had stolen the girl's heart as well as gifted her his.

So the boy was greatly surprised when it was announced to the whole county that the lord's daughter was to be married to the second son of the lord from a neighboring county.

The once-nameless boy left word for the lord's daughter asking her to meet him in their secret place by the water. He waited there all night, but she did not come. He waited the next night and still she did not come; and the next night after that, too. Finally, the night before the lord's daughter was to be wed, the once-nameless boy walked through the walls of the castle and, there, he found the lord's daughter, pale hair spread across a white silk pillow, beautiful and fair in the moonlight. He knelt by her bed and woke her from her slumber and asked her to come away with him, to run away and marry him. He was on his knees, but he did not beg because he never thought he would need to. He never imagined she would refuse him. But the lord's daughter did not take his hand. Instead she laughed at him and called her guards, handing him back his heart on the way out of the castle.

And so he learned then that girls with titles did not marry once-nameless boys.

The boy became determined to no longer be nameless.

So he signed his life to his queen and donned a uniform, pledging to earn his name by fighting for his sovereign and his land. He traveled to a kingdom across the sea, the land without winter.

There, instead of a name for himself, he found blood and guns and sand. He knew that nobody lost their names as quickly as the dead, so he fled once more. He hid himself in the sprawling city of Izman, a kaleidoscope of sights and sounds like he'd never known. When he first grew hungry he remembered what he had once been good at: going places he didn't belong. He stole a loaf of bread his first night in the city, which he ate sitting atop a prayer house, looking out over the rooftops. On the second night he stole a fistful of foreign coins that he traded for a bed. On his third he took a necklace which could have easily fed all his parents' children for a year. As he learned to slip in and out with ease among the streets, he heard a name being whispered. One that didn't truly seem to belong to anyone. A legend. So he took it for himself. He used the name to take other things. Rich people's jewels and careless men's wives. He even stole a princess's heart, like the thieves in the stories he knew. But this time he was not foolish enough to give his back. He had learned not to give things away to anyone who asked.

And so he had a name. And it fit him so well that he almost started to believe it was truly his. Until he met the girl who it belonged to. The girl in the harem with eyes that could light the world on fire. She was asking for his help.

He was to carry a message to a general's daughter. He found her home easily. It was a large house with a red door in the wealthiest part of the city. He waited on a corner, watching the door, servants coming and going, watching people wearing a small fortune's worth of jewels on their hands wave at each other, as he waited for the girl.

Finally he saw the general's daughter.

He knew her before she even placed her hand on the red door. She was beautiful enough that it was as difficult to look at her as it was to stare at the sun. She was like something crafted her whole life with the purpose only to be seen and coveted. And she moved with the easy certainty of someone who knew that her place in the world was above most.

As soon as he saw her he recognized her, though they had never met.

Her hair and skin and eyes were dark, where the lord's daughter had been as pale as milk. Her clothes were colors stolen from the Djinn, where the lord's daughter's had been the colors of the rainy skies and the rivers and the fresh grass. But they were the same. She was the kind of girl who thought she deserved everything just by asking for it.

And he knew that if he knocked on the red door he would be turned away with a scoff and a wave. Because nameless bandits were not invited in to talk to generals' daughters.

So he waited for nightfall in the city. Windows in the street lit up one by one and then went dark as silence drew down across the city. Except for the window that belonged to the general's daughter. He watched that window into the dark hours of the night until finally that light went out, too. And the once-nameless boy did what he did best and walked into somewhere he wasn't supposed to go, straight through the wall and up the stairs to where she slept.

She was sprawled across colorful pillows, dark hair covering her face. He knelt down next to her bed, to wake her from her slumber. But before he could say a word he found a knife to his throat.

It had happened so quickly he hadn't seen the general's daughter move.

"Who are you?" she asked. She didn't look afraid. He saw then that he'd been entirely wrong. She was not like the lord's daughter at all. She had not been crafted to be seen and coveted. She had crafted herself to fool the world. And the easy certainty of her step was the knowledge that she was being underestimated. And she got what she asked for because she asked for it from the right end of a blade. "Answer me quickly and correctly or you'll never speak another lie again." She pressed the blade toward his throat.

And suddenly, the once-nameless boy knew he didn't want a stolen name, tarnished with use. What he wanted desperately was a name good enough to give to this girl. But until he had that, he would have to use another.

"I've come in the name of the Blue-Eyed Bandit."

TWENTY-ONE

I knew something was different when I was woken up by three servants instead of by the sun. I was being propped up to a sitting position and my kurti pulled over my head before I was even fully awake.

"What's happening?" I made a grab for the hem, but something new was being draped around me already.

"The Sultim has ordered that you will attend him in court today." The servant who answered was the same one who'd brought me into the harem. I'd never gotten her name out of her.

And here I thought I was off-limits. But I supposed that was only to being treated as a wife, not as a thing to be polished up and put on display. I yanked my arm back toward myself as a woman scraped something rough along my fingernails. She grabbed my hand back and started again, making me wince at the noise.

"It's a great honor." The servant gathered my long hair up, fastening a clasp behind my neck. Not a necklace, I realized; this was meant to pass for a khalat. It was fine blue cloth stitched with black that matched my hair. Except it left half of me bare. My arms, my shoulder, and half my back were exposed. I almost laughed. This would never pass for desert clothes, not in a place where the sun beat down on every bit of skin it could find. This was the luxury of a city. And the decadence of a harem. She pulled me to my feet so that the clothes fell over my loose shalvar. At least I seemed to be allowed to keep that on.

I could make this real difficult for them if I wanted to. I could resist and make the Sultan dictate my every movement. But the last thing I wanted was more orders.

And I got the feeling that, as hard as I could make things for them, the Sultim could probably make them a whole lot harder for me.

Besides, I was being offered permission to leave the harem, even if it wasn't out of the palace. It'd been seven days since I'd sent Sam to Shazad. Seven days of the same lazy indifference that marked every day in the harem. It wasn't like waking up in the rebel camp. The tension in my bones wasn't matched by anyone else's. The restlessness of an impending battle, the fear of not knowing—they were mine alone. I'd even gone to the Weeping Wall once or twice and strung up the white cloth into the huge tree, hoping the signal would bring him back. Nothing.

Everything depended on a stupid boy who couldn't even tie a sheema right and there was nothing else I could do except wait for news. Wait like Sabriya for Prince Aziz. Helpless and blind to see who would die in battle. I felt like I might lose my mind.

I'd be damn stupid to turn down a shot at getting a look outside.

• • •

THE PARTS OF the palace that they led me through now weren't near so empty as those I had followed the Sultan through. Servants scurried past us, heads bowed, carrying platters heavy with colorful fruit or crisp clean linens. A small gaggle of Xichian men in what looked like traveling clothes sat in a garden that we passed. My neck craned their way instinctively as Jin dashed across my thoughts. A man dressed finely enough to be an emir and trailing three identically dressed women swept down the hallway ahead of us, disappearing up a staircase. A pair of foreign-looking men in strange uniforms stepped aside as we passed. My heart jumped at the sight of them. They looked Gallan. But no, their uniform was wrong. Albish, maybe?

We rounded another corner. I knew the Gallan on sight. Two soldiers flanked an unremarkable-looking man in plain clothes. Their uniforms were glaringly familiar, sending a twist of fear through me. But the soldiers weren't the most unsettling ones. There was something about the plain-clothed Gallan man; his eyes cut right through me. I could feel them in my back as we continued on.

Two dozen curious faces turned my way the second the doors to the Sultan's receiving garden opened. All of them belonged to men, seated haphazardly around the garden on cushions. The Sultan's councilors. They were all soft-looking intellectual types. Like Mahdi. Pale from lack of sunlight, too many hours spent inside studying the world and not enough living in it. Servants hovered around them like a swarm, wielding fans and pitchers of sweet fruit juices.

There was only one man who stood apart from the circus. He was about of an age with Ahmed and Jin and wearing a spotless white-and-gold army uniform. He didn't sit. Instead he stood, straight as a statue, arms clasped behind his back, eyes straight ahead like he was awaiting orders. There was a pang of familiarity as I looked at him that I couldn't quite place.

At the head of the garden, raised above his court, was the Sultan. He lifted his eyebrows a tiny bit as he saw me. So he hadn't known that his son had given me permission to leave the harem. Kadir sat at his right hand. Ayet was draped around her husband's shoulders, wearing the same khalat I was, but in a glaring red with silver threads. She was there to be shown off and she knew it, too, twisting her bare back to the court, showing off the complicated henna designs that decorated her spine. At Kadir's feet was Uzma, wearing the same garment in green across her tiny frame.

I glanced around for Mouhna. She wasn't anywhere to be seen.

Kadir pointedly rested his hand on the cushion to the opposite side of Ayet. I would've given just about anything to not have to sit there. But I didn't have that choice.

An attendant busied herself arranging the long hem of my khalat around me so I was entirely covered. Kadir dismissed her with a wave of the hand. As soon as she was gone I stuck my bare foot out from under the hem. It wasn't much, but it was the best I could manage, as small acts of defiance went. I caught the eye of the the man in military clothes as I looked up. He was watching me, hiding a smile behind his hand, pretending to scratch his eyebrow.

"Kadir." The Sultan spoke across me, low enough that the rest of the court couldn't hear. "Do you not have enough of your own women to keep you entertained?"

"I would have, Father." Something silent passed between Kadir and the Sultan that I didn't understand. "But I seem to have misplaced one of them." He must mean Mouhna. I remembered what Leyla had said about women disappearing from the harem all the time. Like her mother had. "I needed one more to complete my Mirajin set." Kadir reached out and ran a hand lazily along one of the scars on my back. My body shuddered angrily in response.

The way the Sultan smiled would've fooled the rest of the court into thinking he was having the most genial conversation with his son. "Lay that hand on her again and you will lose it." I felt an unexpected surge of gratitude toward the Sultan for coming to my defense. I quashed it. It was his fault I was here, unable to defend myself.

The Sultan straightened. "Bring in the first petitioner." He raised his voice, coming to stand at the gate that led into the court.

"Commander Abbas Al-Abbas," a servant announced. "Of the Eleventh Command."

The soldier who came in bowed low before speaking. "Your Exalted Honor. I have come to plead for a release from my command."

"This is a serious request, in a time of war." The Sultan considered him. "It's clearly not for lack of bravery that you wish to be relieved, or else you wouldn't be here facing me." The soldier seemed to swell with pride for a moment at being called brave.

"News has come from my father's home. My brother, his heir, has been called by God to the Holy Order. My father has no other sons. If I don't return, my sisters' husbands will squabble for his land. I wish to go home to take my place as his heir."

The Sultan considered him. "What do you think, Rahim?" He was talking to the young soldier, the one who'd seemed familiar. Rahim. I knew his name. Leyla's brother, I realized. The only one among the army of the Sultan's sons that she truly considered her family. Sure enough, he had Leyla's same clever, watchful eyes. Though Leyla's years in the harem meant that I could see some of the paleness of their Gamanix mother in her. Years spent outside the palace walls had made Rahim look Mirajin through and through. It looked like he even shared some of his father's stronger features with Ahmed.

"I very much doubt my opinion could add anything you don't already know, exalted Father." Rahim's words were respectful, but there was something else there. I got the feeling the two were playing a game I didn't quite understand.

"Modesty has never suited you, Rahim." The Sultan went on, waving his hand. "I'm sure you have insights, having been a soldier for so long now. Share them."

"I think the eastern border is exposed and that the Eleventh Command needs a soldier leading them who wishes to lead," Rahim said. The Sultan didn't speak again straightaway. He was waiting for something else. A silent battle of wills crossed the court.

"And"—Rahim broke first—"the Holy Books teach us a man's first duty is to his father."

The Sultan smiled, like he'd won some victory. "Commander Abbas Al-Abbas. Your request is granted." The soldier's shoulders sagged in relief. "You will be relieved of your command. Name your replacement and we will raise him up in your place."

I forgot the next petitioner's endless name and title almost before the man was done announcing it. Just like I forgot what he was asking for as soon as he started talking. One after another, the petitioners followed each other in front of the Sultan.

One man wanted money. The next wanted land. The

next wanted more guards in his quarter of the city. Rebels, he reported, were multiplying among the dockworkers. The next wanted the Blue-Eyed Bandit brought to justice. He'd stolen his wife's jewels and seduced his daughter, he reported.

Well, if Sam was still alive to be muddying my name, I supposed that meant at least Shazad hadn't skewered him on sight. Or he hadn't bothered to deliver my message yet.

The Sultan listened patiently before asking the man what more he thought the throne could do about the Blue-Eyed Bandit. I watched him carefully as he spread his hands in sympathy. There was already a price on the Bandit's head for his collaboration with the Rebel Prince, he explained, but no one had been able to find him. The man might as well be a spirit in the desert. Or a fiction.

I resented being called a fiction. But then, I'd resent being found out and tortured out of my mind like Sayyida a whole lot more. I was suddenly stupidly grateful to Sam, even if he did decide it wasn't worth his time getting my message to Shazad.

My foot was falling asleep and I had to shift positions restlessly over and over to keep it from going dead altogether as one boring request followed the other.

I finally gave up all pretense and pulled my knees up to my chin, wrapping my arms around them to keep myself steady.

I was half-asleep by the time the man in chains appeared. Everybody who'd been wilting in the afternoon sun came alive again. "Aziz Al-Asif." The man in fine clothes who was leading the chained man took a bow as the servant announced him. "And his brother, Lord Huda Al-Asif."

"Your Exalted Highness." Aziz Al-Asif stooped low. "It is my deepest regret that I have come to ask that you condemn my brother to death. He has been conspiring to rebellion."

"Is that so." There was an amused edge to the Sultan's voice. "Because that is not what my spies have reported to me. What they *have* reported to me is that you are power hungry and that you are the one conspiring to ally with my son's rebellion. Which can only lead me to believe that you are lying to me in order for your brother to be executed. When he is gone, you can take sole ownership of the seat of your father's lands." A rustle went around the garden. "Release Lord Huda." The Sultan gestured toward the two guards by the door. "And take young Aziz prisoner."

"Your Majesty," Aziz exclaimed loudly, "I have committed no crime!"

"You have." The Sultan cut across him, and there was no mistaking the authority in his voice. "Attempting to kill your brother is a crime. Lying to your Sultan is a crime. Thinking that you can leverage my son's rebellion to your own uses is not a crime but it is not something I will tolerate. Your execution will be at sunset, unless your brother sees fit to save you." The Sultan looked at Lord Huda, who was rubbing his wrists. He didn't object. "Spread the word in the city, then," the Sultan said. "I want the men and women of Izman to see what it costs to try to betray their ruler."

Suddenly I was standing back with Ahmed in his tent as he couldn't make up his mind about Mahdi. As he refused to order an execution. As he failed to give a straight order. All I'd wanted was for him to make a goddamn decision. To be a ruler. A good one. A great one. A strong one.

The Sultan hadn't even hesitated.

Aziz's protests were still fading as the next person was called.

The day was heavy, and as the sun shifted, it turned its full glare onto us. I could feel sweat beading on my neck, running below my clothes. I could feel my eyes drifting shut as the midday heat started to prey on me. The only person who didn't show he felt it was the Sultan.

"Announcing Shazad Al-Hamad."

I came awake as fast as if I'd been shot in the back. For a second I thought I'd dreamed it. That I'd really dozed off and imagined Shazad come to rescue me. But there, standing at the entrance to the garden, wearing a khalat the color of a breaking dawn and that faint smile that meant she knew she was outsmarting someone, was Shazad.

TWENTY-TWO

Shazad was here. Some of the fear that had been crouched in my chest since I'd woken up on a ship escaped. I could kiss Sam's idiot face for getting my message to her.

"Well," the Sultan said, "this is an unexpected honor."

"The honor is all mine, Your Exalted Highness." Her voice was so achingly familiar here in this strange place. It was the voice of a hundred nights in the camp and under desert skies, of conspiracy and treason and rebellion. "I have returned from my pilgrimage." She dropped to her knees. "I come to pay tribute to my most exalted Sultan and Sultim." She dropped into a low bow from her knees until her nose almost touched the ground. She was damn good at that. I supposed she had had sixteen years of practice before the Rebellion.

The Sultan considered her. "I thought perhaps you had come to inquire after the return of your father from the war front." If he meant to throw her off balance with a mention of General Hamad, he'd picked the wrong girl. Shazad started to answer, but I never heard what she said. A screech, like a knife across iron, split the sky, cutting her off.

The entire courtyard stilled. But something inside me woke up.

I knew that sound.

"That's a Roc." Prince Rahim said out loud what I was thinking. His eyes were on the sky and he was on his feet. "And nearby, too."

"In the city?" Kadir scoffed, but he wasn't leaning back so idly anymore. "That's ridiculous."

"Of course, brother." Rahim held himself like a soldier, his hand resting, out of some old habit, on a weapon that wasn't there. "What would I possibly know—I've only been stationed in the mountains of Iliaz for half a decade. I only heard Rocs screaming every night while you were still sleeping in the harem by your mother. But you know better, I'm sure."

Kadir took a step toward Rahim. Rahim held his ground. Kadir was broader than his brother by a good bit. But as Rahim flexed his fists, I saw the scar across his hand. It reminded me of the scars on Jin's knuckles.

Kadir's hands were smooth. Rahim's hands showed the signs of a fight.

The scream of the Roc came again, closer this time, pulling them apart. The gathered crowd, frozen a moment earlier, turned into chaos. Men started to run for cover, and the Sultan shouted orders to his soldiers, sending them toward the walls, unslinging guns as they went.

I didn't move. I just stayed, craning my head backward. Because I knew that scream. And then the shadow passed. Low enough to be seen clearly but high enough that it was out of the range of guns. As it soared overhead two huge blue wings obscured the sun, plunging the courtyard into shadow.

That wasn't a Roc. It was Izz.

A bolt of excitement shot through me, taking me to my feet. Izz was here. In the city.

Something was trailing out behind Izz, scattering in his wake. For a second I thought they were white cloths. But as they flittered down in the wind, I saw they were paper; a rain of paper from the sky.

I reached up as soon as the first sheet came close enough and snatched it before it hit the ground.

Ahmed's sun was printed at the top. I traced the lines of it the way I'd traced the ink on Jin's chest so many times. Printed below it, in sloppy black ink, it said:

A NEW DAWN. A NEW DESERT.

We call for Sultan Oman Al-Hasim Bin Izman of Miraji to step down from his throne and stand trial for treason.

Sultan Oman is accused of these crimes against Miraji and its people:

Subjecting his country to unfit foreign rule in the form of the Gallan army

Untried execution of parties accused of violating Gallan law

Persecution of his own people without just cause

Persecution of Mirajin citizens for unproven Djinni magic in their bloodline

Oppression of working citizens through unfair wages

Enslavement of women across Miraji

The list went on.

We demand the traitorous Sultan Oman be separated from his throne for his crimes and that his rightful heir, Prince Ahmed Al-Oman Bin Izman, true victor of the Sultim trials, be allowed to ascend in his place and return this desert to its rightful glory. If he does not comply and surrender *the throne, we will seize it on behalf of the people of Mïrajï.*

A new dawn. A new desert.

The Rebellion had come to Izman.

I read it over again. I was so absorbed I didn't notice anyone near me until I felt the hand on the back of my neck. I started to spin, but Uzma had already darted up behind me, quiet as a shadow, unclasping the khalat where it was fastened at the nape of my neck.

The fabric came undone, slithering off me toward the ground. I grabbed at it, letting Ahmed's sun slip to the ground, but too late to keep my body totally hidden.

Uzma's nasty little eyes took in my body, judging it, finding it wanting in every possible way with one glance.

"Now, *that* is a nasty scar. Did the tailor Abdul not stitch you together right?" She meant the one on my right hip, where the bullet had gone through in Iliaz. My fingers were still fumbling with the clasp at my neck to tie the khalat back up. I could feel my skin burning under her mocking gaze. "It all makes sense now. Let me guess: you're a whore who got pregnant, and they had to try to cut the thing out of you."

I gave up on the clasp without the servants to help me and reached up to knot the loose ends of fabric together. Uzma took a smirking step toward me as I struggled. One of the pamphlets crumpled under her bare foot, Ahmed's sun wrinkling.

"How about you step away from her." The voice was iron and silk and wholly familiar. "Before I knock you back."

Shazad wasn't armed. But she looked as dangerous as she would've been with both her blades drawn as she stepped between me and Uzma. I tugged the knot tighter at the base of my neck. When I looked up, the smirk on Uzma's face flickered.

Shazad leaned forward, forcing Uzma to stagger backward. "My apologies," Shazad said in a tone that didn't sound sorry at all. "That may have sounded like a suggestion. It wasn't. Go."

Uzma took two steps back, heading straight for Ayet, who was watching from the shadow of one of the pillars. Then Izz screamed again and both of them disappeared, fleeing for cover. Leaving me facing my best friend amid the chaos of the rapidly emptying courtyard.

"I told you about watching your back." Shazad said.

"I told you I knew I could count on you to do it for me." I longed to embrace her, but there were too many people around still. I could explain it away if we were caught talking but embracing might be harder. I had to be satisfied with plucking at the ornate sleeves of her khalat. "I reckon you're the only person I know who can look that intimidating while wearing something with quite so many flowers on it."

Shazad flashed me a messy smile. "All the better to be underestimated in. Come on." Shazad grabbed my hand, glancing around quickly. "We're getting out of here. Now."

She started pulling me toward the gates. Nobody was looking at us as Izz screamed, passing over the palace again. The Sultan had vanished and everyone else was running for cover. It was a good chance to get out. "This is supposed to be a distraction?" I gestured at the pamphlets littering the ground underfoot.

"Things can be a distraction and serve the cause at the same time." Shazad was still pulling me toward the gate. "Can you walk any faster than this?"

My mind caught up too slow. I pulled Shazad to a stop. "It wouldn't matter if I could outrun a Buraqi. I'm trapped." I filled her in as quickly as I could, as chaos reigned around us still. The iron under my skin, and one piece of bronze, allowing the Sultan to control me.

Shazad's face darkened as she listened. She took it in with the same sharpened focus she always had when things were serious. "So we cut it out of you."

"I know I'm not as clever as you but that did cross my mind," I deadpanned to her. "It could be anywhere and I'm as likely to bleed out as anything if you start sticking knives into me."

"I'm not leaving you here," Shazad argued.

"You don't have a choice right now," I said. "Shazad—" I was long on things I wanted to say to her and short on time. Soon enough, the chaos Izz had created was going to die down and someone was going to notice us. There was only one thing that mattered. One last piece I hadn't told her. "The Sultan has a Djinni."

Shazad opened her mouth. Then closed it. "Say that again."

There wasn't a whole lot Shazad couldn't do. She could command armies; she could form strategies that she could see play out eight steps ahead of anyone else. She could fight and maybe even win a war that we were outnumbered and outgunned in. But there was outgunned and then there was fighting a gun with a stick. If the Sultan had even one Djinni, that wasn't anything an army of mortals could stand against.

"So we need to get both you and this Djinni—"

"Bahadur," I filled in, even though I wasn't sure why it mattered. He was just another Djinni. He was a Djinni who had fathered me and whose name was half of mine. But he wasn't my father. Izz screamed and dove low. Guns went off. We both ducked on instinct.

"—both you and Bahadur out of the palace." She made it sound simple.

"Freeing a Djinni isn't like breaking Sayyida out of prison." Not that that had exactly ended well anyway. "He's trapped here, just like I am."

"I'll get some people to look into it." Shazad pushed her hair impatiently off her face. Somehow, even dressed up to look as harmless as a flower, there was no mistaking what she was capable of. "God knows, half of the Rebellion isn't doing anything useful right now. Izman is its own kind of prison. And it's swarming with soldiers since the ceasefire."

"Ceasefire?" I interrupted.

Shazad looked at me, startled, like for a moment she'd forgotten I'd been absent. Her mouth pressed into a grim line as she broke the news. "The Sultan has called for a ceasefire. An end to the fighting with the invaders until their foreign rulers can come to Izman to negotiate a new alliance. That's the news Jin was bringing us back from the Xichian camp before—" She hesitated. "—everything."

The mention of Jin made my heart clench. Something about the way she said his name was off. But I had more pride in myself than to ask about him when we were at war.

"That's why the palace is swarming with foreigners," I said instead, thinking of the crowd of uniforms and strange men we'd passed on our way here. "You think the foreigner rulers will come?"

"Rumor has it one of the princes of Xicha has already set sail. And the Gallan emperor and Albish queen have both sent their ambassadors ahead of them." I thought of the plain-clothed man whose eyes had chilled me. "They'll come. If they don't, there's too great a chance the Sultan will make an alliance with one of their enemies. Meanwhile, soldiers from all sorts of places are flooding into the city from every border to pave the way." Shazad tapped her fingers to her thumb one after the other in quick sequence. It was a nervous gesture. It meant there was more. Problems she wasn't telling me. Complications with the Rebellion that I wasn't privy to.

"What does that mean for us?" I recognized this feeling of being helpless when there was so much to be done. I used to feel like this in Dustwalk.

"Nothing good." She caught the nervous tic and stopped,

balling her hand into a fist. "Especially now. But the Sultan can only ally with one country. As soon as an alliance is struck, war will spark again. The rumors say he's planning to announce his new ally at Auranzeb. But until then . . ." she trailed off. I knew what she meant. Until then we had trouble. And it could only get worse with the Sultan having an immortal being at his command . . .

My mind turned over. There might be another way to figure out how to free a Djinni. I'd just have to get out of the harem long enough to find out. But something kept me from mentioning that to Shazad. We were running out of time. Izz's distraction could work only so long, and we couldn't be caught conspiring.

But I couldn't let her leave without asking: "Shazad, is everyone all right?" I didn't ask what I wanted to ask. It was stupid and selfish. But his name hammered against my teeth. *Is Jin all right?*

"Not everyone." For not being a Demdji, Shazad had always been the honest sort. "Mahdi died in the escape from the camp and we couldn't save Sayyida. A few others. But the death toll is as low as can be expected. Ahmed is alive, Delila, Hala, Imin, the twins. They're all here in the city."

"And Jin?" I couldn't stop myself anymore. She hadn't mentioned him, which couldn't mean anything good. Neither could the hesitation that followed my question.

"No one is exactly sure where Jin is right now," Shazad said finally. "He . . ." She shoved her loose hair up off the nape of her neck. "After you disappeared in the dead of night, he rode a horse half to death to get to the meeting point. When you weren't there, he broke Ahmed's nose and turned back around in the desert. To find you. Thank you for proving me right in my skepticism about the lack of detail in *that* plan, at least." I knew she was trying to lighten the mood, but worry had taken root in my chest. It hadn't ever crossed my mind that Jin wasn't with the rest of the rebels.

"He's still alive." I tested the words out loud. And then I realized what she'd said. "He broke Ahmed's nose?"

Shazad scratched her ear, looking as sheepish as I'd ever seen her. "Ahmed might've implied that if Jin stopped treating you as casually as some girl he'd just met in a dockside bar, maybe you'd stop running away." A surge of indignation that Ahmed thought I'd leave the Rebellion over a lovers' spat struck in my chest. "Jin hit Ahmed so fast even I couldn't get between them. It was impressive, actually."

Izz screamed again. Farther away. The chaos was settling down.

"I have to go," Shazad said. We were out of time. "I'm going to figure out a way to get you out of here. Until then, stay out of trouble." It came out halfway between an order from my general and a plea from my friend.

"You know better than to ask a Demdji to make a promise." This might be the last I ever saw of her. That was true every time we parted. But this time more than ever. Now I was on enemy ground. "And you know better than to believe I'm going to stay out of trouble."

TWENTY-THREE

I had a plan. Well, *plan* might be a strong word. Shazad was the plan maker between the two of us. This was more like the beginnings of an idea that I was hoping wouldn't get me killed. Which was more my style.

I could figure out the rest of it later. For now, I didn't need to get free of the palace. I just had to get out of the harem. And there was only one man who could make it happen.

"Why do you want to leave?" Leyla was making another toy for the harem's children, though I wasn't sure why. Most of their mothers wouldn't let them play with the toys she'd already made. Was this just her way of keeping herself sane in this place where she fit so badly? This one looked like a tiny person. He lay forgotten in her hands, clay limbs splayed, as she looked at me with her huge, earnest eyes. "The harem is nicer than a lot of other places you could wind up."

I liked Leyla. A part of me wanted to blurt out the honest truth, make her a real ally here in this place. But she was still the Sultan's daughter. And big innocent eyes weren't a good enough reason to gamble with the lives of everyone I loved. Jin's face flashed across my mind. The way I'd last seen him, half-shadowed in the tent, on the run, uncertainty hanging between us as the kiss ended. His face was quickly chased away by others'. Shazad. Ahmed. Delila. The twins. Even Hala.

"It'd be nice to be able to get out of the path of your brother," I said finally. "I mean Kadir," I corrected, remembering what she'd told me about her only real brother being the one who shared her mother. Prince Rahim, the soldier among scholars in the Sultan's circle. I'd mentioned seeing him in court the day before to Leyla, but she'd shifted the subject quickly. "Not to mention Ayet and Uzma, who have it out for me." Watching Shazad frighten Uzma might've been satisfying, but the humiliation still burned hot and fierce. "If I could convince your father to give me the run of the palace, we could stay out of each other's ways."

Leyla's eyes dashed back to the ground, and she chewed at her lip anxiously. I knew her well enough by now to recognize when she was thinking something over. I also knew better than to interrupt someone smarter than me when they were thinking. Something else I'd learned from Shazad.

"Bassam turns thirteen the day after tomorrow." Leyla spilled the words out in a rush. Whatever I'd been expecting her to come out with, that wasn't it. "Bassam is one of my father's sons by his wife Thana. My father has a tradition—for every one of his sons on their thirteenth birthday, he teaches them to shoot a bow. As my grandfather did for his sons. And his father before him. They are not to eat again until they eat something they have killed themselves. He has done it with every one of his sons."

Not every single one. How had Ahmed and Jin spent their thirteenth birthdays? They hadn't been hunting with their father. Had they been on a ship, or some foreign shore? Had they even known what day it was to be able to mark it?

I had an image of a scene that never was. The two of them standing side by side with their father's hands on their shoulders, bowstrings drawn back, competing to impress him.

"He'll come to the harem for Bassam." Leyla returned her eyes to her work, the small clay man. She was sculpting a face for him. "If you wanted to ask him for something."

• ● •

THE LARGEST OF the harem gardens was twice the size of the rebel camp—a huge swath of green crowned with a blue lake that rolled down from the walls of the palace, across the cliff that overlooked the sea, before slamming hard into another wall. Another border, the edge of the palace. The water was dotted with fat birds, flapping their glaringly pale feathers lazily, sending water droplets sprawling in a bright arc through the sun.

From my position sitting by the iron gate that led back into the heart of the harem, it looked like a picture printed in a storybook. The Sultan was standing on the shore with a boy I guessed was Bassam. This son was thin and wiry and trying hard to look older than he really was. He held a longbow drawn back across his body, arms shaking just a little bit from the effort, clearly trying to hide it from his father.

I'd watched him miss a dozen shots already, the arrows splashing uselessly into the water. After each shot came an exercise in patience as Bassam tossed a handful of bread into the lake and then withdrew to wait for the birds to come back and settle. Until they felt safe enough again for him to try to kill them. Now his father reached out, resting one reassuring hand on his shoulder. The way the boy swelled happily under his touch, I half wondered if he'd been missing on purpose, to steal a bit more time with his father.

I imagined a younger Jin standing there in Bassam's place. I'd never seen a person need anyone else less than Jin did. It was hard to picture how he would react to his father's hand on his shoulder, if he would have held himself straighter, too, eager for his father's pride.

Bassam loosed the bowstring with one easy gesture. I knew with the practiced eye of a girl from Dustwalk that this shot was different from the others.

The arrow flew true, passing straight through the neck

of the nearest duck. The bird let out a pained squawk that sent the rest of the flock darting up in the air in a panic. A servant scrambled forward, pulling the bird out of the water by its long neck.

The Sultan laughed, throwing his head back as he clapped his son on the shoulder proudly. There was no mistaking the look of pure joy that passed over the young prince's face. For just a moment, in the late afternoon sun, they might've been any father and son sharing a moment of happiness.

And then the Sultan's eyes fell on me, hovering on the edge of the garden. He patted his son on the shoulder again, squeezing it tightly with pride before sending the boy on his way, carrying the dead bird slung over his shoulder.

When his son had vanished, he gestured me over.

"Hardly anybody uses bows anymore, you know," I said when I was close enough to be heard. "Guns are cleaner."

"But not so quiet when you are trying to hunt," the Sultan said. "They scare your prey off. Besides, this is a tradition. My father did it for me, and his father did it for him." And the Sultan had killed his father and now a handful of his sons were counting on following that tradition, too. "What do you want, little Demdji?"

I ran my tongue along my teeth nervously. Chances were, he'd see right through me. But Shazad had said it herself the day Sayyida was brought back: we needed eyes in the palace. The *whole* palace. I could be those eyes. "I want to be able to leave the harem."

I couldn't leave the palace, but information could. Shazad had put Sam on the Rebellion's payroll. The past three nights, since the day Izz had dropped paper from the sky, I'd had a standing meeting with Sam at dusk by the Weeping Wall. Shazad would figure out what to do about him later, but for now, his only task was to slip into the harem every night to meet with me and make sure I hadn't sold out the whole Rebellion on a royal order. It was an awfully boring task. Or as Sam put it, it was the easiest money he'd ever made, being paid to come look at a pretty girl every night. If I succeeded here, I could make his job a little more interesting.

The Sultan played with the string of his bow. "And you want to leave because . . . ?"

"Because I can't stand it there much longer." It was a truth. A half-truth. And it wasn't going to be enough. "And I can't stand your son."

The Sultan leaned on the bow. "Which one?" he asked wryly. There it was again: that faint prickle down my skin, like we were both in on a secret, like we were both playing some game. No, that was ridiculous. If he knew I was allied with Ahmed, all he had to do was command me to tell him where he was. He could use me to lead him to Shazad and from there the rest of the Rebellion.

"Kadir." I shook off the feeling. "He looks at me like I'm a flower in that garden for him to pluck."

The Sultan twanged the string of the bow again, like he was playing a musical instrument. "You know that you are my prisoner, little Demdji. If I wanted to, I could order you to lie in one spot, completely still, until I needed you for something. I could make you grow roots and stay there waiting for an order. Or"—the Sultan paused, twanging the bowstring pointedly—"to be plucked." My skin crawled. "But . . . I admire you coming to find me here. Tell me, little Demdji: can you shoot?"

"Yes," I said, because, as much as I didn't care for him to know just how good I was with a gun, I couldn't lie. Shazad always said our greatest strength was being underestimated. But the Sultan always saw through me when I tried to dodge around a truth with a half-truth. "I can shoot."

He extended the bow toward me. I didn't take it immediately. "You want something," he said. "People who want things have to earn them."

"I know how to earn things. I didn't grow up in a palace."

"Good," the Sultan said, that hint of Jin's smile lingering. "Then you should understand this. Take the bow."

I did as I was told because I didn't have a choice, though I didn't know if he'd meant to give me an order.

"If you can bring down a duck, I will give you free range of the palace—at least, as much as anyone else has. If you don't . . . well, then I hope your bed is comfortable, because you will lie there a very long time."

I ran my fingers down the taut string of the bow. It was an old weapon. Something from the storybooks. Before guns. I remembered some legend about the archer who took out a Roc's eye with an arrow.

I stood in a shooting stance and tried to pull the string back.

"Not like that." The Sultan's hands were on my shoulders. I tensed automatically. But there was nothing lingering in the way he touched me. He gripped my shoulders like he had the young prince's. Like I'd seen fathers in Dustwalk do when they were teaching their sons to shoot a gun. No one had ever done that for me. I'd taught myself to shoot while my father was drunk. And not really my father anyway. Though he cared about whether I lived or died just as much as my real father did, as it turned out. "Widen your stance," he ordered, lightly kicking my ankles apart with his instep. "And draw the bow across your body."

I was keenly aware of him watching me as I drew the bowstring back. I took aim at the nearest duck the same way I would with a gun. I lined up my sight carefully. If I had a gun, my bullet would go straight through the bird.

I'd gotten good at killing birds in the past few months. When you were camping in the mountains, it was helpful to be able to hunt.

I loosed the bowstring. It scraped painfully along my arm. The arrow flew and missed the bird by a foot, plunging into the water. The flock of birds panicked at the noise, spiraling upward into the sky in a flapping mess of feathers and squawking.

I swore, dropping the bow, clutching my scraped arm.

"Let me see." The Sultan took hold of my wrist, another order I couldn't disobey. My forearm was already welting.

"You should have an arm guard," he commanded. "Here." He pulled his sheema off from around his neck. It was the color of the fresh saffron in dishes in the harem. He wrapped it neatly around my arm.

The sight of it brought on a pang of longing as I remembered my old red sheema. Jin.

The Sultan finished tying off the sheema with a final yank, fastening the knot around my wrist. "When the birds return, try again. And this time, draw the bowstring higher—closer to your cheek." I had to obey, though I half thought he had forgotten who he was speaking to. That he meant them as instructions more than orders.

We waited in silence until the birds returned and settled again. I wanted to call them stupid for coming back to something that might get them killed so readily. But then, I was standing next to the Sultan of my own will.

I missed again with my second shot. And my third. I could feel my neck prickling with shame, keenly aware of the Sultan watching me miss over and over. I needed to win. I needed to be able to leave the harem. I needed to save my family from my father.

"Your Exalted Highness." A servant's voice made us both turn. He was bent low. "You are awaited for negotiations by the Gallan ambassador." My ears perked up. It was starting. The negotiations for this country. To turn us back over to them. Why I needed to be able to report back.

"Wait," I called out as the Sultan turned to go. "I can do this."

The Sultan considered for a moment. And then he nodded. "Then find me when you have."

THE SUN CREPT across the sky as I tried. I could feel the sweat running down my neck and I was half-tempted to unwrap the sheema from my arm and tie it around my head. But the throbbing welt there told me not to. There was nothing to be done about the blistering in my fingers, though. Or the creeping ache in my arm as my muscles protested being pulled back the same way one more painful time. Shaking to release the bowstring.

Some servants came and placed a jug of water and a bowl of dates next to me when the sun got high. I ignored them both. I could do this.

I pulled back. Another arrow dove into the water. The birds scattered.

I cursed under my breath.

Damn this.

I had done harder things.

Before the birds could fully escape I reached down and plucked out another arrow. I nocked it quickly and aimed for the still-flapping squawking mess of birds. I found the duck I wanted to hit. And I didn't hesitate. I didn't waste time trying to line up my shot. I aimed with certainty, the way I always had with a gun.

And I loosed the arrow.

The duck separated itself from the flock, plummeted, and hit the grass even as my heart took off.

I BARGED THROUGH the palace, dripping a trail of blood behind me as I held the dead bird by the neck.

The Sultan had told me to come find him when I'd succeeded, and the tug of an order on my gut kept me moving. I didn't think about what I was doing until I'd pushed past the guard, who didn't try to stop me, and burst through the doors.

Dozens of heads turned to look at me as I crashed in. A thought flitted through my mind that I shouldn't be doing this. But it was a little late for that. I strode up to the table, my eyes on the Sultan, and slammed my prize down on the table in front of him, making his cup shake.

The Sultan looked at the dead duck.

It was only then that I took stock of my surroundings. The council room was full to bursting. With men in uniforms. Uniforms of all sorts. Golden Mirajin uniforms and the blue of the Gallan empire.

And they were all staring at me: a wild-eyed girl who had just slammed a dead duck with an arrow through its neck down on the table in front of her Sultan. Prince Rahim was hiding a smile under the pretense of scratching his nose, but nobody else seemed amused.

I had just interrupted one of the Sultan's councils to decide the outcome of the ceasefire and the fate of our whole country, with a dead duck.

I wondered if this was what would cost me my head.

"Well, it seems you are a half-decent shot after all," the Sultan said, too low for anyone else to hear. "You will leave the harem at any time you please." There was a short pause in which a moment of hope bloomed, that he might really leave that loophole for me, one that would allow me slip out of his grip and back to the Rebellion . . . "But you will do so with a guard. And you will not leave the palace." My hope died. I was stupid to even entertain it to start with. The Sultan wasn't an incautious man. And then, raising his voice: "Someone take this duck to the kitchens and my Demdji to somewhere she belongs." I saw the Gallan delegation's heads lift at the word *Demdji*. They'd call me a demon but they knew what that word meant all the same. I wondered if the Sultan was rubbing me in their faces. That didn't seem much of a political tactic.

A servant lifted the duck by the neck gingerly. The papers spread across the desk shifted as he did. I caught sight of a map of Miraji, drawn in faded black ink. Marked with newer blue lines. On our half of the desert. It was barely a glimpse of a corner but it was enough. I saw it. Circled in fresh blue ink was a tiny black dot, labeled in careful print: Saramotai.

My mind dashed to Samira. To the rebels Shazad was going to send to hold the city. To Ikar on the walls. And the women who'd chosen to stay behind. All of them sitting like a bull's-eye inside the blue ink circle.

A servant was already taking my arm, urging me out of the room. Trying to move me on. But I couldn't go. Not without knowing what was happening to the city we'd already given so much to free. My mind started running, trying to find a way to stay. To get those papers.

The Gallan ambassador was talking to the Sultan

now. "We have a command a thousand men strong coming from the homeland with His Majesty for Auranzeb. They will need to be armed if they are to hold Saramotai. Furthermore—"

"He's lying." The words slipped out. The servant holding my arm hissed a warning through his teeth, tugging me toward the door harder now. But the Sultan held up his hand, stopping him.

"What was that, little Demdji?"

"He's lying," I said again, louder this time. I tried the next words on my tongue, looking for the untruth. "The Gallan troops coming with their king aren't as many as he says." There it was.

The Sultan ran one calloused finger in a ring around the rim of his glass. His mind was as quick as Ahmed's. I was a Demdji. If I said someone was lying, then that was God's honest truth.

"Where did you learn Gallan?" the Sultan asked me.

Now, that was a dangerous question. Some of the truth of it was Jin and a long desert crossing and sleepless nights keeping watch.

"The Last County suffered under the Gallan alliance." It was a half-truth folded up in deception, usually too obvious to get past the Sultan. But I was offering him a gift. It might be enough. "And us Demdji, we pick things up fast."

The Sultan's finger made another thoughtful loop of the rim of his glass. "I am sorry that you suffered," he said finally. "Much of my desert did." Finally he addressed the translator. "Tell the Gallan ambassador that I know there aren't a thousand Gallan soldiers arriving with his king. And that I want the real number."

The translator's eyes darted nervously between the Sultan and me as he spoke. The Gallan ambassador looked surprised as the words reached him. His eyes flicked to me, seeming to understand that I had something to do with this. But he didn't miss a beat as he started speaking again in that guttural language of the west. I didn't catch every word, but I did catch the number. "He's still lying," I said again quickly. "There aren't five hundred."

The Sultan considered me as he spoke to his translator. "Tell the ambassador that perhaps lying is more tolerated in Gallandie, but in Miraji, it is a sin. Tell him that this is not the first time since our alliance ruptured that one of his countrymen has tried to deceive me into providing weapons for their troops overseas in order to continue their war in the north, under the guise of arming only those allies coming to our desert. Tell him that he has one more chance to tell me the real number or I will halt negotiations altogether until his king arrives."

"Two hundred." The translator spoke finally, after a tense moment. The Sultan's eyes flicked to me along with the rest of the room.

"It's the truth." It rolled easily off my tongue.

"Well." The Sultan tapped the edge of his glass. "That's a fairly substantial difference, isn't it, Ambassador? No, there's no need to translate that." He waved as the translator started to lean in to speak. "The ambassador understands my meaning. And I think he, and everyone else here, understands that they are better off not lying to me. Sit down, Amani."

He gestured to a seat behind himself. It was an order. I couldn't disobey it. And I wanted to stay. This was what I had asked for. But my legs still shook a little as I folded down onto the cushion behind the Sultan.

It wasn't until I was settled that I realized he had called me by my name. Not little Demdji.

I had his attention now. I just prayed I didn't have enough for him to start calling me the Blue-Eyed Bandit.

TWENTY-FOUR

The duck I'd killed was served dressed in candied oranges and pomegranates, on a platter the color of Hala's skin, my arrow still through its neck. I wondered if that was part of the lesson. When a bullet disappeared inside flesh, you could almost forget it. The arrow wasn't that kind.

The council had gone on well past the sunset, as translators worked frantically, translating Gallan and Albish and Xichian and Gamanix. My head was churning with everything I'd heard in that room, turning it over and over like a prayer until I knew it by heart. I was going to try my damned hardest not to forget a word of it before I could get the news out to Shazad. One wrong detail, one point misremembered, and I could cost thousands of

lives. I tried to sift out anything useless with every rota-
tion through my head, leaving only what I could use.

The Sultan was going to march troops to take back
Saramotai. If negotiations were successful, the city would
go back to the Gallans' hands. A direct access point back
into the desert and into Amonpour. Amonpour was allied
with the Albish. There was an Albish camp on the border
that would be in their path. They would march in three
days. The Sultan was going to march troops to take back
Saramotai . . .

"You seem distracted." The Sultan interrupted my
thoughts as he settled across from me.

"Your rooms are just about the same size as the whole
town where I grew up." It was a quick jab, meant to distract him, lest he think to order me to tell him what I was
thinking about. *I'm considering everything I'm going to tell
the Rebellion about your plans.*

Truth be told, his rooms were the size you'd expect
for the ruler of the whole desert. I was brought in only
as far as the antechamber, but I could see more doors
leading off to a bedchamber with a thick red carpet,
and into private baths on another side. The walls in the
receiving chamber were gold and white mosaics that
reflected the light of the oil lamps around us so well
I almost thought it was still day. Except that above us
a huge glass dome gave a clear view of the sky. And to
one side a balcony overlooked the sheer drop down the
cliffs to the sea.

"Dustwalk." He seemed to pull the name from the far

reaches of his mind. "Tell me about it." It was an order. Whether he meant it to be or not.

"It's a small town at the end of the desert. I grew up there." It was the truth and it was obedience to his order. Even if it wasn't what he was after. One wrong word about Dustwalk and I might give away everything. "I'd rather not talk about it."

For all the size of the room, the table we were seated at was small enough that, if he'd wanted to, he could've reached across it and slit my throat with the long knife he was toying with.

I didn't like being around the Sultan any longer than I had to. Not when he had so much power over me. Not when all it would take was one false word for him to find out who I was. Besides, it was after dark. Which meant I was already late to meet Sam by the Weeping Wall. I hadn't told him about my plan to get out of the harem, seeing as I had no way of being sure I'd succeed or not. I sure hadn't been expecting the plan to succeed so well that it would end with me sitting across from the Sultan. For once I had a whole lot more to tell Sam than he had to tell me. I just had to get back in time to meet him. And before I accidentally revealed the whole Rebellion to the Sultan.

He was watching me now. As if wondering whether to push the point of my hometown or release me from the order. But I was beginning to understand how the Sultan worked. If I gave him some truth, some weakness, on my own, he'd stop circling me. "I hated that godforsaken dead-end town." I gave him that admission. "Please don't make me talk about it."

He considered me slowly. "You hated everything about it?"

I was about to tell him yes, but it wouldn't get past my tongue. *Tamid*, I realized. That was holding me back. I worried at one of the scars healing on my arm, feeling the little piece of metal shift underneath. I ought to hate him now. But I didn't know if I could hate him back then. "No," I said finally. "Not everything."

I thought he would press me. But he just nodded. "Help yourself to the food." Another order I couldn't disobey. I had to make him order me to leave. I couldn't last a whole dinner with the Sultan pulling little truths out of me one by one.

"Why am I here?" I started to spear the oranges off the duck one by one, putting them onto my plate. "You've got a whole garden full of wives and daughters—you could *pluck* one of them out to eat with you if you're lonely."

I knew I was crossing into dangerous territory now. But if I was going to get expelled back to the relative safety of the harem in time to meet Sam, I couldn't mince my words. But the Sultan just sighed in resignation as he knocked my fork aside and started to carve a knife through the brown crackling flesh. "Perhaps I just enjoy your company."

"I don't believe you." I watched the knife work its way through the skin, cutting a perfect round circle off the bone.

"You're right, perhaps *enjoy* is a strong word." He placed the meat carefully onto my plate for me. "I find you interesting. Now"—the Sultan drew back—"eat something."

I ignored the meat and leaned across the table to spear another candied orange straight off the skin of the duck instead. It hit my tongue in a burst of sweet and bitter like nothing I'd ever had. I leaned across again to take another one while I was still chewing the first. I caught sight of a faint smile on the Sultan's face. "What?" I asked, mouth full.

"Nothing." The Sultan was still toying with the knife in his hand. "I just wish you could see the look on your face. If it could be bottled, it would be the elixir the alchemist Midhat was hunting for." In the stories, Midhat was an alchemist of great talent and great misery who lost his mind trying to make and bottle joy since he could not find it in the world. "Then again"—the Sultan switched his grip on the knife, sawing at the meat of the duck I'd killed— "if I could've bottled the look on our foreign friends' faces when you dropped this onto the council table, that would also give me a great deal of joy." He carved a leg of the duck and placed it on his own plate. Last time I'd eaten a duck, it'd been one Izz had caught in Iliaz. It still had the marks of a crocodile's teeth through it, and the fat spat off it into the fire, making Jin curse when a bit sizzled and hit his wrist. Now I was taking food from the same hands that had held his mother down and claimed her by force when the Sultan was the same age as Jin. Probably in these same rooms.

"Your Exalted Highness." The servant had appeared at

the door so silently that I started. He was dropped into a deep bow at the door. "The Gallan ambassador has asked to see you. I advised him you were otherwise occupied, but he has been very insistent."

"The Gallan ambassador summons me to him in my own palace." The Sultan sounded more resigned than anything as he pushed away from the table. "Excuse me." My eyes followed him all the way to the door.

I was on my feet as soon as he'd disappeared.

I flung open two wrong doors until I found the one that led to his office.

Facing me, instead of a wall, was a huge glass window overlooking Izman. From all the way up here, in the night, the city looked like a second sky, windows dancing with lights like stars across an otherwise dark sea. The Sultan's kingdom spread out below him. It was the closest I'd come to Izman since the day I woke up in Tamid's workroom. I resisted the impulse to press my hands against the glass like a child.

The other three walls seemed designed to match the window by night. Blue plaster, inset with what looked like yellow glass stars that would catch the sun in the day.

It reminded me of Ahmed's pavilion. Back in a home that was gone now.

I tried to imagine my prince here, when we took the city, keeping the peace.

But right now we were still in the middle of a war and I wasn't going to pass up an opportunity to find something that might win it.

The room was dominated by a huge desk that was covered in papers and books and maps and pens. I doubted he'd miss some of it if it went missing. It was just a question of what to take.

The Sultan is coming back. I tried to say the words out loud, but they wouldn't cross my tongue. I was safe for now, as I started to carefully lift papers off the desk, holding them up to the glow of light from the city through the window. I tried over and over again to repeat the words as I worked. An early warning system. I found a sheet of paper scribbled with figures and numbers I didn't understand. Another one was a map of Miraji. It detailed troop movements, but those I'd heard about already in the meeting earlier. My fingers faltered over a familiar-looking drawing of armor. It was the suit of metal they'd put on Noorsham. There were words scribbled along the edges. The ones used to control him.

There were more schematics like it underneath. And others for what looked like machine parts. One of the pieces of paper was held down by a tiny piece of metal the size of a coin. My name was carved into it along with a jumble of other words in the first language. So this was what I had under my skin. I fought my urge to fling it through the window and watch the glass shatter.

I took one of the sketches and kept exploring. I pulled out a few interesting-looking pieces of paper. One looked like supply routes. Shazad would be able to decipher that easier than I could. There was another one that looked like a map of Izman. There were dots of red ink interspersed across the paper. I held it up to the light, trying to figure out what they might be marking. But I didn't know Izman.

"The Sultan is coming back." The words slipped out into the silence of the room, setting off a jump of panic in my chest. I didn't have any pockets. I shoved the papers into the waist of my shalvar as I hurried out of the study, tugging my kurti back down over it.

I was back at the table picking at my food when the Sultan reappeared, taking his seat across from me. "What did he want?" I asked as he picked the knife back up. I prayed he couldn't hear the raggedness of my breathing.

"You." He said it in such a matter-of-fact way that it took me aback. "You know, in the Gallans' so-called religion they believe First Beings are creatures of evil. And their children are monsters."

"I know what they believe." My mouth had suddenly gone dry. I reached for the pitcher of sweet wine. The sudden movement made the paper stuffed inside my clothes crackle and I stilled.

"They want me to hand you over." If the Sultan had noticed the noise, then he was doing a mighty fine job of hiding it. "To be brought to justice, they say. Which is a pretext, of course. They are hiding behind religious righteousness because they don't want to admit that you are a serious threat to their being able to lie to my face and sway an alliance back in their favor."

"One of them called me a barbarian." I heard the bile on my own tongue. As far as I was concerned, killing off

First Beings and Demdji was more barbaric than killing a duck.

"Good," the Sultan said. "It would serve all of them well to remember that the people of Miraji can hold their own. Even if it is just against a duck." I wasn't sure where the swell of pride came from. "You want to know why you're here, Amani, dining in my chambers? It sends a message. When we were allied with the Gallan I would have had to hand you over to hang. Now"—he picked up the pitcher I'd been too frightened to reach any farther for—"you are free to be my guest."

"You hate them." I couldn't keep it in any longer. "They hate us. They're using us. Why make another alliance?" My voice had risen without my meaning it to.

The Sultan turned his dark gaze on me. It struck me again how Ahmed had his eyes. Then he grinned, like he was surprised by a child doing something particularly clever. "You sound a lot like the folks who follow my rebel son."

"You asked me about Dustwalk." I diverted his attention away from Ahmed. "I'm from the deepest, darkest parts of your desert. I've seen firsthand what your alliances have done to folks. Cities under Gallan rule where it was the law to shoot a Demdji in the head. Everybody in Dustwalk working for as close to nothing as you can get without starving to make weapons for foreigners. It made for a poor, starving, frightened desert."

"How old are you, Amani?"

"Seventeen." I pulled myself up to my full height. Trying

to look it. Careful of the stolen papers sticking to my skin as I moved.

The bone of the duck leg on his plate cracked under his knife. "You weren't even alive when I took my father's throne. Even those who were have forgotten how things were back then. We were at war. And it wasn't one that we should have been fighting—the war between the Gallan and the Albish. We were a prize in the race between all of our foreign friends. Half the countries in the world wanted to claim our land. But in the end it came down to those two ancient enemies and their never-ending war of false beliefs."

The leg of the duck finally came free in a snap of cartilage and sinews ripping free under the sawing of the Sultan's knife. There was something about the noise of cracking bone echoing around the polished marble halls and glass dome that set my teeth on edge. The Sultan calmly spooned orange sauce across the flesh as he spoke.

"And my father let it happen. He was foolish and cowardly. He thought we could fight the same way our country had in my grandfather's day. He thought we could stand against two armies and somehow not get annihilated. Even General Hamad advised my father he couldn't win a war on two fronts. Well, Captain Hamad then. I made him a general after his advice proved to be so sound."

He was talking about Shazad's father. General Hamad had no loyalty to this Sultan. Shazad had always known her father despised his ruler. But he had backed the Sultan's ideas twenty years ago all the same. There was a time when even a man on our side had thought our enemy was in the right.

"The only way to win was to form an alliance, grant them access to what they wanted from us on our terms. My father wouldn't do it. Neither would my brother who had won the Sultim trials. Just because he was able to best eleven of our brothers in an arena somehow that made him fit to decide the fate of this country?"

Not any more fit than Kadir was. But I didn't interrupt. Getting myself turned out of the Sultan's presence didn't seem so important now. I'd learned history in school. But it was different to hear it from the Sultan's own tongue. It would be like hearing the tale of the First Mortal from Bahadur, who would have stood with the other Djinn at the birth of mortality and watched him face down death.

The Sultan seemed to sense my attention on him all at once. He looked up from where he was sawing at his meat. Glancing between my empty hands and my still-full plate.

"I did what needed to be done, Amani," he said calmly.

He had chosen a side to keep us from being torn apart between two of them. In one bloody night Prince Oman, a nobody among the Sultan's sons, too young even to be allowed to compete for Sultim, had led the Gallan armies into the palace, killed his own father, and slain the brothers he knew would stand between him and the throne: the Sultim and the others who had fought in the trials. By morning he sat in his father's place and the Gallan were our allies. Or our occupiers.

"What I did twenty years ago was the only way to keep this country from falling completely into their hands. The Gallan have annexed enough countries. I couldn't allow us to be next." He sawed at his food carefully as he spoke. "The world is a lot more complicated than it seems when you are seventeen, Amani."

"And how old were you when you turned our country over to the Gallan?" I knew he hadn't been all that much older than I was now. The same age as Ahmed, give or take.

The Sultan smiled around the piece of duck he was chewing. "Young enough that I spent the next nineteen years trying to find a way to drive them out. And I was very close to succeeding, you know." Noorsham. He'd been trying to use my brother, a Demdji, as a weapon to kill the Gallan, and never mind his own people who wound up caught in the crossfire. "A little more time and I could've rid this country of them forever." He picked up his wine, drinking deep from the cup.

A little more time. If we hadn't interfered. If we hadn't saved Fahali. Saved our people. Saved my brother. And he reckoned he could've saved the whole country. They would have been a sacrifice for the greater good.

"You're not eating."

I wasn't hungry. But I speared a piece of cold meat all the same. The orange had congealed into a sticky paste around it. It was too sweet when it hit my tongue now. *You're wrong.* The words, too, were sticky on my tongue. I couldn't spit them out. I wished Shazad were here. She knew more than I did. She'd read up on history and philosophy and had better schooling with her father's tutors than I'd had in a busted-down schoolhouse at the end of the desert. She was better at debating things than I was. But we'd both been in Saramotai. A power play disguised in a just cause. "Awfully convenient how saving this country meant you becoming Sultan without the Sultim trials."

"The Sultim trials are another antiquated tradition." The Sultan placed his wine back on the table, carefully steadying it by the stem. "Hand-to-hand combat between brothers and riddles to prove a man had half a brain might've been the best way to pick a leader when we were just a collection of tents in the desert fighting the Destroyer of Worlds' monsters, but wars are different now. Wit and wisdom are not the same. Neither are skill and knowledge. And Sultans don't go out on the battlefield with a sword anymore. There are better ways to lead."

"You held a Sultim trial anyway." I reached for another orange off the duck, moving slowly so as not to rustle the stolen supply route map hidden in my waistband.

"Yes, and look how well that served me. I acquired a rebel son out for my throne as a result of it." He laughed to himself, as he pushed the gold platter closer toward me. A low, self-deprecating chuckle that reminded me of Jin. "I had to hold the trials, to show the people that though I had taken my throne by . . . other means, I was still upholding the traditions of our country. As antiquated as it is, it can still serve a purpose." He settled back in his seat again, watching me eat. "In some countries, the people love their royals best when they are celebrating weddings or new royal children. If only that were the case with my people, I would never run out of their love. But the Mirajin people are not so easily bought. They never love my family more than when we are fighting to the death for the right to rule them. They never love me so much as they do on Auranzeb when I remind them that I killed twelve of my brothers with my own hands in one night." He said it so calmly that whatever warmth his laugh had brought into the room drained out of it instantly. "I try not to remind them that it was the same night I handed them over to the enemy they hate so much. But really, this is a violent country, Amani. You're proof of that. Our dinner is proof of that." He tapped the arrow through the duck's neck. "I put a knife in your hand and your first instinct was to stab me."

"You tried to stab me first," I objected without thinking. That time he really did laugh, in earnest.

"This is a hard desert. It needs a hard man to rule it." *A harder man than Ahmed.* The thought shot across my mind again. I shoved it away as forcefully as I could. The Sultan had said it himself, rulers were different these days. And what Ahmed lacked in strength he made up for by being good. A better man than most of us. He was so good, in fact, that Shazad and I hadn't even hesitated when it came to taking Delila to Saramotai. We'd disobeyed our ruler without a second thought. Without any fear of consequences.

Shazad would say it was a poor ruler who needed to

rely on fear to make his people obey. I might not be so well versed in philosophy, but it seemed to me like without obedience a man was no ruler at all.

Was Ahmed really going to run this whole country if he couldn't even get me and Shazad and his sister to fall in line?

"There is nothing I wouldn't do for this country, Amani. Still." He smiled indulgently. "I will grant you that Kadir would perhaps have not been my first choice to succeed me were it not for the trials." He played with the stem of his glass, seeming to drift far away.

"Who would you have picked?" I wasn't sure if I meant it as an earnest question or a challenge of whether he actually knew any of his sons well enough to pick one. But the Sultan seemed to sincerely consider my question.

"Rahim is a great deal stronger than I gave him credit for as a boy." Leyla's brother. The prince who held himself like a military man and who had challenged Kadir in court and sat on the war council with him. "He might have made a good ruler, if I had kept him closer. And if he weren't so ruled by his emotions." The light through the glass dome caught the rim of his glass as he spun it. "But truthfully, had he only been raised in my palace, Ahmed might be the best choice." That caught me off guard.

"You mean the Rebel Prince," I said carefully, all too aware I was treading on dangerous ground now.

"My son believes he is helping this country; I know he truly does." He called Ahmed his son. Ahmed always called the Sultan his father, too. Jin never did. To Jin he was always "the Sultan." Like he was trying to sever any strings between himself and his father. But it seemed like Ahmed and the Sultan had less interest in severing those ties. "The trouble with belief is that it's not the same as truth."

The memory rose from the quiet part of my mind where most of my memories of Jin lived. A night in the desert. Jin telling me belief was a foreign language to logic. But what else did we have?

The Sultan let go of the stem of his glass. He wiped his fingers clean of grease and orange pulp before pulling a familiar piece of yellow paper from his pocket. It was folded into smaller squares, and it looked worn out from folding over and over again. From across the table, I looked at Ahmed's sun on it upside down. *A new dawn. A new desert.*

"These are all very fine ideas he has," the Sultan said. "But you sat in that council today, Amani. Do you think my son knows how many guns we can promise the Gallan without overtaxing our own resources? Do you think he knows that the Albish queen, the latest in a long line of sorceresses, is rumored to have hardly any magic left to defend her country with? That the Xichian emperor has not picked an heir yet and their whole country is on the brink of civil war?" He really seemed to expect me to answer.

"I don't know." It was the truth. I wasn't privy to everything Ahmed knew. But if I were being more than truthful, if I were being honest, I'd give him a real answer. *No. He doesn't know.*

"If the world were simple," the Sultan said as he smoothed the tract out across the table, "we could be free of foreign powers, an independent nation. But we are a country with borders, with friends and enemies at all of them. And unlike my son I am not interested in conscripting this entire country to defend it. How many untrained men and women do you think have died fighting for his beliefs?"

Ranaa's face invaded my mind. The little Demdji from Saramotai. The stray bullet. Watching the light in her hands extinguish as her power went, then her life.

The Sultan's army had wanted her. But if it weren't for us trying to save her, she'd be here instead of me. She might be sitting on soft pillows, hair clean and scented with lavender, mouth sticky with candied oranges. Instead of turned to ashes on a funeral pyre and scattered into the desert sand.

"If the throne changes hands, we will be invaded. My son is an idealist. Idealists make great leaders, but they never make good rulers. So I'll tell you what I believe, Amani. I believe that if my son's rebellion were ever to succeed, or even to gain enough of a foothold to cast doubt upon my rule, we would be torn to shreds by foreign powers. It would destroy Miraji, just like my father would have destroyed it before us."

TWENTY-FIVE

I t was closer to dawn than dusk when I returned to the harem. I hated the quiet. I could hear my fears that much louder for it.

Back in the rebel camp there was no such thing as silence, even in the darkest hours of night. There was the clink of weapons on those keeping watch. Conversations whispered in the night. The rifling of paper from Ahmed's tent as he worried long after the rest of us had stopped. Here, any night sound was covered by the gentle running of water or the patter of birds.

My fingers were slick with fat from the skin of the duck and sticky with the sweetness of the orange. I wiped my hands across the hem of my kurti as I stepped into my rooms, starting to pull the clothes over my head.

"What kind of time do you call this, young lady?" The voice made me jump violently. Dropping the hem of my shirt, I reached for a weapon I didn't have. Exhaustion and confusion blurred my vision for a moment. There was a figure sitting on my bed in a khalat. A khalat I recognized . . . because it belonged to Shazad, I realized after a moment. Only the person wearing it was a head taller than Shazad, at least, and had wider shoulders that pulled at the fabric enough to make some of the stitching pop. The face was hidden by a sheema, one blond curl escaping underneath to drop lazily over pale blue eyes.

Sam.

"What the hell are you doing here?" I hissed, glancing around nervously as I dropped down on the mat across from him. "Someone might see you."

"Oh, plenty of folks have." Sam lowered his voice to a whisper to match me. He loosened the sheema around his face. It was tied correctly this time; I could only guess his way of knotting it haphazardly like an infant had bugged Shazad as much as it did me. "But who's going to notice another woman in here?" He had a point. Women seemed to appear and disappear in the harem without anyone batting an eye. "Shazad's idea. She didn't think it was a good idea for you to get caught with a man in your bed. Although I don't know if I have the figure to pull off this khalat." He cinched it around his waist with his hands, like he was trying to make it fit him properly.

"Don't worry, none of us can fill out a khalat the way Shazad can," I said. But there was something nagging at me. "Jin's not back yet." It wasn't a question. I didn't even have to test the truth out on my tongue before saying it. Because if Jin were back, Sam wouldn't be here alone.

Sam kicked back, lacing his hands behind his head. "This is the Rebel Prince's missing brother I keep hearing about? He's the one you wish was waiting for you in your bed right now, I gather." He winked at me.

I dodged the comment. "He wouldn't make nearly so convincing a girl as you do," I said. "Are you wearing makeup?"

"Oh, yes, just a little. Shazad did it for me." He preened a little.

"She must like you. I'm usually the only person she does that for."

"She was worried about you after you missed meeting me by the Weeping Wall tonight." I'd missed my meeting time with Sam by a long ways after I'd given up trying to escape the dinner. "In particular she was concerned you might—and these are her words—'do something typically Amani-ish' and get yourself caught. She's got the entire camp packed up and ready to move again if I didn't find you by dawn."

Somewhere in the midst of dining with the Sultan I'd stopped feeling afraid of him finding out who I was. Sam's words were a sharp reminder that I wasn't risking only my own life. We'd been found once already.

"I've been waiting for so long I was beginning to think she was right and that I'd have to take up the mantle of the Blue-Eyed Bandit permanently. And after being filled in on what 'something typically Amani-ish' means, I'm not sure I'm up to the task. Did you really throw yourself under the hooves of a Buraqi? I'd lose a rib doing that."

I rolled my eyes, letting the joke in his voice burn away some of the guilt. "If there was ever motivation to stay alive . . ." I trailed off. I couldn't exactly tell him that Shazad had been wrong to worry. I had, after all, nearly been trampled by a Buraqi, twice. And I *had* sat across from our enemy and discussed Ahmed over dinner that night. "You can tell Shazad I'm still alive. And I have free rein in the palace now. You should lead with that." I dropped down next to him. "Before you tell her that I missed our meeting because I was dining with the Sultan."

Sam burst out laughing so loud I was worried he might wake someone. The harem had thin walls. "So what does a rebel talk to the Sultan about these days? Though my mother always said to keep politics away from the dinner table—so perhaps you just discussed the weather? Though, best I can tell, you only have one type of weather here."

I could still taste the orange on my lips when I ran my tongue across them. I considered what the Sultan had said about the fact that he was trying to stop a war. A war Ahmed was helping to instigate. That giving over this information would help the Rebellion but might hurt Miraji.

"The Sultan is going after Saramotai." I reached into my shirt and pulled out the map of the supply route. The drawing of Noorsham's armor was wrapped around my upper arm. "Five hundred men are to leave Izman in three days, marching on the city through Iliaz." Sam stayed quiet as I pulled confidential information out of my clothes. Which was commendable, really. "There are too many to stop. Izz or Maz can get there ahead of the Sultan's troops with a warning easily and evacuate everyone."

"Evacuate them where?" Sam said.

"I don't know." I finally pulled the map of Izman out from the waistband of my trousers and leaned back, sprawling my aching legs across the bed of pillows so that they tangled with the hem of his borrowed khalat. "But it's either get them out or someone talks Ahmed into letting Delila try to make a whole city disappear long enough to baffle the Sultan's troops. Tell Shazad. She'll know what to do."

"Seems like you already know what to do."

I shrugged. I'd spent the last half a year listening to Shazad and Ahmed strategize. I'd picked up a few things. "There's more." I laid out the movements of other soldiers for Sam, struggling to remember all the details from the war council. There were more traveling south into the territory that Ahmed had claimed. Sensing a weakness. But it was a diversion; Saramotai was the only city they were going to take back for now.

"When the troops start to leave the city, it won't be so swarming with soldiers anymore," I pointed out. "Shazad said half the Rebellion was short on things to do; well, this is a good chance to change that. Supply routes to the army, and I don't know what this one is marking"—I pointed out the red dots—"but seems worth looking into." I handed him the stack of papers and gave him as much as I could remember from the war council, each a precarious building block toward peace in Miraji that we could dismantle, that we could seize and use as a weapon in the Rebellion. And I tried to shake the feeling that I was a traitor to my whole country with every word I spoke.

TWENTY-SIX

Now that I could leave the harem, I spent as little time as I could there. The palace could've been a barren wasteland to rival the Last County and I wouldn't have cared, so long as it was free of Kadir and Ayet and the rest of the gaggle of wives.

I was required a few hours every day at the Sultan's meetings. He met with each of the foreign delegations separately. The Albish ambassador was an ancient man with pale age-spotted hands that shook so hard he couldn't hold a pen. I overheard him tell his scribe that I reminded him of his granddaughter. He didn't lie as viciously as the Gallan but he didn't come ready to hand over the truth, either. He might wear a kinder face but he wanted something from us, same as the Gallan did. The Xichian didn't have an ambassador. They sent a general who eyed me with distrust with every word I spoke.

I sat behind the Sultan in each meeting, to his right, where he could catch my eye when someone was talking and know the truth of it. I kept the men negotiating the terms of the ceasefire honest. And I learned as much as I could while I was at it. I learned where the foreign troops were stationed along our borders. I learned who the Sultan trusted and what he knew about the Rebellion. His son Rahim, Leyla's brother, attended every single meeting. He scarcely spoke unless his father asked him something directly. A few times I caught him watching me.

After a few meetings I learned that I couldn't avoid Kadir entirely outside of the harem. Every so often, he would turn up at negotiations, too, forcing a place for himself at the table. Unlike his brother, he offered opinions his father didn't ask for. Once I caught one of the ministers rolling his eyes as Kadir spoke.

Kadir was the only person who seemed to be able to get a word out of Prince Rahim unsolicited. The two princes sparked off each other like angry flint. I remembered what the Sultan had said, that Rahim would make a good choice for Sultim if he weren't so ruled by his emotions. So far I hadn't seen any emotion from him except hatred for Kadir.

I returned to the harem every night to meet with Sam at dusk and hand over what I'd gathered.

What was left of the days belonged to me to spend however I wanted outside the walls of the harem. I explored as freely as I could, while carefully avoiding the foreigners who were gradually invading the palace. There were a hundred more gardens that bloomed so thick with flowers I could barely get the doors open, or where music seemed to drift through the walls along with a breeze that smelled of salt and bright air. It wasn't until I climbed a tower that looked out over the water, and the same air picked up my clothes and hair in a rush, that I realized it was the sea. I'd spent my short time on the sea drugged and bound. But that wasn't the memory the sea air stirred up. It was sitting on a dusty shop floor, as far from the water as I could be, with my fingers dancing along the tattoos on Jin's skin.

Once, I rounded a corner to see a figure ahead walking with a limp that was so familiar I was ready to turn and run. I stopped walking so abruptly when I saw him that the guard accompanying me that day walked straight into me. The shame on his face was the most expression I ever got out of one of them. It was nice to know they were human somewhere under that uniform, at least. It turned out it was only an Albish soldier, wounded by a Mirajin bullet before the ceasefire. Besides, Tamid didn't walk with a limp anymore, I remembered.

I was putting on a good show of wandering aimlessly. But the Sultan wasn't stupid enough to give me complete freedom in the palace, either; a soldier waited for me outside the gates of the harem every morning and latched on to me like a silent shadow. The soldier changed every day, and none spoke except to tell me when I was wanted at a meeting. If I tried to take a turn I wasn't supposed to, my guard just became a new wall between me and whatever door or passageway I was heading for. A heavily armed wall that just stared straight ahead until I took the hint.

But I wasn't about to give up. I needed to get back to Bahadur. The Djinni. My father. The Sultan's new hidden weapon. I had to find a way to free him before the Sultan could use him to annihilate us.

• ● •

I WISHED I wasn't so familiar with the feeling of waking up in trouble. But the harem was softening me. Used to be, an intruder's presence would've woken me well before getting close enough to put a blade against my neck.

I wrenched myself to sitting, heart racing in panic, ready to face whatever threat the night was bringing. Soldiers. Ghouls.

Worse. Ayet.

The light of the mostly full moon shivered along the blade in her hand as she drew away from me. Not a knife, I realized: scissors. More dangerous was the smile on her face. In her other hand, her fist was curled around a long dark braid.

My hand flew to my scalp. The last person who'd bothered to cut my hair was my mother before she died. In the years since, it had reached close to halfway down my spine, though it spent most of its time twisted under my sheema. Now it ended bluntly, just above my shoulders.

"Let's see how much he wants you now that you look like a boy." Ayet wound a piece of my slaughtered hair around her finger with a sneer.

Anger rushed through me, fiercer than anything so stupid and vain warranted. But I didn't care if it was stupid and vain. I moved as fast as I knew how, lunging for her. Before she could so much as flinch, the scissors were in my hand. I might not be able to hurt her, but she didn't know that. I pressed the blade against her throat and had the satisfaction of watching her eyes widen.

"Listen to me." I had a grip on the front of her khalat before she could make a run for it. "I have bigger things to deal with than your jealousy about your husband's wandering eyes. So why don't you go take this out on someone who actually *wants* to steal him from you."

Ayet laughed bitterly, throat moving against the blunt scissors pressed to her neck. "You really think this is jealousy? You think I *want* Kadir? What I *want* is to survive the harem. This place is a battlefield. And I think you must know that. Or else what did you do with Mouhna and Uzma?"

"What are you talking about?" Trying as hard as I could to stay out of the way of Kadir and his wives, I hadn't been in the harem enough to notice anything about Uzma since she'd tried to humiliate me in court.

"Uzma has disappeared." Ayet sneered, but I could see the fear behind those eyes now. Girls like her were dropping like flies and all she had to protect herself was a pair of scissors. "Just like Mouhna. People vanish out of the harem all the time. But Kadir only has three Mirajin wives. And then *you* arrive and two of them disappear. Do you think that's a coincidence?"

"No." Coincidence didn't have so cruel a sense of humor. Jin said that to me once. "But I know this wasn't me."

• ● •

IT TOOK ME until midmorning the next day to find Shira. She was sprawled across a throne of cushions in the shade of a huge tree, attended by a half dozen servants. Two women stood guard, while one laid cool cloths on her skin, another fanned her, and another massaged her feet. The last one was immobile but ready, sweat beading down from the lip of the pitcher over her hands. She looked flushed and uncomfortable standing just outside of the shade.

It looked like the future Sultan of Miraji already had his own court, even if he was really the son of a fake Blue-Eyed Bandit. And Shira was taking advantage of it for the few weeks left before she gave birth to him. She was a long way from Dustwalk now.

As I got closer, one of the servants standing guard blocked my path. "The blessed Sultima has no desire for company today." *Sure, the blessed Sultima looks as solitary as a hermit today.* It was on the tip of my tongue, but my Demdji side didn't recognize the difference between sarcasm and a lie. I had to satisfy myself with raising my eyebrow at the small crowd surrounding her. The woman didn't seem to appreciate the irony.

"Shira," I called out, over the servant's shoulder. She lifted her head enough to squint at me, sucking on a date pit between her fingers. She pulled an annoyed face but waved her hand.

"Let her through." The servant moved aside reluctantly. I gave Shira a pointed look. With another dramatic sigh she dismissed them. Everything from the wave of her fingers to the sprawl of her body looked lazy, but her sharp eyes never left me. "So that's what Ayet wanted scissors for," she said by way of greeting, as her court dissipated. "I *was* wondering. You know, I thought about cutting it all off back in Dustwalk when you slept a few feet away from me, but I actually worried short hair might suit you." She tilted her head. "I guess I was wrong."

"You got Sam to smuggle you in a pair of scissors?" I caught myself tugging on the ends where they didn't quite reach my shoulders and dropped my hand. But not before Shira caught the gesture.

"You're surprised?" She ran her hands along her swollen middle.

I supposed I shouldn't be. Shira and Sam might not be anything more than a means to an end for each other, but she was carrying a child that meant something to both of them. Still, I'd figured Sam was with us now. The notion that he might still be getting into other trouble we didn't know about while smuggling information for us made me uneasy. And I'd be lying if I said I wasn't just a little bit angry he could be so chummy with me, all while handing over tools to humiliate me with when I wasn't looking.

"Just be grateful I refused to procure her a knife. A slit throat would suit you even less than"—she waved a hand vaguely—"that."

I swallowed back a retort. I couldn't get into a war of words with my cousin just now. "What kind of game are you playing, Shira?"

"It's called survival." Shira extended a hand toward me, opening and closing her fingers like a demanding child. I took her hand, helping her sit up so she could look at me straight on instead of from the ground. She moved slowly, one hand splayed protectively over her middle. "I would do anything for the survival of my son."

"And what are you going to do if your son is born looking like Sam?" I challenged. "Blue eyes look awfully suspicious on desert folks, I can tell you that much."

"He won't be." She said it with such determination I could almost believe she could truth-tell it into existence even though I was the Demdji here. "I haven't done all this just to fail at the end. Do you know how *hard* I have worked to never be alone here in the harem since it became known that I was pregnant? I traded those scissors for a secret from Ayet that I can hold on to like a shield against her. Because I need to keep her away from me more than I need to keep her away from *you*. Don't get me wrong, you're an excellent distraction, but when I give birth it is *over* for his other wives unless they can give him a son, too. And they can't. And they all *know* that. So do you honestly think Ayet is above doing away with a pregnant girl to keep herself alive? I've seen what you'd do for survival, Amani. I know you understand."

Tamid bleeding out onto the sand. I pushed the image away. "Is that why Mouhna and Uzma have disappeared? Your survival?"

"Interesting." Shira sucked on the date pit between her teeth. "Here I'd been thinking Mouhna and Uzma were your doing. Seeing how you're rubbing elbows with the Sultan now. They weren't all that nice to you. And it looks to me like you've got the power to make them disappear if you wanted . . ."

If I was going to get rid of them, I'd start with Ayet. I shoved that thought away. "So if it wasn't my doing or your doing . . . Girls don't just vanish into thin air."

"Not outside of stories, at least." Shira ran her tongue along her teeth, a hint of worry creasing her eyebrows as she looked far away. Then her attention snapped back to me. "Let's say I wanted your help for something." Shira peeled one of the cloths from her forehead. "What would you want in trade?"

"Why should I help you?" I crossed my arms. "I've got your life to trade you if I need anything. What else have I got to gain from you?"

"You're a lot worse at this survival game than I thought you'd be." Shira sounded really and truly exasperated. Like we were kids again and I was too stupid to understand the rules to some game she'd made up in the schoolyard.

"Then why don't you tell me how you want to play?"

"I want information," Shira said. "I've seen you with Leyla. The scrawny princess with no charm."

"What about her?" I sounded defensive even to my own

ears. Whatever time I did spend in the harem was usually spent with Leyla. We took our meals together. Usually I ate while her food went cold as her whole attention spilled into whatever little mechanical toy she was constructing.

"She's up to something," Shira said simply.

"Leyla?" I failed to keep the skepticism out of my voice this time. "Is it all the toys she builds for children that makes you suspicious, or the fact that she's still almost a child herself?"

"She sneaks around." Shira reached for a fresh cooling cloth. "She leaves the harem and I don't know where she's going. I can't follow her. But you can."

"You want to know where she's going?" It was hard to take her seriously when she was making accusations against someone two years younger than us. "You're worried about *Leyla*?"

"Of course not." Shira rolled her eyes. "I'm worried about her brother." Prince Rahim. Ah. Now, that didn't sound so stupid. "Rumor has it he's in a great deal of favor with his father the Sultan." That much was true. I remembered what the Sultan had said about Rahim over duck that night.

"You think he might have designs on the throne." I suddenly saw where her train of thought was going. There was no love lost between Rahim and Kadir. I just didn't know if he hated him enough to snatch away his wives. But if he did, Shira had to be a target.

"Oh, look at that, you're not as dumb as you act." Shira draped the new damp cloth over her brow; it sent rivulets of water across her eyebrows and down her cheeks. "The rumor was that before Kadir proved he was able to conceive an heir"—she ran her hand along her swollen middle—"the Sultan was close to taking the throne from him. Rahim was said to be the favorite. Why else is he back in court when he's a commander in Iliaz?" That name sparked a pain in my side where the bullet scar was. Iliaz was a sore reminder of being shot. "If he does have designs on the throne and he's using his sister's knowledge of the harem to get to it, I want to know. And there *must* be something you want in return for information on Leyla and her brother."

Leyla had helped me when I needed to get free of the harem. She'd guided me in my first days in the harem. She'd saved me from Kadir's wives. She was as close to a friend as I was going to get inside these walls.

And I wasn't the girl who betrayed friends anymore. Only Shira didn't know that. She knew me as the girl from Dustwalk who left Tamid bleeding in the sand. Who would do what she needed to get what she wanted.

But the beginnings of an idea were sparking in my mind. I'd been looking for a way to shed my guard. This might be one.

"What if I needed a distraction? For the guards."

"A distraction like a pregnant Sultima pretending to go into childbirth weeks early?" She caught on quick.

"And folks in Dustwalk used to say you were as dumb as you were pretty." I couldn't keep it in, petty as it was. I was still angry with her about my hair.

"I made it through sixteen years in that town with a whole lot less trouble than you did," Shira pointed out. "Why do you need a distraction anyway? Are you trying to slip off to see a certain cripple of yours hiding in the palace? Because you ought to know, you might not get as warm a welcome as you're hoping for."

"Tamid is none of your business." My thumb jabbed at the metal under my arm painfully. It was almost a tic now. She'd found my sore spot. And the smile playing over her mouth said she knew it.

"Oh, so you do know he's here." She saw the answer written all over my face. "They took both of us. Because you left us."

"You wanted to go, because Fazim was done with you." That blow landed so hard that I almost regretted it the second the stricken look bloomed over her face. But she'd hit first. It was a bad idea to play chicken with someone who'd known you your whole life. Nobody came out a winner.

Shira pulled the mask of Sultima back on. "Say you'll bring me information about Leyla and I'll be your distraction." She stuck out one hand, heavy with new gold bangles. One of them no doubt already traded to Sam for the scissors that had cut my hair. They clattered impatiently together. "Do we have a deal?"

I took her hand and pulled her to her feet. "Let's go."

⁕ ● ⁕

I HAD TO admit Shira wasn't a half-bad actress. Her screams were so convincing I worried a few times that fate really was cruel enough to send her into labor the same moment she'd been faking it. She sure slumped on me heavily enough as we staggered through the gates of the harem. Her cries and sobs covered my words to the guard waiting for me. He was young and his eyes went wide with panic as his Sultima collapsed into his arms.

And just like that, Shira had shifted from my shoulder to his, grabbing all his attention and weighing him down as I staggered back, out of his view. For a second his head turned to follow me, remembering his duty. But a new scream from Shira quickly drew him back.

And then I was gone, running as fast as I could. Shira's screams faded behind me as I bolted across the courtyard and into the halls of the palace toward the mosaic of Hawa.

• • •

I'D BEEN TOLD that my eyes were the color of the sea on a bright day. That they were the shade of the desert sky. Foreigner's eyes. Traitor eyes.

But the truth was I'd never seen anything exactly the same color as my eyes until I met Noorsham. We had our father's eyes.

It was a foreign feeling for those same blue eyes to watch me from where Bahadur sat in the iron circle as I descended the steps into the palace vaults. He didn't speak when I reached the edge of the circle. Neither did I.

"You're not meant to be here, are you?" Bahadur finally spoke.

I'd only briefly wondered about my father in the years since I'd figured out that my mother's husband wasn't really my father. With my blue eyes, I'd always figured he was some foreign soldier, and I didn't want to be half-foreign. So I didn't think about it.

I'd been a bit more curious since finding out I was a Demdji. Since I'd learned my eyes were a mark my father left me along with my power. I'd wondered what I would feel when I finally came face-to-face with him, just the two of us.

I hadn't expected that I'd feel so much anger.

"I'm here because I need to know how to free you." I crossed my arms over my body, locking my anger inside my gut. There was no room for it here, no time. "Not because I especially care whether or not you ever get to go back to making me some more Demdji siblings who might destroy the world. But I might care if the Sultan uses you to burn all his enemies alive or bury their cities in sand."

"I only buried a city in sand once." He meant Massil, I realized. I'd been there, with Jin. Before I even knew what I was. Before we crossed the sand sea.

"You didn't think that might've been an overreaction?" I asked.

Bahadur watched me carefully, never blinking those blue eyes. "I don't need you to free me, Amani. I have existed since time began. This is not the first time I have been summoned and held by a mortal with more greed than caution. Eventually, I always find myself free, one way or another. When it happens doesn't matter."

"Well, it matters to me." The words came out more violently than I'd meant them to. "You might live forever. But our kind is known for running out of time. This is all the time I have. This is all the time any of us has. And we've got a war to win before it's over and lives that'll get lost earlier if we don't. So tell me, if you've been captured so many times before, are there words to free you?"

"There are, though I do not know them. But there is another way. One you already know. Because you know the story of Akim and his wife."

My mother had told me that story when I was young. I hadn't thought of it in years. Akim was a scholar. A wise man, but a poor one. Knowledge did not often bring wealth, no matter what the holy texts said. And in his studies he stumbled across the true name of a Djinni.

He used this to summon the Djinni to him and trap him in a circle of iron coins.

One day while descending to get more sugar from the basement, Akim's wife found the Djinni. She was much neglected by her husband in favor of his books. And so she was easily tempted by the Djinni. He told her that if she only freed him, he could give her the child she so desired.

So Akim's wife broke the circle of coins that held the Djinni and freed him.

At this point in the story, my mother would usually pause dramatically before throwing a handful of gunpowder in the fireplace and letting it explode. Releasing the Djinni without banishing him with the right words was like releasing a dam of fire.

The Djinni burned Akim's wife alive, and with her, the rest of the house.

"You killed Akim and his wife." It wasn't a question. It was a truth.

"Yes." There wasn't a hint of remorse there. "That might have been an overreaction," he admitted.

We would have to break the circle. Only this circle wasn't made of coins. It was set into the ground. We'd need something powerful. Something like gunpowder.

Bahadur was my father. I didn't think he'd burn me inside out. But there was no telling.

"There were other ways for you to learn how to free me. There are others with this knowledge." Bahadur watched me from inside the circle. He was inhumanly still. He didn't shift with restlessness or fiddle with his clothing as a human would. "Why did you really take such pains to come see me, Amani?"

"Do you remember my mother?" I hated myself for asking. For caring if he remembered one woman out of what I was sure were many in thousands of years. "Zahia Al-Fadi. From Dustwalk. Do you remember her?"

"I remember everyone." Did I imagine the change in my father's voice, the slight shift from the flat empty tone he'd addressed me with so far? "Your mother was very beautiful. You look like her. She was running away from her home. Through the mountains. She wouldn't have made it very far. She had enough supplies for a few days, not a real escape. She would have been forced to turn back or die eventually. I had sprung one of your people's ancient traps. The ones you set for the Buraqi. Crude, but, being iron, it did what it should have. Zahia found me in it. She released me."

"So why didn't you save her?" There it was. The question I'd really wanted to ask. Not whether my mother had made any kind of lasting mark on this immortal, powerful being, but why it hadn't been enough for him to save her life. How he could leave her with me, a child who she'd eventually die protecting, and not have the decency to step in. "You could have, couldn't you? You could have saved her."

"Yes. I could have appeared on the day your people chose to hang her and I could have cut her down and carried her away. Like in all those stories she told you as a child. But to what end? To keep her in a tower for a handful more years as my wife? She was mortal. Even you, who have a little bit of my fire, you will die, too, one day. Dying is what you do. It is the only thing that you all do without fault or fail. If I had saved her then, she would have died another way later."

"But she would have had longer." I could hear the tears in my own voice. "We could have escaped." *Her death wouldn't have been my fault.*

"You did escape," he said.

My temper snapped. "Don't you find it tiring not caring about anything, ever, for all eternity?" I didn't want to cry in front of him. I hated how much I cared if I cried in front of him. But it was too late. Through the tears, I could hear footsteps now, distantly. Soldiers were coming for me. "You let my mother hang. You let me and Noorsham face each other in war—both of us your children." The footsteps were behind me now. I was screaming. "You stood there while I held that knife against my stomach! You made us. Why don't you care about us?" And then it was too late. The soldiers were grabbing me, yanking me away from my father, dragging me up the stairs as I fought against them, still shouting.

Something pricked the side of my neck. A needle, I realized, in the hands of the guard. There was something on the metal. I knew instantly. Something to make me sleep.

Suddenly everything rushed to my head. I felt the floor tip out from under me. I would've hit the ground except someone caught me. Strong arms.

"Amani." My name punctured the storm of feelings. "I've got you."

Jin.

No. When my vision cleared, the Sultan was the one propping me up. He was strong. I tried to struggle, but with one swift gesture, his hands went under my knees and he lifted me into his arms like I was a child. He started to walk, each step shaking me closer to his heartbeat.

"I wanted—" I struggled for some half-truth to cover what I had been doing. My mouth felt fuzzy as the drugs kicked in, the motion making me sick.

"You wanted to see your father."

I waited for the punishment. For the anger. We passed out of the cool shade of the courtyard, through another set of doors. Tree canopies spread out high above me, the sunlight dancing through their branches.

"Yes," I admitted. And that was the simplest truth. I had wanted to face him. I'd wanted an explanation. I was swimming in and out of dreams now. I was starting to shake, too. Every part of me wanted to curl into the warmth of another body holding me. Like I was a small child being carried by my father.

But he wasn't my father. He was Ahmed's and Jin's and Naguib's and Kadir's and Rahim's and Leyla's and he was a murderer.

I was dimly aware that we were in the harem. I felt the Sultan kneel down and then I was being laid down in a bed thick with scattered pillows that crowded around me.

"Fathers often disappoint us, Amani."

TWENTY-SEVEN

There was a gift next to me when I woke up. It had been left while I slept, a conspicuously perfect tidy package of paper and ribbon amid the haphazard mess of pillows flung around my room. It swam into focus slowly as I emerged from the haze of drugs.

I pressed myself up onto my elbows, ignoring the pitcher of water next to me. No matter how dry my mouth was I wasn't about to risk something that might send me back to sleep. I poked at the gift with my foot cautiously, half expecting some trick from Ayet. When nothing exploded, I finally picked it up.

Blue fabric appeared below the paper. It was a khalat. The fabric was the color that the sea had been, the brief glimpse of it I'd had from the deck of the ship. And the hem and the sleeves were trimmed in gold stitching. When I looked at the embroidery closely, I realized it was the story of Princess Hawa, in tiny golden detail. On my right sleeve, where she rode the Buraqi across the desert, there were even tiny gold beads showing the dust kicked up under its hooves. It was the most beautiful thing I'd ever seen.

I'd hated wearing blue most of my life. It just made my eyes more obvious than they already were. It was one of a thousand reasons I'd loved the red sheema Jin stole for me. Only I didn't hate this khalat.

I slipped it on, reveling in the feeling of the fabric against my skin. It occurred to me that I'd never worn a piece of clothing that had never been worn by anyone else before. My clothes in Dustwalk were all castoffs from cousins. I'd bought secondhand clothes in Juniper City when I fled there. Even my clothes in the rebel camp were Shazad's. This was the first thing I'd ever worn that truly fit me. It had been made for me. And I knew what it meant.

It was forgiveness for going to see Bahadur.

• ● •

IN SPITE OF the Sultan's gift I didn't know what I might've lost by tricking my way out of the harem. The Sultan's trust, definitely. My freedom, too, probably. There was nothing stopping him from stripping away the freedom he'd given me with just a few words. He wouldn't be wrong not to trust me to leave the harem. I ran my thumb over the raised golden thread of the sleeve as I headed for the edge of the harem. I was working to destroy him, after all.

But even though my step slowed the closer I got to the gates I didn't meet any invisible barriers there. I passed through the archway that led toward the palace the same way I had yesterday, when Shira and I had been tricking our way out. Still, I didn't quite dare drop my guard just yet. But there was no battalion of soldiers waiting for me at the gates, either. Just one man, same as always. Only it wasn't a soldier. Or rather, it wasn't just any soldier.

Prince Rahim, Leyla's brother, wearing his commander's uniform, was waiting for me outside the gates, hands clasped behind his back. The one who'd spoken that day in court as if he was born on a battlefield. The one who'd watched me with dark eyes that made me nervous so often during negotiations. He didn't speak a whole lot, but when he did, it was always something worth hearing.

"Well, at least I know you won't be able to outrun me in that," Rahim said, taking in my khalat. He offered me his right arm.

"Isn't being my escort a bit below the station of a prince?" I asked, pushing past him and heading toward the now-familiar path to the council chamber. He fell into step behind me.

"I managed to convince my father that you might need someone with a little more experience to watch you. Possibly someone bright enough to know that the Sultima isn't due to give birth for weeks. Not a bad trick, though."

"Am I supposed to be flattered," I asked as we passed under a blue-and-white mosaic archway, "that I get a commander watching me?"

Rahim's lip twitched up. "You don't remember me." It wasn't a question.

We've never met before. It was on the tip of my tongue. But it wouldn't go any further. I looked at him curiously out of the corner of my eye as we walked, my mind racing to place him. I thought he looked familiar when I first met him but I'd chalked that up to his resemblance to Leyla. And to their father. "Then again"—he tapped the place my scar was, by my hip—"you did go down awfully fast with that bullet."

A blast. The smell of gunpowder. A shooting pain in my side. Then darkness. In Iliaz. A soldier behind Jin raising a gun, finger already on the trigger.

I knew him all at once.

I stopped short. "You shot me in Iliaz."

"I did." Rahim kept walking, apparently satisfied now that we were such old friends with a history of gunpowder and near death between us. "Although, luckily for us, it looks like I didn't do an especially good job of it. So here's hoping you can forgive me and we can start over."

He knew. He'd seen me in Iliaz, which meant he knew who I was. He knew I wasn't just a Demdji from the Last County.

Rahim realized I wasn't following him anymore. He stopped, too, turning back to face me. "I had my suspicions as soon as I saw you at court that day. But I wasn't sure until my brother's charming wife decided to . . . expose you a little." He looked embarrassed saying it, at least. But I still felt the heat of the old humiliation prickle across my skin. "I knew as soon as I saw the scar on your hip."

"So why am I walking to a council meeting with you instead of hanging by my ankles in a cell telling your father all the secrets of the Rebellion?"

"We hang people by the wrists now instead of the ankles," Rahim said. "Keeps prisoners more lucid if all the blood doesn't rush to their head." I couldn't tell if he was joking.

"You don't have much of a way with words, anyone ever tell you that?"

"That's why I'm a soldier, not a politician. Or I used to be." Rahim drummed his fingers across the sword on his belt. "My father and I aren't on the best of terms."

"And selling out the Blue-Eyed Bandit to him wouldn't put you back in his good graces?" I asked.

"My father doesn't have any good graces. He's just very good at pretending he does when it suits him. Which puts you and me on the interesting same side of hating my father."

I watched him carefully. This had to be a trick. Some ploy of the Sultan's. Only I was at his mercy. He didn't need to send me a fake traitor; he could just order me to tell him everything I knew about the Rebellion. *You're lying to me.* I tried it out, but it wouldn't get past my tongue. He wasn't lying. But he wasn't telling the whole truth, either.

"What is it you want? From us being on the same side, that is."

"A new dawn." Rahim flicked one of the tracts that had fallen from the sky out at me between his fingers. It was creased from the pocket of his uniform. "A new desert."

"Are you saying you want to put Ahmed on the throne?" It seemed Shira was dead wrong about him having designs on being the new Sultan.

"I'm saying I want my father off the throne and I can help you. On one condition. I want you and your rebellion to get my sister out of the palace."

"Leyla?" Little round-faced Leyla who made toys for the children in the harem and who reminded me of my littlest cousins even though she had a decade on them. "Why? She's as safe there as anywhere else and she told me herself it could be a lot worse."

"If I'm right, she's in danger."

I thought of Shira, asking me for Leyla's secrets, watching her out of the corner of her eye, ready to take down any threats to her child before they could do the same to her. But somehow I didn't think that was what Rahim meant. Men weren't usually aware of the politics of women.

"What kind of danger?"

He didn't answer the question. "You're a Demdji. I've seen you do your little trick every day in my father's war meetings. So, am I telling the truth?"

"Yes." It came out easily.

"Am I trying to trick you?"

I tried yes again, but it wouldn't come out. "No."

"Can you trust me?"

I don't trust anybody in here. "Yes." But I wasn't giving up that easily. "But I want to know why. A lot of folks don't get along with their fathers." I'd learned that firsthand the day before in the vaults. "Doesn't mean most want them dead."

"Fathers don't usually send their children away to die when they're twelve years old, either." Rahim said it so matter-of-factly it surprised me. "Or at least, that's what I've heard. I don't have much of a point of comparison." Rahim started walking again and this time I moved with him.

"How'd you get sent away?" I kept pace with him. "Seems like half the harem would kill for a chance at escape." Me included.

Rahim didn't answer right away and when he did he picked his words carefully, deciding what to tell me and what to keep from me. "I tried to crack Kadir's skull open with my bare hands." I hadn't been expecting that answer.

"And how'd that work out for you?" I asked.

Rahim caught my eye out of the corner of his. "That's what you ask me? Not why?"

"I've met Kadir, I can guess why."

"I wanted to take something from my father the same way he did from me. Women vanish out of the harem every day. Most children just have to accept when their mothers vanish without a word. I wasn't prepared to be one of them." I remembered how calm Leyla had seemed when she told me that her mother had been taken away from her. She shared a mother with Rahim. I had to imagine he hadn't been quite as placid as his sister. "It took three soldiers to pull me off Kadir. His nose is still crooked, you'll notice."

He scratched the bridge of his own perfectly straight nose, hiding a laugh. It was the Sultan's nose, I realized. That was what made him look like Ahmed.

"So how come you're not dead?" I asked.

"It looks bad for the Sultan to kill his own sons. Especially after he already had so much of his family's blood on his hands. So my father decided to send me away to war to die quietly, or at least somewhere he wouldn't hear. My father underestimated me."

"You became the commander instead."

"The youngest ever. And the best." He wasn't bragging, I realized. He sounded like Shazad. Easily certain that he was right. "Now, will you get my sister out?"

I shouldn't be doing this. It ought to be Ahmed or Shazad or even Jin here negotiating with Rahim. This wasn't a job for the Blue-Eyed Bandit. But right now I was the only one here. "That depends what you've got."

"How about an army?" That wasn't a bad opening offer. "The Emir of Iliaz is due to arrive for Auranzeb. He has as little love for the Sultan as I do and the fighting force of Iliaz nearly matches the rest of Miraji's combined. A word from me and that army can be your Rebel Prince's." We'd arrived.

The Sultan looked up as we entered. "Ah, Rahim, I see you managed to get Amani all the way here without her running off." It was a gentle barb. "Congratulations. No mean feat, it would seem."

It would take one word. Just one to his father now, telling him that I was the Blue-Eyed Bandit. And just like that, everything would be over. He could betray me before we'd even made an alliance.

But he didn't. Rahim stepped aside, letting me in the room ahead of him, like a gentleman. As I passed he said in a low voice, "I can get your rebellion an army. Tell me I'm lying."

I didn't say anything as I took my place behind the Sultan. I could only speak the truth.

TWENTY-EIGHT

"You know, where I come from, there's an ancient expression, passed down from parents to children." Sam spread his hands like he was seeing it written out in big letters floating in front of him. "'Don't ally with people who have tried to kill you.'"

"You just made that up." Shazad leaned back against the wall that she and Sam had just walked through. She was the only person I knew who wouldn't be even a tiny bit ruffled by being pulled through a wall by a man we only barely trusted.

"I did." Sam winked at her. "But you can't deny it's a good policy."

"Shazad nearly slit your throat when you first met," I pointed out. "And you're here." I was keeping one eye on the gate into the garden, in case anyone wandered our way. It was morning and the sunlight glaring down on our meeting, with the rest of the harem awake, made me nervous. But dawn had beat Sam back to the rebel camp with Rahim's offer. And Shazad wasn't willing to wait another day.

"Well, that's just because Shazad's charm trumps all wisdom." Sam winked at Shazad, who ignored him. "Besides, I'm just the messenger. That's how I'm going to avoid getting shot."

"What?" He was doing that thing where he talked nonsense again.

"It's an Albish expression, it means—never mind." He shook his head, fighting a laugh. It was one of those rare smiles on him that looked real, not calculated or designed to charm me. The ones that actually made me like him.

But Shazad's eyes had a faraway look. Like she was working through a problem quickly in her mind. I already knew where she would get to. She'd been telling Ahmed for ages we needed a real fighting force. And now I was offering her one. She was taking it seriously enough to come here herself. She hadn't even made a comment about my missing hair, even though I knew she'd noticed.

"We can trust him?"

"He's hiding something," I said. "He won't tell me why he's frightened for Leyla, for one. But he hasn't lied to me. He hates his father, and he has no designs on the throne." No matter what Shira suspected, that truth fell easily off my tongue.

"What do you think?" Shazad turned to Sam. He looked taken aback for a moment by the full force of her attention.

"I think it's not my place to make decisions about whom you should trust," Sam said, recovering. "I mean, you obviously have excellent taste." He gestured to himself.

"She meant about being able to get Leyla out of the palace."

"Oh, well." He cleared his throat. "I can walk her out of here. As easily as I walked you in." Sam's smile looked pasted on again. "Only, in my experience, someone usually notices when princesses go missing from palaces."

"You've got a lot of experience kidnapping princesses, do you?" Shazad said.

"I'll have you know that princesses find me irresistible." He leaned in conspiratorially. "I'm still working on bandits and generals."

"He's right," I interrupted before they could descend into arguing again. "Wives seem to disappear from the harem all too often, but the daughters seem to be a little bit more closely watched. She can't just vanish; she'd be missed."

"And then you'll be questioned. Rahim will get found out along with the rest of us and we'll lose any shot of getting both you and that Djinni out of the Sultan's hands." Shazad was steps ahead as usual. I'd told them about my encounter with my father. Or at least as much of it as mattered. That the only way we were going to get him free was if we broke the circle. We'd need some kind of explosive. And even I knew you couldn't exactly blow something up in this palace without people noticing.

"So we've got to strike a single blow." Shazad was working it through out loud. "We get everyone out at once or no one at all." She was right. If we got my father out, we lost any chance of helping Leyla and Rahim escape. If we walked the two of them out of the palace, my father was left in the Sultan's hands. So we'd have to get all three of them out at the same time. One shot was all we were going to get. One shot for three targets.

"Auranzeb," I said, drawing Shazad's and Sam's eyes my way. "We can use Auranzeb as our cover. This isn't the sort of thing that you and I and a handful of good luck can pull off on our own. We'll need backup, and from what I've heard, there's enough strangers coming in at Auranzeb that we ought to be able to get a few more in."

Shazad considered it for a long moment. Neither Sam nor I spoke as she ran through past celebrations at the palace in her mind. "Auranzeb could work. We could get Imin in easily. Hala, too, if she gets back from Saramotai in time. Maybe two or three more, without pushing our luck too much." She could see the celebration laid out in front of her like a battlefield, and I could tell she was looking for openings and escape routes. A smile started to dawn slowly across her face. It died suddenly as she looked up. "What about you?"

She was right. It wasn't three people who needed to be freed from the palace. It was four. I couldn't stay here. No matter what blow we struck at Auranzeb, everything could be undone if I didn't leave with them.

We could break the circle. But so long as the Sultan had me in his control he could just summon my father back. They could abduct Leyla and Rahim to safety and win a whole army. But the Sultan could make me give away every name in the Rebellion before they could strike.

"Let's cross that bridge when we come to it." I tried to sound easy about it. "For now, I'll tell Rahim that we'll take his deal. We've got a while before Auranzeb yet."

Sam started talking again, laying out the plan. But Shazad wasn't fooled. We were both thinking the same thing.

I couldn't be left behind at Auranzeb. At least not alive.

TWENTY-NINE

War was building. Everybody could feel it. Even those of us who hadn't been alive for the last war, when the Sultan took his throne.

And nobody seemed to know exactly what side they were on yet.

Inside the palace, I saw it in the rising tension in the council room. I saw it in the way the Xichian general's hand slammed down, knocking over a pitcher of wine that drenched the papers sprawled across the table. I saw it in the number of guns and swords that surrounded the Albish queen when she arrived at the palace, taking the place of her elderly ambassador in negotiations.

Having Rahim as my guard made getting around a whole lot easier. After a few days I understood why the

Sultan had allowed Rahim to talk his way into the role of my protector. He and Kadir despised each other. And the Sultan had made clear he didn't approve of Kadir's eyes on me by putting another one of his sons as my shield.

Rahim fed me more information that made it back to Sam as fast as anything. I was able to warn him when the Sultan's city guard thought they were closing in on the new location of the rebel camp in the city. They never found anything. And two days later they had brand-new intelligence that would lead them in circles at the opposite end of Izman.

The news that the Sultan was negotiating with foreigners slipped out somehow, too. Nobody had forgotten how much they hated Gallan rule. New tracts circulated in the streets reminding the Mirajin people what they had already suffered at the hands of our occupiers and our Sultan. But when the soldiers tried to trace where they might have come from, they wound up chasing their own tails.

The Rebellion was rising up like bursts of gunpowder all over Izman. Most exploded in neighborhoods that had suffered under Gallan rule. A NEW DAWN was burned onto walls in the night. Bombs made in kitchens were flung at soldiers in the streets. Folks had started painting Ahmed's sun on hulls of ships. The Rebellion was spreading, further than it ever had before. The Sultan's army came after the culprits. But the names of those they planned to arrest were in the Rebellion's hands before the army's. By the time men in uniform got to their doors, their homes were empty.

I brought Sam a report of thirty Izmani citizens languishing in prison, due to be hanged as examples of what happened when you supported the Rebellion. Last time, it'd been a whole tavern arrested when a bit too much alcohol had them standing on the table chanting Ahmed's name. The Rebellion had managed to get half of them free of the noose before the trap opened below their feet. The rest had choked to death slowly. The Sultan's hangman had made the rope too short, deliberately. So they'd suffer.

So Ahmed would watch them suffer.

We'd get there first this time. Or we hoped we would.

We had the people. We had the city. But there was no taking the palace. Not without the army Rahim had promised us. And there were a whole lot of fires to keep burning until then. Fires we'd started, for the most part. Sam told me it felt like we were trying to plug holes in a wicker basket. I couldn't remember when Sam had started saying *we* instead of *you*.

"There's a plan to rebuild the factory in the Last County," I told Sam when we were a few short weeks away from Auranzeb. "The one outside Dustwalk. Once they've reclaimed our half of the desert." As a gesture of goodwill to the Gallan, of future willingness to continue to provide them with weapons in their war against any other country that didn't share their beliefs. "They're sending a small party down there, soldiers and engineers, to assess the feasibility of it."

"What am I missing?" Sam might be a posturer most

days, but he wasn't stupid, either, even though he behaved like he was half the time.

"Dustwalk is where I'm from," I said, leaning back against the tree. I was tired. Cool air ran its fingers through my hair, lulling me. "I was born there. It might not be that nice a place, but it still deserves better than this."

Sam nodded. "So we make sure their party never makes it back."

He listened to me rattle off the rest of what I'd gathered since I last saw him. But when I was done, he didn't leave straightaway. "You know," he said, still leaning on the wall across from me, "I heard a lot of stories about the Blue-Eyed Bandit. Granted, some of them were about me. I particularly like the one about how the Blue-Eyed Bandit stole the necklace right off a woman's neck, got caught, and still managed to seduce her."

"Is there a point to this, or are you just trying to remind me that the longer I'm in here, the more sullied my reputation becomes?"

"My point," Sam said, "is that none of those stories said the Blue-Eyed Bandit was a coward." That got my attention.

"Oh, so is your point actually that you'd like to get punched in the face?"

"If I'd known the famous Bandit, who fought at Fahali and struck fear into the Sultan's soldiers, was this lily-livered, I probably wouldn't have taken her reputation. It's bad for business to be known as a cowardly bandit. And you should take my stealing your reputation as high praise. I could easily have chosen to be the Blond Bandit or the Dashingly Handsome Bandit or—"

"I swear to God, Sam."

"No, really, go ahead and tell me I couldn't rightfully call myself the Dashingly Handsome Bandit—eh, truth-teller? Tell me I'm not handsome, I challenge you. See? You can't."

"You really seem to think I'm not going to break your nose."

"See"—Sam wavered back on track—"cowardice is the only reason I can possibly think of that makes any sense of why you *still* haven't gone to speak to the person who might be able to get that little piece of bronze under your skin out so that you can leave the palace with us."

I sobered. "Shazad told you about Tamid." I felt a little bit betrayed by that. "It's not that easy."

"It's certainly harder if you don't try. And for all my many feats of bravery, I'm deeply afraid of your general, so I sincerely don't want to bring back the news that you haven't even tried yet. Because guess which of us will get blamed? It's not the one she actually likes."

"Shazad likes you fine," I said offhandedly. "Why do you even care?"

"She depends on you. You don't see it, but she does." For just a moment he actually seemed serious. "And I don't think you're selfish enough to die on her just to avoid an uncomfortable conversation. Besides, if you die, I can't be in two places at once anymore."

I ignored that last part. Sam annoyed me even more than usual when he was right.

I DRAGGED MY feet as we left the negotiations the next day, forcing Rahim to drop back with me.

The Sultan caught his eye, a question mark there. A spark of suspicion neither of us could afford. Rahim saw it, too. He leaned in toward his father, whispering low in his ear. "The Gallan ambassador has the look in his eye of a man about to do something very foolish." He wasn't wrong about that. I'd torn down three of the Gallan ambassador's lies in the meeting, as he got angrier and angrier. "If he were one of my soldiers, I would have him run drills until he cooled off. As he isn't, I think it's best to let him go ahead."

The Sultan considered me before nodding, letting me and Rahim drag back behind the rest.

"There's a—" *Prisoner* wouldn't get past my tongue. "A boy. From the Last County. He only has one leg."

"I know him."

"Can you get me to him?" I pressed.

"Do you want to tell me what you need with him badly enough to risk going places my father doesn't want you?"

"Do you want to tell me why your sister so desperately needs to be saved from the harem?"

Rahim scratched the edge of his mouth, hiding a smile. "This way."

. ● .

I STARTED TO recognize this part of the palace as we came to the foot of a long winding staircase. My first day in the palace, I'd clambered down this, body aching with fresh wounds, fighting legs that couldn't help but obey the Sultan's order to follow him.

I heard voices as we got closer to the top. I recognized Tamid's instantly. It was a voice that went with laughing ourselves stupid after we'd been sent out of the school-room for misbehaving. With nights falling asleep while he read me the Holy Books after my mother died. The other was soft and female. A part of me wanted to turn back. To avoid sticking my fingers in this wound. But Sam had been talking sense for once. I had no right to be a coward in this rebellion.

I pushed the door open.

Two startled heads looked up at me. Tamid was sitting on the edge of the same table I'd woken up on. The sight of him was so heartbreakingly familiar that for a moment I wanted to rush to him and pour everything out. His left pant leg was rolled up to his knee. Or where there ought to have been a knee.

Instead there was a bronze disk hiding the place where his leg ended. It was secured to the scarred skin with a leather strap. There was nothing attached to it. The rest of Tamid's leg—the hollow, polished bronze—was in Leyla's hands, as she sat across from him. She gaped at me and Rahim with wide eyes, mouth moving open and shut in silent panic.

Well. I hadn't been expecting *that*. I didn't think Rahim had, either.

"Don't tell Father!" she blurted out finally. It was exactly the wrong thing to say. Though the fact that she was suddenly flushed from neck to chin wasn't doing her any favors, either. "I was just here to make sure it wasn't . . ." She trailed off.

"Squeaking," Tamid filled in even as Leyla made a noise that sounded an awful lot like a squeak herself. "The joints were squeaking. Leyla came to tune my leg up. Seeing as she built it and all."

"I bet she did." Rahim eyed Tamid in that way that fathers and brothers eyed boys who looked at their daughters and sisters wrong. So this was the secret Leyla was keeping, which Shira wanted so bad. Shira thought she was sneaking off to plot against her with her brother, but she was just an infatuated girl leaving the harem to see a boy.

It might've been funny if I wasn't certain that Shira could use this, too. More than once I'd gotten a beating for sneaking off to see Tamid. And I wasn't a princess. And I hadn't been in love with him. Was this why Rahim was so desperate to get Leyla out of the palace? Would she get punished for this as much as Tamid would? But there was something else passing between the siblings, skipping straight over Tamid. "You designed that, Leyla?" Rahim gestured at the articulated bronze limb in her hands.

She nodded nervously. "I thought—it might be useful." So she didn't just make toys for children in the harem. That was impressive, I had to admit.

But Rahim was angry in a way I didn't wholly understand. "Come on, Leyla, I'll walk you back to the harem. There are some things we need to discuss anyway." Good, it was long past time to tell Leyla about the plan for Auranzeb. The holiday was only a handful of days away now and she needed to know we were getting her out of there.

What followed was the longest, most awkward minute of my life as Leyla reattached Tamid's leg. Everybody was trying their hardest not to look at anyone else. The sound of mechanisms clicking together punctuated the silence as Leyla worked. When she was finally, mercifully done, Rahim practically dragged her out of the room, remembering me at the last second. "Amani, I'll come back and get you."

Tamid and I didn't speak as Leyla followed her brother out. The awkwardness stretched between us long after their footsteps had faded.

"I'd love to be able to storm away, but, you know." Tamid tapped on his leg, below the knee. A hollow sound reverberated back. I winced. "It seems like you ought to be the one to leave. Out of respect."

"Tamid—"

"Do you want to know how I lost my leg, Amani?" Tamid cut me off.

"I know how." I remembered that last dark night in Dustwalk clearer than any of the hazy days that came before.

"No." Tamid slammed his hand down against the table underneath him. I might've flinched if I wasn't so used to the sound of gunfire aimed at me. "You don't. You saw Naguib shoot me and then you left. You weren't there while I lay screaming in the sand. You weren't there when Shira started striking bargains, saying she could help find you. That she knew you better than almost anyone, that she knew where you'd go. Better than *almost* anyone." His hands shook as he clenched them into fists. "You didn't see them tear me away from my mother to take me with them, too, on the off chance I might be useful. You weren't with me on that train that rattled its way to Izman." I had been on that train. I'd seen Shira on that train. I'd kissed Jin on that train. Not ever imagining Tamid might be on board, too.

"Naguib said he'd left you to bleed out in Dustwalk. I thought you were dead, Tamid." The words I'd comforted myself with for months since that day sounded like a poor excuse now he was standing in front of me in the flesh.

"So did I." His right hand was a fist against his thigh now. "I thought I was dead while I writhed in agony and when I got here and the Holy Father said it was infected. That it would have to come off. You weren't here when they sawed off my leg, Amani. But now you are. Let me guess: you want my help. You want me to tell you which little metal bump under your skin is the one you need to cut out to escape." My fingers pressed so hard against the metal on my arm I wondered if it would bruise. Tamid knew me well enough to read my silence.

He pushed himself off the edge of the table. I pretended not to notice the slight wince as his freshly oiled leg hit the ground, or the way he steadied himself for a fraction of a heartbeat before he started to work his way around the small space, tidying up even though it was already spotless. Straightening bottles so the labels all faced out in a perfect line, making them clink with every twist. He slammed a door shut that led toward a small side chamber, where I could see a bed. "You're predictable as anything. You know, back in Dustwalk, you always figured I didn't sleep all that well. But that wasn't true. It was just that, if I knew you'd gotten a beating, I'd lie awake waiting for you to crawl through my window asking for something."

I hadn't known that. I swallowed the tears that were welling up in my throat. "I don't believe you hate me as much as you want me to think you do."

"How do you figure?" Leyla had left her tools behind, and he started lining those up. He sounded disinterested.

"Because if you really hated me, you'd have turned me over to the Sultan as a rebel by now." I saw the truth of it as soon as I said it. "Instead, you pretended not to know me the day I got here. You've been helping the Sultan a whole lot of other ways." This truth came out like an accusation. It was easier to accuse him as a rebel against an enemy than as a girl against an old friend. "You gave him the knowledge he needed to control Noorsham and to control me. And enough first language to capture a Djinni. But you didn't give me up." I saw him wince at the mention of the Djinni. I seized on it. He might not care enough about me anymore to help, but I knew Tamid. If you cut him he'd bleed holy words. "He's going to be able to kill a whole lot more people with a Djinni on his side, you know."

"I know."

"And that's all right with you, is it?"

"Do you mean because it's unholy, or because of how I feel—" Just for a second his fingers slipped, sending a small circular instrument skidding off the table and to the ground. "Because of how I felt, about you?"

How did you feel about me? But that wasn't a fair question when I already knew the answer. I saw it now, written all over him.

"He's our Sultan, Amani. Our job is to obey, not to question."

"You don't believe that." A simple truth slipping out. I retrieved the metal tube off the floor and handed it back to him. "Not you who went to prayers every single day. You don't believe keeping a Djinni prisoner is the right thing."

"It doesn't matter what I think. I've scoured the books in the Sultan's library and I couldn't find the words to release a Djinni, only to bind one—" He caught himself, looking at me straight on now. He ignored the metal tube I still had in my hand, refusing even that peace offering.

"You only know the words to bind them, not to release them?" I imagine my father trapped under the palace forever as we mortals did what we did best: died, and then forgot about him, trapping him there for all eternity.

"What do you care?" he asked.

"Turns out I'm in the business of saving lives now."

"Well, it's a shame that wasn't your line of employment ten months ago when you left me to die."

"They did this to you, Tamid." I held my ground. "Not me."

"Yes, they did," he said. "But it was you who left me behind."

I didn't have anything I could say to that.

Tamid tilted his head farther away from me. On most men I knew, the dark hair would've fallen in front of his eyes, hiding them from me. But Tamid's hair was always perfectly combed against his head. "What do I have to say to make you leave, Amani?"

That was all he needed to say.

THIRTY

I leaned against a pillar in the courtyard at the bottom of the steps. Back on steady ground, pressing my hands back into the marble hard. I forced my tears to dry. I forced myself to remember I was a desert girl. I didn't have water to spare. And this wasn't any kind of place to show weakness. The palace was as dangerous as the desert at night.

Rahim had told me to wait for him. I wasn't meant to be without a guard. I didn't know how long his talk with Leyla would take. But, while it was awful tempting to go snooping around, I couldn't risk getting caught unaccompanied. It would blow Rahim's cover, too. And I doubted the Sultan would forgive me a second time after I'd gone to see Bahadur. As soon as that thought shot across my mind I wondered what it was doing there. It shouldn't matter; I'd never minded getting into trouble before. It was because my head might wind up on the chopping block, I told myself. It was because losing his trust would mean losing access to the information we needed.

So I waited, trying to ignore the itch below my skin to move, to do something, listening to the sounds of the fountain and the birds who populated this part of the palace, trapped here by clipped wings, just like the ducks in the pond. The sudden rattle of a door was as loud as a gunshot.

I reacted on instinct, plastering myself behind the pillar into the shadows. It didn't matter who was coming; I couldn't get caught alone. A fraction of a heartbeat later a door on the other side of the courtyard slammed open. The crack of the handle hitting the stone was so loud it almost covered the woman's cry. I couldn't ignore the itch anymore. I peered around the pillar.

Two figures in Mirajin soldiers' uniforms were dragging a girl between them through the door. She thrashed violently against their grip, screaming so loudly I was sure someone was going to come running. The birds, I realized, remembering that day in the menagerie, what Ayet had said—no one would be able to hear her screaming over the birds. My fingers twitched for a weapon. For a gun. For something to help. But my hands were empty and bound by the Sultan's orders to do no harm. And even I knew I couldn't take on two soldiers with no weapon.

Then they emerged into the sunlight and I saw the thrashing captive's face.

Uzma.

Kadir's wife. Who had made it her duty to humiliate me that day in court and had vanished into thin air afterward. Uzma's eyes were as blank as polished glass, like any spark that had ever lived behind them had been snuffed out. I knew exactly where I'd seen that same look before. Back at camp, on Sayyida after Hala rescued her from the palace. Only Sayyida had been a spy. What had Uzma possibly done to be tortured out of her mind?

They vanished around the corner, the screams fading quickly.

I didn't move right away. I could feel myself torn between following them and staying out of trouble, just once in my life. Trailing two guards and a screaming woman was a surefire way to get myself caught. Besides, it might not be the best way to figure out what was going on. I glanced at the door where they had come from. It was almost definitely locked. But it might not be. It would be stupid and reckless to dart out into the open and risk getting seen regardless.

Well, it looked like I was stupid and reckless, then.

My feet carried me in one short burst across the courtyard. The dying sunlight bounced off the door strangely. As I got closer, I realized why. The door was made of metal. Only someone had painted it to look like wood.

And it was humming.

I stretched my fingers tentatively toward the door. I

could feel the hum building like a pull underneath my skin as I inched closer. My fingertips grazed the door. It was like touching fire without getting burned: all of the power of it, none of the heat. Tiny needles started at my fingertips and traveled up, making my breath hitch and my heart race even though I was standing still.

Suddenly, a pair of hands grabbed me and slammed me into the metal hard, sending pain shooting up my body, an explosion of feeling across every bit of skin that I had.

And then I was staring up into the cruel face of the Gallan ambassador. Behind him was Kadir. Before I could speak a word, the man drove a hand into my middle, pinning me still, knocking the air out of my lungs.

"In my country," the Gallan ambassador said in his thick accent, "we hang demons' children by the throat." His hand tightened on my windpipe, forcing me up straight. "But I don't have any rope with me."

God, the metal door at my back was starting to hurt now. I could feel my thoughts blurring and my vision going black as his hand tightened around my throat. My hands scrabbled uselessly against the back of the hand gripping my windpipe. There were a dozen things I should've been able to do to fight back against him. I could've clawed the soft spots inside his wrists, jabbed at his eyes, driven my leg into his groin. Except the Sultan had ordered me not to harm anyone. I was going to die. The panic started in earnest now. I was going to really and truly die.

And then suddenly I could breathe again. Air flooded back in a gasp as the hand released my throat. I wrenched myself away from the wall, falling to all fours. I knelt there for three long breaths, waiting to remember how to breathe. A crack like breaking bone sounded, and a cry of pain. I looked up in time to see Kadir reel back, clutching his nose.

Over him, blazing with the setting sun at his back, stood Rahim, his brother's blood on his fist. The light blurred his features so I almost couldn't recognize him. He looked like every hero I'd ever imagined from the old stories: the First Mortal facing death instead of running from it; Attallah outside the walls of Saramotai, outnumbered; the Gray Prince against the Conqueror. He didn't look real.

And then he dropped to his knees across from me and he was human again. "Amani." He tipped my head back, checking me with the sure hands of someone who knew a battlefield injury. "Are you all right?" I could see behind him now that there were two soldiers with him and they were holding the Gallan ambassador away from me. "Amani," Rahim pressed. "Talk to me or I'm taking you to the Holy Father."

"I'm fine." My voice came out scratchy but still mine. "I'm sure I have something to wear that'll go well with the bruising." Rahim helped me to my feet. I touched my throat, sensitive where the ambassador's fingers had tried to crush my windpipe.

"Soldiers." Kadir had recovered enough from his broken nose to speak. He pulled his hands away from his face though blood was still gushing across his mouth.

"Release the ambassador. Take my brother away instead."

The soldiers didn't move. Instead they both looked at Rahim for instructions. I noticed their uniforms then. They were Mirajin, but instead of the standard white and gold of the palace they were emblazoned on the chest with the same blue stripe as Rahim's. They were from his command in Iliaz. The emir must've arrived. This was why he'd been late coming back for me. He'd found his men.

"Stay where you are." Rahim gave the order with a controlled ease I'd never seen in him before. I realized this was where he truly belonged, among soldiers, not among politicians in a palace. He was a soldier through and through. No, not a soldier. A commander.

Kadir's gaze flicked frantically between the soldiers and Rahim. "I said let him go. I order you as your Sultim!" His voice, thick with the blood of a broken nose, rose with anger.

They might as well have been deaf. Rahim calmly took his time pulling off the jacket of his uniform and placing it around my shoulders before addressing his brother. "These are my men, brother. They follow their commander, not their Sultim.

"Escort him back to his chambers," Rahim ordered the soldiers holding the Gallan ambassador. "Before we start an international incident. Amani, let's go."

Rahim had already turned away when Kadir pulled the pistol from his belt. I cried a warning, but too slow. The gun went off, hitting one of the soldiers. It was a sloppy shot, the shoulder instead of the chest, but it was enough to make his grip slacken.

The Gallan ambassador wrenched himself free of the soldier's grip. The foreigner grabbed the blade on his belt, diving for the wounded soldier. Rahim moved quickly, his own weapon already drawn, meeting the ambassador's blade in the air in one easy gesture before it could run his soldier through.

Kadir was still raging. He raised his gun again, pointing it straight at Rahim's back. I moved as fast as Shazad had taught me.

He had a loose grip on the gun—I couldn't tell if it was anger or just bad training. I might not be able to hurt him, but I didn't have to let him kill Rahim, either. I slammed my palm flat against the place where the grip of the gun was sticking out from his fist. The gun went off, the bullet hitting the wall, as his fingers flew open. The gun jolted upward, out of his hand. I caught it easily before it hit the ground, flipping it around in my fingers with familiar ease.

I aimed the pistol at Kadir. He went still, staring at me over the barrel of the gun, like he couldn't quite understand what had happened. "You're not going to shoot me."

That was true enough. I couldn't. I had orders against it. But he didn't know that. I pulled back the hammer on the pistol all the same. "Want to bet your life on that?" My fingers were shaking from trying to pull the trigger. And I was that ten-year-old girl again, holding on to a too-big rifle for dear life. Knowing that if I dropped it, I'd be helpless.

"Drop the gun, Amani."

Even if I hadn't known the voice, the tug in my gut at the order would've given him away.

No. I fought against it.

But my arms were already moving without wanting to. I fought it until my arms screamed. The gun clattered to the ground.

When I turned around, the two soldiers were standing at sharp attention, the injured one clutching his shoulder. At their feet the ambassador's body was slumped in the grass. His hands, which had been wrapped around my throat a few moments earlier, were limp now. The blood-stained sword was in Rahim's hand.

And, surveying the whole scene, from my discarded gun to the blood spreading out from under the ambassador's body, his expression unreadable, was the Sultan.

• ● •

THE SULTAN'S FINGERS drummed out a pattern on the ivory and wood chessboard inlay of his desk as his eyes traced the line of my throat. It was going to bloom into an impressive bruise shaped like the Gallan ambassador's hand in a few hours, but for now, it still felt raw and red. We were in the Sultan's study. The same one I'd stolen those papers from a few weeks back. There was a weight to the room with the Sultan in it that hadn't been there without him. Like all the maps on the walls and spread across the desk were extensions of him. Jin had once told me I was this desert. I wondered if he'd change his mind if he saw in here.

I'd been allowed to sit. Ordered, more like. But his sons stood at attention behind me. The Sultan ordered me to tell him what had happened. He wanted the truth, he said. And that was what I gave him. I left out Leyla, but I couldn't avoid Tamid. The Sultan would question why I'd been alone in the palace when I wasn't supposed to be. I tiptoed around that part of the story as carefully as I could, my heart in my mouth. One wrong word and it could all be over. *I asked Rahim to take me to the Holy Father. He left to give us privacy.* I tried not to let relief leak into my words as I slipped on to the next part of the story without any questions from the Sultan.

When I finished speaking, no one said anything for a good few moments. I had a strange feeling like I was back in school, in trouble along with Tamid for something stupid I'd done, facing the anger of a teacher. The three of us lined up in front of the Sultan like we were quarreling children, not soldiers and spies fighting for a country. The Sultan was silent as the last of the sunlight outside faded. Through the huge window I could see the lights of Izman start to flicker to life.

My mind kept running back to the same thought: the gun. The Sultan had seen me holding a gun to his heir's head. Holding it like I knew what I was doing. Holding it like the Blue-Eyed Bandit would hold a gun. He had to know I was more than just a desert girl now.

But I didn't try to explain it. The guilty always talked first. Rahim and I were both smart enough not to interrupt the Sultan's silence.

"Father—" Which made us both smarter than Kadir.

"I didn't give you permission to speak." The Sultan sounded calm. Unnervingly calm. Deceptively calm. "You are a thief, Kadir." Kadir bristled, but the Sultan was already talking again. "Don't disagree with me. You tried to take something of mine." He gestured to me. I hated being referred to as belonging to the Sultan. But I couldn't help the surge of satisfaction over being worth more to him than Kadir right now. "And trade it for the support of the Gallan."

"She's not human, Father!" Kadir's voice rose. He sounded close to stomping his foot in rage like a child.

"Everyone knew that, brother," Rahim interjected. His calm just made Kadir angrier. "If you only just figured that out, I have some concerns about the intelligence of our future ruler."

The Sultan held up his hand. "If you think now is the time for bickering, with a foreign diplomat dead in my palace, then I have questions about _your_ intelligence, Rahim." He nodded at Kadir to continue.

"The negotiations were lasting forever. And the Gallan were never going to make a new alliance with us so long as you were so blatantly flaunting a half-human thing in violation of their beliefs. They came to me"—his chest swelled with pride—"and demanded her death before they would negotiate any further."

The Sultan didn't raise his voice, but even I shrank under the look he gave Kadir. And it wasn't even directed at me. "They demanded her death because she is making lying to me about their resources and their intentions more difficult, and revealing that the Gallan empire is stretched thinner than they would like us to think." He spoke slowly, carefully, like he was explaining something to a child. "And they came to you because you have *clearly* been itching to get your hands on her in some way for weeks now."

Kadir sneered, flopping into the other chair petulantly as his father spoke.

The silence that followed was worse than the glare. "I didn't give you permission to sit."

Kadir started a laugh, like he thought his father might be joking.

"Stand up," the Sultan ordered calmly. "Take an example from your brother for once. Perhaps I should have sent you to Iliaz instead of him."

I remembered what Rahim had told me—that the Sultan had sent him to Iliaz to die. I understood the threat implied in his words. But it was lost on Kadir.

"All that military training didn't help him beat me in the Sultim trials." Kadir stood, shoving the chair so it clattered angrily against his father's desk, shifting some of the papers from the edge onto the floor. "So, what, are you going to put him on the throne instead of me now?"

"The Sultim trials are sacred." The Sultan kept all his attention on his son, ignoring the disrupted papers on the ground. "Overturning them would turn the people more against us than they already are. You'd have to die before we held another Sultim trial, Kadir."

"So unless you're going to do everyone a favor . . ." Rahim muttered.

I snorted under my breath, drawing the Sultan's gaze. I stifled it too late. The Sultan had already noticed the connection between me and Rahim. But his gaze shifted away again without comment.

"The Gallan king is due to arrive tomorrow, in advance of Auranzeb." The Sultan's fingers returned to drumming out the same pattern. "You will come with me to meet him, Kadir. And you will tell him the same story I will. That the ambassador went into the city without a guard and was killed by rebels on the street. Do you understand?"

Kadir's jaw worked angrily for a moment. But if he thought his father was going to give in first, he was badly mistaken. "Yes."

"Good. You are dismissed."

Kadir slammed the door behind him on his way out, like an angry child.

"That lie may not be wise, Father," Rahim said. "If it looks to the Gallan like you can't control your own people—"

"Then we may look weak. I had considered that and I don't in fact need a lesson in political strategy from my son." The Sultan cut him off impatiently. "If we are *lucky*, it may give the Gallan soldiers who come with him some incentive to help keep the peace in Izman leading up to Auranzeb. The only alternative is to turn *you* over to Gallan justice. Perhaps you'd prefer that."

Rahim's jaw screwed itself shut.

"Rahim saved my life." I couldn't keep quiet any longer. The Sultan's attention swung to me and immediately I regretted talking. But I was already going now. "He ought to be rewarded, not *threatened*." The Sultan didn't speak and I didn't back down. I couldn't afford to now. "I figured I was here to tell the truth."

Finally he seemed to check his temper. "She's right. Your soldiers did well today, Rahim." Somehow it still didn't sound like praise. "At your orders, no less." More like veiled suspicion.

"Yes, they did." Rahim was as smart as his father. He didn't offer excuses for his men obeying his orders over Kadir's. He kept his answers short. Like a good soldier would. Or a traitor. Waiting to be dismissed.

"The rebels raided an incoming shipment of weapons at the south gate yesterday." The Sultan spoke again. "How do you think they knew where those were, Rahim?"

I was sure the Sultan could hear my heart speed up. I knew exactly which shipment he meant. They knew because Rahim had told me and I'd told Sam. Did he suspect us? Was it an accusation? Or was he asking his son's military advice as a peace offering? I prayed wildly that he wouldn't turn the question on me, that it wouldn't be in this moment that we lost everything.

"There is a war going on." Rahim kept his eyes straight ahead, over his father's head, like a soldier at attention. "Your soldiers are unhappy. Unhappy soldiers drink and they talk." He chose his words so carefully that they were true. That I could have repeated them without hesitation. Though not carefully enough not to insult his father's rule.

"We killed two rebels in the raid," the Sultan said. My stomach clenched. A list of possible rebels I knew cascaded through my head. Imagining them all dead. Suddenly I desperately wanted to run to the Weeping Wall and Sam and find out who. Find out if I'd never be seeing Shazad again. Or Hala. Or one of the twins. But the Sultan wasn't watching me. His gaze was on Rahim. Waiting for a reaction? "Next time, I want one alive for questioning. Your soldiers from Iliaz seem well trained. Have Lord Bilal designate half of them to join the city guards on patrol." My shoulders eased in relief.

"As you wish, Father." Rahim didn't wait to be dismissed. He just offered his father a quick bow before turning on his heel.

And then it was just me and him. A long moment passed in silence. I half thought the Sultan had forgotten me. I was about to point out that I hadn't been dismissed when the Sultan spoke again.

"You're from the end of the desert." It wasn't what I'd been expecting.

"The very end," I agreed. There was nothing after Dustwalk but uninhabitable mountains.

"They say your people's blood runs thicker with the old stories than elsewhere." That much was true. That was how Tamid had known how to control Noorsham. How to trap a Djinni. All the things that the north had forgotten. "Do you know the stories of the Abdals?"

I did.

In the days before humans the Djinn made servants out of dirt. Simple creatures made from clay and animated only when they were given orders by a Djinni. Good for nothing except to follow orders from their immortal masters.

"The Abdals were as much their creation as we are, and yet the holy texts refer to humans as the first children of the Djinn. I understand why now." He riffled his hands through his hair as he leaned back in his chair. It was an exasperated gesture that looked so much like Ahmed it made me homesick. "The Abdals didn't have it in them to be nearly so difficult as children."

"Abdals would be a fair bit harder to leave a country to, though." It slipped out before I could bite my tongue. I was too comfortable with him. He might look like him, but he wasn't Ahmed. But the Sultan surprised me by laughing.

"True enough. Though it would be easier to govern over a country full of Abdals. I wouldn't have to constantly try to convince them I am doing what is best for them." One of the maps pinned up on the wall showed the whole world. Miraji was in the middle. Amonpour crowding our borders on one side. Gallandie looming over the north, swallowing countries as it went toward Jarpoor and the Ionian Peninsula and Xicha, the country that had sheltered Ahmed, Jin, and Delila for years. Albis a fortress holding against Gallandie's expansion in the sea and Gamanix on land. It was a big world. "The people of Miraji are rising up in protest of the Gallan, of the Albish, of the Xichian, of all our foreign friends and enemies."

I swallowed and felt the pain in my throat from where I'd almost just been choked to death by one such foreigner. "So don't renew an alliance with them."

I knew I'd overstepped. I knew as soon as the words left my mouth. But the Sultan didn't rage at me the way he had at his sons. He didn't sneer at me. He didn't try to explain to me like he had when we sat across from each other over dinner in the next room.

"You're dismissed, Amani." And somehow that was worse than anything else he could've said.

THIRTY-ONE

"I think they're fading." Leyla inspected the marks along my throat. They'd bloomed into a glorious necklace of purple fingerprints by the next day. "They ought to be gone by Auranzeb." That seemed to be everyone in the harem's biggest worry on my behalf. That my near death would clash with my khalat. Across the garden I could see two women whispering behind their hands, casting me looks. Good God, I hated this place. Leyla's gentle hands dropped away. "I really think you ought to go see Tamid, though; he might be able to give you something for that."

"I'll survive."

Her big eyes were wide with something unspoken.

"What?" I asked.

"Rahim told me, about Auranzeb. About getting out. And just . . . I wouldn't want to leave Tamid behind."

I started. Had Tamid told her about me? That I'd done exactly that? Was that a jab meant to hit me in that old wound? But there didn't seem to be any kind of malice behind her words.

Leyla bowed her head, brushing her hair nervously behind her ear, avoiding my gaze. She was in love with Tamid. Or at least she thought she was. She was still shy of sixteen. And she'd spent her whole life trapped in a palace. Tamid had to be one of the first men our age she'd ever encountered who wasn't a brother to her. No wonder she'd think she was in love with him.

And he was clever and he was kind. No wonder she'd really fall in love with him.

And she was right. I couldn't leave him behind a second time.

● ● ●

WHEN SAM WALKED through the wall that night he had a split lip and he was walking like he might've bruised his ribs. It was the one sign he brought with him that things were getting close to boiling point on the outside. He only ever gave me good news from the Rebellion. That Saramotai was safe. That an ambush had been successful. That the delegation meant to inspect the remains of the factory in Dustwalk had never made it that far.

"You want me to break out four people from this palace now, and I only have two hands." Sam scratched at the scab on his lip. I slapped his hand away. He was going to make it scar.

"Three people."

"Four," Sam said. "I'm counting you. How long have you known me now? Do you really still underestimate the prowess of the Blue-Eyed Bandit?" He flung his sheema over his shoulder. It snagged on one of the branches of the Weeping Wall tree.

"Is it just me, or have you gotten more ridiculous?" It was so like Sam to try to dodge anything even a little bit serious. Like the real possibility I might not be able to escape at Auranzeb with them.

"Ridiculously smitten with you." He'd managed to extract the sheema with some dignity. I realized he was trying to make me laugh. And it was working.

"You're not smitten with me, you're—" *In love with someone else.* It almost slipped out, but I stopped myself in time. Sam spent a lot of time bragging about conquests. I was more than sure half of them were invented. But I'd never heard him talk about anyone in particular that he actually cared about. I searched his face now, looking for a hint of something truthful under there. But I was the one with traitor eyes, not him.

"You sound awfully sure of yourself, my beautiful friend." He was all swagger as he planted his hands on either side of me against the tree. "Want to bet on that?"

He was going to kiss me, I realized. Or he wanted me to think he was. To prove some stupid point.

"Your lip is bleeding." I reached out to where the split was, but Sam caught my hand playfully as he leaned in a little closer. I didn't feel anything. Not the way I did when Jin looked at me the way Sam was. Or was pretending to. No rush of heat invading my whole body. The world around him was still as sharp as it had been before he touched me. He wasn't Jin. But he was here when Jin wasn't.

The laugh was unmistakable. Our heads snapped around, pulling us apart before his mouth could find mine.

Ayet was in the gateway to the Weeping Wall garden, head thrown back to the sky in a laugh, like she was thanking the heavens for the gift that'd been sent to her. Seventeen years of desert instincts reared in my chest. Only I wasn't in the desert now. And this was a different kind of danger.

"You know, in all this time looking for a way to keep you out of my husband's bed," Ayet said, "I never thought it would be as incredibly *obvious* as this. You're just one of the hundreds of women in the harem *stupid* enough to take a lover."

"Ayet—" I took a step forward and she took one back. I stopped, keenly aware that she could bolt like a startled animal any second and run to sell me out. "Don't do this. It's not—"

"Oh, it's very much too late to negotiate, Amani." And then she whipped around, racing back into the harem.

"Well," Sam said. "This seems like it might be a problem."

•••

IT WAS A matter of hours until the Sultan and Kadir were back from greeting the Gallan king. From lying to him and saying it was the Rebellion who had killed his ambassador. A handful of hours to stop Ayet before she got the chance to spill the news to her husband. Stop her or get everyone out.

Sam was making a run for it back to the rebel camp for help. I still didn't know where it was and I was grateful for that. If the Sultan ordered me to tell him, my ignorance would buy them some time at least. But they still had to be prepared to run.

In the meantime, I was going to try to stop Ayet.

If there was one person who was a bigger threat to Ayet than I was, it was Shira. And she was still standing. I needed to know how. Shira bartered in information. She had something that kept Ayet off her back. And I needed it.

I burst back toward the core of the harem, breathing hard. Something was different. I felt it immediately. I spotted Leyla, dark hair gathered up off her neck, staring across the garden, worrying her thumbnail. "Leyla." I dashed across to her. "Listen to me. Ayet just found out— it's complicated. If she speaks to your father or to Kadir, we're not going to be able to get you out of the palace at Auranzeb like we planned. So you need to be prepared to leave tonight if I tell you to. And I need to find Shira," I summarized quickly. "Do you know where she is?"

Leyla looked startled as I spilled the information out at her. But she grasped on to the last question. "The Sultima? Her baby's coming. Someone has sent word to Kadir."

That was it, I realized. That was the restless wildness filling the harem. Damn. Bad timing. "Leyla, where is she?"

Shira's screams got louder as I burst down the hallway. There were a handful more harem women, sprawled in prayer outside the door. A servant woman rushed out, carrying a blood-soaked cloth. Shira's screams followed her out. Then the door slammed shut again, muffling them.

And then, suddenly, silence dropped like a stone in Shira's rooms.

I held my breath. Trying to count out heartbeats as the silence stretched. Waiting. Waiting for it to be broken by something. A shout. An accusation. A midwife stepping out to let us know that Shira hadn't survived.

It was a baby's wail that ended it.

I let a sigh of relief escape. It wasn't even all the way out of my lungs before there was another scream.

Not Shira's this time.

I moved like a shot for the door, tearing it open. Shira was collapsed in a heap of sweaty hair and bloodied cloth, clutching a small swaddled bundle to her chest, her knees pulled up around the baby, like she could protect it. The three women around her were staring like they'd been turned to stone. A fourth was slumped against the wall, hands clasped over her mouth, shaking.

I took another step forward, until I could clearly see the small bundle Shira was holding. The baby didn't have

Sam's blue eyes. He had blue hair. Like Maz's hair. A bright violent blue. Like the hottest part of a flame.

This wasn't Sam's son. It was a Djinni's. Shira had given birth to a Demdji.

Suddenly Leyla and Rahim weren't the most important people to get out of here. "Shira." I dropped by her side. "Can you walk?"

Shira finally lifted her eyes from the baby. "I can run if I've got to." Whatever polish the city'd given to her accent, it was gone now. She sounded Dustwalk through and through. She pushed herself off the bed slowly, but without so much as shaking. I'd never seen Shira look so impressive before. She'd had an air about her when she stood as the Sultima, in her fine clothes and unearned arrogance. But that was different from the fierceness she wore now, wrapped in a ruined khalat and sheets, holding her son.

"Let's go, then."

The lack of guards in the harem had made Shira scared for her life since she conceived, but it might be what saved her life now. There was no one to stop us as we pushed our way out of her rooms. Mothers, sisters, wives, sons, servants—they all gaped mutely, unsure of what to do. Though I was sure somebody'd had the sense to run for help.

We didn't have much time. But we had some. My heart was racing.

"Shira." I glanced around a corner. It was a quiet garden thick with flowers, and empty now. We were close to the Weeping Wall. I just prayed that Sam would be there to help us when we got there. "I need to know. What did you hold over Ayet all these months? What did you have that kept her away from you?"

Shira stumbled, and I caught her. "I'll tell you if you get me out of here alive," she joked. Even now, with death on her heels, Shira was still the bargainer of the harem.

"Shira, please."

"A husband," Shira said finally. "Another husband, outside the walls of the harem. She put poison in his food after he broke two of her ribs. She bribed her way though her . . . inspection." She tried to put it delicately. "A few words of truth in the Sultim's ear and I could've made her disappear. Silk rope around the throat in her sleep and disposed of in the sea. That's how they go when the Sultim wants to make them disappear quietly." I clung to the words. I had to get to Ayet before she got to Kadir. I had to let her know I could ruin her in return if she tried to blow my cover.

We were almost at the Weeping Wall. So close to freedom.

I heard the familiar click of pistol holsters against belts. The sound of boots hammering into the ground.

It was moments before we were surrounded by men in uniform with the Sultan and Sultim with them.

Kadir shoved his way through the ranks. He surged toward Shira. I started to move between the Sultim and my cousin. But two soldiers grabbed him first. Kadir started to fight them. "Stand *down*. She's my wife. And a liar and a whore." He was struggling. "It is my right to do with her as I see fit. And I am going to make her bleed for her treason."

Shira shifted her child against her chest, staring down Kadir, as fearless as I had ever seen her. "I did this to stay alive. Because you are a vicious, stupid, impotent man."

Kadir lunged for her. The Sultan gave a flick of his wrist and Kadir was pulled back by the soldiers again. "Take my son somewhere he can regain a level head."

"My *wife*—" Kadir started, but the Sultan cut across him.

"This is business for rulers. Not petty husbands."

I could hear Kadir's protests as he was dragged across the garden.

"You know what the penalty is for violating your marriage vows, Shira." The Sultan's voice was calm as they disappeared. I had an image of a moment like this, fifteen years ago: Delila being carried away as the Sultan wrapped his hands around Ahmed's mother's throat.

"Kadir will *never* father a child. He can't. And I reckon you know that, too, Your Exalted Highness." Shira pulled herself up straight. "I did what I had to do for our country."

"I believe that some part of you thinks that you did," the Sultan said. "I always liked you, Shira; this is a shame. You were cleverer than most. I've heard that you like to strike bargains. I have one last one for you. Your son's life, in exchange for the name of the Djinni who fathered him."

"Shira—" I warned. But it was too late.

"Fereshteh." She raised her chin in defiance, oblivious

that she had just given the Sultan another Djinni's true name. "He told me he would make me the mother of a ruler. A true prince. A great Sultan. A greater Sultan than Kadir could ever hope to be."

I had never seen uncertainty on the Sultan's face before. But I thought I saw it there for just a moment. And I couldn't blame him. A truth out of a Djinni's mouth was a powerful thing. If Shira wasn't lying, she might be holding a future ruler.

"Fereshteh," the Sultan repeated. "Good. Take the child, Amani." It was an order and I was already fighting my arms' urge to obey.

"What will happen to Shira?" My arms were moving without my meaning them to. The Sultan had never looked so much like Ahmed as he did in that moment. It was the same face Ahmed wore when he told me something he knew I didn't want to hear but that had to be done anyway. "Please," I said. Shira was whispering to her son, making him promises she wasn't going to be able to keep. Clutching at the only moments she was going to have with her child. My mind was racing, trying to find something. An escape, anything. But we were trapped. Some things there was just no way out of. Her child was in my arms. "Please don't kill her."

My cousin's eyes met mine. Her lips parted. The Sultan's words came back to me. Shira was good at making bargains. And she had one last thing to trade. One last coin she could try to buy her life with. Me. She could offer the Sultan the Blue-Eyed Bandit and the whole Rebellion in exchange for her life.

She could destroy me now. I didn't have anything.

"His name is Fadi," she said. Fadi was our grandfather's name. The name our mothers had before they were married.

"Lock her away," the Sultan ordered dispassionately, already turning. Already forgetting her now that she was just another useless girl in the harem. "Amani, come with me. Bring the child."

Fadi wailed louder in my arms the farther away we got from his mother.

THIRTY-TWO

THE TRAITOR DJINNI

In the days that only immortals remembered, the world was changeless. The sun did not rise or set. The sea had no tides. The Djinn had no fear, nor joy, nor grief, nor pain. Nothing lived or died. Everything just was.

Then the First War came.

It brought with it dawn and dusk. It brought with it high seas and new mountains and valleys. And more than anything, it brought mortality.

The humans were made with a spark of Djinni fire, but they were not endless. And that seemed to make all the difference in the world. That changed everything. They didn't just exist. They were born and they died. And in between they felt so much that it drew the immortals to them, though they were only sparks to the Djinn's greater fires.

As the war ended, the Djinn of the great desert gathered and gazed across a changed world. The land that had been theirs. The war had ended. The mortals had served their purpose. They had fought. They had died.

Then they multiplied.

The Djinn looked on incredulously as the humans built walls and cities and found a life outside of war. They found new wars to fight. The Djinn wondered if they should let the humans carry on. The Djinn had made the mortals; now the war was over, they could unmake them if they so chose.

Some of the Djinn argued that humanity had served its purpose. Humans would only cause trouble. Better to burn them now, all at once. Return them to the earth from which they had been made before they overran it.

The Djinni Fereshteh agreed with this. The world was simpler before mortals. He had watched his own son, born to a human woman, survive a dozen battles with the Destroyer of Worlds' creatures, only to die in a brawl with another mortal. And though the Djinn had quickly forgotten to be afraid of death when the Destroyer of Worlds was defeated, they were slower to forget this new thing the humans called grief. It seemed like a feeling too great to contain for a Djinni who was eternal.

But the Djinni Darayavahush argued against destroying them. He said humans should be allowed to live. They had earned their right to share the earth by defeating the Destroyer of Worlds. They were remarkable; they had fallen in waves on hundreds of battlefields but had somehow continued to stand in the way of the Destroyer of Worlds' armies. Such will to survive should not be ignored.

The Djinn argued as years passed and a generation of humans passed into another. They argued as cities rose where there had been none before and new rulers succeeded old ones for the throne. As the mortals slowly forgot the time of the Destroyer of Worlds.

Finally, when the last of the mortals who had lived to see the First War passed into death, the Djinn gathered at the home of one among them who had claimed an old battlefield as his domain, a place where the earth had been ripped into a great valley where no other Djinn wished to live. They decided on a vote. They would cast a black stone into the water if they believed it was best to end mortality, and a white stone to let the mortals live.

The stones piled up, black, then white, one after another, until the two sides were exactly equally matched and only the Djinni Bahadur was left to cast a vote that would decide the fate of all of humanity.

Fereshteh felt sure that Bahadur would cast for his side. Bahadur, too, had watched a mortal child of his die. A daughter with blue eyes and the sun in her hands who the humans called a princess, one of their foolish words to pretend any one of them was more powerful than another. Surely Bahadur had felt the same pain Fereshteh had. He would want to end it just as much.

And yet when Bahadur finally cast his stone, it was as white as bone. Fereshteh's side lost. And thus all the Djinn made an oath—that none among them would annihilate mortality. And because they were Djinn that oath was the truth.

Centuries passed.

Fereshteh didn't know how many, for only those whose days were numbered counted them. He tried to stay away from the humans at first. But they were constantly changing. It was hard not to watch them. Every time Fereshteh thought he had grown bored of them they did something new. They made something new, sometimes out of nothing. Palaces rose higher than before. Train tracks carried them across the desert. Music sprang seemingly from their minds to their fingers. And every so often Fereshteh could not resist temptation anymore. But time taught him ways to avoid the grief. He never looked over the children he gave mortal women. He had no interest in watching little pieces of himself be destroyed by the world his fellow Djinn had allowed to continue.

Then there came a day when Fereshteh heard his name being called with an order he could not disobey. And so it was that he came to stand prisoner in front of a Sultan and a Demdji. A Demdji holding a child that Fereshteh had marked as his own, though he had already forgotten the child's mother. It was easier that way.

But he remembered all his children. And he remembered the pain he had felt when each of them died. So when the Sultan held a knife above this child, and asked for the names of his fellow Djinn, he surrendered easily. He could not watch this spark of himself die.

He gave Darayavahush's name first. He gave the Sultan only the names of the Djinn who had been stupid enough to think that humanity was harmless and worth saving. The ones who had cast a vote to let them live. Half the Djinn in the desert.

And he laughed as, one by one, they became trapped by the creatures they had chosen to let live.

THIRTY-THREE

The Sultan had been dangerous enough with one Djinni. Now he had an army of them. They might've created humanity to fight their wars, but there were stories of what happened when immortals entered the wars of men, too. Cruel conquerors who leashed them in iron and turned their powers against helpless nations. The heroes who won Djinn over to their side by sheer virtue and flattened their enemies. No matter what the circumstances, immortals were unstoppable.

My thoughts were in a storm as the Sultan led me back to the harem, one firm hand on my spine. There was too much to do and not enough time.

I had to get news of the other Djinn to Sam. And I had to make sure Fadi, who was screaming in my arms, was safe in the palace. I had to find a way to save Shira. And I had to do it before Ayet betrayed me to the Sultan. Shira giving birth had distracted everyone, but it was only a matter of time now before Ayet got Kadir or someone else to listen to her and the Sultan found out I was the Blue-Eyed Bandit. And then it would be over. I had to do everything I could to help before it all ended.

"Father." My thoughts were interrupted by Rahim. He was striding down the hallway toward us, his collar unfastened, hair disheveled, trailed by two servants. Dawn was just breaking but he looked like he hadn't had any sleep all night. He would be in trouble too when Ayet sold me out. What was he still doing here? "A word."

He drew his father to one side, out of earshot from me, leaning in close to say something rapid-fire under his breath. I was suddenly nervous. He was still here, and there was no way Rahim would let Leyla's life be put in danger. He'd choose her over me in a second. I had no doubt about that. Same as I'd do for any of the Rebellion over the two of them. I didn't begrudge him that. But it hadn't ever crossed my mind that he might save his own skin by selling mine out instead of waiting until Ayet could do it for us.

"Forgive me." The two servants with Rahim stepped in front of me, blocking my view of my so-called ally. One was reaching for Fadi in my arms expectantly, her head bowed.

"No." I pulled Fadi closer to my pounding heart. I wasn't going to hand him over. I might not be able to do anything else before I got found out, but I wasn't about to let another Demdji get swallowed up in the harem and disappear.

"He needs to be fed." The second servant spoke up, a note of exasperation in her voice. "Now's not the time to be difficult." It was the closest I'd ever seen to insolence in one of the harem servants. It made me look twice at her, but in spite of her voice, her head was bowed low in respect. She'd said it loud enough for the Sultan's eyes to dart over.

"Hand it over, Amani." The Sultan gave me a distracted order as he continued his conversation with Rahim. I tried to catch his eye over his father's shoulder, but Rahim might as well never have known me for all the attention he was giving me.

"It's all right." The first servant, too, sounded familiar somehow, although I was sure I'd never seen her in the harem before. "We'll take good care of him."

In that moment, as the Sultan turned his back entirely on us, the first servant dared to lift her head fully and I was face to face with Hala.

She was hiding her golden skin from sight with an illusion but it was still umistakably her. It was unsettling; she was both wholly familiar and completely strange. Her high, arrogant cheekbones and long nose were unmistakable, but she looked younger and more vulnerable without her golden veneer.

And the other servant. I looked closer now. Her eyes were wrong. They weren't the desert dark they ought to have been. Instead they were the color of liquid gold.

Imin.

My heart sped up. Something was in motion. But I wasn't sure what.

Imin winked at me. It was so quick that even if the Sultan had noticed it would've been mistaken for a blink. I loosened my grip on the baby in my arms as I passed him over to Hala. I'd been given an order, yes, but there weren't many people in the world I'd trust with Fadi more than Hala. She might not scream maternal instinct, but Demdji took care of their own.

I didn't have time to watch them disappear into the harem before Imin grabbed my arm. "Walk quickly. And don't look back."

"What's happening?" I asked under my breath as we moved fast down the hallway. Too quickly, I realized. If the Sultan took his eyes off Rahim for even a second, he'd realize I was all but running.

"Something that passes for a plan on short notice, that's what. Take a right here." We turned the corner and then we were out of the Sultan's view. Rahim wasn't betraying us, I realized; he was a distraction. I felt suddenly ashamed for believing he'd turn on us so easily. By the time he was done talking to his father, the Sultan would think I was back in the harem. If he wondered at all.

"Fadi, the baby," I started. "The Sultan will look for him, you need to—" Imin's eyes rolled to the sky, cutting me off.

"Believe it or not, we *can* make a stab at executing a

plan without you." Imin slowed down as we left the cool of the marble palace walls and passed into one of the huge, sprawling gardens. It was only early morning, so the unrelenting heat of the day hadn't set in yet, but I still squinted against the sun after the dark of the vaults.

We stopped, ducking behind a tree, out of sight of anyone who might walk by. Imin yanked the servant's clothes off in one quick gesture. Underneath was a palace guard's uniform that had been made for someone a whole lot taller and broader. Imin started unrolling the sleeves and loosening the belt buckle, making room for a new body. "We can't just walk a baby out of the harem. Someone would notice he was gone. Unless the Sultan thinks he's dead, that is. If, say, half of the harem were to see Kadir drown the baby in a fit of rage, for instance."

Hala could do that. That's why they'd risk bringing her into the palace. All she'd have to do was take Fadi back to the harem and then play the scene out in the heads of whoever happened to be nearby. She could even put it into Kadir's head if she wanted to. She could make him believe he'd really killed him. And even if she didn't get to Kadir, who would the Sultan believe, a dozen wives and daughters in the harem who saw it happen, or a son with a violent temper? Especially when the child was nowhere to be found. "Then my dear sister can just walk him out the palace door to safety under the cover of an illusion." Imin shook out the long sleeves so they fell over the dainty hands of her female form. "It's almost easy."

Imin was right. This could work. We could save Fadi.

"And his mother?" I asked, anticipation building in my chest. "My cousin Shira—how do we get her out?"

"We're not going to—" Imin started, then quickly stopped herself before she could truth-tell the future. But I knew what she had been about to say. *We're not going to save Shira.* It didn't matter whether she said it or not; it seemed like it was already decided.

"Why?" I asked. "If we can get Fadi out, why not Shira? Sam has clearly just walked you and Hala through the walls, he could—"

"The prison is iron bars all the way through; there's no way for Sam to walk in there and walk her back out." Imin didn't meet my eyes. "But I can walk *you* in there to see her before she's executed." So that was what the guard's uniform was for. "She's asking for you."

"That's not a good reason not to save her." Imin was holding the truth back. I just didn't know why. "If Hala wanted to, she could get a soldier to unlock Shira's cell and walk her out under the Sultan's nose. Which means there's some other reason saving Shira's not part of the plan." It wasn't a question. "Why?"

Imin straightened. She was drowning in the guard's uniform. She looked liked a child playing dress-up in grown-up's garb. But her face was wise beyond her eighteen years. "Because we haven't given up on saving *you* yet." Understanding hit me all at once. Because if Shira disappeared, I might as well turn myself in. An infant could disappear believably, but Shira's death couldn't be faked near so easy. If she was gone, she'd be counted as escaped. And sooner or later the Sultan's eyes would turn to me, the girl who had already tried to help her once. And he would ask questions and I would sell out the whole Rebellion with a word.

It was Shira or everyone else.

"But Ayet—" I started to tell her that I was already done for. That I'd been stupid and careless and gotten myself caught. That it was over for me anyway.

"You don't need to worry about Ayet." Imin started to shape-shift, to fill out the uniform. He was a head taller than I was in a few seconds.

"What do you mean?"

He didn't answer, scratching at his chin angrily as it filled out with a beard. "I hate these things." Whichever soldier's shape he was stealing had a voice for giving orders, deep and ponderous. "Navid has been growing a beard since we fled camp so now kissing him is like rubbing my face against burlap. You're lucky Jin's always been clean shaven, you know."

"At least Navid doesn't occasionally vanish to parts unknown on you," I offered back. I pressed my palms against my eyes, pushing back against the exhaustion. "So we're supposed to just let Shira die?"

"The way it seems to me, one of you has to," Imin said. "If you really wanted me to, I could save her. But I'd have to kill you here and now so that you couldn't betray us." He drummed his fingers along the knife at his belt. I knew Imin meant it. He'd do anything for this rebellion, just like any of us. And that'd include killing me. "You can do a lot more for the Rebellion alive. And she—" Imin hesitated, like he didn't want to say it. But he was a Demdji. He had to be truthful. "She can do a lot more by dying."

• ● •

EVEN IN SUMMER it wasn't warm in the palace prison. I felt the chill sink into my bones as Imin and I descended the worn stone steps. The guard at the door hadn't even tried to stop us after one glance at Imin in uniform. We would be left alone down here.

Shira was shivering in a corner, wearing the same clothes she'd given birth in, her back turned to the door. I took a step toward her, but Imin stopped me, one hand on my shoulder. He pointed toward the cell neighboring Shira's.

It took only a few steps closer to the cell to realize that what I'd thought was a pile of discarded clothing was moving. Just barely. Only the faint rise and fall of breathing. It was a woman, collapsed on her side, dark hair spilling across her face. But I knew the khalat she was wearing, the color of roses with stitching the same shade as over-ripe cherries. It was the same one she'd worn that day in the menagerie.

"Ayet?"

"It's no good." Shira still had her back to us. "She doesn't talk anymore. She might as well be dead except she's still breathing." Like Sayyida and Uzma. Driven mad. This was what Imin meant by saying that I didn't need to worry about Ayet betraying me. Slowly Shira turned over, work-ing her way to sitting with the help of the wall. "You wanted to know where girls disappear to." She waved one hand in a gesture so grand she might've been showing off a golden-domed palace. "This is where we go. I told you I had nothing to do with it." She dropped her arm; it fell limp to her side. "Good news is, only one of us has to die today."

"Shira—"

"Don't try to comfort me." Her tone was the same one she'd used when we shared a floor in Dustwalk, dripping with disdain. But she didn't fool me that easy anymore. She was a desperate girl. "And *you*," she shot at Imin, who was hovering behind me on the stairs, "you don't have to watch us like that, you know. I'm already condemned to die. What else am I *possibly* going to get up to between now and sundown?"

Well, being condemned to death sure hadn't made her any more polite. I thought about telling her that Imin was on our side. But that wasn't what really mattered to Shira. I gave Imin the tiniest nod and he retreated back up the steps, out of earshot.

"So." I slid down the wall next to the cell so we were sitting side by side. Seventeen years, I couldn't think of a single time we'd sat together. Not in Dustwalk. Not in the harem. It'd been us facing off against each other every single time. Now we were sitting side by side with a row of steadfast iron bars between us. "You asked for me."

"Funny, isn't it? The last person I ever want to see is the last person I get to see alive."

"You don't have to explain, Shira." Half a year and I'd started realizing every conversation I had with someone in the Rebellion might be our last. Sometimes it was. But it was harder to push that out of my head when I knew for sure that Shira was a dead woman. "Nobody wants to die alone."

"Oh, good God, don't be so pathetic; it's depressing." Shira rolled her eyes so far back I thought she might lose them inside her head. "There's only one thing I want from you. Your rebel friends were here. They said—" She swallowed hard, like she was trying to hide from me that she'd hoped, even just for a second, that this might not be the end. "They said they couldn't get me out." A stab of guilt went through my heart. They could. But they were saving me over her. I was choosing my new family over my old. "But they said they would help Fadi." She opened her eyes, her fingers curling around the bars. "I didn't become Sultima by trusting anyone and everyone. I want to hear it from you. You might not be much, but you're still the only blood I've got here. Tell me my son is safe."

"Hala's gotten him out of the palace." As the words spilled off my tongue I knew they were true. "We can protect him."

A tension I hadn't even realized was there fled her body as I spoke, a fear she'd been holding deep in her bones since the first time I'd seen her in the baths. Had she looked at me that day, my Demdji eyes, and understood that she was going to be done for on the day she gave birth? Before I knew the harem, I might've asked why she'd taken the risk of lying with anyone other than her husband. If she was really stupid and arrogant enough to think that she wouldn't suffer the same fate as Ahmed and Delila's mother. Of every other harem woman who had ever strayed into another man's arms. But I'd seen enough since entering the harem to know there were other ways to die here. Ayet was proof of that.

"Why didn't you try to sell me out to the Sultan in exchange for your own life?" It slipped out. I never believed anyone ever did anything that wasn't for themselves before the Rebellion. And there were parts of me I couldn't shake from before the Rebellion. The parts that kept me alive. "You know who I am. You knew your life was all but forfeit. If survival in the harem is one big game, why not play your last piece?"

I knew the look she gave me from days together in the Dustwalk schoolhouse. The one she saved if you said something particularly stupid in class. The one that made sure that you knew not just that you were stupid but that she was a whole lot smarter than you. "The Sultan doesn't make trades. Everyone knows that. He hasn't traded anything since he traded Miraji's freedom for a throne. That's a mistake you only make once. He *takes* instead. And he would've taken the knowledge of your treachery from me and then we would've both been dead. And I want *one* of us alive. I'd rather it be me, of course, but you'll have to do." A slight smile appeared on her face at her own joke at death's doors. But it was gone quickly. "When I'm gone I want you still around with your idiotic idealist rebellion to gut the Sultan and Kadir." The more she talked, the more her accent leaked out through the cracks. Our accent from the Last County. "I hate *them* and I hate what they did. And I almost succeeded in taking their throne, too."

"Wait." I cut her off before she could chase her own thoughts too far away from me. "What do you mean you almost took their throne?"

"Fereshteh promised." She said it with the certainty of a child repeating something she truly believed. Who didn't understand that promises were just words. But Fereshteh was a Djinni. If it was dangerous for Demdji to make promises, how bad was one from a real live Djinni? A thousand stories of Djinni promises granted in horrifying torturous ways tumbled toward the front of my mind.

"I figured out that the harem was an unwinnable game, early on. The only *real* way to win is by becoming the mother not just to a prince but a Sultim. Only Kadir can't sire any princes. And Fereshteh was just there, in the harem gardens one day. Like he'd stepped out of a story and into my life to save me. And he said that he could give me a son. And just like that I had a way to win the unwinnable game. To survive past Kadir losing interest in me in his bed and become the Sultima." Her eyes were far away. "And when I touched him he turned from fire to flesh. And he asked what I would wish for our child."

"What do you mean, what would you wish?" My mouth had gone dry.

Shira's bloodshot eyes snapped open, like she'd been

startled from the edge of drifting to sleep. "He said he could grant me a single wish for his child. Every Djinni can."

"Shira." I chose my words carefully. "You've heard the stories as well as I have. A wish from a Djinni—"

"In the stories men *steal* wishes. They trick and lie and cheat for an easy way to change their fortunes. That's why the Djinn twist them. Thieves don't prosper from wishes. But if the wish is given freely . . ." Then there was no need to twist it. They could really give someone their heart's desire.

"You wished for more than a prince." But my mind wasn't wholly with Shira anymore. It was racing across the sands back to Dustwalk. To my own mother. If she'd been given the chance to wish for anything, what had she wished for me? What great boon had my father granted to me? "You wished for your son to be Sultan."

"The only way to win the game." Shira tipped her head back against the cold stone wall, a small sigh slipping through her lips. That was when the tears started to come. "I wished to be the mother of a ruler. I wouldn't have to scrape to survive anymore. I could have everything I ever wanted." A Djinni's word was truth. If Fereshteh had promised Shira that Fadi would be Sultan one day, what did that mean for Ahmed? "But I lost." Tears rolled down her face. I'd never seen Shira cry before. It looked unnatural on her somehow.

"Shira, do you want me to go?"

"No." She didn't open her eyes. "You're right. Nobody wants to die alone."

I expected to feel grief. But all I found inside was anger. And suddenly I was furious. And I didn't know who I was angry at. At myself for not getting her out quickly enough. At her for being stupid enough to get caught. At the Sultan for doing this to both of us.

"I should have wished for something else," she said finally as the tears stopped. When she opened her eyes again there was a fire there I'd never seen in her. One I suddenly realized had been there all along. Back in Dustwalk when I thought I'd been the only one who wanted to get out as badly as I did. In the harem when I thought I was the only one hiding something. She'd just veiled it a whole lot better than I had. "Tell me that you're going to win, Amani. That you're going to kill them all. That you're going to take our country away from them and that my son will be safe in a world that doesn't want to destroy him. That's my real wish. Tell me that."

I opened my mouth and then closed it again, fighting for the words. Truth-telling was a dangerous game. There were so many words I wanted to say. *No harm will come to your son. I'm not going to let it. Your son will live free and grow strong and clever. He will live to watch this rotten rule crumble. He will live to see tyrants fall and heroes rise in their place. He will have the childhood we never could. He will run until his legs are tired if he wants to, just chasing the horizon, or he will grow roots here if he'd rather. He will be a son any mother would be proud of and no harm will ever come to him in the world that we are going to make after you are gone.*

It was too dangerous to promise any of that. I wasn't an all-powerful Djinni; I couldn't make promises. All I could manage was, "I don't know what will happen, Shira. But I do know what I'm fighting for."

"You'd better." Shira leaned her head against the cool metal. "Because I'm going to die for it. That's what I traded your rebellion for." Her tears had dried now. "I promised them that if they got my son out, I would show this city how a desert girl dies."

•   •   •

THE CROWD IN the square outside the palace was restless and roaring with noise. I could hear it before I even reached the balcony at the front of the palace. It was nearly dusk and they'd taken Shira away. They had offered her fresh clothes, but she'd turned them down. She hadn't been dragged; she hadn't fought or wailed. She'd stood up when they came for her, like a Sultima going to greet her subjects instead of a girl going to die.

She'd made me promise I would stay with her until the end. I might not be able to follow her onto the execution platform, but I wasn't about to break a promise to a dying girl. Nobody tried to stop me as I strode through the palace halls, Imin trailing me like a shadow.

I stepped through the curtains and got my first good look at Izman since the day I'd arrived. The balcony was half-shielded by a finely carved wooden latticework screen so that we could see the city without the people of the city seeing us. It overlooked a huge square, twice the size the rebel camp had taken up in the canyon. And it was filled to bursting. News of the execution of the Sultima had spread quickly. People were crowding to see a harem woman die for giving birth to a monster. It was like something out of the stories, but they were going to witness it.

The crowds jostled for a view around a stone platform that sat directly below the balcony. Looking down on it from this angle, I could see the stone wasn't as smooth as it would look from below. It was carved with scenes from the darkness of hell. Men being eaten by Skinwalkers, Nightmares feeding off a child, a woman whose head was being held aloft by a ghoul with horns. That would be the last thing anyone led to the executioner's block would see.

That was the last thing Shira was going to see.

I almost missed Tamid. He stood in the shadows of the corner looking miserable. Shira and Tamid had barely ever traded a word at home, no matter how small Dustwalk was. I got the feeling they would've hated each other if they had. But it occurred to me that Shira and Tamid had made it out of Dustwalk together. They had survived. They had survived what I'd done to them. They'd been together when I'd left them behind. That had to mean something.

"It was a mistake to arrange this execution without consulting me, Kadir." I caught the edge of the Sultan's conversation as I brushed by. He was furious. "The city is already restless. You should dispose of her in private. Like you did her child." Hala had succeeded in convincing the

Sultan that the harem had watched Kadir murder Fadi. Good. He was safe.

"She is my wife." Kadir sounded violent, even in the face of his father's calmer anger. "She is mine to do with what I please."

Kadir spotted me as he spun away on his heel from his father. A nasty smile spread over his face. "You"—he shot the order to Imin—"you're dismissed. Go find somewhere else to be."

I sensed the other Demdji tense behind me. But he couldn't refuse. He sketched a quick bow before ducking out.

"I'm glad you're here." Kadir sidled across the balcony toward me. My eyes darted for the Sultan, inadvertently, looking for help. But his attention was elsewhere. Rahim was nowhere in sight, either. Tamid was watching us. But there'd be no help from him. Even if he didn't hate me, he was no match for a prince.

Kadir's hand found the small of my back like he thought I was some puppet and he could pull all my strings. He shoved me past two of his wives, who were watching from behind the lattice screen, hiding from the crowd, out into the open at the edge of the balcony, where I was exposed. A few eyes from the crowd drew up toward us as we appeared.

"You tried to help her get away." Kadir leaned into me, the pressure of his body forcing me against the railing, trapping me between him and open air and the sight of my cousin below. I could feel every inch of my body that he was touching fighting back against the feeling of him pressed to me. I hated more than anything that I couldn't fight back. His breath was hot on my neck as he spoke. "And now I want you to watch her die."

I didn't need him to make me watch her die. No matter what happened, I would give her that. I wouldn't do it for Kadir. I'd do it for Shira. Because whatever else she was, she was my flesh and blood and she deserved that much from me. She deserved a whole lot more, in fact. But this was all I had to give.

A roar came with Shira's appearance onstage. Some of it was jeers, but those were drowned out quickly.

She had been right not to change, I realized now.

Shira in her silks and muslins and jewels and fine makeup looked like nobility. But as she was now, dressed in a plain white khalat, she looked like a desert girl. She looked like one of the crowd she was facing, not something out of the palace. Folks were cheering *for* her, I realized, not for her head.

When she stepped up onto the stone, she was still shaking, her naked feet barely holding her up.

The restless crowd settled enough to listen as the executioner started to announce her so-called crimes. Shira stood with her head held high, back as straight as an iron bar. A light breeze picked up her hair. It was long and loose around her shoulders and it moved enough to expose her neck. The wind seemed to draw her eyes up. She tilted her head back, spotting me and Kadir on the balcony easily. She ignored her husband, locking gazes with me instead. There was a slight curve to her mouth. That was the only warning I had.

The executioner was still reading. "For treason against the Sultim—"

"I am loyal to the *true* Sultim!" The words burst out of Shira's lips, startling the executioner into silence. "The true Sultim, Prince Ahmed!" Her words stirred an answer in the crowd. "He was chosen by fate at the trials! Not by the hands of his father! A father who himself defied our traditions! I know the will of the Djinn, and they are punishing these false rulers. Kadir will never be able to give our country an heir!"

A rush of pride swelled in my chest. The Sultan had been right. It was a mistake to execute her in public. Kadir had given his legendary Sultima the biggest stage in Miraji to spill all their secrets on. She was one girl, seconds away from death, and she was using her last breath to do more than a rain of pamphlets from a Roc could. Even if they silenced her now, this story would spread all over Miraji and get grander with every retelling.

"If Kadir ever sits on the throne, he will be the last Sultan of Miraji!"

Kadir shoved away from me as his Sultima spoke, pushing back inside, shouting orders. But he was far too late. The damage was done, and silencing her now looked like they were trying to stifle the truth. I didn't move, though I caught the Sultan's gaze for just a moment. He looked resigned. As if he knew this would come out of his son's stupidity.

"He will die without an heir to take his place and our country will fall back into foreign hands." Shira was still talking, her voice carrying over the beginnings of restlessness in the crowd. "The same foreign hands that the false Sultan makes deals with behind closed doors. Prince Ahmed is Miraji's only hope! He is the true heir—"

She was still shouting as the guards wrestled her forward, forcing her head down onto the block. "A new dawn!" she screamed as a guard forced her head down so hard that her chin connected with the block, opening a huge gash.

The din of the crowd was drowning out anything more she would have said, but she held my gaze as the executioner stepped up. I leaned forward, closing the distance between us as much as I could, my hips pressed against the railing, my body craning over the balcony.

I held her eyes until the axe came down.

THIRTY-FOUR

I couldn't tell where the first stone came from. It sailed out of the crowd, smacking into the wall next to the balcony.

"A new dawn!" someone screamed from the crowd. "A new desert!" The rebellion's cry picked up all around the square. The crowd below turned into a mob with frightening speed. Another rock flew, smacking into the screen around the balcony. The closest guard flinched back. Those out in the open with me were already retreating.

I saw the bomb as it prepared to sail. A flash of fire in the crowd. A bottle stuck with a burning cloth, aimed toward the balcony. I dove for cover inside. Even as I prepared to hit the ground, I spotted Tamid, staring through the screen, eyes pressed to the openings, fingers laced through the carved wood. I grabbed him and pulled him to the ground sprawling, even as the bottle struck the screen, exploding in a burst of flames and glass against the wood.

When I looked up, coughing, some of the screen was missing; the rest was catching fire. There was another soldier who'd been standing too close sprawled near us, crying out in agony as blood bloomed across one ruined side of his face. Tamid stared at the man, eyes wide. I supposed he wasn't quite so used to dodging death as I was.

"Bottle bombs, just like we used to make back home," I offered, pushing myself off him. I checked around quickly, making sure no one had noticed. The chaos was a distraction. The Sultan had already vanished. Gone to safety or to give orders to fortify the palace, I figured. To quell the crowds. I just hoped the Rebellion was ready to protect them. "We need to find cover." I offered my former friend a hand up. "Come on."

Tamid got us back to his rooms safely, through hallways choked with soldiers, headed into the streets to keep the peace. Hundreds of men passing us, their boots pounding into the marble floor. He slammed the door behind us and bolted it shut. He leaned on the door for a moment, out of breath, as I slumped into the chair at his desk while he took another by the balcony.

We lapsed into uncomfortable silence. I could hear the rioting outside over our ragged breathing. Shouts of rebellion; gunfire. Once, something that sounded like an explosion. I thought I might've seen the flash of light it gave off across Tamid's face as he peered out over the city. And I was stuck in here. Helpless.

Gradually my breathing slowed as night fell outside. The rioting faded to the back of my consciousness. I was left listening to the roar of grief in my head instead. I'd been helpless to save Shira, too. I'd watched her die. I might not have always liked her. But I'd never wanted her dead. And now she was gone. Another casualty of the cause.

I could've gone back to the harem. But I wanted to be there even less than I wanted to be here. So I waited.

When it got too dark to see, Tamid started to work his way around the room, his metal leg clicking with every step, lighting oil lamps as he went.

There was a book open on the table. I noticed it as the lamp above it came alive. A picture fiercer than any of the faded drawings I'd ever seen in the books that found their way down to Dustwalk glared out of the pages. It was a Djinni made of blue fire standing next to a girl with blue eyes with the sun in her hands.

Princess Hawa.

"Do you have anything to drink in here?" I asked finally when the last lamp was lit and I couldn't take it anymore. "Remember in Dustwalk, when anybody died, everybody got together for a drink to honor the dead. Or are you too holy to drink now?"

"Did you drink to me, after you left me for dead?" Tamid asked, shaking out the match.

After leaving Dustwalk I remembered drinking with Jin in a bar in Sazi. I didn't even know why I was drinking then. I wanted to say I was sorry again. But my silence spoke for me.

Tamid pulled open a cupboard. It was lined with jars and bottles of stuff that looked more like poison than booze. But he reached toward the back and pulled out a half-empty bottle with the label scratched off. There was no mistaking the amber liquid inside. "I only drank because you were a bad influence, anyway." He pulled the cork from the bottle.

"I only have one glass." He poured a measure into a glass and another into an empty jar. "I don't get that many guests around here." He handed me the jar.

That wasn't what it had looked like with Leyla, but maybe they had better things to do than drink together. "The jar is clean, I promise. If I wanted you dead, you're right, I could've already done it."

"To the dead," I said. I took a sip, burning away the smart retort on the tip of my tongue before I could say something I'd regret. "Who weren't so lucky as me."

Tamid rolled his glass between his palms. "I didn't think you'd care about Shira."

I wished I had it in me to be angry about that. But he wasn't wrong. The girl I was when I'd left Tamid bleeding in the sand wouldn't have cared. But the world was bigger than Dustwalk, it turned out. "Well, I guess you were wrong."

We fell silent again as I sipped at my liquor, letting it burn on the way down. Tamid just stared at his own glass. Finally he seemed to decide something. "Leyla says you're planning to abduct me."

"*Abduct* is an awfully strong word." I'd accused Jin of abducting me once. But we'd both known that was a lie. I'd wanted to go. Even if it had meant leaving Tamid. "But yeah, more or less."

"Why? Is it just that you don't want me helping the Sultan anymore?" He didn't look at me. "Or did Leyla just ask you too sweetly to refuse? Or is it that—what was it you said? You're in the business of saving lives now?" There was scorn on his tongue but he was giving me a chance to be honest with him. I couldn't waste it.

"Because I wouldn't leave you behind if I got the chance again." It slipped out as easily as only the truth could. My gaze was fixed on his fake leg. "You never wanted to run away with me."

"And that was a reason to leave me to die, was it?" It had been the wrong thing to say. He leaned away from me, taking away whatever small distance I'd closed between us by saving him on the balcony. By sharing a drink with him here.

"That's not what I meant and you know it." I didn't want to fight with him. I didn't want to fight anymore at all today. I just wanted my friend back when I'd already lost one to the executioner. "I'm just saying, you wouldn't even run away from somewhere you hated with your oldest friend. I'm having trouble imagining that you've now become the sort to run off with a princess. Are you really going to leave with Leyla? You're not going to try to snitch on us to her father?" I tried to sound disinterested. But a lot of folks would die if Tamid decided he was loyal to the Sultan. "You can't blame me for having my doubts. Between the two of us, there's only one who's in a habit of running away with royalty."

Tamid looked up at me over his glass so fast I knew he'd been faking disinterest in me. "That foreigner who stole the Buraqi was royalty?"

I realized I'd said it without meaning to. Slipped out as natural as if I could still trust Tamid.

"His name is Jin," I said. "And yes."

"Where is he now?"

I'd managed not to ask myself that question since Ayet had caught me with Sam in the garden. But in that moment, when I was sure she was going to turn us in and it was all going to end, one stupid thought had flitted through my head.

I wasn't ever going to see Jin again.

I might die and he was off doing God knew what, God knew where, with God knew who.

The thought that had chased it was selfish: If he were here, Jin wouldn't let me die. He would leave the captured Djinn in the Sultan's hands, risk everything, before he'd let me die.

"Your guess is as good as mine." I drank.

"Not all that great being left behind by someone you're in love with, is it?" Tamid raised his glass in a salute before taking a sip.

You only ever thought you were in love with me. But I couldn't say it out loud. That caught me off guard. "No," I admitted into my drink. "It's not." We were silent. "What about you and Leyla?" I asked finally. "Where will you two go if we do get you out?"

"Maybe home." Tamid shrugged. "Back to Dustwalk."

I scoffed without meaning to. Tamid looked up, offended. "Oh, come on," I defended. "Maybe you didn't want to leave like you did, but don't tell me after seeing everything else that's out here, you just want to go back to that hellhole. Or do you have fonder memories of all the names that town called you than I do?"

"I'm not like you, Amani. All I ever wanted was a simple life as a Holy Man with a wife. I always figured you'd change your mind and see it my way eventually." Dark eyes darted to me before sliding away again. The memory of him proposing marriage was heavy between us.

There was a part of him that still didn't understand. I could see that now, more clearly than I'd ever been able to back in Dustwalk. I'd move the whole world to make up for what I'd done to Tamid. But I wouldn't ever give it up for him. Not for anyone. The difference was, Jin had never asked me to. He'd taken my hand to show it to me instead. "This life—Djinn, princes—it's too much for me. I haven't changed my mind about what I want in this life, Amani. And neither have you."

A thought struck me and I couldn't hold back the laugh that bubbled up. I pressed the back of my hand to my mouth as I nearly choked on my drink. Tamid looked at me askance. "I'm not laughing at you." I waved a hand at him, my nose burning from the liquor. "I was just—I was trying to picture your father if you brought a princess home for a wife."

I saw it dawn on Tamid's face, too. He rolled his eyes

skyward. "God save me." Tamid's father was a hard man. He'd tried to drown Tamid as a baby when he was born with a crooked leg. He was also patriotic to the very core. He invoked the Sultan's name at every occasion. *What would the Sultan think of my weakling of a son, Tamid? What would the Sultan think that a boy in his country can be bested by a girl, Tamid?*

"What would the Sultan think of you taking his daughter to wife, Tamid?" I did my best imitation of Tamid's father, like I had when we lived in Dustwalk. Tamid dropped his head into his hands, but he was smiling as I laughed, the alcohol making me feel lighter.

"What about *you*?" Tamid rolled his glass between his hands, the faint smile lingering. "You can't leave. In this grand escape plan, what happens to you?"

I'd been wondering that, too. The thought was suddenly sobering. Shazad had always been willing to give up her own life for the Rebellion. But I didn't know whether she'd be willing to give up mine or if I'd have to do it myself. Imin had already volunteered if she couldn't. "I don't leave this palace so long as the Sultan's got control over me." I tried to shrug casually. But Tamid had known me far too long. He could read me better than anyone.

Almost anyone. Jin had understood who I was better than Tamid ever had. And Shazad had seen who I could be. Tamid had always seen who he wanted to. But he still knew when I was hiding something. *Traitor eyes.*

"I'd die for this, Tamid. I don't want to have to. I'd do just about anything to not have to." I listened to the roar of the crowds outside. "But it's a whole lot bigger than my life or anyone else's."

Tamid set his glass down. "I want you to know I don't believe in your rebellion."

"I figured." I downed the rest of my drink.

"And your prince is as likely to destroy this country as anything else." I figured that, too. But I didn't say that. "But you were right: I don't hate you enough to want to watch you die. Take your shirt off." That wasn't what I'd been expecting him to say.

"Do you say that to all the girls?" It slipped out. It was a stupid thing to say to someone who wasn't my friend anymore. Who'd been in love with me once. It was stupid to make a joke when Shira's blood was still cooling in the square and the riot in the streets was still raging. But against all odds, Tamid laughed. He laughed exactly like he used to, with a slight roll of his eyes, like he wanted me to think he was humoring me by laughing. But I knew him better than that.

"No." Tamid picked up a tiny knife with a blade no longer than one of my fingernails. "Just the ones I'm about to cut a piece of bronze out of."

He was serious, I realized. He was going to help me. He knew where the pieces of metal in my skin were. He could take out the one controlling me. That forced me to stay here.

He was going to save my life.

THIRTY-FIVE

I could hear Auranzeb already starting on the other side of the wall. The sound of laughter drifted through, high and clear like a bell, a riot of voices, Mirajin and foreign alike, and music running like a soft current underneath.

We stood in the shadow of the harem walls outside the gate, whispering knots of perfectly made-up girls all around me. They kept their distance from me. Nobody in the harem seemed to know exactly what I'd had to do with the events around the blessed Sultima, but that hadn't stopped the rumors from spreading. Some were even saying they'd seen me help Kadir drown Fadi. I knew they were lying because Hala wasn't stupid or spiteful enough to plant that image in their heads. I cast around for Leyla, an ally, but I couldn't find her in the dim light leaking through from the other garden. The shuffle of cloth and breathing and the occasional excited whisper were the only sounds to be heard on our side. We were like penned creatures, waiting. I forced out a long breath, trying to calm my racing heart.

This was it. Tonight we freed the Djinn and Leyla. And one way or another it was my last night in the harem.

My left hand strayed to my side, a nervous habit I'd been trying to break the last few days. The last thing I needed was anyone noticing the tiny healing cut under my arm where Tamid had sliced the piece of bronze out of my skin. The iron was still there. He told me without meeting my gaze that he hadn't exactly planned on getting the shards of metal out, that I might bleed out if he tried. But I understood the truth of it. He was willing to help me escape, but he wasn't going to help the Rebellion by giving me back my power. He wasn't a traitor like me.

The riots had lasted all night after Shira died. They were being called the Blessed Sultima's Uprising, for now. But stories were written by the winners. If we lost this war, chances were the name would change to the Disgraced Sultima's Uprising. They'd left a tension in the air that put a frantic damper on the preparations for Auranzeb. I could feel it even inside the safety of the palace walls.

When daybreak had come after the night of rioting, the Rebellion had claimed part of the city. Sam told me our side had used the riots to erect barricades all the way, hemming off most of the slums and some other parts of the city to claim them in the name of the Rebellion.

In one night we'd taken rebel ground in the capital itself. If that didn't send a message, I didn't know what would. There were suns painted on buildings across the city and, most unsettlingly, there was one in bright red paint smeared on a wall at the heart of the palace. Nobody could account for that, except for Imin, that is. But she was now a tiny, doe-eyed servant in the kitchen, and no one would suspect someone so small to be able to reach that high.

The dawn had also found the streets littered with bodies. A whole lot of them were wearing uniforms. According to Sam, Shazad had run a flawless strategy even if it was in city streets instead of a battlefield. And even if some of her troops thought they were just loot-ing and burning, she'd managed to nudge them carefully one way or another, leading them like soldiers even if they didn't know it.

Still, even though we'd won more than we'd lost, there was a nervous edge among the rebels. If there was ever a time for the Sultan to turn his new Djinni army out against us, it was now.

But it'd been three days and no immortals walked the streets yet. This was still a war among humans. And Demdji. And tonight I was about to get back to the side I belonged on.

The servants of the harem had dressed me in Mirajin colors. White and gold. Like the army. Only I looked like a different kind of soldier. The white glowed pale and rich next to my desert-dark skin. The cloth clung to my skin like a lover's fingers, ending in a hem heavy with golden stitching that climbed upward, scattered with pearls. I imagined walking past Kadir's wives, and them grabbing at my khalat like they did at the pearls underwater. My arms were bare from the elbows down, except where golden bracelets rattled heavily at my wrists. In the burnished light, the gold powder that had been dusted over my whole body made it seem like the sun lived under my skin.

They had clucked over my shorn hair before finally resigning themselves to running sweet-smelling oils through it so that it stayed straight. They wove my hair through with strands of pure gold, threads of it that mixed in with the black and caught the light. I found it hard to care about my shorn hair anymore. Whatever anger I'd ever had at Ayet left me when I saw her curled up on the floor of the prison, dead eyed. She'd fought and she'd lost and I felt sorry for her.

When they were done they crowned me with a tiny circlet made of miniature gold leaves with pearls as berries. My mouth had been stained darker gold.

Every woman from the harem who was being allowed into the party was dressed in the same colors I was, Mirajin gold and white. But I was blinding. Like some untouchable gold sculpture that had been crafted to place in a palace and be admired. There was nothing of the desert girl left. I looked more beautiful than I'd ever seen myself, but unnatural, like a stranger.

But I knew who I was. I was still a rebel.

And tonight we were going to strike a real blow.

"Announcing"—the call came from the other side of the door—"the flowers of the harem." A hush fell over the crowd, expectant. The doors swung open. The girls around me rushed forward like children toward a new gift. I was jostled as I followed at a slower pace. I imagined for the guests it was like watching birds burst free from their cages, a surge of white and gold as we were released among the people.

The gardens were seductive in the late afternoon light. Fountains bubbled happily among guests in their finest clothes, music twisting its spell with the smells of jasmine and sweet food. High above us the sky was strung with golden ropes from one side of the garden to the other; small glass decorations hung from them, catching the light. When I craned my head back I saw they were crystal birds hanging from the golden wires. A servant passed me with a tray of soft cakes dusted in white powder. I took one and shoved it into my mouth, tasting the sugar exploding on my tongue as it melted there. I tried to savor it, but it dissolved quickly, until only the memory was left between the tip of my tongue and the top of my mouth.

I heard whispers go up in the crowd as we passed. The Albish queen's eyes swept over one of the girls, who was wearing a sheer muslin dress that showed a whole lot more of her than you'd expect, and glanced away in disgust, smoothing her hands over her own full, heavy skirts.

I ignored her, my eyes darting around for faces I knew, for Shazad or Rahim. I caught the Sultan's gaze through the crowd. Some of the revelers looked like they'd already started celebrating like the next dawn would never come. But not our exalted ruler. He was as sharp as anything. He raised a still-full glass to me in greeting before his attention was pulled elsewhere. I let out a long breath. I couldn't look suspicious. I took a slow route around the gardens instead. Like I wasn't looking for anyone at all.

Rahim found me before I could make it very far. "I've been assigned to keep an eye on you tonight by my exalted father." He was wearing a crisp white dress uniform and a sword at his side that didn't look decorative to me. "There are a fair few foreigners around and apparently even after nearly getting you killed once I can still be trusted."

"Once I lost someone a hand during an ambush." It'd been early days in the Rebellion. After Fahali, before getting a bullet to the stomach. "It was my fault. When Ahmed sent me out again in a similar raid, I asked if he was really going to trust me. He said I was a lot less likely to make the mistake a second time than someone else was to make it the first."

"Well, let's hope that's the only thing my brother and my exalted father have in common. On that note, let's go find your rebellion." He extended an arm to me. I held up my gold-dusted hands apologetically. "Ah." He dropped his arm. "Of course: look but don't touch."

We walked side by side through the glow of the garden. On a night like this, it would be easy to forget we were celebrating the Sultan's coup. Two decades ago to the day, he had allied with the Gallan and taken our country by force. The sun had gone down with Sultan Oman's father on the throne. Dawn had found him dead in his bed, and the palace packed with Gallan uniforms. The Sultim was found facedown in a garden, like he had tried to run. Many of the Sultan's other brothers met the same fate. He couldn't afford any challenges to the throne. He'd left only the women and the brothers who were younger than him alive . . . Twenty years ago tonight the palace had been full of death and blood; now soft lights and music drifted through the walls and the buzz of conversation seemed to lull us all away from any memories of that night.

Except there were the statues. Among the guests and the musicians and the servants passing around wine and food, the garden was dotted with statues made of what looked like clay and bronze. They were frozen in agonizingly twisted shapes, buckled to their knees, arms up like they were protecting themselves.

"I knew Prince Hakim when he was a boy, you know." The speaker was some Mirajin lord or other, talking to a young, pretty girl. He was gesturing at a statue.

They were the princes. Bronze sculptures of the twelve princes the Sultan had killed when he took his throne.

Someone had rested a glass in one of their upturned palms, leaving the dead prince's agonized face to stare up at a half-finished wineglass smudged with oily fingerprints.

"Well, those are in bad taste," a voice said in my ear, making me jump. A server was standing by my elbow with a tray piled with basbousa. I had an odd feeling of recognizing him, only I didn't. Until he rolled his eyes skyward.

"Imin." I cast around carefully in case we were overheard.

"Those colors don't suit you at all, by the way." His eyes swept me appraisingly. If I'd had any doubt left in my mind that it was him, it evaporated at the disdain in those bright yellow eyes that betrayed him as a Demdji.

"He's one of yours?" Rahim guessed. "How did he get in?" He didn't know the half of it and now wasn't the time to explain that Imin was the same tiny female servant Rahim had helped to abduct Shira's baby a few days earlier.

"I've got my ways." Imin took a piece of the sweet cake off his own tray and put it in his mouth. "Shazad is looking for you two." He licked his fingers clean and pointed. Shazad was a little way off, hair wrapped in tight braids around her head, like a crown. "She says it's high time you kept up your side of the bargain and introduced us to whoever's got this so-called army of yours."

"*She's* with your rebellion?" Rahim inspected Shazad skeptically across the garden. "General Hamad's daughter? I always thought she was just a pretty face."

"So does everyone else," I said. "That's how we figured she wouldn't get searched too closely on the way in. Shazad's the one who carried in enough explosives to free every Djinni down in the vaults."

"Explosives," Rahim repeated. He sounded nervous.

"You didn't tell him the plan?" Imin asked, shoving more food into his mouth.

"We didn't even *have* a plan until a few days ago," I said

defensively. "I've been busy since then." My hand drifted again to the tiny cut in my side.

Imin turned to Rahim. "According to Shazad, every Auranzeb, when the sun sets, the Sultan gives a speech, which means that all eyes will be on him. Using that as cover, Sam will sneak Amani and Shazad through the walls and out of the party." Imin jerked his head sideways, indicating our imposter Blue-Eyed Bandit. My eyes skated straight over him before I spied him. He was dressed in an Albish army uniform. So that was how he was getting around inconspicuously.

"Isn't it a crime to impersonate a soldier?" My heart was starting to beat painfully in my chest now. There was so much that could go wrong tonight. Not being wholly sure I could count on Sam was just one of them.

"I hear it's a crime to desert the Albish army, too." Imin sucked on his teeth, moving around a seed caught there. He made a terrible servant. It was amazing that he'd gotten this far without getting caught. But he was right: the uniform fit Sam too well to have been stolen. Too well to be anything but tailored for him. My eyes went to the congregation of Albish soldiers, accompanying their queen here. It was a huge risk he was taking, as a deserter in their midst. And he was taking it for us.

Even as I watched him, his eyes dashed across the garden, landing on Shazad, who had started to cross the garden toward us. Sam's eyes never left her. No, I realized, not exactly for us. Damn. I'd seen men fall for Shazad before but I'd never seen her fall back. This couldn't end well.

"Hala will meet you on the other side of the wall," Imin went on. "She'll make you disappear long enough that you can get to the Djinn and set the explosives."

"And my sister?" Rahim asked. He was casting around the garden for her. Come to think of it, I still hadn't seen her, either.

"You're not a very patient man." Imin took his time, deliberately chewing. "If everything goes according to plan, Sam will get Shazad and Amani out of the palace straight from the vaults, and then double back through *that* wall for you and your sister." He nodded again, the other way this time.

"You get Leyla, and wait for Sam in the southeast corner of the garden, away from the chaos that's bound to come when something blows up in the palace," I said, shifting carefully as someone brushed past us, dangerously close to overhearing our conversation.

"Then we figured Hala will get Tamid out under cover of an illusion, and I will get out in the chaos, just looking like another servant running from an explosion. What could possibly go wrong?"

"A lot could go wrong," Rahim pointed out.

"It's still far from being the worst plan we've ever come up with." I tried to comfort him.

"No, the worst we've ever come up with ended with you flooding a prayer house," Imin offered, which was true but far from helpful right now. "So that's not really saying much."

"Everybody survived that," I said defensively. Rahim was looking at me, an uneasy look on his face.

"Welcome to the Rebellion." Shazad had reached us; she greeted Rahim with a devastating smile. "We make do with what we can get. Now, are you going to give us an army or not?"

• • •

WE FOUND LORD Bilal, Emir of Iliaz, leaning against one of the grotesque sculptures, eyes hooded. He was young, but he looked like he was already exhausted by life, or maybe by his own importance. It didn't seem smart to tell him that out loud when we were trying to form an alliance. I probably ought to let Shazad talk.

"So." Lord Bilal looked me over. "You're the blue-eyed rebel everyone is talking about." He glanced at Shazad. "And you must be the face of the operation. You're too pretty to be anything else." I watched my friend bite down on her annoyance.

"And you're the emir looking to turn rebel." She wore a bright smile the whole time and flapped her hands airily. Looking at her you'd think she was just a beautiful girl flirting with a man. Not a rebel planning a full-scale war. I realized why he'd chosen to wait for us here, in this corner of the garden. The music that drifted through the walls covered any conversation around us. I could only guess it covered our words, too. Still, Shazad spoke quietly.

"I'm my father's son." Lord Bilal shrugged one elaborately tasseled shoulder lazily. I thought I caught what looked like a skeptical eyeroll from Rahim. But when I looked at him head on, he was ever the soldier. Rahim had served under Lord Bilal's father first. He'd know better than anyone if the son lived up to the father. "My father had no loyalty to the throne. He never forgave Sultan Oman for turning Miraji over to foreign hands. He used to go on and on about how Iliaz is the most powerful county in Miraji, how the rest of the country depended on us. He'd tell you until your ears bled how Iliaz didn't need the rest of Miraji. It could survive as an independent nation."

"Are you saying you want your own country, in exchange for your army?" That sure wasn't asking for much.

"Are you in a position to negotiate that with me?"

Abducting Delila without permission was one thing. Giving away part of Ahmed's country without his permission, that wasn't something even Shazad and I could do. "No," Shazad said finally. "Even I'm not *pretty* enough for that." I snorted under my breath. She went to elbow me in the side, almost forgetting where we were, but she caught herself before she did, turning it into a gesture rearranging her sleeve. "But we can get you to Ahmed." Shazad paused pointedly. "Provided you can give me some numbers that will impress me."

Lord Bilal raised an eyebrow at Rahim. His commander stepped in easily. "There are three thousand men garrisoned at Iliaz. Twice that number retired in the province who can be called upon."

"And you have enough weapons to arm them all?" Shazad disguised the tactical question with a careful laugh, touching Rahim's arm as if he'd just said something hilariously funny.

"Amani." Imin, in the guise of a servant, appeared again at our side with an elaborate bow. "The Sultan is headed this way."

I traded a glance with Shazad. "Go," she said. "I've got this."

My stomach was too tied in knots to eat or drink as I left them. I made a show of inspecting the horrible statues that surrounded the garden to keep from glancing over my shoulder every few moments at Shazad and Lord Bilal in negotiations, Rahim in between them. The statues' bronze faces reminded me of Noorsham. Only his bronze mask had been smooth and featureless. These were wretched reminders of what the Sultan could do to us if he caught us in our treason before we could escape.

"Announcing"—the voice rang out through the courtyard again—"Prince Bao of the Glorious Empire of Xicha."

I felt that tug of something that reminded me of Jin.

A small crowd of Xichian men stood at the top of the stairs. They were dressed in bright clothes that looked as foreign as anything I'd ever seen the Gallan wear, but entirely different at the same time. I'd seen the occasional Xichian dress on Delila, but there wasn't a single woman among them.

A green-and-blue robe was draped over the narrow frame of the man at the head of the party. The six men around him were of similar builds. They reminded me of Mahdi and the rest of Ahmed's scholarly set.

Except for one figure at the back. He wasn't taller, but his shoulders were broader than those of the scholarly looking men that surrounded him, and he held himself like he was ready for a fight.

My mouth went dry.

Instead of snapping, the string tugged harder. I took a step forward without meaning to, trying to get a closer look. Through the crowd, among the mass of people, his face swung straight toward me. Like we were tied together by some invisible bond. Like we were the needles of the paired compasses.

Jin's eyes found mine. I was wrong. He didn't have his father's smile. Because that troublemaker curve to his mouth was all ours.

THIRTY-SIX

There was an entire garden between us and we were on enemy ground. One mistake, one false move could cost the whole Rebellion. And still it took everything in me to keep my feet grounded. Not to obey that tug.

It was more painful than any order the Sultan had ever given me.

Jin leaned in and whispered something to the Xichian man next to him as they descended the steps into the garden. The man nodded, turning to say something back. The crowd shifted, and he vanished. I battled my instinct to move toward him. To fight my way through the crowd and damn the Sultan watching me.

I started to move slowly toward where I'd seen him disappear. Or as slowly as I could with my heart beating out the rhythm of gunfire. I dodged around foreigners in strange clothes, Mirajin folks in fine colors, dangerous men in uniforms. Only I couldn't see him. I'd lost him. Again.

"Amani." His voice by my ear sounded exactly the same way it had the last time I'd seen him. In the desert. On the run. Breathless from kissing me in the tent.

When I turned around he was so close I could've reached out and touched him. Only if there was one sure-fire way for us to both die as gruesome a death as the bronze men around us, that would be it.

His eyes traveled the length of me, from the top of my perfectly combed head all the way to my bare feet. I was suddenly more keenly aware of my appearance than I'd been all night. That I was a golden-glowing girl, not wearing a whole lot, who'd been polished like the other harem girls for the express purpose of being looked at by other men but not touched. The other Xichian man with Jin was doing exactly that, his gaze snaking across every piece of uncovered skin I had. But Jin didn't seem to notice that I was painted gold and on display as if to taunt him.

"You cut your hair," he said finally. It was such a thing for him to notice, among everything else. The clearest wound I wore in the open of everything that had happened in the walls of the harem.

"Not deliberately." It was too much to explain to him now everything that had happened. But Jin could read some of it on my face. In the two-word answer.

"Amani, did they—" He stopped himself. *Did they hurt*

you? stalled there. I knew why. If someone had hurt me and he hadn't been able to stop it, I didn't know what the chances were that he'd forgive himself. "Are you all right?"

Now, that was a heavy question. "I'll live."

His face changed, hand curling into a fist at his side. And when he spoke again his voice was low and urgent. "I swear to God, if he's hurt you, Amani, I will make him suffer for it." I didn't have to guess who *he* was. The Sultan.

"You don't believe in God." It was all I could think to say.

His hand twitched forward, like he wanted to pull me to him, away from everything else happening around us. "Then I swear to you."

I had to ball my hands together to not reach for him. I remembered being little, my arms shaking from the effort of holding up a rifle too heavy for a ten-year-old. All I wanted in the entire world was to let the gun drop. To release my hands and let it fall. The effort of holding it up was too much. It was tearing into my muscle.

But staying alive depended on me holding that rifle up. Learning to shoot.

I kept my arms where they were. Shaking with effort.

"Jin," I said as low as I could in Mirajin. "It's not safe for us to talk."

"I really don't give a damn about safe or not." His voice was low and sure. And for a moment I thought he really might grab me. Just take my hand and run us both out of there. Then he remembered himself; the gesture turned into a bow as he stepped out of the way of the man behind him. It was one of the Xichian men, trailing him like a shadow. "I'm the translator for Prince Bao tonight, of the Xichian Empire. So long as we talk through him, we'll be fine." The man inclined his head, oblivious, saying something in Xichian.

"What happened to his other translator?" I asked through what I hoped was a deceptively polite smile.

"He came down with a bad case of broken ribs this afternoon." Jin winked at me over the prince's head, which was still bowed in front of me. "The prince has a weakness for beautiful women so it wasn't all that hard to steer him over to you. Say something back, as if I've been translating to you."

I hadn't seen Jin in two months. And last time we'd been fighting and his hands had been inside my clothes, and his mouth over mine. There were months of unspilled words between us. Not to mention I probably ought to let him know that as soon as the last of the light that was currently stretching our shadows faded, there was the small matter of freeing a whole lot of Djinn. There was too much to say and too little time, and it was too hard to spill it all through a polite smile. "Where the hell have you been?" I asked finally, through a forced smile at Prince Bao, as if I was talking to him and not demanding an explanation through my teeth.

I didn't catch Jin's expression as he turned away from me and said something quick in Xichian. I recognized it as some sort of polite platitude. The man said something back, nodding and smiling, handing it to Jin to translate. And finally Jin could turn back to me.

"I was looking for you." His right hand was still curled into a fist, bouncing tensely against his leg.

"Well, that was stupid," I said, and Jin stifled a laugh as I pressed my lips together and tried to radiate politeness at the foreign man who seemed to think I didn't know he was staring at my chest. "I was right here."

"Yes, Shazad has already gone into great detail about my choices."

"Shazad knows you're here?"

It was starting to get dark. It wouldn't be long before need tore us apart again. "In Izman, yes. Here in the palace . . . less so." Then there it was. That smile that pulled me into trouble straight after him. I fought the impulse to return it. "You'd better say something back to your prince."

Jin said something quick in Xichian; I only caught the edges of it, but it sounded like he was telling him that Mirajin wasn't so economic a language as Xichian. He barely waited for Prince Bao's answer before turning back to face me. "I came to make sure you leave this place tonight. Even if we don't manage to get anyone else out, you're coming with us. Do you understand?"

A smile pulled at my mouth in spite of myself. I ignored the grin Prince Bao gave me back, clearly thinking I was smiling for him. "Are you saying you're here to rescue me?"

Jin raised a shoulder. "Well, when you put it that way . . ."

I wanted to reach out to him. More than anything. I

wanted to fold into him. I wanted to remind him that this was a war. That we could fight and run and stay together all we wanted, but we weren't always going to be able to keep each other safe. "Jin—"

"A Demdji *and* a budding diplomat, I see." The new voice sent pinpricks down my spine before I could answer. We'd been so wrapped up in our covert conversation that I hadn't noticed the Sultan approach. The Sultan placed a hand on my back.

Needles climbed the length of my spine. I felt Jin's tension, and he turned it quickly into a bow. Prince Bao followed suit. And then he rose, and I watched Jin stand face-to-face with his father for the first time since he'd been a child in the harem.

I knew exactly what he saw because it was what I had seen: Ahmed aged by another two decades. His brother, our prince, and our enemy becoming muddled into one. But I couldn't even begin to imagine what he felt, having to stand toe to toe with the man who had bought his mother and enslaved her in his harem. Who had killed his brother's mother with his bare hands. Who had taken me. And having to smile politely.

Don't lose your head, I willed silently under my breath. *Not now. Don't get us both killed.*

And then he bowed his head in front of his father and, keeping the smile fixed on his face, he made the introduction, presenting the Xichian prince to the Sultan with a long string of titles as Prince Bao nodded along deliberately.

"You speak Mirajin very well," the Sultan said in compliment to Jin when he was done, barely sparing a glance at the foreign prince. I held my breath. The stories spoke of Ahmed and Delila disappearing into the night as if by magic. But the stories were only a sliver of the truth, twisted after passing across so many tongues.

The Sultan was a smart man. I'd learned that much here. Surely he must've known how the two of them really escaped. He must have figured out that the Xichian woman who'd disappeared the same night as his son and the Demdji baby had been responsible. Surely he remembered that, while the stories had forgotten him, there had been another son who had vanished that night, too.

But if he did, none of it showed on his face.

And nothing showed on Jin's. "Thank you," he said in his perfect Mirajin. "Your Majesty does me a great honor."

But the Sultan wasn't done with him yet. "Your mother was Mirajin, perhaps?"

Don't lie. I'm standing right here. Don't lie. If he asks me I can't lie for you.

"My father, Your Exalted Highness."

The Sultan nodded. "If you will excuse me," he said to Jin, extending an arm for me. "I need to steal Amani. If your prince doesn't mind, of course."

I knew Jin well enough to see what the idea of letting me go did to him. That he'd rather square off against his father right here in the middle of the garden than let me walk away with our enemy. With the man who'd already taken me from him the first time.

Jin inclined his head slightly. "Of course, Your Exalted Highness. I will make your apologies to Prince Bao." The Xichian prince's head bobbed along cheerfully, oblivious to the tension around him.

And then the Sultan was clasping my arm in his, ignoring the gold dust from my arm rubbing off onto his sleeve, and I had no choice but to follow him away from Jin, and not look back.

"You shouldn't be on your own," he said as he led me away. "There are a great many enemies of your kind here tonight. I had asked Rahim to watch you."

"He found an old friend of his from Iliaz." It was as good as I could give him.

"He found more than that, by the looks of things." He gave a pointed look to where Lord Bilal, Rahim, and Shazad were still deep in conversation. That he'd noticed that at all made me nervous as anything. "He found a pretty face." My chest eased a little. So long as he didn't suspect Shazad and Rahim of doing any more than flirting, then we didn't have to worry. "Though I suspect that one could be a match for him in wits as well."

I'd watched Shazad get underestimated time and time again. Even Rahim had doubted her value tonight, in spite of my word. It frightened me that the Sultan had sized her up so easily.

"Why am I here?" I asked, trying to draw his attention away from my wayward guardian and my friend. "If it's so dangerous."

"Because . . ." The Sultan stopped walking. We'd come

to an alcove in a wall of the garden, shielded from the crowd. "You asked me why we must renew our alliances with foreign powers who place their own countries over Miraji. I want you to have the answer to that question, Amani." He released my arm. "Stay here." The order didn't come with the old pull. But the Sultan didn't know that. As far as he knew, I'd grow roots.

The Sultan stepped up onto the raised platform in the garden. The tension that had been rising in my chest since dawn was nearly bursting me. Night was falling around us and nobody had lit any lamps around the garden to ward against it. The only light came from the lamps strung above the platform, plunging the crowd into darkness.

It was almost too perfect a cover to slip out under.

"Esteemed guests! Welcome. I am honored by your presence," the Sultan called through the gardens, summoning all attention onto him. Conversations went out like snuffed matches all around us as clusters of people turned into a crowd around the raised platform.

I started to push my way through against the bodies pushing toward the platform. I was headed toward the edge of the garden. To rejoin the Rebellion and get the hell out of here. Assuming I didn't wind up burned alive like Akim's wife for releasing the Djinn.

The Sultan's voice carried on from the stage. He was talking about peace and about power. Meaningless platitudes. Around me snatches of translation drifted out of the crowd. Shazad appeared next to me as I dodged around a Mirajin woman who rattled with rubies. Neither of us spoke or broke our pace as we came together, like two currents merging into a river.

As we got farther, Sam dropped into place between us, splitting off from the other soldiers in the same uniform as him, but with different loyalties. We broke free of the crowd finally. Sam pulled ahead of us as we approached the wall, and he grabbed our hands, the gold dust from my palm staining his as we pressed between two of the clay-and-bronze sculptures. "Hold your breath," he instructed as I fought my instinct to flinch away from walking straight into a wall.

We should've met hard stone. Instead it was like stepping into sand. Like the wall had changed its form for us, from solid to soft. Only it was reluctant to. Even as we pushed through I felt it trying to trap us there. The stone was pressing against my skin, fighting back to the shape it had been for thousands of years. I squeezed my eyes shut. After surviving the harem and the Sultan I was going to die here anyway. I was going to be entombed in the walls of the palace forever.

And then air hit my skin again and I was through, stumbling out the other side. Away from the Auranzeb celebrations. Into the quiet of the polished palace halls.

"Took you long enough." Hala greeted us on the other side. She looked like herself, golden skin and all, dressed in simple desert clothes, as she waited. Sam had gotten her in a few hours before. Waiting seemed to have put her in an even better mood than she was usually in. Her eyes swept me. "That color doesn't suit you."

"Yes, I've already been over this with Imin. Thank you for your input." I decided to ignore Hala, turning to Shazad instead. "You knew Jin was back and nobody thought to mention it to me?"

She paused, unwrapping the sash around her waist, revealing rolls and rolls of gunpowder hidden inside. Sam and Shazad traded a sort of conspiratorial look. The kind Shazad and I used to share. I was reminded with a pang of how long I'd been gone.

"Don't lie to me, Shazad. Of all people, don't you lie to me."

"Yes, he got back yesterday," Shazad admitted. "Izz found him. When we went down to Dustwalk after your tip about the factory. He was looking for you down there. He seemed to think you might have changed your mind and headed home with that aunt of yours. Idiot."

"For what it's worth"—Sam piped up—"I did vote to tell you."

"For what it's worth," Shazad said, "you're a thief, not a rebel, so you don't get a vote—"

"I really don't think you've got the moral high ground here," Sam returned, leaning against the wall looking all too pleased with himself. He was enjoying Shazad's attention, whatever form it came in. "And another thing—"

Hala groaned, cutting him off. "While *someone* might be fascinated by this, they are not people currently trying to get you across a palace unseen. Do you mind?"

I led the way.

We stayed close to Hala, moving as slowly as we could.

It made it easier for her to fool the minds of the soldiers we passed standing guard inside the palace. They were few and far between. Resources were spread thin tonight. But not a single one of them blinked as we walked straight in front of them; their minds were twisted firmly by Hala's power so all they saw was empty hallway. We moved quietly down now-familiar hallways and around corners until finally we came face-to-face with Princess Hawa's mosaic. Sam didn't wait for me to speak, grabbing our hands again, pulling us through the wall.

We came out, half stumbling, at the top of the old stone stairs that I'd walked down the first time I'd woken in the palace, the Sultan holding a lamp in front of us, so I could see only one step in front of me at a time.

Only I could see the bottom of the steps now. We weren't alone in the palace vaults. My arm shot out, stopping Shazad from going any farther. She understood the signal instantly, pausing where she was.

We moved carefully, lowering ourselves on the stairs like ghouls in the night, crouching until we were at the edge of the shadows, until we could see clearly into the crypt.

The vaults flickered with the movement of the captured Djinn. There were eighteen of them now. Eighteen names that I had called one by one to be trapped. And though they'd all taken the form of men there was still something unnatural about them. They stood like pillars of immortal power around the vaults, sometimes catching light that couldn't come from anywhere. The sheer force of their presence felt like a physical blow.

A half dozen men in uniform carrying torches were huddled around Fereshteh. He was exactly where I had left him after calling him, trapped inside the iron circle. Only somebody had placed what looked like a cage over him. It was made of brass and iron and gold and glass all interlocking in complicated patterns, jointed in a thousand places, arches of metal curving into each other.

The other captured Djinn looked on curiously from within their own circles, like parents watching something their child had made and they didn't wholly understand. For a fraction of a second Bahadur's eyes darted up our way before going back to the other immortals.

Something shifted in the circle of soldiers and the figure who had been working at the machine came into view. I knew Leyla instantly, even from this far away.

So this was why I hadn't been able to find her in the gardens. She was moving anxiously, hands dancing across complicated-looking pieces of machinery as easily as they ever did with the little toys she made in the harem.

She twisted something, stepping back suddenly. The whole circle of soldiers took a step back with her.

For two heartbeats nothing happened.

And then the machine came alive.

The bars of the cage started to move, slowly at first. Then faster.

Inside the machine, Fereshteh watched curiously as the blades moved. He didn't look afraid, but panic was starting to rise in my chest. The machine whirred faster and faster, huge blades swinging in evenly paced circles, like each one was a moving horizon across a huge globe. The bronze blades rising like dawn, the dark iron blades cutting across bringing the sunset. Faster and faster. Until it was a blur of machine around the Djinni.

A sense of dread filled my chest. We had to free him. We had to free him now before it was too late. I started to move forward, blind to the danger. And then one of the pieces of the machine, an iron blade, snapped into place. It swung suddenly, arching upward toward the sky. It froze there for a moment. I saw what was going to happen a second before it did.

It drove straight through Fereshteh's chest.

Inside, the immortal Djinni, one of God's First Beings, who was made at the same time as the world, who had seen the birth of humanity, who had watched the first immortals fall and seen the first stars born, who had faced the Destroyer of Worlds, died.

THIRTY-SEVEN

The Djinn were made from a fire that never went out. An ever-burning smokeless fire that came from God. And in the early days of the world the First Beings lived in an endless day.

Then the Destroyer of Worlds came. And with her she brought the darkness. She brought night. And she brought fear.

And then she brought death.

Wielding iron, she killed the first immortal Djinni. And when he died, he burst into a star. One after another, the Djinn fell that way, filling our sky.

Watching Fereshteh die was like beholding a star on earth. White burned across my eyes, and I was blinded. I heard someone scream. I heard Shazad shout something I couldn't make out.

Slowly the light retreated from under my eyelids, leaving me blinking but able to see again. Inside the machine, Fereshteh's body was gone. What was left was burning bright as a star, and the metal of the machine around him was blazing incandescent. I felt the hairs on the back of my neck stand up painfully. I knew where I'd felt this before. The metal door, before the Gallan tried to kill me. Even as we watched, the light whipped up a wire I hadn't seen before, igniting, racing along the ceiling, darting above us.

There was a shout from below as the flash of light above our heads illuminated us too sharply to miss. The time for subterfuge was over. Sam grabbed us both by the hand, wrenching us up the steps and back through the door so fast I barely had time to take a breath before we plunged through.

Hala staggered back as we stumbled through.

"Hala." I tore my hand out of Sam's for a moment. He stumbled to a stop, but Shazad didn't. She was a few paces ahead of us, already running back toward the garden. "Leyla—she's down there. Get her out."

She didn't even argue with me. I didn't give her time. I was running, chasing on Shazad's heels back toward the gardens. I glanced over my shoulder before we rounded a corner, just in time to see the door in the mosaic open, unsuspecting soldiers spilling out toward a waiting Hala, who grabbed hold of their minds before they'd taken a step. And then Shazad wrenched me around the corner. Hala and Leyla were on their own.

Sam grabbed hold of me as we approached the wall, dragging me toward it.

We burst through the wall, gasping, just as the Sultan's speech ended. Applause burst around us and for a moment I felt destabilized, plunging away from what we'd just seen, chasing the starlight, back to the normality of the palace.

And then, all around the darkened garden, lights started to come on. Not oil light. Not fire and flickering torchlight. Just light. Fire without heat. And it was coursing out from the machine that had just killed the Djinni, and then getting trapped in the crystal birds that I'd seen earlier, hanging from strings and staying there, flaring to life.

Bottled starlight.

Awed sounds filled the garden as the lights illuminated the amazed faces of the Auranzeb guests.

And then, in the corner of the garden, something moved. I snapped around in time to see one of the statues shift. One of the figures of the Sultan's dead brothers straightened his head. And then the one next to him. And the one next to him.

The metal men straightened up and took a step. And another. The crowd started to turn around, expecting another party trick. But this wasn't a trick.

"What are they doing?" I heard the fear in Shazad's voice. It was rare to hear her afraid. But I knew she was remembering the same thing I was. A train. A boy in a metal suit. Burning hands. Bahi's screams.

A foreign man in the crowd was forced to stagger back as a statue advanced on him.

I was sitting across from the Sultan in his study when he spoke about the servants of clay the Djinn made before humanity. The Abdals. Creatures of clay who obeyed any order. I was listening when he talked about the first time he had made a mistake thinking he could control a Demdji. That our power wasn't worth the risk of disobedience.

It didn't mean he'd given up on having that power.

It meant he'd given up on disobedience.

The metal things were stepping past the Mirajin, toward the foreign guests. Penning them in.

I heard the Sultan telling me Mirajin forces alone couldn't stand against the threats on our borders.

It was a trap. Auranzeb. The ceasefire. Everything. It was a trap to lure them here.

I knew what was going to happen the second before it did. One of the Albish soldiers lunged between the metal man and his queen. The statue raised one hand.

I was watching his face when he burned. He burned like Bahi had burned in Noorsham's hands. He burned like something lit with Djinni fire.

THIRTY-EIGHT

The screams started, some of them snuffing out before they could start, as the Abdals turned their stolen Djinni magic on them. Mirajin soldiers were pouring into the gardens now, too, cutting off anyone who tried to run. The smell of blood mingled with the smell of burning.

I realized that I was waiting for an order from Shazad that hadn't come yet. That she was frozen next to me. Pressed against the wall, watching men and women burn the same way she'd watched Bahi burn. If she wasn't going to take charge, someone else would have to. My eyes darted around the garden for Jin. I couldn't see him.

"Sam," I ordered, "you need to start getting people out from our side. As many as you can, and then you get out.

Shazad—" She jolted as I grabbed her arm. I did my best imitation of her. We needed someone to be Shazad and she wasn't herself just now. "I need you to pull yourself together." She was pale, but she nodded. "How do you feel about using that gunpowder to blow the gates?"

The gates were on the other side of the garden, chaos and death blooming in between us. I saw her mind working. The Abdals were attacking only the foreigners. They wouldn't cause her any trouble, seeing as she was Mirajin. But there were too many soldiers. There was no crossing that. "I need a weapon," Shazad said, finally sounding close to normal. She was wrapping a sheema around her face, hiding her identity.

"I might be able to help with that." Rahim appeared by my elbow. There was already blood on his uniform. He held out a foreign-looking sword to Shazad. "Are you as good as Amani says you are?"

"No, I'm even better." Shazad grabbed the blade out of his hand. "Together?"

The Sultan had been right. They were a well-matched pair. They burst into movement as easily as if they had been trained as one person their whole lives. Soldiers' bodies fell around them as they moved, fighting their way across the chaos. At the same time, Sam turned, plunging into the crowd, discarding his Albish uniform jacket as he went.

Tamid.

He darted across my mind all of a sudden. Hala was supposed to get him out. But the plan had changed. She was getting Leyla now. I had to get to him. I couldn't leave him behind again.

I was running before the thought had even finished, dodging around the chaos in the garden. I plunged into the hallways, headed for Tamid's rooms, the noise from the garden fading into the distance.

The sound of clattering feet in pursuit replaced it. I glanced over my shoulder as I ran. My escape from the gardens hadn't gone unnoticed. A handful of soldiers were behind me. A gunshot sounded just as I flung myself around a corner. The bullet hit where my head would've been. Plaster sprayed like blood, peppering my skin. Orders must not be to capture me, then.

I careened around the next corner, my bare feet skidding on smooth marble.

And then, like a Djinni blossoming from the sand, Jin was there at the other end of the hallway, firing at something I couldn't see. My heart took off and I felt myself speed up.

He turned, gun up, raised toward me as I bolted down the hall. The soldiers were close behind me, but he wouldn't have a clear shot at them, not with me in the way. I pumped my legs harder; I had to get to him before they got a shot off at me.

I could almost hear the hammers pulling back on the guards' rifles.

I crashed into Jin full speed. His arm curled around me. He turned me sharply just as the guards lined up their shots, until there was nothing but his body between me and the bullets.

I could feel the pistol pressing into my back. I curled one hand around it and Jin's grip yielded.

It was like being home.

I aimed in the space around Jin's body that was still shielding me. Three quick shots. And then there weren't any more. Not from me. Not from them.

Because I didn't miss.

I pulled away from Jin. There were three bodies slumped on the ground, dead, and then there was nothing but Jin filling my vision.

"You're bleeding." Jin's hands were frantically searching my body.

I was shaking hard. The sensation of being back in his hands. Of us being together again. Of pure relief.

"Not mine." I shook my head. I had no idea where the blood had come from. "We have to move. We need to get people out—"

"We are." Jin grabbed my hand. "They're getting as many people out as possible. Shazad is taking care of the gates and Imin escaped with your friend Tamid in the confusion. We need to—" We burst around a corner. Kadir stood in our way, flanked by two of the Abdals, their twisted bronze faces staring at us blankly. Like Noorsham. But without any eyes. Without any flesh or blood inside. Or any doubt.

This was what the Sultan had wanted. Soldiers who couldn't turn traitor. Demdji who didn't have a conscience. Who wouldn't fight his control.

I fired on instinct. My last bullet. It plunged straight

through the clay where its heart should have been. It didn't even stagger.

"Well, little Demdji bitch." Kadir raised his gun toward us. "No traitor brother of mine around to save you now."

"Want to bet?" Jin stepped in front of me, shielding me from Kadir, ready to fight him. But Kadir wasn't interested in a fair fight; his finger was already pressing down on the trigger.

That was when the gates exploded.

The Sultim staggered, his shot going wide. It was enough. I grabbed Jin's hand. We bolted for the stairs, a spiral leading up and up and up. Our feet pounded against stone as we climbed, Kadir close behind. We burst out onto a hallway. And I realized suddenly that I knew where we were.

I spun toward the room at the end of the hallway. It was Tamid's workroom. The one where I'd been able to see the roofs of Miraji. When I'd thought about jumping.

I slammed the door behind us, shoving the bolt into place a second before Kadir crashed into it, making the wood shake. In the corner of the room, one of the glass bottles fell from the shelf and shattered across the ground.

There. A coil of rope among the bottles and the bandages.

I grabbed it with one hand and ran to the balcony, Jin close on my heels. It was a narrow jump between the edge of the balcony and the wall. And from there it'd be an easy climb down.

"I think we can make that." I was breathing hard. I was

trying to be sure. I thought it was about the same distance as it was between Tamid's roof and the one next to it at his house back in Dustwalk. I'd made that jump before. But that was so long ago it was hard to remember. And the drop here was a whole lot farther.

"I wish I shared your confidence, Bandit." Jin's breathing suddenly sounded shallow. I looked over and saw him clutching his side.

I grabbed his hand and pulled it away. It was a long cut. A stray bullet, maybe. "Damn it." I looked around desperately. Kadir was hammering on the door behind us.

We were trapped. No way back. Only forward. "If I can make it"—I tied the rope to the banister of the balcony—"can you crawl?"

That smile pulled at the edge of Jin's mouth. "Have I told you that you're exceptional lately?"

"No." I looped the rope around the edge of the balcony again. "You disappeared on me for a few months without explanation instead."

Jin spun me around to face him. "You"—he kissed me quickly, on the left corner of my mouth, sending a rush through me—"are"—the right corner of my mouth this time—"exceptional."

I didn't wait for it. I pulled him to me, kissing him fiercely before pushing him away. "We don't really have time for this now."

"I know. I'm distracting you." He tugged on the piece of rope and the loop I'd made came untied. "As exceptional as you may be, you're also exceptionally bad at knots." He started doing something complicated, his fingers working deftly. And then he turned to me. In a few quick motions he'd looped the other end of the rope around my middle. "If you're going to risk your life, might as well do it safely."

"You're sure that will hold?" I looked at the tangle around the railing uncertainly.

"You can trust a sailor with knots," Jin said. "And you can trust me with you."

He steadied me with one hand as I climbed up. No matter how far down the drop looked from the balcony, it looked a lot worse standing on the balcony's railing. The jump might not be all that far, but it was a long way to fall and a narrow landing.

I could probably make that.

The door rattled behind us. Kadir pounding his way in.

I was half-sure I could make that.

I took a deep breath.

I was about to find out.

I jumped.

Open air yawned below me. For a second I wondered if this was how Izz and Maz felt, when they shifted into animals.

When they flew.

My bare feet hit the wall, stumbling. I grabbed on to one of the crenellations for balance. I teetered there for a second before I found my footing. I pulled the knot around my middle and wrapped it around the crenellation. The rest of the rope hung down the other side of the wall, almost to the bottom. At least close enough to get us out of the palace.

It looked solid enough and, God, it had better be.

On the other side of the balcony, Jin swung himself over the edge. He locked his hands and legs around the rope. The knot next to me tugged as Jin leaned his weight onto the rope.

It held.

And still held as Jin tugged his way across. One inch at a time, leaving a trail of blood behind.

All I could do from the wall was watch, heart in my throat, as every tug brought him closer to me. He was nearly halfway across when the lock to the door broke.

Kadir burst through in a storm of rage.

I had my gun up and pointed before he had made it to the balcony. I didn't have any bullets. Just a bluff. "Touch that rope and I can make you sorry that you were ever born, Kadir."

"You're lying." But he didn't come any closer, rooted, chest heaving with rage.

"I'm a Demdji." I pulled the hammer back on the empty gun. "I can't lie."

Neither of us moved. We were in a standoff now. I stood on the wall, gun up, pointing it straight at Kadir as Jin dragged himself the rest of the way across the rope. One inch at a time. Slowly. Slowly. He didn't have to be fast; he just had to be faster than Kadir's brain worked. Faster than the Sultim would take to realize I had nothing but an empty gun.

"Kadir." The voice at the door made me jump so hard that I had to steady myself on the wall.

The Sultan was alone, stepping through the door. There were no guards with him. No Abdals.

"Father." Kadir held out one hand. "Careful, she has a gun."

His gaze darted from me to Kadir, to the gun, back to Kadir. His mind wouldn't work nearly so slow as his eldest son's. I urged Jin silently to hurry. He was a handbreadth away now.

The Sultan dropped a hand on his firstborn's shoulder. "Oh, my son. You are a fool."

Then the Sultan pulled out a knife.

I started to shout, started an empty threat that I couldn't finish with no bullets left in the gun. A promise to stay in the palace if he let Jin leave. Anything that might buy Jin the last few moments he needed to get across before the Sultan cut through the rope and killed him.

He didn't slash toward the rope. Instead the blade in his hand went straight through Kadir's throat.

It was a clean kill, like with a hunting prize. So clean that when Kadir dropped to the ground, the annoyed protest was still written all over his face. So fast that I didn't have time to cry out before he was on the ground.

The shock rippled through me, freezing my tongue, my whole body.

The Sultan looked up at me calmly, wiping his firstborn's blood onto the dead prince's shirt. And suddenly I was sitting across the table from him again. Listening to him tell me that his sons would drive this country into dust under foreign heels. That Kadir wasn't any more fit to rule than Ahmed.

There is nothing I wouldn't do for this country, Amani.

The Sultan turned to face me. He wasn't stupid. He was going to figure out I was out of bullets pretty fast. I had to keep him busy, just a few moments. Until Jin made it across.

"You know, it's been a while since I went to prayers." There was a weight crushing my chest as I spoke. I had hated Kadir. But, God, seeing him like that, with his eyes staring glassily up at the night sky, blood still gushing from his throat . . . "But I'm pretty sure God frowns on killing your own son."

"Ah, yes." The Sultan smiled placatingly. "Cursed is the one who kills his own blood. Remember what we are celebrating, Amani: my ascent to this throne. I think I am past being able to escape that curse. Besides, Kadir would not have made a good ruler. It's my own fault, really. He was born too early in my reign. I was scarcely older than he is—was." He spared a glance down at the body bleeding out on the balcony. "I'd planned that the throne would pass him by, go straight to my grandchild, but of course, that wasn't to be. I hadn't counted on that power-hungry little wife of Kadir's to be so resourceful." Shira. She had been dead a few days and already her name was being erased. When they told the stories of what happened in this war, was that all she would be, the power-hungry Sultima? He looked back at me. "And I have to admit, I had not anticipated you managing to get yourself free." He almost looked impressed. "How did you do it?"

"You've overestimated the loyalty of your own people."

I wasn't going to give him Tamid's name. "Do you really think this is going to save them? Make them rally to you again? Slaughtering anyone who stands in your way?"

"It's not about the dead foreigners downstairs, Amani. It's about all the ones left alive overseas." The Sultan looked at me over the barrel of the gun. "Do you know what happens in a country when the throne changes hands, Amani? Turmoil. Civil war. Too much war for them to turn their minds to invading us again anytime soon. And by the time they do, I will have an army of Abdals ready to defend our borders."

An army of clay men with Demdji powers. Put that at our borders and he was right, we'd never be invaded again.

"The Demdji before you . . ." He meant Noorsham. He never used his name, like he never had mine until the day I'd killed that duck. Like we were things to him. "He burned so bright. But I lost the protection he would've given this country." Because I set him free. "I wondered if I could re-create his fire. If I could create a bomb out of metal with the power of a Djinni. And instead I found the right fire to create life. Because that's what the Djinni fire is. It's life. It's energy. It gave us life. And I have just harnessed it. Not to destroy. To power this country. The Gallan claim the time of magic is over and turn to machinery. The Albish cling to their old ways. We will be among the countries that unite the two."

"All at the cost of slaughtering our immortals."

"The First Beings made us to fight their wars. But where

have they been in our wars? While our borders are harried by foreigners with their greater numbers? While my people make it easier for them by turning against each other at the urging of my son?" He spoke patiently. Like he might do for his own children. Explaining a difficult lesson. Only he wasn't my father. My father was a Djinni. My father was a Djinni trapped inside the palace at his mercy. And for the first time since the Destroyer of Worlds was defeated, at very real risk of dying. My father hadn't cared when I had been about to die. Why should I care about him? But I did.

"The time of the immortal things is long over. We have taken this world from them. There is a reason that Demdji like you are rarities now. This world belongs to us. And this country belongs to us. It is the role of children to replace their parents. We are the Djinn's children." The Sultan smiled a slow, lazy smile. "And I think you're out of bullets."

And then Jin was across. He grabbed the edge of the wall and pulled himself up with a grunt of pain, and then his arms were around my waist. He half leapt, half dropped, his hand looping around the rope as he went. And we were falling. On the other side of the palace walls.

And I was free.

THIRTY-NINE

I zman was blazing still with Auranzeb celebrations, even in the ruins of the Blessed Sultima's Uprising. News hadn't reached the city yet of what was going on in the palace. That we were free of foreign rule. That the Sultim was dead.

I trusted Jin to lead us through the unfamiliar streets. The journey was painstakingly slow as we laced our way under the shadows of windows spilling out light and noise, through the winding side alleys of the unfamiliar city. Avoiding the big streets flooded with drunks and celebrations.

"Here." Jin pulled me to a stop finally, by a small door in a white stucco wall in an alley so narrow the wall before us almost touched the one behind us. A gutter ran from the door through the narrow paved streets.

I wasn't sure what I was expecting on the other side. For it to lead to another world maybe, like our old door. Or that it would spill down into a secret passage that would lead to wherever the rest of the Rebellion had set up since we'd lost the Dev's Valley.

Instead we stepped into a large kitchen warmly lit by the embers of a dying fire. It was about the most normal kitchen I'd ever been in. Just like my aunt's back in Dustwalk. Except this one didn't seem to be in low supply of food. Gleaming pots and pans hung from the ceiling between drying herbs and spices. Tinned supplies lined the shelves.

I slammed the door shut on the night behind us. I didn't have time to consider where we were, except safe. Jin and I collapsed next to the fireplace, his back against the wall. I was on my knees facing him.

"You're covered in blood." I eased him down off my shoulder. "I need to see."

"I'm fine." But he let me tug the hem of his shirt over his head all the same, wincing as his arms went up over his head. His bloodstained shirt hit the floor in a ball even as he rested his arms on top of his head, stretching his chest out and giving me unhindered access. He wasn't lying to me, at least; the better part of the blood didn't seem to be his. Some stained his skin, but aside from the wound in his side that had kept him from jumping to the wall and a huge bruise blooming like a cloud under the tattoo of the bird over his ribs, he didn't seem too badly hurt.

I noticed it then. A bright red cloth wrapped around the top of his left arm like an armband. I might've thought it was a bandage, but I'd know my sheema anywhere.

I reached out without thinking, fingers skimming the edge of where the fabric met his skin. His eyes snapped open at the touch, and he looked down, like he'd forgotten he was wearing it. "This is yours." His fingers started to fumble with the knot on the inside of his arm.

I sat back on my heels. "I thought I'd lost it." It was stupid. It was nothing but a piece of cloth. It wasn't the Rebellion; it wasn't Jin. It was just a thing. A thing I didn't think I'd ever get back.

"I thought you'd left it." He didn't look at me. He was still fiddling with the knot. It was fastened tightly. Like he'd been desperate not to lose it.

"Left it?" Finally the knot came apart in his fingers.

"The morning after you vanished." His shoulders were taut as he unwound the red sheema from his arm. "You were gone, and this was outside my tent." I must've lost it in the scuffle with Safiyah. When I'd been standing outside his tent. Deciding whether to go in. "It seemed like a message."

The skin under where it had been tied was paler. Like it hadn't seen the sun in a while. He handed me the sheema. I took one end. Our history hung between us, a dozen tiny reminders of the first days we'd known each other. When things had been simpler. He'd been the Eastern Snake and I'd been the Blue-Eyed Bandit and it'd been just the two of us, not the two of us and a whole revolution. A whole country.

I started to say something about how stupid it was to think I'd leave and tell him with a discarded sheema. But then, we hadn't been all that good at telling each other things.

"You left first." I pulled at the edge of the sheema. "When I was hurt, you left me."

"You walked into the path of a bullet, Amani." He smoothed back a piece of hair from my face gently, his fingers running down it to where it ended bluntly from the wound inflicted by Ayet's scissors. He looked at me like he was relearning my face. I didn't need to memorize him again. He looked exactly the same as when I'd left him. Did I look different from my time in the harem? "You walked into it without a care for your own life."

"That's what I do," I said. "That's what you do, too."

"I know." Jin's hands fell away from my hair, settling on my shoulders instead, lacing at the nape of my neck. "But that doesn't mean I had to like it."

"You were mad at me for almost dying?" I was so close to him that all I had to do was breathe for us to be touching. I felt like he was holding me together between his hands, but the heat of them made me feel like I might vibrate out of my skin.

"At you, at Ahmed, at myself, at everyone." He was finally looking at me square on. The dying embers cast his face in a warm glow as his thumb ran circles over the back of my neck. "I'm not good at losing people, Amani, and you know I don't give a damn about this country." The rest of him was still now, something solid to hang on to. But his fingers were sliding into my hair, making me shiver. "Not the way Ahmed does and not the way Shazad does. I came here because I give a damn about him, and I give a damn about Delila, and they both love this place. I give a damn about you and you are this place. I thought I had to do without you if you were so determined to leave the world. But then you were gone and I would have torn the desert apart looking for you."

I wanted to say something that would help. I wanted to say that he didn't have to be scared of me dying. But that would be a lie. We were in a war. No lives were safe. I couldn't promise him a future where I didn't take another bullet and he couldn't promise me one, either. The same reckless hope that had us fighting at all was as likely to kill us.

So I didn't say anything as I closed the last of the distance between us.

He said he would have torn the desert apart looking for me. And I felt in that kiss his desperation as his mouth found mine.

It wasn't enough with Jin; it was never enough. His hands were in the mess of my torn palace clothes, trying to find me under the too-heavy stitching and the weight of the gaudy khalat. One hand tangled into my hair, pulling away the delicate gold circlet that still clung there. He freed it from my hair, casting it aside, pulling pieces of the palace away from me, trying to return me to him.

It was like being caught in a wildfire, desperate for breath, like if we stopped we would extinguish. Without thinking, I pulled my hands away from his chest. It took one quick movement for my torn khalat to come off and join his shirt in the heap on the ground, until I was wearing nothing but the thin linen chemise underneath.

His fingers found the hem, pushing it up, and then they were against my stomach, grazing the scar on my hip. I suddenly realized I was shaking. I pressed against him, skin to skin, looking for some kind of warmth. His hands found the small of my back, stilling me against him.

I felt us slow. My heartbeat slow. The wildfire turned to embers as Jin held me flush against him. I realized how close we were to the edge of doing something more. His skin against mine, his hands climbing my body, sinking me into him.

The door to the kitchen clattered open, wrenching us violently apart. Sam stumbled into the kitchen carrying an unconscious Leyla.

"What happened?" I was on my feet in a second. Jin was easing himself up the wall carefully behind me.

"She made the crucial error of resisting." Hala followed through the door, dropping the illusion of looking human as she did, her skin going back to its normal golden hue. "She was fighting us, saying she couldn't leave her brother behind. Turns out she could." She took my still-glittering skin in with one sweeping glance, though half the gold dust had faded in the escape. "Well, this is a sorry sight," she said by way of greeting. Her eyes danced to Jin.

Some of the dust from my skin had rubbed off on Jin, a smear of gold from his left ear to his mouth. Jin wiped a hand absentmindedly across his jaw. It was no good; the gold from my skin was all over his hands, too. I might've been embarrassed if it wasn't for the unconscious princesses and old friends in this tiny kitchen pulling my mind in other directions.

"The others?" Jin asked, giving up.

His question was answered before Hala could. Imin stumbled in, servant's garb badly torn. Shazad pushed her way into the kitchen behind Imin. She had Tamid by the arm. He tried to shake her off angrily as she pushed him ahead of her. Shazad let him go slowly, making it clear she didn't have to before she did. And then she saw me and that sloppy smile broke over her face as she closed the distance with a hug. I felt my own arms, like they were finally untethered, fling themselves around her.

"Rahim?" I asked.

"Alive." She released me. "Captured. He's a soldier through and through. We needed someone to cover our escape. And he wouldn't run." She looked at me. "We're going to fix this." And I believed her. Because I was back. I wasn't a prisoner anymore and we could do anything. Her hand tightened on my back. And then Imin was demanding her attention and she split away from me. And I was facing Tamid, who was staring at the ground intently, leaning wrong on his fake leg.

And then my arms were around him. Relief wracked through my body. "Thank you." I pulled him close.

But Tamid didn't return the gesture. He pulled away. "I'm not a traitor, Amani. I didn't do it"—his eyes went to

Jin—"for your rebellion." The only time Tamid had met Jin he'd been pulling me up onto a Buraqi while I left Tamid bleeding in the sand. My guess was that wouldn't particularly endear him to my childhood friend.

"Well, then." Shazad clapped a hand on his shoulder, as I swallowed the lump in my throat. "I guess we'll be keeping both you and the princess under lock and key for a while. Come on."

"Where are we?" I asked finally, glad my voice sounded normal as we started toward the door leading out of the kitchen and into the house.

"My house," Shazad said. I tripped on the bottom step of the kitchen. Jin steadied me. "My father is away and I sent my mother and my brother to our house on the coast. I didn't want to put them in danger."

"We're camping out in General Hamad's house?" I asked.

"No." Jin's hand was at the base of my back. "That would be like asking to get caught. We are using it, but most of the camp—" He winced as he reached for the door, grasping his side. I opened it for him. A fine dining room, dark now, waited on the other side. "There's a garden, not far from here," Jin explained as we crossed slowly. "It's linked to this house by a tunnel."

Jin led me through another door, his hand looping tighter on my waist. I realized he'd scarcely let me go since we'd left the palace. We were propping each other up.

The tunnel started in the cellar, behind two huge boxes that were labeled as being flour but that sounded a lot like guns when I disturbed one of them as we pushed by. Shazad struck an oil lamp to life and led the way.

I wasn't sure how far we walked. It was more than twice the length of Dustwalk, though. I counted my paces for that long before giving up. And then a pinprick of light appeared ahead of us. Another door, I realized.

I hesitated. Dozens of memories of coming home to the Dev's peace flooded in. Of standing outside the door in the cliff face, and waiting for it to let me leave the desert dust and come home. That was gone now. That home wouldn't be waiting for me on the other side of this door. It wouldn't spill open onto an oasis that had been built out of magic and turned into the Rebellion's refuge. The people who had died in our escape wouldn't be on the other side waiting for me. I didn't know what to expect. But I wanted to come home all the same.

I stepped through.

It was quieter than the old camp. That was the first thing I noticed. And I realized why in an instant. The huge walls that stretched up around the property might block everything from sight except the sky, but we were still in the middle of a city. There were ears all around.

But the place was still blazing with light and with movement.

It wasn't the desert, but the memory of the desert was still there. Tents were scattered among the campfires and a makeshift armory had been set up against one of the walls. Lanterns and laundry crisscrossed patterns over the sky. It almost looked like hope.

"Amani!" Delila was the first person to see me. She was sprinting across the garden and flung her arms around me, pulling me from Jin's grip. "You're alive! They got you out! What happened to your hair? I like it, though! You look older. I wanted to come and help, too, but no one would let me."

I realized as she pushed her hair behind her ears that it looked darker. And not just by some trick of the light or because of an illusion she was casting. It had been dyed black, hiding the telltale Demdji purple. A safety measure in the big city. Ahmed was taking no risks with his little sister.

"We've been over this," Shazad said. "We need to keep one of you two in the camp at all times just in case we need to hide it." She gestured between Delila and Hala, who smiled tightly.

"And somehow I'm always the expendable one."

"Nice to see you, too, little sister," Jin joked as she pulled away from me. With a foolish grin Delila flung herself at Jin. I was sure the greeting I was getting was a pale shadow in comparison to what Jin had had when he finally returned.

Navid was on us, grabbing Imin, still in the bloody servant's garb, in a tight embrace. All those days with Imin roaming the palace and no news couldn't have been easy on Navid. But Imin had been right—the beard didn't suit him.

And then I was being passed from hand to hand, friends and rebels I barely knew alike patting me on the back, hugging me, congratulating me on staying alive. On escaping. Thanking me for my sacrifice when I'd stayed so long in the harem. The twins turned into two cats and twined themselves around my legs, almost tripping me with every step I took. I felt like a piece of myself was being returned to me with every person, pulling me out of the harem, pulling away the grief over Shira, the anger over my aunt, everything that had happened in the last few months, as I slipped from one hand to another.

And then like the parting of a curtain I was standing face-to-face with Ahmed. I was sure that every moment of doubt I'd had in the past months, all of it, was scrawled across my traitor eyes. Every time I'd seen his father decide more quickly. Every time I'd feared that the Sultan was right and Ahmed wasn't ready. Every time I'd been stupid enough to listen to a murderer and a tyrant.

"Ahmed—"

"Amani." He grabbed me roughly by the shoulder, jolting me forward into a hug. I collapsed gratefully. Ahmed was a lot easier to believe in when he was flesh and blood in front of me. "Welcome home."

FORTY

The ripples of the night before hit us one by one.

The events of Auranzeb were twisted by the palace before being spread among the people of Izman. The Sultan announced Miraji's independence from foreign rule. Any country that threatened our borders would burn for it.

The announcement went on to say that in the fighting of the night Prince Kadir had been killed. He had died bravely in combat, killed by his own brothers, the Rebel Prince and Prince Rahim, who had turned on his family unexpectedly, along with Lord Bilal, who had escaped. Prince Rahim had been apprehended trying to flee like a coward. He would be cursed forever for killing his own blood. The Sultan was grieving his son. There was no news about an execution for Rahim. After what had happened at Shira's execution I could see why the Sultan might not want to risk another public beheading.

There were going to be new Sultim trials. To choose a new heir to Miraji. The Sultan had told me the people never loved the throne so much as when princes were killing each other for it. He'd murdered his own son and now he was using his death to win the people back over from the Rebellion to the throne.

But we could use it, too. We would remind the city that the Sultim trials had already chosen an heir. Prince Ahmed.

In light of the recent events, the palace announced there would be a new curfew. The Sultan's army of Abdals would patrol the streets. They could not be reasoned with or argued against. Anyone found on the streets between sundown and sunrise would be executed. It was for safety, the palace said. After all, only dark intentions belonged to the dark hours of the night. They didn't say it was to hobble the Rebellion, but we all heard the meaning behind the words.

And we were hobbled.

It was strange, hearing it from the outside, after being on the inside for so long. We were operating blind again just when we couldn't afford to. It was agreed that Imin would go back to the palace, to be our eyes.

"Isn't there another way?" I knuckled my eyes tiredly as I went over it with the others. We were in Shazad's father's office. It had been set up as a war room of sorts. Not that much had needed to change for that. There was something comforting about it even though we could scarcely have been further from Ahmed's pavilion back in the rebel camp. The walls were pinned with maps and notes. The map of Izman I'd stolen from the Sultan's desk the night we'd eaten together was right in the middle. I recognized a lot of the rest as information I'd passed on from inside the palace.

Some of it Rahim had given me.

I'd escaped, but he was still inside. And we needed to know what was happening to him. So I felt a stab of guilt as I voiced my objection. "I'm not sure it's smart to put another Demdji in the Sultan's hands." Rahim had been my ally, but no one knew better than I did the risks of Imin getting found out.

Navid looked hopeful at my objection. He was sitting in a huge armchair in the corner, arms circled around Imin. She was wearing a petite feminine shape, small enough that she fit into her husband's arms like she was a missing piece who'd belonged there all along. Her legs were tucked under her as she leaned against his chest comfortably, eyes closed. She was exhausted but awake. The night before had taken its toll on everyone. Hala was truly asleep in a corner. Jin was sitting on Shazad's father's desk, shirt flung over his back, as Shazad inspected the wound on his side.

"You need to get this seen to properly," Shazad said to Jin. "Somewhere you won't bleed all over my father's study. Go find Hadjara." We'd lost our Holy Father in the escape from the Dev's Valley. Until we had someone new, Hadjara was a decent seamstress.

"If you don't need me—" Jin said, easing himself to his feet.

"We've done fine without you so far, brother," Ahmed commented. It was a low blow. Shazad and I shared a look. This new tension that hung between Ahmed and Jin wasn't good for anyone.

But Jin didn't say anything as he brushed past me on his way to the door, fingers dancing across the back of my hand like he wanted to take it. "Don't volunteer for anything stupid while I'm gone."

"We don't have that many other choices that I can see," Imin said as the door closed behind Jin. "Unless someone else would like to reveal now that they've been sitting on a secret shape-shifting skill so I can take a break. Anyone? No? I didn't think so."

"I'd offer, but I don't think foreigners are all that welcome in the palace at the moment," Sam offered. He was watching Shazad. "And I don't make a beautiful enough woman to pass in the harem very long. Amani can vouch for that."

"It's true," I admitted. "He doesn't have the cleavage to pull off a khalat." Shazad snorted.

"Someone has to go," Imin said, uncurling herself from her husband's grip, shifting easily from wife to rebel. "If I get caught I can always take poison before he gets his claws into me like he did Amani." I wasn't entirely sure she was joking.

We stole a few hours of sleep after daybreak, when we were sure the palace was done feeding lies to the people and the rush of the night before had worn off. We were in Shazad's home, which meant she had her own rooms inside the house. That was the moment it hit me in earnest that our old home was gone. Our tent was gone. The small space that we had shared for half a year and that had become as familiar as my bed in Dustwalk had ever been.

I figured I could've found my own tent. If I'd wanted to. Start getting settled into this new camp. Instead, I found Jin. He was dozing in the shade of an orange tree with huge, sprawling branches. His shirt was riding up and I could see the place Hadjara had patched him up. He startled awake as I stretched out next to him, stilling as he realized it was me. I knew he was watching me. In the scarce few months we'd had between Fahali and the bullet that caught me in the side, we'd stolen plenty of moments together in the desert but never slept side by side. He shifted slightly so he was on his side facing me as I settled down, pillowing my head with my arm. The grass was still cool from the night. I might be sleeping on the ground again, but I had the feeling I would rest easier here than I had on a hundred cushions in the harem. "I haven't gotten around to setting up a new tent yet." His arm found the small of my back. "Seeing as I only just got back from chasing down this girl I know."

"Next time you should try to keep better track of her," I said as I closed my eyes, leaning my head into him.

"I'm counting on it." He settled me against him. That was the last thing I heard before I dozed off.

Shazad woke us both sometime in the afternoon; her hair was wet from a bath and twisted up into a knot at the back of her head. I wondered if she'd had any real rest since Auranzeb. Leyla had finally come to, she told us.

Shazad had made good on her promise of chains. Tamid and Leyla had been confined to two of the many empty rooms in the house, chained and locked until we could count on them not making a run for it. I'd tried to go see Tamid in the room adjoining Leyla's, but he'd pretended to be sleeping, which was a clear enough message for me.

Leyla looked like a trapped animal, her knees pulled up to her chin, eyes darting between me, Jin, Ahmed, and Shazad, like she was trying to watch us all at once.

No. Not a trapped animal. She was looking at us like we might be the animals. About to tear her apart at any second. I remembered the day I met her, in the menagerie. When she'd been building a small mechanical elephant and I'd been the one being circled by Kadir's wives. But this was different. At least I figured it was.

"So," Ahmed said conversationally, sitting down at the end of the bed. She drew her legs in a bit farther. "You built an army of machine and magic for my father."

"I didn't—" Leyla had always sounded young, but her small voice was almost gone now. "Please, don't hurt me. I didn't have a choice in helping him."

"Nobody's going to hurt you," Ahmed said gently at the

same time that Shazad made a disbelieving noise at the back of her throat.

"Everyone has a choice," Shazad said when Leyla looked at her with wide, startled eyes. I kicked her ankle. Hard. The last thing we needed was to scare Leyla too badly to talk. She looked at me sharply.

"My choice was to help my father or watch my brother die." Leyla buried her face in her chained-up hands miserably. "What would you have done?" And then she started to cry. Out of nowhere, big ugly sobs that shook her whole body violently.

"Your father threatened Rahim?" I asked, instead of letting Shazad answer that question. "He told you he would hurt him if you didn't help him?" Rahim had been worried about Leyla being in danger in the harem, but it looked like he was the one being threatened.

"Rahim has no idea. He never knew what happened to our mother." Leyla wiped at her running nose with her sleeve as best she could with tied hands. "All those years back. She told my father she could make him a machine that could power all of Miraji. That could change the world." Her mother had been the daughter of a Gamanix engineer. The country that melded magic and machines. "And she did it. Except that it needed to take its energy from somewhere. It took it from her." Leyla wiped angrily at the tears welling in her eyes. "Just like it did for all the other people who came after her."

"Like Sayyida," I realized. "And Ayet." And Mouhna and Uzma. Girls who had disappeared out of the harem without a trace. A place where girls disappeared all the time without causing any ripples.

"They were tests. You can take—" Leyla squeezed her eyes shut. "The Holy Books say that mortals are made with a spark of Djinni fire. The machine takes that spark and can give life to something else. Not true life, but— what they have. My father figured if he could do that with a mortal life, what could be done with an immortal one?" Leyla looked pained.

"You can power an army that doesn't fall when faced with bullets," Shazad filled in, understanding what it was we'd all seen the night before. The gravity of what we were facing moved between the four of us. "That doesn't tire or eat. That can stand against Miraji's enemies."

"Including us," I said, grimly. "How do they work?"

Leyla shrugged, looking miserable. "The same way all magic docs. Words, words, words."

"So how do we stop them?" Shazad interrupted before Leyla could tumble down some rabbit hole of self-pity.

"It's almost impossible." Leyla shook her head, tears squeezing out of her eyes. "You'd have to destroy the power source and—"

"The machine," Jin said. He took a step forward and Leyla flinched away from him. I put a hand on his arm, stopping him. He might technically share the same blood as Leyla, but he was a dangerous-looking tattooed stranger to her, not a brother.

"How do we do that?" Shazad asked. "We've got enough gunpowder to blow the whole thing if we can—"

"No," Leyla said hurriedly, her eyes wide and panicked. "You'd destroy the whole city!" Like in the story of Akim and his wife. Djinni fire out of control. "The Djinni has to be released, not unleashed. The energy released with the right words." Then Leyla looked straight at me. "Amani bound him. She's the only one who can unbind him."

And just like that, everyone was looking at me. If I'd known I was doomed to get this much attention I might've brushed my hair.

FORTY-ONE

"**I**'m not going to lie to you all." Ahmed looked around the kitchen crowded with rebels. "This is going to be a challenge." It was a good thing for morale that Ahmed wasn't a Demdji. If he couldn't lie, I was pretty sure he would've struggled to use the word *challenge* instead of, say, *disaster*.

We were two dozen or so packed to the rafters around Shazad's kitchen, leaning against the colorful tiles that swirled around the walls like steam off a fine dish, our heads bumping pans that hung from the ceiling. Shazad stood next to Ahmed, at his right hand like she always did. Jin was leaning on the fireplace; if you didn't know he was injured, you might not even guess he was using it for support. Sam had retreated to the back, letting his hand pass in and out of the wall absentmindedly.

I cradled the cup of strong coffee in my hands. I'd slept a few more restless hours, but not enough. There were faces that should have been here that weren't, people who had died in the escape from the valley. There were new faces I didn't know. Still, even in the strange setting, it felt just like it used to in Ahmed's pavilion in the camp. We'd lost that home, but we were still fighting to make a new one.

The curtains in the kitchen were red, drawn against peeping eyes on the street. They turned the room bloody as the dawn.

A new dawn. A new desert.

"We're outnumbered," Ahmed said, "outmaneuvered and outgunned."

Jin caught my eye across the room, an eyebrow going up as if to say, *Not much of an inspirational speech.* I snorted.

"And out-Demdjied, judging by those things at Auranzeb," someone muttered from the back. A ripple of assent went through the room. The rumors of the Abdals and their strange powers had spread frighteningly fast. Shazad said there were already signs of it snuffing what sparks of dissent we'd been able to ignite in the streets.

"Yes, thank you, Yasir. And that's where we start." Shazad took control easily as she stepped up to the table. Ahmed ceded the room to her. I had an image of Shazad next to Ahmed on the throne. As his Sultana as well as his general, her head dipped over some problem with a golden crown slipping down her brow. It would suit her. "We have three problems of pressing urgency right now, and thanks to our real Blue-Eyed Bandit, now returned to us—no offense," she tossed over her shoulder at Sam, "we might have solutions for them."

"Even if she did create one of those problems in the first place," Hala muttered.

I ignored her. As I stepped forward, eyes followed me. I might not have been back long but I'd already noticed the change. I wasn't just the Blue-Eyed Bandit anymore; I was the girl who had made it out of the palace alive, who had stood toe to toe with the Sultan and escaped. "The first problem is that we need an army, a true army that can go up against the Sultan's. If we can forge an alliance with Lord Bilal, then we have a fighting force. We've arranged a meeting with Lord Bilal a few hours from now. Before dark. By the end of it, here's hoping we'll have an army."

"Assuming he hasn't already fled the city," Hala added.

"Did you get more pessimistic since I left," I asked, "or did I just forget what a pain in the ass you are?"

"Well, you know what they say about absence making the heart grow fonder." Hala shot a fake smile my way. "Isn't optimism what got you captured in the first place?"

"Please keep in mind how many ways I know to kill you both if you don't shut up," Shazad interrupted before we could descend into an all-out brawl. A laugh went around the room, lightening the weight of the mood.

"Our second problem," Ahmed said, trying to get the room back on track, "is that even if we do get an army, we can only stand against another army of flesh and blood. Not one made out of mechanical parts and magic. Which is why we need to get Amani to that machine."

"And right now it'll be too well defended. There's no way we can get anywhere near it," Shazad said. "Not unless we draw the Sultan and his whole army away from guarding it. Which, as it turns out, wars are very useful tools for."

Everyone stared at Shazad. "Are you suggesting we start a war just to get Amani into the palace?" someone said from the back of the room.

"No," Shazad said. "We need to start a war anyway. I'm suggesting we use the war to make our odds of winning a little better by giving Amani the opportunity to sneak into the palace."

Even if I could get inside I wouldn't be able to deactivate the machine without the right words to free the Djinn in the first language. Words not even Tamid knew.

"Bringing us to our final problem," Ahmed pressed on. "Which is that Amani is currently . . . incapacitated." That settled the room soon enough. I self-consciously rubbed the spot on my arm where I could feel one of the pieces of iron sewed into my flesh. It was like prodding at a loose tooth. An instinct, a tic, feeling that little shoot of pain when I pressed it in, reminding myself this wasn't truly part of me. Reminding me I was useless with my body riddled with iron scars.

"Where are we on finding a Holy Man we can trust?" Shazad asked, leaning her knuckles on the table. "Someone to cut the iron out of Amani?" I knew what the words cost her. In the months since Bahi had died, I didn't know if I'd truly heard Shazad talk so plainly about Holy Fathers. Not even when I'd been shot through the stomach. But then again, I had been unconscious for most of that.

"More or less exactly where we were the last three times you asked me that," said Sam. He was on edge. "Holy Men are largely in the pockets of your Sultan. They'd all sell you out in a heartbeat sooner than they'd help you."

And Tamid couldn't be trusted not to stick a blade in me either, given how he felt about the rebellion.

"Can't we take a chance?" I rubbed my finger along my forearm, worrying at the piece of metal below there. I wanted to claw it out of my skin myself.

"No," Jin said without hesitation, speaking for the first time. Everyone's head swiveled toward him. Jin didn't tend to speak up at war meetings, unless he had something that needed saying. Which meant folks tended to listen. Only there was an uneasiness among the rebels now. He hadn't disappeared on just me. He'd abandoned the whole Rebellion. "We're not taking chances with you."

"So either we find someone," I concluded, "or I've got to walk into the palace more or less defenseless."

"Welcome back to being human," Shazad said. "I'll get you some guns."

• ● •

"SAM." I CAUGHT him as the kitchen emptied. He was peeling an orange stolen out of one of the baskets hanging from the ceiling. "I need your help." I stopped speaking as Shazad brushed past me, calling out to someone quickly about the weapons supply. That earned me a raised eyebrow from Sam.

"Something your general can't help you with?"

I lowered my voice as I pulled him into an out-of-the-way corner. "I think I know somebody who might be able to help get the iron out of my skin. Not a Holy Man. A woman. My aunt."

Sam paused, orange wedge halfway to his mouth. "The woman who drugged you and kidnapped you and sold you to the harem? Yes, she seems very trustworthy."

"Please, Sam, I need help. You walked in and out of the harem at will for months. You have no idea what it's like to be in there and feel powerless to leave or defend yourself." I tugged up my shirt, showing the scar on my hip, the same one I'd shown him the first time we met. "This happened even when I had my power. If I have to, I'll walk into the palace again without it, but I'm twice as likely to get killed doing that and you know it. But I'd take just about any risk not to. Now, will you help me?"

Sam considered, peeling off another piece of the orange. "How much?"

"How much what?"

"How much are you going to pay me to find your oh-so-very-trustworthy aunt?"

My shoulders sagged. "Really? After all this, you want to keep pretending you're doing it for the money?"

"Why else would I be doing it?" he asked. "I'm a bandit, remember?"

"Because you want to be something more than that,"
I said finally. It had been a gamble. A guess. But the way
it fell off my tongue so easily I was sure I was right. I'd
watched Sam walk through walls with injuries for this rebellion. Walk into Auranzeb as a traitor to his own people
for this rebellion. He wasn't doing this for money anymore. "That's why you're still here."

"That'd be an awfully stupid reason." Sam scratched his
eyebrow. I stayed silent. "I'll see what I can do."

FORTY-TWO

As it turned out, the Hidden House wasn't all that hidden. It was a bathhouse at the intersection of two twisting streets lined with colorful awnings in the middle of Izman. To me, they looked exactly like every other street we'd passed through on the way there. The city was an immense maze, and if it wasn't for Ahmed gently nudging me around twists and turns, I'd have gotten lost sooner than I'd ever been in the desert.

As we got closer, steam heavy with the smells of flowers and spices curled out of lattice windows, sliding its fingers into my hair, taunting me with memories of the harem. Ahmed gave me a small nudge, indicating I should look up. As I did, the name finally made sense. All the buildings in this corner of Izman seemed to stand an even three stories tall. The Hidden House stretched up two stories higher than any of the others around it. And the roof was shielded by canopies of vines and desert flowers that tumbled down the walls, hiding it from prying eyes.

Shazad had picked this place for the meeting with Lord Bilal. Except she'd told him to meet her elsewhere first. With no guards and no weapons. It was up to Shazad to meet him there and bring him here. We were taking our precautions. We were asking him to put an awful lot of faith in us.

Jin had gone first, out in the open, to see if he drew any attack and to sweep the place for traps. Ahmed and I followed, looking like an ordinary couple walking the streets of Izman instead of a prince and a bodyguard with a gun secreted in the folds of her khalat. But we made it as far as the house without incident.

Ahmed pushed open the door and let himself in. At a desk a girl's head darted up. "Well, if it isn't our Rebel Prince." She flicked a book shut and shot me a look. "You can take your finger off that trigger—you're safe here." I hadn't even realized I'd been gripping my gun. I eased my finger off. But I didn't reholster it. "Your brother is on the roof," the girl said to Ahmed.

"What is this place?" I asked, as we started up the stairs.

"It's a safe haven." Ahmed stepped aside, letting me go first. I wasn't sure if he was being polite or if that was what I was supposed to do as his guard. "Not ours. Sara's." He tilted his head backward at the girl at the desk. "She was married at sixteen. Widowed at seventeen. Nobody but Sara knows what her husband died of, since no one could prove that it was poison, but he left her with broken bones and a great deal of money." My mind darted to Ayet without meaning to. If she'd wound up here instead of in the palace she might not have been my enemy. She might have been one of us. She might still be all right. Or she might have taken a bullet for the Rebellion and died outright. "She took the money and made this. It's a place for women who might not want to be with their husbands. For whatever reason. A place that keeps women safe from them. Sayyida came from here. And we found Hala here, too."

"Hala's married?" I almost tripped on the step.

"Who do you think took her fingers?" Ahmed steadied me. "You all right?"

"Fine." I waved him off. "So how come it looks gaudier than a whorehouse at Shihabian?" I asked.

Ahmed laughed, catching me off guard. Ahmed had a good laugh; I'd forgotten that. It'd been a damn long time since I'd heard it. "Sara's theory is that if folks think they know what you're up to, they don't dig much deeper and risk finding the truth. And everybody thinks they know what we're up to, with a house full of women, with men coming in and out every day, and the occasional child appearing." Sara. Now I remembered why that name rang a bell. Standing on a mountain in a desert, the day before Bahi died, Shazad teasing him about a child with a woman named Sara. "She likes to say she just added some pillows. We sent Fadi here. He'll be safe."

We climbed four flights of stairs until we reached the roof. Jin was there, waiting, shadowed under a canopy of greenery. His shoulders eased visibly when he saw us. "No trouble on the way?"

"We're fine," I said. "No trouble here?" He shook his head.

We lapsed into tense silence as we waited for Shazad. It was meant to be a half hour before she arrived. It was closer to a full hour and panic had my guts wrapped in a knot wondering what had happened to her when she emerged at the top of the stairs with Bilal, hooded and blindfolded.

We'd told him to meet Shazad unarmed and alone. We'd set almost all of the terms of our meeting and we'd set them high, expecting a negotiation. But Shazad said he hadn't even flinched. He'd agreed to come to us, defenseless. That was the sort of thing that made you suspect a trap. Shazad kept scanning the skies around us warily as she pulled the hood from his head and uncovered his eyes.

"Don't worry," Bilal said lazily, "I don't have anything up my sleeves. You can ask any one of your Demdji if you don't believe me."

Everyone looked at me. So he knew what I was. "He's telling the truth," I said. I could tell what Shazad was thinking. There was something wrong with a man who had so little regard for his own life.

"Good." Bilal stuck his hands in his pockets. He was wearing an ugly purple-and-gold kurta that was too loose on him and billowed around his arms. He fit right in with the gaudiness of the Hidden House. "So you're the famous Rebel Prince." Bilal looked Ahmed over. "I thought you'd be taller."

"You shouldn't believe everything you hear," Ahmed said.

"I hear you might actually be able to topple your father," Bilal offered. "With some help from my army."

"That," Ahmed said, "you should believe."

"Good," Bilal said. "I want to end this parade of invaders. It's tiresome. If my army can topple your father, it is yours to command. I never had much interest in commanding anyway. That was always Rahim's strength. He was like a second son to my father. But I will want something in return."

"When I am Sultan"—Ahmed was prepared—"I will declare Iliaz independent. You can be the ruler of your own kingdom, as long as you are prepared to swear allegiance to the throne of Miraji."

"Oh, I don't care about that." Bilal shook his head. "That was just a pretext to feed your pretty general something big enough to get me face-to-face with you. If I'd told her what I was truly after outright, I had the feeling she'd turn me down on the spot on your behalf. Women—they can be so unreasonable."

"And what is it that you're after?" Ahmed asked. He was careful with his wording. He didn't say, *Name it.* Even though we all knew how desperate we were.

"You can keep your kingdom, every last piece of it."

Bilal said. "In exchange for my army, all I want is one of your Demdji as a wife."

The silence that filled the moment that followed was tangible. It was the silence of shock from all of us on the roof. It was the silence in which Ahmed didn't immediately refuse him.

"The Demdji are not mine to offer," Ahmed said finally, picking his words carefully. "Iliaz, on the other hand—"

"I have no interest in being the king of my own country." Bilal waved a languid hand. "An independent Iliaz was my father's dream. He was an ambitious man. A great man. I'm a dying man. The Holy Men say it's in my blood. I have a handful of years left to live. If I'm lucky."

I saw it now, in the loose-fitting clothing, the pallor of his skin, the way he held himself like he was always tired. It wasn't arrogance. It was illness. "Even if you did win the war and grant me my own kingdom, I would rule over it for how long? One year, two?"

"So where do we come in?" I couldn't keep my mouth shut any longer. Not when he was negotiating for one of us. "If you just want a wife to give you a son before you die, I'm sure you can find someone who's not a Demdji."

Bilal smiled wanly. "Everyone has this notion that the Demdji have powers to heal. That is why on the black market you can buy scraps of hair or strange skin. Or floating blue eyeballs to heal you." His eyes traveled across us. "But that is a watered-down story. Some will say that the true healing power lies in taking a Demdji's life." I remembered Mahdi holding his knife to Delila's throat, trying to drag her to Sayyida, to save her life. Saying Delila would die so she could live. "It's a mistranslation from Old Mirajin, you see." Bilal looked at us. "The true phrase is not whoever takes a Demdji life, but whoever owns a Demdji life. Whoever is *given* a Demdji's life. Surely you know the story of Hawa and Attallah."

Hawa and Attallah had made oaths to each other.

The stories said that theirs was a love so great that it shielded Attallah in battle. But if she was a Demdji . . .

Wedding vows. It hit me like a punch in the gut.

I give myself to you. All that I am I give to you. And all that I have is yours. My life is yours to share.

Until the day we die.

They were nothing but ritual for most. But in the mouth of a Demdji, they were truth-telling. That was how the legend had been born—Hawa had kept Attallah alive with her words. So long as she watched him on the walls, her life tied to his, he lived. When she fell, he fell, too. He didn't die from grief. He died from a Demdji truth.

Dead silence had fallen around us as that understanding sank in.

"Give me one of your Demdji," Bilal said, and his eyes scraped across me. "She will be treated well. I will not harm her. Though I will expect her to perform all her wifely duties." I saw Jin's hand tighten. "I will ask only one son of her. And in return, I will honor her by taking no other wife. I want to live to see my hair turn gray and meet my grandchildren. And I will give you an army and a country. One girl, in exchange for a throne."

He let the weight of his words settle over us. "I see you need to consider this. I ride for Iliaz in the morning. If you want an army, come find me there with a wife. If you don't—" He shrugged. "I will watch you and your rebels burn under your father's new weapons from my fortress and die in my own bed long before the war is over and the Sultan comes for me. And if you hate me for it, we can settle that after death."

FORTY-THREE

I missed the desert nights like an ache. Shira had been right, you couldn't see the stars from Izman. The city was too flooded with noise and light, too bright to make out the constellations of the dead.

But I knew it wasn't really the stars I missed. Everything had changed. We weren't an upstart rebellion in the desert anymore. I missed the simplicity of being sure that what we were doing was right. That it was worth it.

We were starting a war. And a war demanded sacrifice. I could feel the uneasy restlessness in the camp.

"There's an easy way out of this, you know." When Jin talked, with my head leaning against his chest, I felt it in my bones before I truly heard him. It was long past dark and we were both already half-asleep.

It'd been a long, quiet walk back after Bilal's proposal. Even Shazad hadn't had anything to say. Ahmed and Jin had fallen into step ahead of me, deep in an angry conversation. They were working it out at the same time as everyone else was. Hala and Imin were both already married. Which left me and Delila. The two of us were the only ones who were able to offer ourselves up to Bilal in sacrifice if we wanted that army. If we wanted to make this a real fight, not a slow massacre.

I knew what Jin meant. If he and I got married, I was off the table, too.

"I know," I said. I didn't say anything else. I didn't say that I knew Jin would never forgive himself if he saved me over Delila. That if Ahmed tried to force my hand he wasn't the kind of ruler I'd want leading an army anyway. I didn't say that I'd walked across the entire desert to *not* wind up having marriage chosen for me, even if it was to Jin.

But my silence spoke for me.

He wrapped his arms around me and pulled me against his chest. He was warm and solid. I tucked my head low, my mouth resting against his heartbeat, over the sun tattoo.

He fell asleep eventually. I didn't.

After a few restless hours I pulled myself out of his arms. We were mostly sleeping without tents in the warm summer air. I picked my way through the bodies that were strewn across the grass. Like dead on a battlefield. The house was quiet as I made my way back to the kitchen.

It looked a lot bigger without half of the Rebellion

stuffed into it. I started rifling through the tins on Shazad's shelf. Looking for coffee.

The door to the kitchen crashed open, making me jump so violently I knocked a glass bottle to the ground with an ear-splitting shatter. An unfamiliar man staggered into the kitchen. I was about to go on the attack when he got close enough to the fire that I saw yellow eyes. "Imin?" I relaxed, even as he collapsed into a chair by the fire, breathing hard. "Are you all right?"

"I had to run all the way here," he panted. He was wearing a young man's face and his beardless cheeks looked flushed. "The city is swarming with those Abdal things. One nearly saw me a few streets back. But I couldn't get out of the palace all day and I had to tell someone. Rahim . . ."

That name got my attention. "Is he all right?"

"No," Imin deadpanned. "He's a prisoner. He's obviously *not* all right. But he's not dead, either. And judging by all the talk in the kitchens, he's not going to be. Rahim is respected in the Sultan's army. Executing him would be bad for morale, they're saying. And bad for the Sultan among the people. So he's being sent away, transported to some work camp where he can die quietly."

That sounded like good news, the first in a long while, but I didn't get my hopes up yet. "When are they moving him?"

Imin treated me to another eye roll. "Do you think I ran through Abdal-infested streets for my health? Tomorrow night."

I FOUND AHMED in the general's study. There was one flickering lamp that leaked its light under the bottom of the door. It made me think of the story of the jealous Djinni who flickered a tempting light in the night, luring children out of their parents' homes, making them chase the fire far enough into the night that he could snatch them up and keep them as pets.

I could hear voices from halfway down the hallway.

"Delila . . ." Ahmed sounded tired. "You can't—"

"Yes, I can!" Delila raised her voice. I paused, just shy of the threshold. "You're the one who can't, Ahmed. There wouldn't even be a war if it wasn't for me. This whole thing started because I was born. That's why Mother—I mean Lien—had to run. That's why you two had to start working when you were younger than I am now to feed us. I'm the reason you and Jin grew up in Xicha and that's why this whole revolution started in the first place. That's why Bahi is dead, and Mahdi and Sayyida and everyone else. I started this war and you will not even let me fight it. So I'm going to help finish it."

I stepped back just as Delila stormed out of the study, the door hitting the wall loudly enough to wake half the house. She didn't even see me as she pushed her way down the hallway. I waited until she was out of sight before I stepped into the light on the threshold.

Ahmed's head shot up as my shadow crossed into the study. It had been resting on his palms, his elbows propped on the desk. His gaze struggled to focus on me. There was an empty bottle next to him. I wondered how full it'd been when he started.

"Amani." He stretched up, and the candlelight traveled across his face, flicking one side into light then the other, so he looked like two people. I'd never seen Ahmed drunk before, I realized. "If you're here to do the selfless thing and offer yourself up to Lord Bilal for an army, I'm afraid my sister just beat you to it."

"Doing the selfless thing doesn't sound a whole lot like me." I sank down into the chair across from him without being invited.

"Jin would never forgive me if I were to let you go." Ahmed shook his head. "If I let Delila go, he won't, either, but I'll probably never forgive myself, so at least we'll both hate me equally then." *Let you go*, he said. Not *make you go*. Ahmed was my ruler; he could order me to do the self-less thing. To surrender myself instead of his sister. But that hadn't even crossed his mind.

Because he wasn't his father.

There had been moments in the palace when that had frightened me. That he might not be strong enough, knowledgeable enough, that he might be too idealistic. But that was what Miraji needed. Miraji needed a ruler like Ahmed. I was just afraid that a ruler like Ahmed could never seize the country from a ruler like the Sultan.

"It should be easy, shouldn't it? One person for an en-tire country. My sister or an army."

"No," I said. I thought of the ease with which the Sultan

had ordered an execution. "I don't think ruling is ever supposed to be easy. But, what if there was another way?"

"To win the Rebellion without an army?" He cast me a wan smile. "With more riots and lost lives? More cities falling out of my hands like Saramotai? With a death count rising as my father creates machines to make slaughter easy?"

"No. What if there was another way to gain control over the army from Iliaz?"

Ahmed looked up at me, a flicker of hope on his face.

"Rahim," I said. "He was commander of Iliaz's army before Bilal was ever the emir. They know him. They respect him." I thought of how easily his soldiers had fallen into line when Rahim had ordered them against Kadir the day the Gallan ambassador almost strangled me. "I think they would follow him. With or without Bilal's consent."

"Are you suggesting we send Imin—"

"No." I shook my head. "Imin might be able to take his shape, but wouldn't be able to take Rahim's place."

"Imin's done it before," Ahmed said. "Impersonated someone for us."

"Not for so long. You don't think that if Imin walked into camp with your face and started giving us orders, everyone would notice it wasn't you quicker than anything? We need the real Rahim. No more tricks, just a good old-fashioned rescue."

Ahmed leaned back in his chair. "Is that the only reason you want to save him?"

"I don't like leaving people behind." Especially not people whom I owed my life to.

"Amani, with the whole city looking over their shoulders and Abdals patrolling the streets every night . . . this sounds like a suicide mission." Ahmed rubbed his eyes. "And we're going to need the others here if we're planning one of those."

FORTY-FOUR

It was dawn before we had a plan that wouldn't end with us all dying by Abdal fire.

We started looking for the most likely place to intercept the transport taking Rahim out of the city. We needed to get to it before it left Izman. Fighting in the confined space of the city streets was to our advantage; if it got out into open ground, we didn't stand a chance. Sam stepped through the wall as we all stood craned over a map of Izman. There was an ugly bruise on his cheek that hadn't been there last time I saw him.

"Where'd you get that?" Shazad asked, distracted for a moment.

"A friend," Sam said cagily before joining us around the table. He shot me a meaningful glance I couldn't quite read. And then it was gone. "What are we doing?" he asked. "Picking out summer homes?"

"Picking a good place for an ambush," I said. The Sultan was sending Rahim's transport across the city with human guards and Abdals alike. We weren't worried about the mortal soldiers. Hala could take care of them. And if she couldn't, bullets could.

The Abdals were a different story.

We needed Leyla.

She was messy with sleep when she was brought before us in chains. But her eyes were wide and awake and frightened. Even though she wasn't so much younger than us, she looked like a child standing across from Shazad.

"Leyla." My friend leaned on the desk. "Think very hard about the answer you are going to give me before you speak. Is there a way to stop the Abdals? Any way you can think of?"

Leyla's eyes darted around the room nervously, between me and Imin, and the men who were her flesh and blood without being her true brothers. "I'm not sure—" she whispered. "I don't want anyone else to get hurt if I'm wrong." Her voice was thick with unshed tears. I resisted the urge to comfort her. There'd be someone to feel sorry for her if we rescued Rahim. Until then she was going to have to grow up.

"This is your brother's life at stake, Leyla," I said. "He would've done anything to save you. The least you can do is try to save him."

She chewed nervously on her lower lip. I couldn't tell if she was looking for an answer or if she already knew it and was deciding whether to tell us. "You could try destroying the word."

"The word?" Ahmed asked.

"The one that gives them life. It channels the Djinn's fire into their spark. I put it inside their feet." Leyla shifted nervously. "It was the hardest place for anyone to do them damage," she said. "They look like people so folk will naturally aim for their heads or their hearts. Who would think to aim for a foot?"

"That's smart," Shazad admitted. "And very inconvenient for us."

"Do you think they could be fooled by an illusion?" I asked. "Not like Hala climbing into their heads; like a veil." Like one of Delila's illusions. But I didn't mention her by name. It would be an argument to take Delila with us if the answer was yes and that was not an argument we'd be having in front of Leyla.

"They might," she admitted. "Do you have someone here who can cast illusions like that?"

"Thank you, Leyla." Ahmed's voice carried dismissal. "You've been very helpful."

Ahmed looked at me as Leyla was led back away, steeling himself.

I was ready for a fight. "You can't protect her forever, Ahmed; we need Delila—"

"I know." He held up a hand to stop me. "I know I can't protect her forever. So I will count on you two to do it."

Ahmed rubbed his hand tiredly across his face. "Get some rest before you go save my brother."

• ● •

SAM HUNG BACK with me as the others made their way to their beds even as the sun made its way into the sky. Jin cast a look back for me, but I waved him on.

"I found your aunt," Sam said when we were out of earshot of the others. "She is in a very fine set of rooms above a gold merchant's, living beyond the means of a simple medicine trader, by all accounts. It made her easy to find." She was living off the gold she'd traded me for. It was a sort of poetic justice that it had allowed Sam to find her.

"Fine." I shook my head. It was heavy with sleep and too many plans, too many things that could go wrong in rescuing Rahim. "We can go in a few days and—"

"If you do that, you'll be finding an empty house," Sam said, interrupting me. "She's packing up her life and leaving the city tomorrow. A lot of people are. Too much unrest in the city. And now the curfew. Cities are never a good place to be in times of war."

Of course. It'd sounded too much like good luck to be true.

"So we'd have to go tonight to have a stab at getting her to cut the iron out of me."

I would need more than Sam's help for that.

• ● •

"AND YOU'RE COMING to *me*." The circles of exhaustion under Hala's eyes made the skin there look a deeper shade of gold. "Me, instead of your darling Shazad or your beloved Jin?"

They don't know how to crawl inside someone's head like you do. It was on the tip of my tongue. But she wasn't wrong. Shazad or Jin and a few well-placed threats could probably get me the same thing. That wasn't the real reason I was here. We were both Demdji, and we owed each other the truth.

"They're human," I said. They would fight beside me. We would die for each other. But no matter what, they would never understand this the same way Hala did. To have a part of myself trapped away. That someone had hurt me because of what I was. That I wanted to hurt her back. "The story around camp is that your mother sold you in marriage to the man who took your fingers."

Hala's face changed at once. "Do you know what our mothers get," she replied as I watched the motion of her golden fingers through her inky hair, "along with us, from our fathers?"

"A wish," I said, remembering my conversation with Shira in the prison.

"Do you know what your mother wished for?"

"No," I admitted. I supposed I ought to ask my father, if we ever succeeded at getting me back into the palace.

"Mine wished for gold," Hala said. It was such a stupid simple wish. The one that every peasant and tinker and beggar made in stories. I didn't press her. I just waited.

She had this look like she wanted to tell me, her golden lips parted slightly. If I didn't push, she would.

"My mother had grown up poor and she wished to be rich," she said finally. "And maybe she meant it well. Maybe she found out she was going to have a child and wished for wealth to be able to raise me in comfort instead of in the gutter where she'd grown up. That's the lie I used to tell myself when I was little. But I could never say it out loud." Her smile was bitter. "And then the money ran out, and what she had left was me, her golden daughter."

She leaned back, and the light in the opening of the tent made her skin flash. She was one of the only people bothering with a tent. It occurred to me she might be hiding. The golden daughter of a woman who loved gold too much. We'd both been traded in for gold in our own way.

"I'll help you."

● ● ●

I FOUND JIN shaving inside the house, in a small room set off from the study. For the long nights when the general didn't get to his bed, I guessed. A beaten brass basin was half-filled with water underneath a cracked mirror. It was just a little bit too low for him, so that he had to stoop over. His shirt was flung over the door handle. From behind him I could see the way the muscles on his bare shoulders bunched, moving the compass tattooed on the other side of his heart. There was a new tattoo on the opposite shoulder. A series of small black dots across his skin. Like a burst of sand. As he straightened he spotted me in the reflection, leaning in the doorway watching him.

"That one's new." The room was small enough that I only had to take one step to be close enough to touch it.

"I got it done while I was with the Xichian army." His skin was hot under my hand as my fingers danced across the dots, one at a time. "I was thinking about this girl I knew." He turned around quickly, catching my hand. He smelled of mint mostly, but there was an undercurrent of desert dust and gunpowder when he kissed me that made me desperately homesick. That made it harder to speak what I had to say next.

"Jin, I'm going to tell you something," I said, pulling away, "and I don't want you to ask me any questions about it. I just want you to trust me. Tonight, there's something I've got to do before we rescue Rahim. And I need Sam and Hala for it, and I don't want to tell you what it is in case it doesn't work."

"I hate everything about this already." Jin wiped a stray streak of water off his jaw with the back of his hand.

"I had a feeling you might. But I've got to tell someone, and Shazad is more likely to try to stop me. And she needs to get to the ambush point. You both do. We can't chance this falling apart on my account."

"One way to be sure of that is for you to just come with us." Jin toyed with the ends of my shortened hair, considering me carefully, trying to read me. But for this I was determined not to let anything show.

"Get to the intersection." I stood my ground. "Wait for

us there. If everything goes right we can still get there in time to intercept Rahim."

"Is that a promise?" I knew when Jin was saying yes without really saying it. I had him on my side.

"Djinn's daughters shouldn't make promises." I pushed myself up, reaching for a shadow near his ear where the razor had missed, close enough to him to feel his heartbeat. "It usually doesn't end well."

Jin turned his head instead, catching me off guard with a kiss, fast and sure. He broke it off quickly, but he didn't pull away. He just smiled against my mouth. "Then this had better not be the end, Bandit."

FORTY-FIVE

The rooms my aunt kept above the gold merchant's were cluttered with chests, half-packed, some of them stuffed to overflowing. When Sam walked us through the wall I smacked my shin into one of them, and barely kept in the string of curses that sprang to my tongue.

We picked our way through the mess carefully; silks and muslins spilling out of a trunk brushed against my leg like clinging cloth fingers. A rope of pearls was wound carelessly on top of another chest. So this was what selling someone out to the Sultan bought you.

And in the middle of it all, sprawled across a bed, slept my aunt.

"Ready?" Hala whispered. I nodded because I wasn't sure I'd be able to answer truthfully. Hala didn't deign to wave her hands over my aunt's body like the street performers did. There was no sign that she was doing anything at all except a slight crease of concentration on her forehead.

My aunt came awake with a violent gasp as Hala seized control of her mind.

For a second, she looked around, wild-eyed. Then she saw me and her gaze focused in recognition.

"Zahia," she gasped out. I watched her fight it for a moment, the line between reality and dream. Between the knowledge that her sister was dead and what she was seeing standing in front of her. It took only a few blinks before the illusion won.

"Safiyah." I sat on the edge of her bed. "I need your help." I rested my hand next to hers on the cover. I couldn't quite bring myself to clasp it in pleading.

But Safiyah did it for me. She laced her fingers with mine and pulled my hand to her lips. "Of course." There were tears in her eyes now. "For you, I would flood the desert." She paused expectantly, looking at me. And I realized it was one half of a saying. Something that'd passed between Safiyah and my mother. Some secret bond between sisters.

Only it wasn't secret. I knew it. My mother had said it to me before. But there was no way I could say it to Safiyah.

I thought of Shazad. My sister in arms. We had recognized something in each other the first time we met and we were tied. By more than blood.

I would probably want to destroy anyone who stole her life, too. The way I had my mother's.

"For my sister . . ." I willed the words off my tongue. "I would set the sea on fire."

The rest was like walking my aunt through a dream world. She led me into her kitchen. It was a small room crowded with hanging spices as well as jars and jars of things that belonged in an apothecary. She cleared the kitchen table, talking the whole while, snippets of conversations meant for my mother which I barely understood. It was eighteen years of all the pent-up things she'd wanted to talk to her sister about while there'd been a desert between them. All the secret private jokes between sisters in a life before this one. The language of two women I'd never really known.

"You need to strip," she told me. As one, Hala and I turned to look at Sam meaningfully.

He held up his hands like we had him at gunpoint. "I'll, um . . . keep watch," he said, backing through the wall.

I stripped and lay down on my aunt's table. She plucked a tiny knife out of the pile and started cleaning it. I'd been stabbed and shot and beaten and plenty of other things in my life. But I still didn't love the look of this knife. With a roll of her eyes Hala slipped her hand into mine as my aunt stepped forward, swiping a piece of fabric, wet with something that made my skin tingle, across the spot where the first shard of metal was embedded.

The tiny knife pressed into my arm. I felt the needle

of pain shoot through me. I tensed instinctively, squeezing my eyes shut. But the feeling of my skin breaking never came. And then the hard table below me was gone. I moved my fingers and found soft sand beneath my skin.

I opened my eyes. I was staring up at stars. Desert stars, the way they blazed in the open nothingness against the dark, the last burning light of the desert.

This was an illusion. I knew that because I knew Hala. And I knew I was lying on a kitchen table with a knife cutting metal out of my arm and being stitched back up by my aunt.

But knowing the stars above me weren't real didn't matter—same as realizing you were in a dream didn't help you wake up. I didn't fight it, this unexpected kindness of Hala stealing away the pain from my mind. Instead I stretched my fingers out across the sand, reveling in the feeling of it against my skin, even if it was all in my head.

The illusion Hala had woven in my mind shattered. The desert and the stars were gone and the kitchen was back. Pain across my body woke up. I hissed and quickly Hala grabbed my mind again and the pain faded as she pulled it out of my head.

I must've been under the illusion for a good long while, because there were twelve tiny pieces of iron lying in a glass dish next to the table. There was a symbol printed into each of them. The Sultan's seal. I got angry all over again. That was so like him. He could've just shoved iron under my skin from a scrap pile, but these pieces had been specially made.

"The last one . . ." I felt my aunt's fingers exploring my skin; I felt the slight pressure on my stomach, just above my hip, a handbreadth away from my navel. Her dreamlike expression looked worried now. "It was so near your stomach, Zahia," she said to me. "There were scars here already, like an old healed wound." She frowned, like she was struggling to remember what had hurt her sister. But I knew what it was. That was where Rahim had shot me. Where the wound had healed over a long, torturous month. "The scar tissue makes it almost impossible to remove it all without making it worse," Safiyah was saying now. "I'm worried I've made it worse."

I pushed myself up, ignoring the returning pain of the smattering of twelve tiny wounds across my skin. This might be the city. But it was still desert land. There was desert dust everywhere. I pulled on it. A stabbing pain tore through my side as I did, right where my old scar was, blinding for a moment. But sure enough, I felt the ground shift, a thousand tiny grains of sand rushing toward my fingers.

I felt the rush of using my power through the pain. It would have to do. I released the sand and the pain receded.

"We need to go."

"Hold on." Hala stopped me as I started to get dressed. "What do you want to do with her?" She meant my aunt. "Do you want me to tear her mind apart?" Like Hala had done to her mother who had sold her. Who had used her daughter so selfishly.

I wanted her to hurt.

Ahmed would tell me that an eye for an eye would make the whole world blind. Shazad would tell me that was why you had to stab people through both eyes the first time around.

"Did it make you feel better?" I asked. It wasn't an accusation. It was a real question. I wanted to know. I wanted to know if hurting my aunt like she'd hurt me would take away this anger rotting in my chest. "When you tore your mother's mind apart? Did it help?"

Hala turned away from my aunt first. "We need to go."

FORTY-SIX

Moving through the streets of Izman after dark wasn't exactly easy—not with the Abdals and not with my skin rebelling with pain at every step. Without Hala in my mind, the kingdom of cuts on my body screamed in pain.

But speed was essential.

We rounded a corner, and moonlight bounced off metal and clay. Hala grabbed my arm, shoving me between two houses, into the shadows. We didn't dare move. The Abdal passed by the mouth of the alley, close enough that I could've reached out and touched it. And then the sound of steps again, closer, coming from the other end of the street, working their way toward us. Penning us in. Sam didn't hesitate, grabbing my hand and Hala's. "Hold your breath or get dead very fast."

I just had time to suck in a lungful of air before he dragged us both backward through the wall. We stumbled into a small kitchen. I could hear the rushing of my own heartbeat in time with the steps outside, slowing as they passed. We waited a solid few breaths until Sam dragged us back out.

We reached the intersection where we were due to meet, with seconds to spare.

A rope ladder dangled from the rooftop as promised. I started to climb as Hala and Sam slipped into a side alley. Jin reached a hand down for me, clasping my arm as he pulled me up the last few feet on top of the roof. A hiss of pain escaped through my teeth as his thumb hit one of my wounds.

"Is there a reason you keep coming back injured when I leave you for five seconds, or is it—" His voice carried too loud, and I clapped a hand over his mouth, shutting him up.

"Don't flatter yourself," I said quietly. "I'm always getting injured when you're around, too." I was raw inside and out. I didn't feel like explaining my encounter with my aunt just then. I pressed a finger to my lips. When he nodded, I slowly peeled my hand away.

We flattened ourselves on the edge of the roof. Jin handed me the rifle a second before the Abdal appeared around the corner.

Its steps echoed around the empty streets, accompanied by the rattle of the wheels of the prison wagon that followed behind and a dozen more boots, on human feet this time.

A word carved into metal, powering the Abdal like a heart, in the right heel. Somewhere no one would ever have the instinct to hit. We didn't need instinct; we had insider information.

Another step.

Two more.

I took a deep breath.

I squinted against the dark, trying to track the glint of metal in the moonlight. Somewhere high above, a curtain twitched, then fell shut, casting the street back into shadows almost as quickly as it had illuminated it.

But it was enough.

I pulled the trigger.

It was a perfect shot. It clipped the edge of the bronze heel guard, bending it at an angle. I almost laughed. Thank God for soft metal.

The men surrounding the carriage were pulling out weapons already, looking for the threat. But that wasn't my problem.

Jin's gun went off next to me even as Shazad stepped through Delila's veil of illusion, appearing like an avenging spirit below, blades drawn.

I took a second shot. It went through soft clay flesh. And a third. And I saw it. The shine of metal under the clay skin. Somewhere inside there was a word. Giving the thing life. A soldier turned a gun toward me and fell.

And for a moment it was like old times. Like the days before Iliaz. The three of us against the world. The simplicity of rebellion, where every little victory could win a war.

My next bullet hit hard.

When mortal things died, they fell. They fell like the soldiers littering the streets under our gunfire. But the Abdal didn't. It stopped. Just stopped as abruptly as I would have when the Sultan gave me an order.

And the streets were still again.

I clambered down after Jin.

The Abdal stood unnervingly frozen. I'd seen enough of Leyla's little inventions close up to know this one was different. It was as much a creation of a Djinni as I was.

The lock at the back of the carriage splintered under another gunshot, taking my focus with it. I joined Shazad and Jin at the back of the wagon, as the door swung open. Rahim was bound and gagged, a sack pulled over his head. I held up a hand, stopping Jin and Shazad. Rahim had rescued me once; I owed him the same.

The wagon rocked gently under my weight as I entered.

I pulled the bag off Rahim's head. He jerked, like he was ready to fight, arms bound and all. He stopped when he saw me, holding still long enough to let me pull the gag from his mouth. "What's happening?" he rasped.

"This is a rescue," Shazad said from behind me, framed in the doorway, one arm braced against the roof of the carriage. "Obviously."

"You got us an army," Jin added as I sliced the ropes around his arms free. "Now how do you feel about leading it?"

Rahim glanced over his shoulder uncertainly between us. The impossibly beautiful general, a half-Xichian prince he didn't yet know was his brother, an imposter Blue-Eyed Bandit, a Demdji with purple hair dyed black toying nervously with an illusion of a flower, another doing nothing to hide the gold of her skin. I didn't have to imagine what he was thinking. I'd been in his place eight months ago. His gaze finally landed back on me.

"Welcome to the Rebellion," I said. "You get used to it."

• ● •

WE MOVED AS quickly as we could back through the darkened and deserted streets of Izman. The Abdals patrolling the streets in a steady checkerboard rhythm might not be called by the commotion, but that didn't mean we were going to make ourselves a moving target. We caught Rahim up in interrupted whispers as we worked our way back toward Shazad's home.

We told him that Leyla was safe.

That we were going to take the army from Lord Bilal by force.

That he was going to help us do it.

Rahim didn't even blink. Maybe rebellion ran in the blood of the Sultan's sons. Maybe it ought to be called treason. Whatever it was, we were going to use it to take the throne.

Shazad's house was quiet when we pushed through the kitchen door. It was late, I supposed. But still, something about the quiet needled at me. The tension of returning from a mission was missing.

Ahmed waiting to make sure we were all coming home alive. Waiting for his sister.

Imin waiting for Hala.

My senses had reached a fever pitch by the time we were climbing the stairs at the end of the tunnel into the garden. I was on the last step when my boot hit something that rolled away with a familiar ping. A bullet. It skittered into the silent garden and then vanished.

A feeling of wrongness hit me a fraction of a second too late. I heard the click of two machine cogs slotting together. The whirr of metal pieces working, spinning faster and faster, and then snicking into place. That was the only warning I had before the illusion disappeared.

Chaos bloomed as the serene front dropped away. Bodies littered the ground, rebels mostly, only one or two men in uniform, weapons still in hand. The corpses sprawled across shattered tents, staining the ground red. Survivors were shoved back against the walls, bound by their hands. They were on their knees with soldiers gathered around them. Ahmed. Imin. Izz and Maz. Navid. Tamid. All still alive, at least.

And facing us was a whole host of Abdals.

They had created the illusion, I realized. They didn't just have Noorsham's power to destroy. They were as powerful as Demdji. And leading them . . .

"Yes, Amani." The Sultan smiled Jin's smile at me. The one that meant trouble. Like he could read my mind. Out of the chaos around him, our bound and dead rebels, one figure emerged. Leyla unbound. And unafraid. She was wearing a jacket that looked like it belonged to the Sultan over the same clothes she'd been wearing since Auranzeb. That trapped-animal look in her eyes was gone. She wore a satisfied smirk instead as her father spoke.

"It was a trap."

FORTY-SEVEN

I pulled out my gun, already knowing it was too late. Two dozen guns clattered to attention, ready to shoot us if they had to. Shazad and Jin had weapons drawn, spoiling for a fight.

They would die; they both would. I could see it now. We were all trapped. Me, Jin, Shazad, Rahim, Delila, Hala, and—I looked around for Sam. He was gone. Nowhere to be seen. We were surrounded. We were outnumbered. But that wasn't going to stop them from going down fighting.

"Stand down!" Ahmed ordered from where he was kneeling. "Everyone stand down, weapons down."

I could see Shazad struggling with every fiber of her being against the order as Jin's hand opened and closed on the gun in the corner of my vision. But my attention belonged to the Sultan. His eyes were locked on me. I could almost hear him. That weighted, reasonable voice that made me feel like we were all just children acting out. *You know how this ends if you fight, Amani.*

"Do as he says," I said. "Weapons down." I tossed my gun to the ground. The iron left my skin with a sigh of relief.

Finally Shazad's swords clattered to the ground noisily. Jin's gun followed. I was unarmed. But I wasn't helpless. The Sultan might have choreographed this, but there was something he wasn't expecting.

Somewhere at the edge of my awareness, beyond the city walls, I reached for the desert.

"Very wise." The Sultan nodded to Ahmed, tied and trapped. "You know, it never ceases to amaze me how ironic the world can be. That the son who is most like me is the only one who wants to denounce me."

"Well, that's just not true." Rahim stepped between me and his father. I used the shield of his body to shift my hands a tiny bit. I tried to pull without my arms, without any sweeping movements. I pulled from deep down in my gut, the part of me that had kept me alive against all odds until now. It came with a shooting pain in my old wound.

"I'd denounce you in a second, Father."

Far away, the desert surged up in answer.

"That's why you're on that side of Father's guns and I'm on this one." Leyla finally spoke. Her shy, lilting voice, which had always sounded sweet, took on a different tone now as it bounced around the walls of the garden. Gone were the wide, tear-filled eyes. "I'm the one who didn't betray my family."

Her brother met her gaze across the courtyard. "You were my family," he said softly. "I was trying to save you. After I found you were as talented as Mother with machines, I knew our father would try to use you the same way he did her. That *destroyed* her, Leyla."

"I didn't need saving." She tugged the jacket closer around herself against the night air. "I took care of myself from the day you left me among those women and their plots. I learned to survive. To make myself useful." She had said that to me once in the harem, as Mouhna and Uzma and Ayet disappeared, one after the other. If you weren't useful, you were liable to vanish, invisible. And who was more invisible than a princess alone in the harem?

So invisible, I hadn't even considered that Ayet had disappeared after I'd told Leyla that she'd caught me and Sam in the Weeping Wall garden. That Uzma and Mouhna had gone missing after the incident with the suicide pepper and humiliating me in court. So invisible it hadn't crossed anyone's mind that she'd witnessed their nastiness, too. That it had been her idea to select them to put into the machine, not the Sultan's. "You were gone and I was here, finishing what Mother started." Leyla's smile was as sweet as ever, and she aimed it at Rahim like a weapon. "She would have wanted that. It was the Gallan she hated. Not our father."

"You lied to me," I said. And I hadn't spotted it because she was a big-eyed, shy girl with a sweet face.

"Demdji are *always* the easiest to lie to. Your kind never expects it," the Sultan said. "What good daughter wouldn't obey the word of her father?" He made a motion, like he was pulling back a bowstring and loosing it. I was holding an entire sandstorm in my mind on the edge of the city, dragging it forward over walls and rooftops. I felt it stagger as something punched through my heart. The horrible, humiliating memory of wanting to impress him, of wanting to please him. Of doubting Ahmed for him.

"Little Blue-Eyed Bandit, so very trusting, over and over." I flinched at the nickname as he started toward me. Jin shifted angrily at the edge of my vision, but he knew better than to try anything as his father drew closer. "Oh, yes, Amani, I knew from the moment I saw your little blue eyes."

All those desperate attempts to hide it from the Sultan, to keep Ahmed from coming up so that the truth wouldn't slip past my traitorous tongue. And he'd been letting me get away with it, letting me dance around the subject. Because he already knew I was allied with Ahmed.

The Sultan chucked me under the chin gently as he reached me. "I could've made you tell me what you knew, but that wouldn't have gotten me to Ahmed. It was a great deal easier to use you to feed fake information to your prince. Once Leyla told me Rahim was a traitor, I could use him to pass information to you."

I caught a flash of movement behind the Sultan. A figure in the shadows. I looked back at the Sultan, quick as I could. Trying not to betray what I'd seen. I tightened my fist, keeping my grip on the desert.

He turned away. "I have to say I rather enjoyed watching you scramble around putting out fires, never noticing the others I wanted you to look away from. While you were looking at Saramotai, I was taking back Fahali. While you were saving traitors from the gallows, I had men arresting dissenters in their own homes. And while you were running around trying to save my traitor son, I was emptying your traitor camp and arresting my other traitor son." He dropped one hand on Leyla's shoulder. "She's done a great deal of good work. How did you think we found you in your little valley hideaway?" He held something up. It was a compass. Just like the ones Jin and Ahmed had, only smaller. They'd told me once, I remembered, that those were of Gamanix make. Leyla's mother was a Gamanix engineer. "We hid one of these on your spy before we released her to be . . . rescued." Sayyida. She was a trap, too.

"And when I found out from Rahim you were planning to escape . . ." Leyla bounced, excited. "Do you want to see?" It was that same light in her face that I'd seen when she was showing some new toy to the children in the harem. She turned, gesturing to the soldiers. Two of them dragged Tamid away from the wall. He struggled to keep up with them on his fake leg.

I took a step forward and this time, it was Jin who caught me, pulling me back. They forced Tamid to the ground, sitting with his bronze leg splayed out in front of him. Leyla unfastened it with practiced ease. She had made it, after all. Proudly she turned the detached leg toward me. Perfectly fitted in the hollow bronze of Tamid's calf was a compass.

"I fitted it after I convinced you Tamid should come with us, and he was none the wiser that I was using him to help bring my father to your camp."

This was my fault. I had led them to us. I had saved Tamid. I hadn't left him behind and I was still being punished.

I pulled, one last violent yank on my Demdji powers.

And then the sky darkened. The sandstorm was on us.

The Sultan's head shot up as the shadow fell across us. The raging cloud of sand had rushed in to crown the garden. I raised my hands, taking full grip of it—there was no point pretending now.

I poured everything I had into the sand. All my anger. All my defiance. All my desperation. I whipped the storm into a frenzy before slamming my arms down, pulling the full force of the desert around us.

I looked for the Sultan. He was watching me. The last thing I saw was him smiling at me the same way he had that first day in the war room over the dead duck. Like he was proud.

Then the sandstorm swallowed us.

"Amani!" Shazad's voice shouted some order to me that was swallowed in the chaos. I turned to face her just in time to see an Abdal rising up behind her, raised hand glowing red. I swung my arm. I felt something tear in my side where my wound had been as the sand turned into a blade and crashed through the Abdal's leg, cutting into clay flesh and metal bone and severing it, sending the thing toppling to the ground.

"Watch your back!" I shouted at her. I didn't need orders for once. I knew what I was fighting for. I knew who I was fighting. I knew what I needed to do.

We needed the rest of the Demdji. And we needed them out. I couldn't leave any Demdji in the Sultan's hands. I couldn't let him do the same thing to them that he'd done to me.

I slammed my arms down, severing the iron around Izz, then Maz. The twins burst into motion, flesh turning to feathers, fingers to talons as they plunged into the air, then back down. Delila was running for Ahmed as I freed him. And then Imin, who staggered forward, toward Navid.

A bullet caught Hala in the leg. She screamed, staggering forward. She would've hit the ground except Sam was there. He grabbed her, arms under her legs, and the two of them vanished through a wall. I turned my attention elsewhere. I'd lost Ahmed in the chaos.

We weren't winning, but we didn't have to. We just had to get as many people out as we could. I grabbed a fistful of sand and twisted hard. A stab of violent pain answered in my stomach. And then it was gone. The sand staggered, then dropped. And just like that our cover was gone.

The pain in my side doubled as I tried to grab hold of the sand again. And suddenly, it was blinding. My body was made of pain where it ought to have been flesh and blood. I staggered to my knees, gasping.

"Amani." When I could see again I realized Shazad was kneeling in front of me. The way she said my name made me think it wasn't the first time. She looked scared. Two other rebels were standing over us, covering her back while she had mine. "What's happening?"

I didn't know. I couldn't even talk for the agony. Something my aunt had cut open so carefully inside me felt like it'd ripped in my side.

"That's it, you're getting out of here."

"No!"

But Shazad was already helping me to my feet. I tried to pull away, to stand on my own. But she kept her grip.

"Don't argue. Last time you got left behind, *this* happened." She meant the Djinn and the Abdals and everything else. "Demdji get out first, and that's an order from your general and your friend. Jin!" She caught his attention across the chaos of the garden. He was with us in a second. "Get her out of here."

He didn't need to be told twice and I was in no state to fight an order. His arms were under my knees and shoulders, lifting me off the ground. I remembered the night of Auranzeb.

Are you saying you're here to rescue me?

This was how to rescue a girl. I might've laughed if everything didn't hurt so much. Shazad covered us as he lifted me toward Izz, who was wearing the shape of a giant Roc, carrying people to safety as fast as he could.

Jin and I were on his back and off the ground with one powerful wingbeat, carrying us high over the rooftops of Izman. Shots punctured the night behind us. They had a clear aim without the cover of the sandstorm. But Izz dodged expertly, moving too quickly to be a target. As we rose I could see Izman spreading out below us like a map, houses dotted with tiny pinpricks of light at the windows among dark streets. And just beyond the rambling walls and roofs was the sea, looking pink with the dawn. We were almost out of range. Even through the blinding pain I could tell. Almost. Just a little higher, just a little farther, and we'd be out and gone and Izz could drop me and Jin somewhere safe and go back for the others.

I didn't hear the gunshot that hit us. But I felt it. In the sudden jerking motion of Izz's body as iron punctured his skin. In the scream that erupted from him. In a blur of pain, I realized they'd hit his wing. Jin's arms tightened around me.

For a moment I was back in the harem, looking out over the water with the Sultan at my side, bow drawn as I took aim for the birds. The moment my arrow went through my kill. Watching it plummet to the ground and we were falling, too.

Izz was fighting not to plunge us back into the camp. To carry us farther away. To get us out. The Sultan couldn't capture another Demdji. I could feel the iron biting into him, and the pain hobbling his injured wing.

A last few frantic wingbeats carried us forward, the wind grabbing at us. And then we burst free of the city, of the roofs and streets and the walls that would shatter us when we crashed. We were out over the sea, a sheer drop of a cliff face from the city into the water.

We were falling. Izz's body flipped, spilling us out as he screamed in agony, frantically beating his wings. Jin's grip left my waist.

I had just a moment to catch sight of the water below as I slipped from his back, plunging toward it.

I didn't even feel it when the water swallowed me whole.

FORTY-EIGHT

I'd never understood drowning.

I was a desert girl. The sea was made of sand where I was from. And that obeyed me. This. This was an attack.

Water invaded every part of me. Rushing to swallow my body hungrily. Rushing into my nose and my mouth. I was suffocating and the world was narrowed to black. Turned out I was good at drowning for a desert girl.

And then I was surging out of the depths of the water; air hit my face. Something slammed into my lungs. Light burst across my vision. It bloomed then faded to black. And then again. Pain and light wracking through me. Battling for my body.

And then stars. Stars above me. And a mouth was on mine.

I wasn't dying. This was one of Hala's illusions. Except it wasn't. Jin hovered above me. I saw the lines of his face, etched in the predawn light as the pain slammed into my lungs again. Burning. Burning.

I was a Djinni's daughter. Burning was what I did.

And then the stars vanished and I was staring at the ground and the sight of bile and water spilling out across sand. Expelled from my lungs as I vomited half the sea out. Even after it was all gone I was on my hands and knees retching violently.

I felt a gentle hand on my back. "Remind me to teach you how to swim sometime." The joke sounded strained. But I laughed anyway. It turned into more coughing as I knelt doubled over, shaking, trying to put myself back together.

The shadow of Izman, set high on the cliff above, loomed over us. It was an awfully long fall. I saw the pain written across Jin's face, his hair sticking to his brow. I pushed a piece away. My heart was slowing. The chaos of the fight. Of surviving. Some of the pain in my side had subsided.

It was quiet and calm here on the shore as the sun rose. Just for a moment. But the stars were glaring down accusation at me. And I had to let the rest of the world back in eventually.

"Izz?" I asked. I didn't see a giant blue Roc anywhere. He'd been hit by a bullet. He wouldn't be able to shift again with that in him.

"I'm not sure." Jin shook his head. "We got lucky; we fell and hit the water. Izz didn't fall with us. By the time I'd surfaced with you, I'd lost sight of him." The water lapped innocently at our bodies, but out there it was a churning mass that'd swallow you whole.

"And the others?"

Jin shook his head. "I don't know. Sam got some out. I saw others fall. I lost track of Ahmed and my sister in the fighting and then you dropped." He sat back. He was shaking. "So this is what you didn't want me to know about."

I reached for the sand in my mind, but I could feel the stabbing sensation where my old wound was and I stopped. I might have the iron out of my skin, but it wasn't so easy to shift back. I sank my fingers into the waterlogged sand under myself and forced my heartbeat to slow. "Ahmed is alive." It fell off my tongue easily. The truth. "Shazad is alive." The names tumbled off my tongue one after the other. Delila, Imin, Hala, Izz, Maz, Sam, Rahim. Our people were still alive.

"Anyone who made it out will head for the Hidden House." Jin pushed his soaked hair back off his face as he stood up, reaching down for me. "We need to get back there; it'll be safe—"

"Maybe not for long." I took Jin's hand, letting him help me to my feet. I was still unsteady from how I'd stopped breathing for a bit. "It just takes one person to talk."

It was painfully slow going to get back up the cliffs to the city. As the sun worked across the sky, we waded where the water was shallow enough. Jin swam some of it with me hanging on to his shoulders until finally we found a place where the ground up to the city sloped enough to climb. The sun was high over us by then and still we did not move quickly. Jin caught me when I stumbled, but a few times we still had to stop to rest. For me to catch my breath as the pain in my side throbbed. We finally found flat ground just outside the city walls. We were far from alone. A crush of people were fighting their way in through the gates.

Someone shoved by me, jostling me back into Jin, who steadied me.

"Hey." Jin caught a man by the shoulder. The man turned, clearly spoiling for a fight. He backed down when he caught sight of Jin, who had the look of knowing how to kill a man and being half-desperate, too. "What's going on?"

"The Rebel Prince," the man said. My heart jumped at the mention of Ahmed. "The Rebel Prince has been captured. He's going to be executed on the palace steps."

"When?" I shoved forward; I couldn't keep it in anymore. The man's eyes swept me disdainfully, from my disheveled hair to my clothes dried stiff with seawater against my body. He might not want to mouth off to Jin, but I wasn't half so intimidating as my foreign prince.

"Answer her," Jin pressed.

"Sundown," the man said, shaking Jin's hand off, already pushing toward the crowd. "He's lifting the curfew for one night for it. And if you don't let me go I'm going to miss it."

Jin and I traded a glance before our gazes went to the horizon, across the sea.

The sky was already darkening.

FORTY-NINE

THE REBEL PRINCE

When men and women on long desert roads sat around campfires, where only the stars could see them, they told the tale of the Rebel Prince as best they knew it. And they told the truth as best they could. But not all of it. Never all of it.

When they told of his days in the harem, they never told of his brother the Foreign Prince, born under the same stars. They told of the night his half-Djinni sister was born, but they never knew of the young woman who risked her own life to take three children away to safety as the Rebel Prince's mother died. And when they told of the Sultim trials, they left out the general's beautiful daughter who trained him and fought beside him until he was ready to face the challenge.

In years to come in the desert, when the caravans warded against the fear of the night with stories of great men, they would tell of the day that the people of Izman gathered at dusk in the thousands to get their first glimpse of the Rebel Prince since the Sultim trials, as he stood on an executioner's stage. Waiting for the axe to fall.

The stories would never tell that the Rebel Prince was not the only captive of the Sultan on that day. They would never know that he could have escaped capture had he not made so many of his people escape before him. They would never tell that he had laid down his weapons and surrendered himself to his father in order to save those others who were left behind.

The storytellers never knew that the man who stood on that stage did it by his own choice. That he could have escaped his fate if he were a less good man. A less brave man.

On that day, a hundred thousand men and women would come to watch and each would tell the story of what they saw there. The tales would cross the sands in the months that followed, repeated across the desert and on foreign shores. The same stories would be told again among caravans in the centuries that followed, when the time came to teach their children of all the great heroes who had come before them in the desert.

But there would only ever be six people who would

know the story of what truly happened that day. The people of the caravans would never know what came to pass in the prison cells below the palace between dawn and dusk. Before the moment that all of Izman saw on the stage.

Six people, who had all fought side by side and were imprisoned side by side for it. They sat in the dark, awaiting their fates like thousands who had sat there before them. They passed whispers inside their cell, swearing that the Rebellion would not die there with them. Though by dawn, two of them would be dead.

Six people who would never tell the story of what took place on the day that would be known forever as the day the Rebel Prince died.

FIFTY

When the legendary Princess Hawa died at Saramotai, time lost all sense. The sun rose to watch her fall. It stopped in the sky in the dead of night. And the stars stared down alongside to witness the birth of grief in a new world. The entire world held its breath as Attallah dropped dead because his heart was torn in two.

Time didn't stop now. It was already running out. There was no time to plan. No time to race for reinforcements or even a gun. I didn't know what to do. Or even what I was running toward. I just knew that I was running, pressing through the mob in the streets, racing toward the palace.

No time to get help. No time to plan a rescue. That was what the Sultan was counting on.

He was going to execute Ahmed and we barely even

had time to get there, let alone plan how to get him out. We were going to have to make a plan on the fly. Like we always did.

We were good at that.

I saw a man with a gun as we shoved by. "Jin." I grabbed his arm. He stopped, looking where I was pointing. I didn't need to say anything further. Jin grabbed the man, wrenching his arms behind his back, holding him as I grabbed the gun. And then we were moving again, rushing away from the man's shouted accusations.

The crowd started to get too thick before we were even within sight of the palace. I pushed. The streets were choked with people and I couldn't move anymore.

I couldn't even see the square. I shoved forward, but soon I was trapped in the mass of bodies. I squirmed through until I was shoved up against a wall. I looked up.

I couldn't climb that. Not alone. But I could get up there with help. Jin knew what I was thinking before I'd even finished thinking it.

"You'll be alone," he said. Someone jostled him, pressing us closer together, until we were flush against the wall. Alone, with a gun, powerless and bleeding from a half dozen places.

"I know." I ran my tongue along my lips. They were caked with salt.

Jin lifted me up. I grabbed the ledge above, dragging myself up painfully. And painfully slow, fighting through the stabbing in my side.

My feet hit the ledge and I started to run, ignoring the

shooting pain in my body. A jump carried me easily over the narrow gap onto the next roof. I landed hard, scraping my knee. I was back up, leaving a streak of new blood behind. I jumped to the next roof, startling some birds into flight. I kept going. Shoving forward, onward and onward, until there was nowhere to go. And I was standing on a roof overlooking the square in front of the palace.

Ahmed stood alone, chained by his wrists to the stage set above the heaving mass of people. His eyes were cast down. I knew what he was seeing. The images of pain and death. The writhing monsters.

The last thing Shira had seen.

The last thing Ahmed would see.

Unless I saved him.

A man was reading out what I could only guess was a list of my Rebel Prince's supposed crimes. I couldn't hear him over the din of the crowd. Above him I spotted the balcony from which I'd watched Shira die. They had shielded it with iron instead of carved wood after the riots. Through the gaps in the lattice I thought I could just make out the Sultan, surveying the scene, come to watch another son die.

As the list reached its end, Ahmed finally looked up, out over the sea of Mirajin citizens. Facing his people.

"The Sultan," the man cried, "in his great wisdom and mercy, has agreed to grant leniency to any other rebels. They will keep their heads but be condemned to a life of penance serving this country, which they betrayed." Leniency my ass. The Sultan had told me himself he needed to win back the love of his people. I remembered him chastising Kadir for Shira's execution. The people didn't love you for killing an innocent. "But, for his crimes against his own blood, Prince Ahmed has been condemned to die." But Ahmed, he'd told the people, had killed Kadir, his own brother. They had to see Ahmed die.

I aimed my gun at the balcony, squinting. That was a small target from this far. Even for me. And I didn't know if I had a shot to waste.

Over the roofs of Miraji behind me, the sun was setting.

I flattened myself on my stomach and aimed the gun. God, I hoped it was a good gun. I didn't have a plan beyond shooting the executioner. But that had to be enough, for now at least. I had to save Ahmed and then I could worry about whatever came next.

The executioner stepped onto the stage and my heart stuttered. They hadn't sent a man to kill Ahmed. The Sultan had sent an Abdal.

Even I couldn't make that shot.

I had the executioner in my crosshairs and I was helpless. I aimed the gun all the same. I fired. One clean shot, through the knee. A scream went up from the crowd at the sound of gunfire. But the executioner didn't so much as stagger. I fired again and again and again, aiming desperately for the tiny target of its foot. Until the gun in my hand was empty.

Until the Abdal had reached Ahmed.

It forced him to his knees in front of the wooden block they'd laid there. Ahmed didn't fight. He knelt down with dignity, his eyes going down to the gruesome scenes below as he laid his head on the executioner's block.

I reached out for the desert. I could feel it scattered through the streets, sand invading the city. I started to gather it to me but the pain stabbed through my side, sending me down with a cry, scattering the sand back to street dust.

The mechanical man took one step backward. Swinging the axe upward. And I was helpless. I was helpless without my Demdji powers, without any bullets. Unable to stop it. Unable to do anything.

"Ahmed!" His name ripped out of me. Through the crowd. Over the din of people calling out, pressing forward, calling for his head, for his freedom.

I was too far away for him to hear me. Too far away to reach him. But somehow from the block his head tilted up just as the axe swung high. He looked straight at me. His eyes met mine.

The low rays of the sun struck the iron of the axe, turning it into a blazing light as it reached its pinnacle.

But the sun didn't stop. Time didn't stop. The world didn't show any sympathy for my grief.

The axe fell. It turned from sunlight to iron. To blood.

FIFTY-ONE

I didn't cry until I was safe.

I wasn't even sure how we got back to the Hidden House. All I knew was a hand leading me through streets that had turned to chaos as soon as the axe fell. Through a world that had stopped making sense. Jin. He could've been leading me to the executioner's block and I wouldn't have known until I was looking up at the crowd with the axe hanging above me.

But then we were through the doors, into the safe haven of the Hidden House, where we'd all been together only two nights before. Sara was waiting inside the doors, a screaming baby on her hip. Her lips were moving, but I didn't hear anything she said. Jin pulled me past her. And it came on like a punch to the gut. My knees gave out below me on the stairs.

I sobbed. For all the dead. For all the losses. For the things that had been taken away. It was seared into my mind forever. The blade. The blood. The eyes.

The look in his eyes as they met mine across the crowd. A second before he died.

And it was my fault. Mine and someone I trusted. Someone I thought was innocent.

The scream came on so sudden and violent that I had to stuff my sheema into my mouth to keep it from being heard through the walls of the house. It tasted of sweat and sand and of Jin's skin somehow.

I could hear the sounds from the next room. Voices dropped low, tentative with uncertainty and thick with grief. What was left of the Rebellion. The folks who'd escaped the attack at Shazad's.

The murmur was soothing. I closed my eyes and leaned my head against the wall.

Too many people had traded their lives for someone else's now.

Bahi had burned to save Shazad.

Shira had walked to the executioner's block for her son.

Rahim had thrown himself on the mercy of his merciless father for Leyla.

My mother had bowed her head to a noose for me.

I thought about revenge and about love and about sacrifice and the great and terrible things I'd seen people do. I thought about how many people I'd seen lay their lives down for the Rebellion, over and over.

I thought about the moment the axe fell. The eyes locking with mine a second before the light left them.

The stairs creaked with a new weight next to me. I knew it was Jin without opening my eyes. I knew before he leaned his weight into my side. Before he laced his hand with mine, running his thumb across my palm in a slow circle.

"We're not done yet." My voice scraped out. Almost gone but still there. I finally opened my eyes.

"I know."

• ● •

THE LOW MURMUR of voices died with our entrance, leaving nothing but the chanting in the streets below. A constant thrum like a heartbeat. Good. Silence was death. And the Rebellion wasn't dead yet.

And every eye in the room was on me. Rebels I knew well and rebels I didn't.

Hala's golden hands were wrapped around a steaming cup someone had given her, dark hair all over her face. Sara sat in a corner, her son asleep in her arms, staring through the shutters into the street below and blinking back tears. Sam was running his finger around the rim of an empty glass, over and over. Maz was wrapped in a blanket, shaking violently, blue hair sticking up at all angles. Tamid was stitching the wound in Izz's arm from where the bullet had torn through his wing, obviously grateful for something to do.

There was only one spot left free, at the head of the table.

Half of the people in the room were sitting on the floor rather than take that place. I felt Jin tense behind me as he saw it.

I cleared my throat, but my voice came out steady. "We need a plan." I fought the instinct to look for Shazad to start making one with me. She'd been taken with Ahmed. Delila. Imin. Rahim. Navid. They'd all been captured, along with dozens of others.

"What is there left to plan?" Hala was looking into her coffee cup instead of at me. She squeezed her eyes shut. "You don't think it's only a matter of time before that axe comes down again, and again and again—"

"Hala." Maz cut her off with a hand on her arm. She pulled herself up short, opening her eyes, staring me down. I flinched at the gaze. Her eyes might be the dark brown of any desert girl's, but they still reminded me of Imin's golden eyes.

"—until everyone else is gone, too," she finished.

"No." I held my ground. The Sultan might've thought he was using me, those months in the palace. But I hadn't spent all that time there without learning a thing or two about the man who ruled over Miraji. The Sultan was smart. Too smart to risk more rioting in the streets. "The Sultan is losing his grip on his people. He knows that. That's why Rahim wasn't executed. He needed Ahmed to die publicly." Someone in a corner made a noise like a sob, quickly smothered in their sheema. "But for the rest of them, he gains more by showing mercy than by showing force."

"You're thinking he'll send them away," Hala said.

"Instead of executing them," Maz filled in. A spark of life flared back in the room briefly.

I had to tell them the rest, the thing I'd figured out. I was going to have to tell all of them. But my eyes kept drifting to Hala in her corner. Waiting was not going to make it easier.

"There's something else." The room went quiet. "We lost someone today." I could see it all in my mind. A head lifting on the block. Meeting my eyes. Creatures of illusion and deceit. "But it wasn't Ahmed." My eyes the color of the sky. His the same shade as molten gold. Staring straight at me. I knew those eyes. But they weren't Ahmed's.

My meaning dawned slowly through the room. Slowest across the golden-skinned Demdji's face.

Imin.

"Hala, I'm so sorry."

Grief and rage warred across her face while the rest of us were silent for Imin. Her head dropped into her hands.

Ahmed wouldn't have let anyone go to the executioner's block for him. But he wasn't the only one being kept prisoner. Half the Rebellion would've sooner walked onto that stage than let Ahmed do it. Shazad would've worked out the plan, in all the confusion of the attack. Delila with her hair dyed dark, concealing her Demdji side; she might not be able to hide a whole rebellion but she was good enough to hide her brother, for a time, conceal his identity under an illusion of a different face. Whichever one Imin had been wearing when they were taken. And Imin was good enough to take Ahmed's place. Not just good enough. More than good.

Imin had walked into an execution for our prince.

"Ahmed is alive."

I looked around the table, the small cramped room in this, our last refuge. "The Sultan might've bested us today, but he *can't* plan for everything. He didn't plan on me slipping out of his grip." I met Tamid's eyes. "He didn't plan on us escaping. And he sure as hell didn't plan on Ahmed living. So he's not planning on us saving him, either."

"Who is going to lead us?" Izz asked. His eyes turned to Jin.

"Don't look at me," Jin said. He was leaning against the door frame. Like he might disappear on the Rebellion again any second.

"I can lead us." That drew every eye in the room to me. I waited. But there wasn't a single word of protest. Not a word of argument.

I was a Demdji. I was the Blue-Eyed Bandit. I was their friend. I had learned strategy from Shazad. I had been among the enemy. I hadn't left them when Jin had. And they believed me when I said that I could lead.

We were going to rescue our people, our friends, our family. And when we had them all back we were going to march Rahim to Iliaz for an army. I pressed away from the wall. I was unsteady, but I was still standing. We were still here.

And this time, the Sultan had given us an advantage— the only thing that was truly invincible. Not an immortal creature. But an idea. A legend. A story.

The Blue-Eyed Bandit was always more powerful than I was. The Rebel Prince was always more powerful than

Ahmed. And now, we could write a better story than the prodigal prince. One no one would ever forget. One the entirety of Miraji would stand behind.

The prince who returned from the dead to take his throne and save his people.

ACKNOWLEDGMENTS

I owe a lot of thanks to a lot of people, both for all the support since the release of *Rebel of the Sands* and all the support in writing this book. And even though I haven't even started I'm already worried about forgetting someone. So to everyone who was there for these books and for me, friends and family who offered anything from a kind word or a drink to help get the book from my brain to the laptop, publishing professionals who helped get this book from my laptop to the bookstore, booksellers and librarians who helped get it from the shelf into readers' hands, please know that I am grateful!

First always, my parents, who somehow managed to raise me with both the absurd belief that I could achieve anything I set my mind to and the very pragmatic understanding that I would have to work hard for it. I wouldn't have aspired to or achieved one book, let alone two, if not for them. And I probably wouldn't have finished if they hadn't provided a steady supply of both encouragement and alcohol in the final weeks of drafting.

I'm still not sure who I sold my soul to in order to land an agent who is as smart, passionate about books, and supportive (and a million other things I don't have room to list here) as mine. I can probably do without a soul, but I know I can't do without Molly Ker Hawn in my corner.

Thank you also to the rest of the Bent Agency and the wonderful foreign rights agents they work with for all they have done for *Rebel*.

I think the trick to putting a good book on shelves is to work with people who are smarter than you are. So thank you to Kendra Levin, whom I suspect of being psychic because she understands what I'm trying to achieve even before I do, as well as somehow always managing to time encouraging emails exactly when doubt is about to get the better of me. And to Naomi Colthurst, who brought so much positivity and enthusiasm to this book that I'm pretty sure I siphoned some of it from her to be able to finish editing.

To use the old cliché that it takes a village: to my two transatlantic villages at Penguin Random House and Faber, thank you.

Ken Wright and Leah Thaxton for being so wonderfully supportive of me and of *Rebel* throughout the whole process. As well as Stephen Page. And to Alice Swan, who brought Amani and crew to their UK home in the first place.

My publicists on both sides of the pond: Elyse Marshall, who I'm pretty sure could power a small country with her positivity, and who can organize a bookish jaunt around the US and make it look easy. And Hannah Love in the UK, who kept me (semi) sane in my jaunts around the UK and who sometimes goes as far as to dress as my creepy twin. Thank you for getting my book to readers!

To Maggie Rosenthal, Krista Ahlberg, Janet Pascal, Natasha Brown, Sarah Barlow, Mohammed Kasim, and Naomi Burt, for all the hard work you do on this book day to day that I don't see, and the parts I do see that are a lot of seriously smart contributions and comments about this book. The kind that clearly come from a great deal of care. I'm so grateful to have so many additional eyes and brains on these words.

To the people who make my books look good: Theresa Evangelista, Will Steele, and Emma Eldridge for my covers. And to Kate Renner for designing the inside, including the awesome map, and for having an endless amount of patience when dealing with my complete geographical incompetence.

To the whole of the marketing and social media teams: Emily Romero, Rachel Cone-Gorham, Anna Jarzab, Madison Killen, Erin Berger, Lisa Kelly, Mia Garcia, Christina Colangelo, Kara Brammer, Erin Toller, Briana Woods-Conklin, Lily Arango, Megan Stitt, Carmela Iaria, Venessa Carson, Kathryn Bhirud, Alexis Watts, Rachel Wease, Rachel Lodi, Susan Holmes, Niriksha Bharadia. And especially Amanda Mustafic and Kaitlin Kneafsey for all your support on the road. And Bri Lockhart and Leah Schiano for being early readers of this book and just in general endlessly awesome human beings when it comes to book love.

To the whole of the sales teams on both sides of the Atlantic, especially Biff Donovan, Sheila Hennessy, Colleen Conway, and Doni Kay, who were kind enough to guide me as I traversed the US and introduce me to some awesome booksellers. And to the Faber sales team, David Woodhouse, Miles Poyton, Clare Stern, and Kim Lund.

And to all the incredible booksellers I met in Boston, Chicago, Seattle, and Raleigh, who were kind enough to be readers of a very early draft of *Rebel*. In particular Kelly Morton, Allison Maurer, Lauren D'Alessio, Betsy Balyeat, Rosemary Publiese, and Kathleen March, who wrote such nice things about that early draft. And Gaby Salpeter for your enthusiasm about a later draft. And to every bookseller in the UK who has been such a wonderful champion of the book, in particular Aimee and Kate at Waterstone's Piccadilly, Chloe at Foyle's, and Jamie-Lee at Waterstone's Birmingham.

And though you are too many to name, thank you to all the awesome bloggers, vloggers, and general YA supporters who have been so enthusiastic in spreading the word about a new author online.

This book is dedicated to my friend Rachel Rose Smith, who is one of the smartest, kindest people I know and who has been there for me in the best and worst times around writing and outside of the bookish world. She only begins a long list of people I have been lucky enough to accumulate in my life. And who I will wear out my fingers trying to name. But particular thanks go to Michella Domenici for being my first fangirl always, Amelia Hodgson who always has the time to help dig me out of a plot hole, Justine Caillaud for being a creative support since I was able to pick up a pen, Meredith Sykes for the early read and the necklace made of sand, Christie Coho for keeping me sane, Cecilia Vinesse for coffee, food, and puppies, and Roshani Chokshi for actual medical advice about scars and metal under the skin.

For being kind enough to write nice blurbs for *Rebel*: Rae Carson, Alison Goodman, and Erin Lange.

And to everyone else who has been there through this, who has pushed this book into the hands of others or offered a kind word, advice, or an ear in the good times and the less good times, personal and writerly alike: Jon Andrews, Kat Berry, Anne Caillaud, Emma Carroll, Lexi Casale, Sophie Cass, Traci Chee, Jess Cluess, Noirin Collins, Laure Eve, Max (Hamilton) Fitz-James, Maya (M. G. Leonard) Gabrielle, Stephanie Garber, Jeff Giles, Meave Hamill, Janet Hamilton-Davies, Heidi Heilig, Bonnie-Sue Hitchcock, Mariam Khan, Rachel Marsh, Kiran Millwood-Hargrave, Anne Murphy, Elisa Peccerillo-Palliser, Marieke Peleman, Chelsey Pippin, Harriet

Reuter-Hapgood, Marie Rutkoski, Melinda Salisbury, Samantha Shannon, Tara Sim, Evelyn Skye, Carlie Sorosiak, Solange Sykes, Emma Theriault, Annik Vrana, Katherine Webber, Anna Wessman, all of my fellow '16er authors for getting it, the whole of my book club crew for being bookish with me, and the very nice people at Artisan coffee who basically fueled this book and have let me spend more hours in their establishment than in my own home. And so many more, thank you all!

And finally, thank you to all the readers of *Rebel of the Sands* who have taken the time to share your enthusiasm for my first book, and your anticipation for this one. I think I'm supposed to write for myself first. But I've always wanted to write for others. And you make that possible.